# Year of the Amphibian

········  *A NOVEL*  ········

## CHRISTOPHER PICKERT

WINGSEED
PRESS

Dear Dani,
Thanks for reading, and
I hope you enjoy it.

ISBN  978-1-7324720-0-6  (Hardback Edition)
ISBN  978-1-7324720-1-3  (Paperback Edition)
ISBN  978-1-7324720-2-0  (Ebook - ePub)
ISBN  978-1-7324720-3-7  (Ebook - Kindle)

Library of Congress Control Number:  2018907287

Printed and bound in the United States of America
First Printing, 2018

Wingseed Press
wingseed-press.com

Follow the author:
christopher-pickert.com

Front cover illustration by Eroyn Franklin:
www.eroynfranklin.com

Dedicated to my sisters
— all of them.

# Late August

"I found a toad!"

Words echoed up into the trees. Conrad stood for a moment, but hearing no response he crouched down to peer under the wood-pile. The leaves above him resumed their quiet breathing in the wind, while the far-away sound of a motorboat buzzed in his ears. A musty odor wafted up his nostrils from the overturned boards at his feet. The lumpy captive squirmed inside his cupped fingers.

Then came tennis shoes scraping on dirt. Conrad looked up to see his two sisters panting toward him with their eyes on the prize in his hands. For Conrad, Levy and Beth, toads were always prizes, especially this one.

"A black toad!" Beth whispered as they squatted close and tickled it between its eyes. Black toads hardly ever turned up. Really they were normal brown toads that had changed color, but most toads didn't bother. Levy lifted this one by its bulgy sides and lowered it legs-first into The Can, their old coffee can. Holes had long ago been punched into its sides with an ice pick, for air. Inside it smelled of dirt, freeze-dried coffee and the urine of previous prisoners.

"Ooooh," said Levy, squinting her eyes and holding her long brown hair straight out in her fists like handlebars. "It's a black magic toad. We'll die in agony for disturbing it".

"No it *is not*," said little Beth, standing upright and speaking with the air of a child princess. "It's a forest spirit trapped in a toad, until it grants us each three wishes, of course."

They turned their eyes to Conrad, who at fourteen was the oldest. He looked away while deciding. Dying from black magic would be too short, he thought, plus Beth would fuss about the manner of her death.

"Toads are never malevolent," he intoned. "We must free the forest spirit."

Beth flashed a grin. Behind her Levy rolled her eyes, but in a moment she went back to normal, which meant folding parts of her body in ever-new ways.

"OK fine, but where?" she asked.

"There's only one place it will work," Conrad said as though speaking from ancient knowledge he didn't just make up. "The Church."

The afternoon's adventure was decided, so they sealed the can and set off.

Beyond their father's house was endless forest, their private kingdom, threaded with deer trails winding up over the crests of hills and down through miniature valleys. Each place had a name and they knew them all, because over the years they had made them up. But first was the way in, The Gate: a pair of old birch trees sagging like enormous white candles at the edge of the property. From the first day the kids had dared enter the woods, they felt that the only way in was between these two trees, though you could enter the forest anywhere.

Today was the same. They couldn't just walk up to the gate — it might be ghoul-guarded, or snap shut and sever their bottoms from their tops. Instead they crept along the low rock wall where the yard ended, out of sight.

"You'll have to be quick," Conrad whispered.

"Whoah-so-whammy!" Levy sang as she sprinted through, arms and legs flaying the air.

"Itsy-bitsy-betsy!" Beth squealed.

"Zeekagga!" Conrad yelled, crashing on the soft moss at the other side while holding the can out in front of him, the toad tumbling inside as he rolled.

Now inside and down a slope, they came to The Nursery, a

close-growing sea of baby trees always in shade that hid the ground under an unbroken surface of leaves.

"Snakes, big ones, slithering," Conrad murmured.

"Bigfoot's taking a nap, and you're about to step on him," said Beth.

"Bear trap," said Levy, "steel teeth."

They shuffled through faster. Over a rise they came down into The Black Hole. Less light made it through the forest canopy here, leaving the low-lying ground dark and soggy.

"Why couldn't we go the easy way down by the lake?" Beth whined as she struggled to pull her short legs over one of the fallen pines that crisscrossed the mud.

"We can't cheat," said Conrad. No further explanation was needed. But next was worse: the Dead Woods. Here an unseen force had sucked out all life, leaving a grove of closely-packed, dried-up little pine trees armed with dry branches that tore at them as they pushed through.

"I'm being sliced into a thousand pieces!" Beth screamed.

"They're grabbing my hair!" Levy screeched. "They're pulling me back!"

Scraped and jabbed, they emerged into Bigfoot Alley, a long stretch of woods with a steep rise on the right and huge old pines rising like Roman columns that cast the pathway in mysterious shadow. This was Conrad's favorite place, but they continued through without speaking. Over the top of the next hill the woods opened up with the soft glow of summer light filtered through leaves. This was The Church, a dimly-lit gathering of lichen-crusted glacial boulders that together resembled a ruin. In the middle was a patch of forest grass, an oasis of silken green. The grass didn't belong to this forest, they felt, making it enchanted.

Levy and Beth luxuriated while Conrad gathered sticks. He made a wide circle of them and told the girls to sit on the outside. Following his lead they took their places on their knees, equidistant of course, then placed their hands flat on the ground and bent their bodies low.

"I will place the toad *dead center*," Conrad said in his grandest voice. "We must each inform the spirit of our wishes before its host body escapes this circle of swords, at which point the spirit will be freed, so calm your hearts and be ready."

Conrad pulled out the toad and gently lowered it into the middle under his hands. As if on cue, the wind picked up: a slightly chill wind off the nearby lake with an *autumn is coming* urgency in its whisper. The wind made Conrad sure of his wishes — really he only needed one. He looked at his sisters, lifted his hands and pulled back behind the sticks. The toad sat still in the center.

"The youngest must go first," he whispered to Beth.

"Please Mr. Toad," she said, "I wish for a new bicycle so I don't have to use Conrad's old piece of junk anymore. One with gears and a cushy seat." She paused to think.

"Two more," Levy whispered.

"Please Mr. Toad, I want Mrs. Gavil to stop telling me in front of the whole class to wash my hair. That's just the way it looks. I can't help it."

The toad's head made a little jerk to the right. The leaves above made papery sounds in the breeze.

"Go on," Conrad said.

"I know, just wait ...and please, Mr. Toad, can you *please* make me a better ballet dancer? My toes never turn out right and Ginny always teases me. Please help me with my legs and-"

"Levy's turn," Conrad said.

Levy sat considering with a leg bent out and her head hanging sideways. Meanwhile the toad blinked and moved its head straight again as if its nugget of a brain was turning over its options.

"OK," Levy said, "I've got all three. Please Mr. Toad, I want to win the lottery and have a really big house designed by my handsome husband who's a famous architect."

Beth couldn't resist this. "Ooh Mr. Toad!" she mocked in flowery tones, "I want to kiss you *and* turn you into a handsome prince *and* marry you *and* live in dollhouse-land *and* have seventeen children *and-*"

"And shut up!" Levy barked with a wave. At this the toad tried a wobbly hop — then a leap.

"Hurry say it!" the girls hissed. The toad popped to the edge of the circle.

"Please Mr. Toad," Conrad said as the toad paused halfway across the sticks, "let me stay here. I don't want to go back."

The toad hopped out of sight behind a tree trunk. Beth sprang up to chase it.

"Sorry, buddy-o!" said Levy, pointing her legs up the side of a tree and arching out her belly. "Yours doesn't count! The spell was broken. Now you'll just have to go back to stinky Los Angeles with the rest of us."

○ ○ ○

Conrad cast his eyes around his father's little house and wondered why he loved it so much. The living room was nothing but a jumble of this and that: worn lime-green carpet, a tacky dude-ranch couch, a fireplace rug that resembled the shaggy hide of a yeti dyed a shocking yellow, and — to top it all off — a huge tiger musky looking down sideways on everything, mounted as if peeling from the wall like old paint. Conrad was sure that his mom would have put this house in order, if she had stayed.

But the state of the house didn't matter because while the kids were there they mostly went in and out of it: in for food and towels and clothes, and out for adventure. All through the day, the wooden screen doors in the front and back slammed shut with a gunshot 'bang!' as kids sailed through, always preceded by the twanging sound of the long metal springs that struggled to hold them shut. The door sounds, the sight of the lake and trees through the windows, the smell of ashes in the fireplace, and the sad whistle of a summer bird they had never actually seen — all these things together were what the house felt like for them. Their dad went to work all day and left them there in paradise, this beat-up cottage on a clear lake in the woods. They knew exactly how great it all was, and nobody had to tell them they were lucky, least of all Conrad. The first days of each summer hatched a private, epic story: all the ideas they had, all the things they built and all the ways they celebrated being free that summer in that place was the story, and the end of summer was the death of the story and it could never live again in quite the same way.

*The school year in L.A. has a beginning and end just the same,* Conrad thought. But it never felt like a story. And it didn't give him this ache in his stomach when it was over. He pressed his face against the window, watching the winds whip up the surface of the lake to pull out the summer warmth. What had been the story this year?

Well, for one they had set out to live in the woods. Down a deer trail they built a lean-to out of sticks with fern-leaf beds inside. But mosquitoes swarmed as the light dimmed, forcing the kids into the campfire smoke for protection. Then later, staring up from their prickly beds in the blind night, the scratching of circling raccoons and the snorting of nearby deer yanked them from sleep again and again. And after midnight the temperature plunged, leaving them shivering in the dark. Sleep-deprived, hungry, and smoked like beef jerky, they stumbled home and slept for half the next day. But later on, of course, they tried it three more times.

What else? So many scenes drifted together in Conrad's mind: waking each cool summer morning with nothing and everything to do, followed by so much swimming, fishing, building, biking and hiking, so much planning, scheming, sneaking, arguing and laughing, so much moving under the trees and through the water.

A shout.

"Dad's home!" Beth's voice echoed. Conrad made his way out to the front where their father's car could be heard approaching a ways down the road. Cars came by only once in a while here, and there was something about their dad's old sedan and the way he drove it that his kids could recognize like early-warning radar.

The car rolled up the sandy driveway and came to a stop. Their dad Henry eased out of it looking large and out of place in his light blue business suit, soon to be replaced with old jeans and a ratty sweatshirt.

"What have you rascals been up to?" Henry asked with a look on his face that meant that he was happy to be home, relieved to see his kids unhurt, and worried that he might find some disaster unleashed by his monsters during the day. As always, Beth took the lead.

"We swam in the morning," she reported, secretarial, "and we rode our bikes to Other Beach and tried to read our books, but Levy wouldn't stop fidgeting so we swam instead, and this afternoon Conrad found a black toad so we made wishes on it at The Church."

"Oh, uh, that sounds like a fun day," said Henry with a passing look of confusion about where and what The Church was. "Now, I have chicken for dinner. Do you want to fry it, bake it, or grill it in back?"

"Let's eat outside!" the girls begged. "We hardly have any time left outside."

"Oh, you kids!" Henry said with a dramatic groan, dragging his suited body to the door, "you always choose the hardest job for me. After my long day I have to go stoke the coals in back like a servant."

"Oh dad!" Beth and Levy whined, playing their parts with pouty lips.

○ ○ ○

"Dad," Conrad said later as they ate at the picnic table overlooking the lake, "what if I don't want to live in L.A. anymore? What if I want to stay here... could I do that?"

His sisters' eyes widened. They hadn't taken him seriously about this before.

Henry sat up with his mouth open and didn't move. But then he looked down at his plate and scooped up another spoonful of baked beans.

"You know that's OK by me," he said with a grunt, "but the

courts gave your mother custody, so you'll have to take it up with her. I doubt she'll agree to it."

○ ○ ○

That evening Conrad asked if he could go night fishing. Asking was a formality, so Henry could go through his worried father routine: counting out the points on his big fingers irritatingly close to Conrad's face while Conrad nodded and mumbled "uh-huh."

"Don't ever turn off your running lights." Finger one.

"Uh-huh."

"Always listen for other boats. And if you do hear a boat coming, wave your flashlight in its direction." Fingers two and three.

"Uh-huh, uh-huh."

"And if you catch the big one, use your net and don't lean out of the boat. There'll be nobody to fish you out if you fall in." Finger four.

"Uh-huh."

After a few more fingers, Conrad zipped himself tight in his old life jacket and went out into the dark carrying his pole and tackle box. Down at the dock he untied his little aluminum boat and put in the oars. He had done this before. Soon he was gliding out across the dark liquid, pulling at the oars with squeaking strokes that exposed him to imaginary watchers. But after reaching the other side of the bay and stowing the oars, the quiet set in.

The moon had risen. He used its light to avoid casting too far into shore where his spinner bait might get hooked in a tree. In the distant future, he was sure, scientists would dig up fossil trees and wonder about the strange shapes petrified in their branches, but tonight's lure didn't matter much since he hardly ever caught anything and didn't expect to now. He continued to cast, and reel in. Cast and slowly reel in. Again and again. And then he stopped and sat looking out, not moving. He stared at the moon in the sky and its perfect reflection on the lake's surface. Two moons, just the same. He stared on and on, and the moons didn't move, nothing moved and there was hardly a sound.

A feeling of perfect clarity flowed through him: the clear water and the clear moons and the clear him. He was not a boy in a boat, he was the water and the moons, all in perfect focus against slick blue-black.

The woods whispered now, leaning into sleep, and a breeze shattered the moon into a thousand dancing shards. Conrad caught his breath. Then he put in the oars and pulled himself back across the bay.

# 2

# Early September

*Smaller...*
*Smaller...*
*Still smaller...*

Crackling cracks would form first, all across his skull, then his thoughts would take wing in a desperate attempt to escape, rushing and flapping in pointless circles until his head was compressed to a dimensionless point.

Flying toward summer, the ceaseless drone of the jet engines had been the sound of splashes and hoots, of motor boats and wind in the trees all blending into a happy white noise, but now it pressed on him as the rush of freeway traffic and unkind voices in the school hallways.

Conrad pulled his eyes from the clouds to peek at his sisters playing Mad Libs and wondered how they could both go either direction like it was all so very natural. But then Levy squirmed in her seat and jabbed Beth in the ribs.

"Quit it!" Beth whined.

Levy lifted her nose. "Why are you so sensitive?"

"I'm not! That hurt."

Conrad turned back to the hum and followed it to its sinister source: it was brain-erasing technology, trying to wipe away his summer.

*They can try, yes they can, but they'll never get to the middle of me!*

Now Conrad wondered what was actually at the middle of him. There didn't seem to be anything in there at the moment. Whatever it was, it must have shut down for the season.

Levy poked him. "Let's play woulda," she said.
"OK you start."

The plane's fuselage accordioned into a remote mountainside.

Or it would have, but an alien mother-ship zoomed in to gobble it up first.

Or it would have, but a time warp sucked the plane back to the previous June.

Or it would have, but the plane landed, and Conrad found himself tramping up a tunnel at the L.A. airport behind his sisters. Their mother Sueanna waved at the other end.

"Oh, I've missed you!" she cooed as she hugged and smooched them, now suddenly her children once more. For their part, Sueanna hadn't been forgotten so much as papered over for three months, becoming gradually flatter in their minds until popping out now in all three dimensions, the same but somehow not. Of course people always looked strange after being away for ages, but Sueanna never stopped buying new pins to tie up her hair and never stopped changing her clothes — though a common theme of buttons and belts and sharp collars ran through her outfits. She was always presentable, and stylish and trim, even today at the airport for her kids, as if she would lead them outside to a limo.

"I can't wait to snatch you home again!" Sueanna enthused. "Just wait till you see. I've completely re-done the sun room. It's like having a brand new house."

"But what about the herd?" Beth implored.

"Oh don't worry. They're all fat and happy."

Conrad followed the chattering of mother and daughters to the baggage carousel. He stood staring at its clinking silver scales until their bulging summer-sized suitcases came tumbling down. He helped yank them onto the floor and drag them toward the exit.

The exit. The end. The place where Los Angeles really began. Every time Conrad stepped through the airport doors, where the warm L.A. air hit his body and the warmed-over L.A. smells went up his nose, he thought of the man in The Twilight Zone who woke to find that he wasn't himself.

The kids' bags grew heavier with every tug, but when they arrived at the parking space the car was missing.

"Was it B or D?" Sueanna asked herself out loud.

"Oh Mom!"

"You go wait over there, I'll find it."

The kids dragged their bags back to the walkway and sat on them.

"I can't wait to see Weetie!" Beth breathed, referring to one of her many guinea pigs.

Levy shook her head. "Nah, I missed Beastmaster the most. He's the cutest."

"No he's not. Weetie has cuter eyes."

Conrad had no opinion. He stared at the parking garage ceiling.

*How did those stains get up there?*

*Should somebody worry about those cracks?*

*Why is one section of cement a lighter shade than the other?*

The station wagon pulled up. After heaving their bags into the back, the kids piled in and were off. A stressful series of turns and merges kept Sueanna's eyes glued to the road, but they soon appeared in the rear-view mirror.

"How was your summer Conrad?"

He didn't want to get going about it. Anything he said would be less than it was. He stared out at the dusty-dry neighborhoods passing one after another below, at the empty-looking houses tinted yellow in the lowering afternoon sun like ghost towns between the traffic jams. "You know..." he mumbled.

The car pulled off the freeway. Conrad watched the familiar scenes pass by: the same plastic signs, the same mini-mart, the same bag-lady muttering behind the same stolen shopping cart. Then the car turned a corner onto a block of mismatched little homes with patchy brown lawns. Up the driveway, there it was: the old white house again. His sisters bolted from the car and ran to the back where their animals lived, but Conrad paused in his seat. He looked out at the house and thought.

*Now I will walk through that front door.*
*Now I will go to the kitchen and have some milk.*
*Now I will go to the back and pet the dog.*
*Now I will go up to my room.*
*Now I will see my stuff that hasn't existed for three whole months.*
*Now I will be this person again, the one that lives here.*

That was his only choice, so he pushed open the car door and went inside.

○ ○ ○

Inside was too confining, but outside was too bright, so Conrad squinted at the sidewalk passing underfoot, every square stained with what looked like dust-encrusted spit, and spotted with something like tar that might once have been gum, and broken by cracks thatched with dirty little weeds, and bordered by patches of grass fertilized with a confetti of ground-up litter. Up close, everything in Los Angeles was like this — L.A. was made of this stuff. Every trendy new thing stood right above it, always looking up as if the cracks would never spread. But nothing trendy lived here, not east of La Brea anyway. Crusty buildings baked at their corners like the prows of beached ships, the rich having receded toward the coast decades before.

At a particularly wide crack Conrad crouched to tie his shoe, hoping to see all the way down to the original soil, trodden by the native people, or at least to an older sidewalk from the Buster Keaton days. But he saw neither, only grit and specks of paper. He stood and continued walking, but after another block he lifted his eyes toward salvation: above a disappointed mini-mart and a dirty-looking dry-cleaners, along a walkway on the second floor where he would see Taqueria El Sapo, a hole-in-the-wall offering a burrito so delicious it was a mood-altering drug, able to make Los Angeles temporarily bearable for him. He'd been craving this burrito for three months straight — in fact without the thought of it he might have faded entirely into the woods. But now he didn't see it. The shop was dark and a 'For Rent' sign sealed the fact of it.

"God dammit!" he screamed. He could do that here, just like he could do in the woods. The trees didn't listen and neither did the parked cars. He was just another crazy person wandering in the heat.

What now? There were other burritos, loads of them, but Conrad was loyal, so he would mourn — for a day anyway. He'd seen leftovers in the fridge. Pointing his attention back to the ground he traced the blocks back home, square by square. But then-

*BOOM*

So loud it had to be nuclear, the eye-squeezing terror of the end! *Here it comes*, he thought, a microsecond of bleaching absolution: blades of grass washing green, sidewalk squares melting, buildings bending back — then powder, then white, then nothing...

Then nothing. Conrad opened his eyes and blinked: same cracks, same weeds. The sound had been a car backfiring, or that's what people always said. He'd never seen it happen in person. But this wasn't a fear that ever released him so fast. For a moment he stood shuddering in place. He had seen the movies: people's skeletons glowing white as the blue-screen fire swallowed them whole. In the woods he always imagined it happening far away, but now he'd returned to the target, his body exposed to the sky on the open streets. Any unsuspecting minute he could find himself going see-through — though not even a neutron bomb could make him more invisible than he already felt.

But would it burn him from the top down? *It couldn't be that simple.* Maybe the bomb's rays would reflect from the ground and fry him from below as well, or maybe from all sides... There wouldn't be time to feel, people said, but if somebody slowed the reel, his end wouldn't be instantaneous, would it? Something had to go first, from the outside in: his clothes blazing away like flash paper, his rubber tennis shoes goofifying, his skin flaking clear off the gristling fat and bone, his brains exploding and feet and arms and chest and legs and stomach sizzling shorter like fuses. And then, for the smallest slice of time, suspended in midair: his penis, glowing white-hot in a swirl of flames.

"What are you doing?"

It was Beth, walking Doonie, their grumpy little terrier, or rather dragging it behind her at the end of a leash. Beth was also standing still, but that was just how she was, as if she were going on fifty instead of fifth grade.

"Nothing," Conrad said.

"I can see that, but why?"

"I thought it was the end of the world."

Beth yanked the dog past him. "Well Mom's looking for you," she said.

Conrad turned the corner toward the house: still sitting there not vaporized, still rumpled as if a giant hand had accidentally dropped it from three feet in the air. Ever since their arrival Sueanna had been slowly altering its interior room-by-room — scraping off wallpaper then putting up new wallpaper, sanding old paint from the trim then painting over it, ripping up the old stained carpet then putting down fresh carpet — for the time being leaving everything outside looking as abandoned as when they first arrived. Scraggly grass hovered close to death, and actually dead plants still stood in pots left by the previous owner. This time of year it was good, however: Conrad was already planning the ghosts he would yank from gravestones when people walked by on Halloween. But for now he only floated in through the back door and slumped into a kitchen chair.

"Where did *you* go off to?" Sueanna asked.

"El Sapo's gone."

"Oh that place again? Didn't you get sick from there once? There's food in the fridge you know. You shouldn't waste your money."

"Uh-huh. Hey Mom can I have ten dollars?"

"What? I just gave you five."

"Yeah but the pawn shop has a whole box of oil paints."

"Since when do pawn shops sell paints? Are all the artists starving for real? And why are you going into that place? It's full of lowlife characters. You could be kidnapped by some old pervert and we'd never see you again."

"Yeah I know but what about the paints? I'd be saving so much money! There's even a cobalt blue."

Sueanna sighed. "I don't know... Why don't we go get you new ones? I always did like the art store. Your sisters said they needed something, now what was it?" She pointed her eyes at the ceiling.

"No! Last time we went there you said it was too expensive, and then you said you had a catalog with super-low prices, but you never found it because there's a million catalogs piled around here so I only ended up with a couple colors."

"I don't know, it just seems gross to use someone else's paints."

"It's just paint Mom, come on."

"Well I'll think about it."

Conrad dropped his chin into the heels of his hands. Sueanna changed the subject.

"Hey are you sure you're ready for school tomorrow? Got all your binders? Your pants are all ratty you know." A note of pleading crept into her voice. "Don't you want to go out for some new clothes, or shoes maybe?"

Conrad mumbled through his fingers. "I'm fine."

"Well don't get all excited or anything."

"Why should I."

"Well it's high school now. You'll make new friends." She said this as a matter of course as she packed cereal boxes into the cupboard.

"I don't care."

"What, you don't care about school and friends? That attitude won't get you anywhere there."

"I don't care about getting anywhere there. I don't even want to be there in the first place."

"Well that's not up for discussion so you'll just have to make the best of it."

It was always the same at times like this. Sueanna stood taller, and withheld her eyes, and faced away to whatever she happened to be doing. Conrad burned from the inside, not to be seen, but not being seen left him free to escape, so he did — up to his room where he fell onto his bed.

Now he had escaped, and it was just stupid, and he was stupid and everything was stupid. Scanning his eyes across his shelves he noticed a little package. He jumped to take it down and rip it open: sure enough, it was the silver minnow lure he had ordered from a bass-fishing catalog back in May. It had arrived too late, ending up high and dry in its clear-plastic sarcophagus for the whole summer. Now it would have to wait again for nine more months.

○ ○ ○

Sueanna leaned over as Conrad retreated from the car. "Maybe you could try smiling this year," she said, then blinked as if to repeat the suggestion before speeding away. Now there was nothing between Conrad and the noisy throng on the other side of the street: shouts and squeals and smiles and laughter that he couldn't imagine being party to. An overwhelming urge to escape rooted him to the spot. This would be his third year at The Divergent School, but once again he'd gone away and put the place completely out of his mind. Now he'd be forced to cram it all back in, even though it was completely pointless because nobody would see him anyway. He'd walk through all those sun-lit faces and none would turn. *Just one neutron bomb*, he thought. They would all go invisible, too.

Third period: history. Students sat in little study chairs along the walls of a windowless room while a gray-cotton sphere, cratered at the belly button, orbited between them. This was Mr. Sebastien. He passed in front of Anise, Conrad's dark star, briefly eclipsing her. Conrad diverted his attention to his folding desk, pushing it up with a finger to allow an imaginary boat to pass through to freedom, then lowering it, but as he raised it again a palm stretched from the side to stop him. Conrad followed the arm to its owner: Peter Fronton — darting goofball, incorrigible instigator. Anywhere else Peter would jump right into it, wild eyes gleaming, but not here, because Mr. Sebastien was exempt from the ninth-grade laws of nature. A legend had passed through the years: that History with Mr. Sebastien was both the best and the hardest class in school. If you didn't like history, you'd better start — doing poorly was a mark of shame. It didn't matter that the man was a grab-bag of easy targets: cloddish feet turned outward, unbending knees, a rotund middle that dragged the legs forward instead of walking, and a head intent on swallowing the face. It didn't matter because in that face were eyes you did not want to disappoint.

"Welcome back to 1983," the teacher said, as if he knew that Conrad needed reminding. "This year, mmph, will be special, for all of us." Mr. Sebastien pushed and grunted and barked his words. Conrad peeked beyond him to Anise, Anise of the dark flowing hair, Anise the brown-eyed, creamy-skinned, dimpled, deep-voiced spirit of pure somethingness. A curtain of hair fell to shield her face while she took diligent notes, leaving Conrad free to stare.

*Here I am,* he thought, *just like before.*

*Bad.*

*This has to be bad, looking at her like the summer never happened.*

*There's something wrong with this...*

But Anise was beautiful, so bad was good. Conrad lulled in her direction, soon finding himself alone in a room glowing white under skylights. But this wasn't heaven, and he wasn't dead: he was a celestial creator, hovering at the edges of existence but endowed with the power to draw life itself! Lifting his pencil, he began reeling a line from the eons of his memory, a never-ending stroke cohering gradually into a face. A door opened behind him — he heard footsteps, but no matter: he almost had the eyes! Yet when two warm hands grasped his shoulders, his pencil came to a halt. A tingling warmth spread all though him, turning him flesh again. Arms slipped around his chest. Dark hair blocked the light. Hot breath met his cheek.

"Our goal this year..." said Mr. Sebastien.

Conrad flinched — Anise was looking straight into his eyes from across the room.

"...is to understand how World War One came to pass, umph, and to do that we must begin at least in the previous century."

Conrad snapped his head sideways and scribbled the words 'previous century' in his notebook. In the corner of his eye Anise's pen also moved.

"Having completed the first section of your reading list within the coming weeks, you must bring me your project proposals the first Friday of October. Does everybody understand?"

"Yes, Mr. Sebastien!"

Books and papers flurried into bags. Conrad ran outside.

Divergent styled itself as a progressive school, but that was the only aspect of its style it had gained control over thus far. Its campus was still spreading like a cheerful fungus down a rag-tag string of formerly industrial buildings, far from any hint of high society and surrounded like an island by the impersonal rush of multi-lane streets, but despite the school's never-ending pleas for donations it would have hardly been conceivable for many of Conrad's classmates to be richer than they were. Little about the place made outward sense: young people in the latest fashions wandering a rutted alley between faceless buildings, attempts at public art colorizing the drab concrete walls, and here and there a 'shelter' built with found pallet wood and palm leaves — apparently constructed by those less-lucky students who hadn't been given their own BMWs to lounge in during the breaks (the administration had actually begun tearing the shelters down, until students staged the now-legendary 'palm frond revolt'). But the school's lack of ivy was exactly the attraction to the parents who sent their kids there. The barrenness of the campus promised that anything was possible, that the school's commitment to the arts and humanities wasn't just marketing — yet the students who were themselves committed to the arts were still the freaks, just like anywhere else.

One other thing the school lacked was a cafeteria. Instead a food truck parked in the alley where students rushed out at lunchtime to claim what was edible before it was gone. Being late was punishable by cucumber sandwich. But today Conrad had been quick. Standing by the food truck as usual was its hulking, expressionless owner, known to students simply as Food Truck Man. Conrad had tried and failed many times to make this man smile. Today would be no different.

"Long time no see!" Conrad said.

"Mmm."

"Got anything good today?"

"Uh-huh." The man stared over Conrad's shoulder. Conrad glanced in the same direction, to a parking area lined with pricey cars. Well-to-do teens sprawled across some of them with their smiling, gossiping faces turned up to the sun, their eyes protected from overabundant rays of good fortune by sleek black sunglasses. *I'll never be one of them,* Conrad thought. *Makes me sick.* He looked back at Food Truck Man and wondered if he felt the same, but only received the change for his chicken salsa burrito, vinegar chips and tangelo juice.

Conrad carried his feast to the sitting area next to the arts building, where the benches were enormously tall to make people feel like they had been shrunken (the product of a long-since-graduated art club). Dusty pines towered in the outer ring to complete the effect. From one of the benches a pair of skinny legs dangled down.

"Hey man," came an idle voice.

Conrad scrambled up the rungs on the side of the bench to see his friend Joey Mackal wearing the same ill-fitting black jeans, the same old Converse sneakers and the same Van Halen t-shirt, as if there hadn't been a three-month interruption to their lunchtime ritual.

Joey met Conrad's eyes only briefly before slipping back into cool-and-detached mode. "Got any good stories?" he asked as if not really expecting any.

"Oh you know, the usual stuff," Conrad said. It wouldn't be

polite to say that every fiber of his body strained to return to paradise and that Divergent and the whole city around it was at best a purgatory he would have to endure for the duration, because what would that mean about Joey?

"So no summer love?" Joey pressed.

Conrad shook his head.

"Bigfoot?"

"Nope."

"Bigfoot love?"

"You should really come visit next time."

Joey blew through his lips. "OK let me get this straight. I could be here, at the beach maybe, babes everywhere. *Or*, I could be roasting a possum on a stick in the middle of the tundra, not a girl in sight."

"There's no tundra," Conrad said, "and don't be so sure."

"Oh, so you've got something to tell me, huh?"

Joey was one of the rare people at school who could see Conrad, or so he'd always thought. It somehow felt less so today, but he played along anyway. "Well tell you the truth," Conrad said as if revealing a secret, "I did run into this pack of wild girls deep in the woods. Once their leader saw me they gave me so much trouble I swear, trying to drag me back to their huts."

"Aw hell!" Joey gurgled, tilting his head in mock desperation. "Mud and leaves and sticks, plastered all over my body! Take me there now!"

"Oh yeah? So what was so grand about summer in the concrete desert? Tell me that." Conrad waited for new and improved tales of sleazy romance from the mouth of a fourteen-year-old he knew had never had a date, let alone a kiss.

"Fine, I'll tell you, but just keep it between you and me." Joey paused and inhaled. His eyes narrowed to wistful slits. "First... there was Shalula," he sighed and squeezed voluminous air breasts with his hands. Conrad laughed at him.

"What's so funny up there?"

Conrad looked down to see Anise and her friends passing directly below. He didn't answer.

"I said, what's so funny, Conrad, huh?"

Conrad looked to Joey then back again. Anise stared up to him with an expression he couldn't read.

"It's, uh..." He slowed at the sight of her eyes — mottled brown like polished agates. "It's just that, uh..." He pointed at Joey. "He said Shalula."

"Oh, that's *real* funny. We'll be on our way now, bye!" Anise led her friends away, all smirking.

"Dude..." Joey also smirked. "I don't think your musky forest scent reached her down there."

"Yeah whatever," Conrad said, pretending to shrug it off even as his heart thumped.

"Man you are *so* pathetic."

o o o

At 3:30 Conrad stood near the exit. *I've sampled enough,* he thought. *Beam me out of here.* But the hallway was cool, so he hesitated at the gateway, squinting out at the glossy vehicles arriving one after another to fetch the incomprehensible beings he'd been observing all day. Confident light glinted from their eyes and metal and teeth.

*I'll have to be quick.*

A blast of September heat pursued him as he emerged. As if to out-pace the air, he scooted along the curb looking straight through the blur of passing faces before turning up and out of sight.

A freeway overpass took him closer to the sun, to a bus stop that was nothing more than an aluminum signpost sprouting from sun-baked cement. Here he moved as little as possible, slowing his blood as the minutes dragged by. He leaned his backpack from his shoulder against the post, to at least shade his face from the searing light. And he kept his legs straight, leaving an air gap between his pants and his skin so only the material would burn. He knew all the tricks.

Still more heat, broiling him, until a bus came squealing to a halt, driven by the same tough old lady as before. Her eyes twinkled a silent 'welcome back' as Conrad jumped up to sit near the front where he could watch her weathered arms stretch around and around, pulling the wide steering wheel to swerve the bus to and away from each curbside.

*She's been doing this the whole time,* Conrad thought. *I was sitting in the boat, or swimming, and her arms were doing that.*

*Weird.*

The bus soon filled to standing-room-only. Bodies swayed around him like carcasses in a meat locker, a collage of human detail he struggled to ignore: elbow wrinkles, and stomach bulges, and dandruff-specked shoulders, and belt buckles and finger hairs and scars and moles and acne. The eyes were the worst: gazing dead ahead unseeing. Conrad was a ghost here, much as at school — except the bodies on the bus weren't quite so white. He wasn't one of *these* people it seemed, and he wasn't one of *those* people either. He turned his eyes to the buildings passing outside, to the sun-cracked scenes looking more so through the smoke-tinted, knife-scratched, graffiti-covered plastic bubble windows. Months in the woods had scrambled his memory, but it all came back to him now as he spied the guitar shop, the little corner taco stand, the pet groomers... all set back behind repeating patterns of parked cars and buckling concrete and faded signs and dust-coated bushes. Long stretches appeared abandoned despite the traffic.

Conrad sank deeper down, propped his knees on the seat in front of him and closed his eyes. Now he only felt the regular tide of the bus roaring to accelerate, then slowing, then again. It all began to lull him.

What!

Dim shapes blurred by the window, but then Conrad saw the unmistakable neon sign of an old diner, which meant... *two stops late.* "Back door!" he yelled and squirmed through warm flesh out the rear exit, dropping out to stand dazed on the sidewalk. But as the bus roared away he looked up at the 'XXX Arts' movie theater and the 'Peekshop' adult book store next to it and remembered that the pawn shop was just down the block.

By the time Conrad made it back up near home, the sun was low and a light was on in Mr. Onter's house, a little old-world bungalow set back from the street behind drooping avocado trees. Conrad cut the lawn here for cash, while in Mr. Onter himself he had found a never-ending source of interest. He decided to stop and knock.

"Conrad, back from the wilds," said Mr. Onter, his face impassive as he pulled open his ornately-carved front door. "Come in. You're just in time to hear my new acquisition."

Mr. Onter didn't bother with small-talk questions about Conrad's summer, as if it had only been a weekend, and instead led him to the side room, a sanctum of floor-to-ceiling books and records neatly arranged on polished wood shelves. A long antique sofa at one end of the room faced a pair of imposing speakers at the other. Conrad perched himself on the sofa and scanned around as Mr. Onter fiddled with the stereo.

Mr. Onter hadn't changed, but of course he never did. Today he was clothed in his usual after-work attire (the informal kind of formal-wear), and his wavy gray hair was brushed back in the same way at the same length. The books however had changed positions, and a large set of leather-bound volumes now took up half a shelf. Conrad figured he would be hearing about these very soon.

"What's in the box?" asked Mr. Onter.

"Used paint."

"Oh? What an excellent idea. If the painting's no good, just put the paint back in the tubes."

Conrad nodded. "That's right."

Mr. Onter pulled a record from its sleeve. "Happy to be back?"

"No."

"I should have guessed. I seem to remember you saying that last time."

Conrad scowled. "I hate it here." But after a moment he added, "well not *here* here."

It was true — Mr. Onter's house was a kind of sanctuary. Even now Mr. Onter refrained from judgment. "Well we should talk about that some time," he said. "I take it you're in high school now?"

"Yeah. It's so weird."

"Mmm-hmm. Nothing about being your age *isn't* weird, but don't worry, four years is the blink of an eye. Anyway, listen to this." Mr. Onter dropped the needle and stood up to watch Conrad's face.

The needle floated with quiet pops, then a piano pounded into the room, hammering forward at first, then pulsating, then thrashing and whirling in cycles, then rushing to an end.

Mr. Onter squinted with satisfaction at the sight of Conrad so absorbed. "Can you believe that's from 1848? It's called *Allegro Barbaro*."

"It's like a punk-rock song," Conrad suggested.

"I don't know about *that*, but it sure was ahead of its time. It's by Charles Alkan. I've been looking into him lately."

Conrad fidgeted at his comparison being waved off, thinking that Mr. Onter had likely never heard a punk song. But he liked the music so he asked to hear it again. "Wow, that's nuts," he said when it had finished the second time.

"Yes and just wait till you hear this other one he wrote, it's called *Minuetto alla Tedesca*. It's incredible! But maybe next time, judging by your restless legs. This weekend then, the lawn?"

"Yessiree."

Conrad plopped himself at the dinner table and looked from sister to sister: both had turned to stone, but their eyes still burned with eternal fury. Conrad looked to Sueanna.

"Mom, what's, uh..."

"Oh let's not mention anything about it," she said with a quick shake of her nose. She laid down a foil-covered casserole dish and sat at the end of the table. "Let's all just be nice. What took you so long to come home?"

"Mr. Onter stopped me about his lawn," Conrad said. He never mentioned hanging around inside Mr. Onter's house listening to music or peering at old maps. But now Levy's rage began to wear off — an elbow twisted upside-down and a gremlin voice leaked out.

"Mark - my - word," she croaked. "That man will rape you one day."

Beth cracked a giggle.

"Levy!" their mother scolded. "That is not appropriate language for a young girl! Especially not at the dinner table."

Levy pooched her lips in pretend shame. Sueanna eyed her for a moment but then turned to Conrad.

"You have to be careful of that man. He lives there by himself."

"Wait, Mom?" Conrad said, caught off guard.

"You can't be too trusting. He could try to take advantage of you."

"Oh he's fine. Don't worry so much."

"Well I just think he's probably, you know... And he might very well like young boys."

"Mom! He just needs his lawn cut. Sheesh."

"Don't talk back to me like that. I hear stories all the time about what some disgusting men do."

Conrad groaned and reached to lift the casserole foil in a bid to deflect the subject. It worked.

"SPSP!" Levy and Beth called out, the last of their anger vaporized by the sight of dark orange waves in the casserole dish: sweet potato shepherd's pie (olive-oily whipped sweet potatoes on top, spicy fatty meaty goodness on the bottom). Conrad stood up to cut out heaving portions to drop on each plate while the girls commenced a show of piggy snarfing.

"Mmm num num num, must eat more."

"Face – not – enough – full, num num."

"Stuff more, num num num."

Their chins were soon slick with orange dribble. Sueanna's posture straightened. "That is not ladylike behavior!" she said. "I expect better of you both. What if you did that when guests were here?"

"Oh we would never embarrass you, Mom," said Levy. Beth shook her head in earnest agreement. Both wiped their faces and sat prissy-straight. "We would eat like this." Little fingers held out stiff, they took minuscule bites.

"Oh isn't this divine?"

"Yes, quite my dear. Quite."

Their mother decided this was a more acceptable show and let it pass.

○ ○ ○

A storm passing above the rain-forest washed the trees, and shushed them. Conrad's face bobbed just above the river's surface as he drifted downstream, calmed by the rush of misty rain and the rhythmic dripping from nearby branches. He liked it here in the Peruvian jungle. He would stay.

Thunder.

"Conrad what are you still in there for?"

Beth was at the door. It was always Beth, pounding and questioning. He didn't answer, but now he heard Levy outside as well. "He's in there with his imaginary friend Jack," she pretended to whisper.

"Oh yeah?" Beth said back.

"Mmm-hmm. She's real pretty too."

"Wait, Jack's a girl?" Beth was genuinely perplexed.

"That's right. Her skin's like *oh* so smooth, like butter. Conrad's always going off with her."

"Would you two go away?!" Conrad yelled. The river was the tub, the rain came from the shower head, and the forest canopy was a large green beach towel from the closet. He liked to cover himself in the water, steaming and meditating under the loud patter of the shower rain on the towel. But somebody always ruined it. "Leave me alone!" he yelled again.

"You mean leave *us* alone?" Levy corrected.

"Just shut up and leave!"

There was no Jack today, though she wasn't wrong — but that was none of her business. And now to make it worse Sueanna's voice joined in.

"What are you girls bothering him for? Don't you have homework to finish?"

"He's been in there since before eight," Beth informed her.

"Conrad is that true?" Now Sueanna knocked.

"I'm showering!"

"For three-quarters of an hour? You have shares in the water company?"

"That's what Dad says!"

"He's acting weird again," he heard Levy murmur.

"I don't want to hear about it," Sueanna scolded her, then spoke through the door, "and I don't want to hear about *him* either! You come out, and you girls go back to work."

When the giggles had retreated, Conrad emerged from his jungle into a world of drab beige tile to dry himself off. In the hallway, after slipping into a t-shirt and cut-off pajama bottoms, the air felt cooler on his skin than it was, so he moved like a sloth, arms and legs wide apart, to prolong the tingles. He caught sight of Sueanna in her room, facing away at her desk writing checks under a lamp. He crept closer and leaned on the door-frame. A minute passed before Sueanna turned her head with a little start.

"Oh! It's my son," she said, but turned back to the checkbook. "I half-expected a prune."

Conrad squished his nose against the enameled wood. "Mom?" he murmured. "I just don't get any of it."

"Any of what?"

"All of it. Everything's so weird. People just running around. I can't see why they're doing the things they do."

"Well all you have to do is ask them."

"OK. So why are *we* doing all these things? It's like we're just as crazy as them. I mean, why are we even here? We could've moved to New York instead, or I don't know, Iceland or someplace..."

"Oh what do you know about Iceland."

"But why did we have to move at all? We're just doing the same things here we'd do there."

"It's better here, that's all."

Conrad grumbled at this. "That's not saying anything. You always say stuff like that."

"Well I'm sorry to disappoint you." Sueanna ripped off a check and started another. Staying on task helped her to stay firm. "You're thinking too much. Maybe if you put some of that thinking into your homework your grades would improve. You have homework don't you?"

"Yeah."

Conrad drifted back to his room and pulled out his history assignment, but the Peruvian river had been too relaxing and his mother the opposite. He stared at the pink mimeographed sheet without comprehending until his head sank sideways onto his desk.

# 3

# Early October

"Listen to your eyes!" Mrs. Pelora, the art teacher, coached her students as she paced the perimeter of the room.

*Feet... so strong-looking, and her toes are spread apart.*

Really Conrad was talking *to* his eyes, he felt, not the other way around.

"Emphasize the lengths!" the teacher pressed again.

*Calves... toned and curvy, like rolling hills...*

"Follow from the limbs! Their volume defines the torso!"

*Knees... indented on the straight leg but not the bent one. I never noticed that.*

"Look, people! What are your eyes telling you?"

*Vagina.*

That's what his eyes were saying.

*Vagina.*

"Look first, then do!"

*Vagina... It's so soft-looking, how the hairs sweep toward the middle like that...*

At Divergent you could actually fail art, and nude models started in the ninth grade, a titillating prospect until it wasn't: all business, Mrs. Pelora had begun with models sure to scramble expectations. First came a very elderly British lady, reclining proudly across an ottoman, her limitless wrinkly folds posing such challenges that few students finished their drawings before the bell rang. Then the next week brought a towering god of a man, all sinewy muscle woven under burnished deep-brown skin, his penis too prominent to overlook. A notable day that was: girls quick-peeking from behind their easels, boys sitting ridiculously upright as if to suggest that they were also men. Also Mrs. Pelora, silently enraged, dragging a boy out by his collar for implying that Gabby, the only black student in class, would be especially interested in the model's endowments. Sweet quiet Gabby, hot-faced in the corner — Conrad had wanted to say something nice to her after class but didn't know what.

But this time...

Conrad sketched with purpose despite today's model being a young woman of exceptional fitness facing him naked just ten feet away. He looked around his easel to follow the woman's sandy hair curving down along her ivory chest. The edges of her nipples, he noticed, weren't flat — they had little bumps. Did the bumps have a name? And he could see a faint blue vein going up the side of a breast.

*We say 'woman,' or 'girl'...*
*But this is an animal...*
*With a vagina.*

Conrad felt his gaze drawn down by gravity. He imagined brushing his fingers on the hairs. But then he caught himself and pressed his legs together, catching the attention of Stacy Branden next to him. Stacy's thick-braided head turned slowly, expressionless. But then she made horsey-teeth and bugged out her eyes. Just as quickly she turned away as the teacher arrived.

"Longer, longer! The legs are longer. Look!" Mrs. Pelora leaned down to look with Conrad, her vanilla-scented body oil causing the little moles on the model's skin to appear to him as chocolate chips. She pointed at the model's legs. "See, they're much longer than your brain assumes. Make your hands obey your eyes."

Conrad erased both legs, then looked at the model again to count how many of her heads would line up along the leg that was outstretched. He measured with his fingers on the paper. He looked again. What was the outer shape? And the 'negative space' on the inside? He drew careful lines and erased them each time as they failed to match what he was seeing. *Ugh!*

Running out of patience, he winged it, drawing an entire new leg from instinct. There! He sat up with a rush of satisfaction: it looked just like the real leg, a perfect gesture in just a few lines. But then again, no: the new leg was too big for the body, like a balloon animal gone wrong. Should he erase the perfect leg, or the rest of the body he had so carefully penciled?

"Let's all thank Linda, our excellent model for today!" Mrs. Pelora called out. "Please sign and turn in your drawings."

Mrs. Pelora unhooked a white bathrobe and carried it across the room, and Conrad spied sideways as the model reached to accept it. At rest her shape had been magazine-perfect, but now it wiggled outside the lines and it was alarming, *alien!* All those parts could shake and bend and fold, and did so whenever she moved.

*Girls are weird.*

*People are weird.*

Conrad shoved his drawing into the middle of the stack and shot out into the alley where his naked art dream bubble vaporized under the hot sun, leaving him wide open. Sure enough, a feeling that dogged him rushed right back in. *You have to get out of here*, it growled day after day. He was always aware of the fence at the end of the campus, as if he might just up and scale it. *Run,* the feeling said now: he hadn't finished his history proposal. But instead of running he stopped to think. Skip chemistry? *Impossible.* An important lab was planned for that day and he'd only be in new trouble.

Trouble!

Anise was standing at the other end of the alley, all by herself. He could pass near her if he hurried! His feet launched him forward, but a sudden dark squish bounced him backside-first onto the asphalt. Looking up he saw it was the model, standing tall and toned above him in shorts and a polo shirt. He had sunk face-first into her warm giving chest, and his hands had pressed onto her legs to stop himself. The thrilling after-impressions of both lingered in his mind.

*Girls are nice.*

"Oh I'm sorry!" he whispered. The woman reached a firm

smooth hand into his to lift him up, then straightened her clothes and said it was nothing before going on her way. Dazed, Conrad watched her legs walking away, but then he became aware *down there*, aware that he *had better not stand straight*. He glanced up: Anise was closer this time, with a hand over her mouth. But she couldn't see, could she? *About face!* He swiveled and retreated, scooting between two buildings where he folded himself up to wait.

*Boys are weird.*

*And jeans are better, not these stupid khakis.*

*Please...*

*Please just stop already.*

*God dammit!*

By the time Conrad could stand, something else had grown: a smoldering mortification. And he was late for chemistry, but when he arrived the teacher was missing and two boys in the corner were threatening each other with their lab equipment.

"I daresay I shall transform you into a newt!" Todd Barnes squawked in a hammy British accent, waving a flask in the air. Robb Cott defended himself with a test tube brush yelling "bugger off!" Both wore pricey plaid shirts, creased trousers and penny-loafers, and as far as Conrad could tell their roles had always been to saunter around campus deciding who was a freak, to make chortling noises, and to bask in the giggles. Conrad's resentment of these two had long since thickened to a paste, furthered by the eighth grade catch-phrase, whispered from girl to girl: "Robb or Todd?" — not to mention an old rumor about Robb and Anise that some people said was made up.

The classroom chatter had grown deafening when Miss Lanto tramped through the door, but she launched straight into the day's task.

"Right! OK! As you know, today we'll be working further through methods of chemical separation!" Miss Lanto was young and attractive but exuded a toughness that sent the students scurrying into action. "Your first experiment today is called Paper Chromatography. As always, please read the instructions carefully with your lab partner. Get to it!"

Conrad's lab partner was Stacy Branden, of the braids, noted for winning the science fair two years in a row. Normally Conrad let her run the experiments, but this time he pressed ahead stiff-faced and mute as if unaware of his own hands. Behind his eyeballs a separate scene played out: the first time he had embarrassed himself in front of Anise, then the second, then the third, the fourth, the fifth...

*Idiot!*

*Yes, you.*

*You are an idiot.*

*Go back to where you belong, idiot.*

Stacy squinted sideways as they worked through the steps. "Don't forget the stopper!" she said, poking a finger on the directions. "It says the solvent will evaporate. We wouldn't want you breathing that, now would we. You've already had a big distraction today I seem to remember."

Conrad jumped.

Stacy leaned back. "What?"

Now it occurred to Conrad that Stacy had meant the model in class, not the model in the alley, and certainly not Anise. He turned to Stacy and made horsey teeth to cover himself, and Stacy smirked, but traces of doubt lingered in her eyes.

After that Conrad stayed quiet until the lab was finished, only then giving a curt thanks. Stacy watched him leave. "Don't forget your face!" she yelled after him.

Conrad squeezed through a throng of students blocking the exit and ran, hoping to get a word in with Mr. Sebastien before class, but the halls were already empty. Then at the classroom door he froze: the last open seat was his usual spot with Peter Fronton on the left, but to the right was Anise, impossibly separated from her friends Carrie and Amy across the room.

The teacher looked over and grunted. "Take a seat mister," he said.

The seat took Conrad, his limbs all turning to rubber as he bent himself in, but mercifully Anise was busy inscribing the date at the top of her notebook. Mr. Sebastien stood up.

"Mmm! OK folks, the time has arrived to pass in your proposals."

Rather than break out in lazy groans like in any other class, here the ring of students moved like nervous junior lawyers presenting their dockets. Mr. Sebastien began making the rounds, personally extending a hand to receive — or rather *expect* — each student's work. Conrad pulled out his proposal, such as it was, and hastily jotted a plea at the top of the first page:

I am stuck on this and need help.

At least his disaster was bound in a folder, so Anise wouldn't see.

"Thanks Anise," said Mr. Sebastien. Anise's folder was gray and professional, with a clean white title card glued to the front, but before Conrad could peek at it the teacher had laid it on the stack in his arms. Anise relaxed back into her chair and smoothed her hair behind her ears.

Mr. Sebastien pulled in front and the hand came out. Conrad raised his folder and forced a stiff smile. At this the teacher cocked an eye, but an instant later he said "Thank you Conrad" and continued on his way.

"Psst. What's your proposal about?"

"Thank you, Peter."

"Conrad, what's your project about?"

It was a whisper, from the right.

And...

Anise was the whisperer.

And...

She had whispered his name.

"Psst!"

Conrad's eyes strained to the side but his neck turned only halfway. Words separated from their meanings.

"It's uh, it..., um, it has to do with painters," Conrad managed to say. He looked for one instant to her face then away again.

"Painters? What does that have to do with World War One?"

Conrad felt the face heat coming on, the instant lockjaw. He had to say something quick.

"Well, the idea is, um, German painters, they, you know, show how people thought... before the war." Conrad felt relief at having put together a nearly coherent sentence. He figured this would satisfy her.

"Oh that's a cool idea. So what is it the painters show about them?"

"Thank you, Brenda," said Mr. Sebastien across the room, at the last student in the ring.

*Please, Mr. Sebastien, start talking.*

Conrad looked to the right again, to the clear eyes so alarmingly open to him. "They show that the Germans really liked sausages," he said all of a sudden, as if the words had burped up uninvited. Anise began to blink.

"Very good!" said Mr. Sebastien. "All of you gave me a proposal today, which makes me, mmph, very happy. Now let's get back to our discussion of industry and warfare."

When Conrad looked again Anise had turned herself forward with her mouth folded in, again taking charge of her notebook, etching her little letters. Conrad did the same, but with less straight shoulders than hers. He didn't look in her direction again.

At lunch Conrad and Joey both moped on the high bench, Conrad not speaking unless spoken to, Joey twisting in frustration.

"Just look at that," Joey said breathlessly, motioning toward the other side of the alley where their classmate Lacey Flanigan stood facing a junior named George, the latter known for being 'cute' on a level above other boys described the same way. As for the girl, Joey's considerable infatuation was split between Lacey and another named Angela, thankfully not present. Conrad imagined Joey's head melting into pudding if both girls were to come into view at the same time. Lacey was blond and fit and brightly pretty, while Angela, also blond, passively glowed with an old-movie allure. In both cases Conrad felt nothing. It was nice. He could enjoy their attractions without finding himself curled into a blubbering pretzel like with Anise. But if pressed to choose between Lacey and Angela he would say Lacey, since Lacey liked to wear tight pastel jeans and moved like she could run to save her own life.

"Oh man," Joey groaned, still gazing and suffering. "I bet her pussy's so tight."

"What good would that do?" Conrad asked.

"Someday, man. Someday you'll know."

"Wouldn't that just make it hurt more, for her I mean?"

"You're such a dumb-fuck," Joey said, craning his neck to get another look. "How are we supposed to compete with that guy?"

"Who, George? I'm not competing with him."

"Sure you are. Just wait. He'll be talking to Anise next." Joey turned back to his sandwich. "Shit man. I can't take this anymore."

"Yeah," Conrad grumbled. "I just want to get out of here."

At 3:30 Conrad stuffed his books into his bag, slammed his locker door and escaped outside where the school and everyone in it would recede behind him into a separate, less desirable dimension. But cars jammed the street. Waiting for a chance to cross, he bounced up and down on his toes while studying the fine texture of the curb, the pitted surface of the road, and the jagged, imperfect place where they met. He pictured the background din of teenage goodbyes as a liquid that the little pores in the cement were absorbing. But then the shape of his name floated by — someone was pointing at the other end of the block, someone female.

Conrad glanced toward the school building. Whoever had pointed was now pretending she hadn't, but Anise was among them and was looking in his direction. He was being watched. That couldn't be good. He focused on the passing cars.

*Smile at her? That's silly.*

*Wave? They're all laughing at me, calling me a dork.*

As a compromise, Conrad rotated his head in Anise's general direction and raised his eyebrows a few times. With that he crossed and headed for the overpass without looking back.

○ ○ ○

A winding tunnel constructed from chicken-wire covered with ratty old clothes snaked for twenty feet across the grass. Beth placed a bit of lettuce at one end, while Levy sealed a guinea pig into the other and proceeded to chameleon-crawl back to her sister. Halfway she stopped and extended an arm.

"Don't you dare peek!" Beth yelled.

Levy retracted her hand and crept on. "I just wanted to see where it is," she said.

"No cheating."

A slam reverberated through the house — the front door. After a moment they could hear Sueanna in the sun room calling out "Conrad, you didn't answer me!" Seconds later, Conrad emerged from the sliding back door and made for the garage.

"Conrad, look what we did!" Beth called.

"That's very nice," he said without looking.

Levy stood up to watch him pass. "The ghoul has been released," she whispered. Beth nodded.

Conrad entered through the garage's side door and surveyed the dusty collection of family artifacts piled up beyond the rows of guinea pig cages. Reaching up to the back shelf, he yanked down his old easel with a clatter that sent a rustle of alarm through the herd. When he came back out his sisters were on their knees looking into the tunnel exit.

"It's coming!" Beth squeaked. A guinea pig's nose could be seen twitching in the shadows. In another moment it scurried out to the lettuce and began to chew with sewing-machine precision. Conrad pretended this wasn't funny and headed back into the house.

"I don't appreciate being brushed off when I greet my son," his mother said as he attempted to pass through the kitchen. He stopped but faced the exit.

"I didn't have anything to say."

"It doesn't matter if you're in a bad mood. If your mother greets you, you respond. It's not my fault you're grumpy." She held herself imperiously when talking like this, but without looking his way. Conrad peered beyond her to the counter. Kitchen tools and bits of food covered the entire surface. "A friend of mine is coming over for dinner and I need you to be nice," Sueanna added. "She's bringing her son, too. He's your age, and very nice. Gets all A's in school and he does magic, too. Maybe you can make a new friend for once. Go clean up and change."

"But why change? We're not going out."

"I need you to look *nice* for my friend. I'm not going to have my kids looking like a bunch of sloppy hicks when I have guests."

"But I have stuff to do! You didn't even tell me about this."

"I don't have to tell you, I'm your mother. And anyway you were just going to go mess around with your paints. A little socializing won't hurt you."

Conrad stomped up to his room and collapsed face-first onto the wool blanket that covered his bed. It was the exact twin of the blanket on his bed at his father's house, with the same label at the corner, but here it never felt as cool to the touch.

Levy and Beth came pounding upstairs and burst in.

"I call the shower!" Levy announced. "I'm all stinky and covered in grass." She stood with her arms and legs far apart from her body, apparently to keep them from sticking.

Conrad's voice came out muffled from inside the mattress. "Who said you guys could come in here?" he demanded.

"What's eating you anyway?" Levy asked.

Conrad sat up. "Nothing. Get out of here."

"What's eating you anyway?" Levy asked again.

"Would you get out? I need to change!"

"What's eating you anyway?"

Conrad jumped up but Levy bolted out of the room and locked herself in the bathroom across the hall where she could be heard repeating "What's eating you anyway?" behind the door.

Beth however stood staring up at Conrad's face. "I'm sorry you're having a bad day," she finally said.

Conrad stood for a moment close-lipped. He wondered where she had learned to talk that way.

"So what do you plan to wear?" she continued. "I only have normal clothes, plus a dress that's too fancy. I'm not sure how changing will make me look any better."

"Same here. I only have that one suit…"

They looked at each other again, squinty.

"Right then!" said Beth, turning to leave. "I'll tell Levy."


"Kids! Kids! Our guests have arrived!"

Sueanna had been too harried to check upstairs in person. Now she stood at the front door greeting the guests, Karen and her son Tony. Both were dressed casually.

"Kids, hurry down!" Sueanna called again. Her children flew down the steps on cue.

"Oh hello!" said Levy, uncharacteristically first to speak. "My mother has told us so much about you both."

Sueanna blinked, seeing that her monkey-daughter had transformed into a princess wearing a bright pink gown, with even her hair tamed and clipped.

"I'm Conrad! It's very nice to meet you. And your name is…?"

"Uh, Tony?" said Tony, hesitant as Conrad squeezed his hand in close confidence. For his part, Conrad was buttoned up tight in his seventh-grade suit, complete with a florid tie and non-prescription glasses from an old Halloween outfit.

"Hee hee!" Beth giggled like a cutie-pie, her ballerina dress bouncing as she curtsied.

"Sueanna your kids are adorable!" Karen cooed. Whether this was sincere Conrad couldn't tell. Sueanna however was cornered.

"Oh, well, we'll see about that," she said, "Let's all go sit down."

The table was laid out with real cloth napkins and the good silverware, with a cut glass water pitcher standing among a great number of tea-plates populated by appetizers that Sueanna had learned to make from cooking magazines. Conrad leaned his nose closer to the Figs In Savory Sauce. Beth made a wall with her hands to defend them.

"Kids let's make sure to let our guests try these first, OK?" Sueanna said, her voice high and unsteady. "Tony, any chance you'll give us a show today?"

Tony nodded. "You bet!" he said with a smile. Noticing Conrad watching, he narrowed his eyes.

Karen leaned in. "Oh he's been learning so much from his mentor these days" she said. "He comes home with a new trick every week."

"Where did you find him?" asked Sueanna.

"Him? Oh no, the mentor's a *she*, from the Magic Castle. Her name's Alexandra. Isn't that a perfectly magical name? And *such* a lovely woman."

Tony shook his eyebrows at Conrad.

"Hmm," Sueanna hummed, staring through her plate. After a pause she turned. "Say Conrad, that gives me an idea. Maybe you should have an art mentor?"

Conrad blinked. *Art Mentor.* The concept had never entered his mind. But his mind calculated.

"Um, yeah," he said. "But who?"

"How about Mr. Onter?" Beth proposed, still using her baby voice.

Levy sat up. "Oh good idea! He's been *such* a good influence on Conrad."

Conrad glared at them both.

"We'll think about it later," Sueanna cut in. "Who'd like to try the crusted chicken?"

After dinner Sueanna herded everyone into the living room and dimmed the lights. Tony disappeared, then, striding from the kitchen wearing a black satin cape, launched immediately into his first trick in which the number of balls in his hands kept changing.

"Did you say five balls? Take another look, just to be sure..."

Levy and Beth watched from the floor. Conrad watched them watching: Beth kept perfectly still, tracking Tony's every gesture to spy the secrets, while Levy rolled in circles on her bottom, boy-stoned, gazing at Tony's face.

Tony soon finished with the balls and moved on to card tricks, speaking to his audience in deep-velvet words. "I think you will all agree that *this* is the card you saw earlier. Am I correct?"

Conrad saw what he didn't see: through trick after trick, never a moment of awkwardness, not a single unscripted feeling or brow-bead of sweat. In Tony he saw not a boy his own age but the offspring of an alien race, ice-blue certainty coursing through its veins and glimmering in its eyes. Conrad had encountered these beings before: they could shrink him with a look.

The show ended to claps and hoots as Tony glided out of the room.

"Well that was just excellent!" said Sueanna, standing up. "Now Conrad, why don't you take Tony to your room to study? I want to hang out with Karen a bit more. Girls, same for you."

Conrad led Tony upstairs. "This is it," he said, hiding his reluctance. "You can sit at the desk."

Tony scanned around Conrad's bedroom with the look of smiling curiosity that people wear in art galleries. "Nice place!" he said. Whether this was sincere was impossible to read.

Now Conrad saw his bedroom as an outsider: wrinkly clothes, failed drawings and old fishing magazines formed a lasagna that obscured the floor. Summer t-shirts still flopped from a suitcase standing half-open against the wall. But it was too late to fix, so Conrad unbuttoned his costume and folded it on his bed. His confidence folded with it as Tony watched. Conrad unpacked his books onto his bed, then laid out his various assignments in a row, Tony's eyes following his every movement. After long minutes of this Conrad felt like a zoo animal.

"So what's the deal with your family?" Tony asked. "You guys always dress up like church for dinner?"

"Oh no, we were just pranking my mom," Conrad said, smiling

with hope for some common ground. "She kept bugging us to look good." But Tony only stared, so Conrad added, "I don't always get along with my mom like you do."

"My mom's a total bitch," Tony said, hardly blinking, "and I'm her only kid so she never leaves me alone."

Conrad rifled through his drawer for a pen. "Huh," he said after a pause, as if he'd learned a mundane fact.

"So who decided it?" Tony asked. "Did you and your sisters, like, have a meeting or something?"

"Meeting? No... We were complaining I guess, then the idea just came. It's always like that, like chemicals."

"Oh," Tony said, still appearing to feel that it was some sort of sibling black magic.

Conrad turned to his reading. Not catching the hint, Tony sat facing Conrad as if expecting more attention.

"Want to see something?" he asked.

Conrad gave up on his book and rolled off the bed. Smiling keenly, Tony reached into his bag to pull out a large leather volume with a built-in combination lock.

"I tell my mom it's my journal, but really..."

Tony covertly dialed the lock, pulled off the strap and opened to the first page.

"...it's my *collection*."

Conrad looked down to what at first glance appeared to be some sort of grisly collage — crime scene closeups maybe, or human remains from a plane crash. But his vision soon resolved: it was breasts and vaginas, a crazy-quilt of lady parts close-cropped from magazines, covering the page to its edges.

"These are the big ones," Tony said, flipping to another page covered exclusively in round bulging boobs. Conrad couldn't see how these were necessarily bigger, since there were no bodies to compare for scale, let alone faces. He started to fidget.

"This page has the really bushy pussies," Tony continued, turning the page. Like in a bird species book, every variation of plumage covered the available space. He turned the page again. "And these are the shaved ones. I can't decide which I like better."

Tony waited as if expecting an opinion one way or the other. Conrad stifled an urge to laugh. Whatever was mystically thrilling about seeing a woman's body had gone missing from this, while every animal detail was horrifically enlarged. Nevertheless he reached over to flip the page back and forth between 'bushy' and 'shaved' like an animation, faster and faster.

"I can't decide," he answered. "How long did it take to, uh, collect all these?"

"Oh, long long time." Tony lowered his voice to bank heist level. "I have to sneak the magazines into the house, and then I go through them and find the best parts. How about you? Got any good magazines?"

Conrad shook his head. "No, just bass fishing stuff," he said, lying. A Playboy was hidden right over their heads in the attic, with a sly woman hanging her long brown hair over the edge of a sofa, but Conrad wouldn't mention it. Tony might try to cut out her 'best parts.'

"Boys!" Sueanna called from the stairs. "It's time for Tony to go!"

Tony shoved the folder into his bag. "Great hanging out!" he said, standing up and shaking Conrad's hand with a smile that beamed out of proportion to the short time they had spent together. Conrad nodded and followed Tony downstairs just far enough to lean around the wall.

"Bye! Nice to meet you!" he called, waiting for Karen to wave back before hurrying back up and locking himself in his room. He pulled his easel over to the desk to inspect the malfunctioning screws that locked its legs. Soon enough, Sueanna was at the door.

"Conrad, I want to talk to you," said her voice through the wood.

"I have homework."

"Open the door so I can talk to you."

"I still have reading to do! Tony just talked the whole time."

For a few moments it was quiet, but he could tell Sueanna hadn't moved.

"Open the door this minute!" she yelled, making him jump.

Conrad leaned his easel at the end of the desk, scooted over to unlock the door, then retreated to his bed.

Sueanna stepped just into the room. She crossed her arms and stared at her son, who had engaged himself in the careful placement of his books and papers in relation to each other on the bedspread.

"Conrad, I don't appreciate you trying to embarrass me in front of my friend," she said.

Conrad didn't look at her. "You told us to dress up," he said.

"I told you to look nice, meaning look less scruffy."

"But how were we supposed to know *how much* less scruffy you wanted? None of us knew what to wear."

"That's not the point," she said, more heated this time. "You and your sisters put on a silly act for my friend. Now how do you think we seem to her?"

"We seemed adorable. That's what she said."

Sueanna stood breathing through her nose. "You just don't care how we look as a family, do you," she said. "It's so hard for me to have a social life, but it's all a big joke to you isn't it."

"Who says I want to be in this family anyway?" Conrad said louder, facing her now. "I didn't want to be here in the first place!"

Sueanna's mouth clasped shut. Conrad turned back to his papers and sulked.

"That's very hurtful," Sueanna said after watching him for a moment. "You're so ungrateful." Then she left and closed the door.

o o o

The stifling loaf of air hovering in Conrad's bedroom refused to pass through his open windows. It was waiting to smother him, he was sure, the moment he dozed onto his homework. He had to get out! Hearing nothing in the hallway, he crept down the stairs and out the back door, then scurried along the side of the house to the street. There he sat on the curb against a streetlight pole and closed his eyes.

Now he could breathe. The warm Santa Ana winds, lately dehydrating the city, soothed him as they blew down from the darkened hills. He leaned back to allow the streetlight to glow sky-blue through his eyelids. Soon he was lying on the dock again, drying himself in the sun. His beaded skin shivered in the breeze and warmed when it paused. The air was always moving somewhere, now at the far end of the bay, crossing back again.

"What's up, buddy-o?"

Conrad jumped to his feet, but then he groaned and deflated back down to the curb as Levy emerged from the shadows.

"Dammit Levy. Mom didn't send you, did she?"

"Nope. I've been hiding in my room. She's really pissed."

"I'll say."

Conrad didn't have to ask how Levy knew where he was, since sitting under the street light was an established ritual. At first Levy balanced back and forth along the curb as if crossing a log over a gorge, but she soon folded herself down into a gargoyle, resting her head sideways on her knees. The warm wind was too calming for even Levy to fidget now.

"I can see the hills," she murmured.

Conrad raised his head and squinted through the glare of the streetlights to the outline of nearby hilltops cutting across the night sky. In those hills were trails. "Mm-hmm," he drawled. "It's high time we get outta here, girl."

"Yep."

"So Levy..."

"Yeah?"

"When girls look at guys, what do they think about?"

Levy blinked her eyes. "Oh all sorts of things."

"Like what?"

"Oh, so you want to know if girls think about what's down there all jingly-jangly when guys walk around, every one of 'em? Wouldn't the boys like to know if that were true."

"No! I mean other stuff, like, I don't know... like what they think guys are thinking. It's all this big mystery and nobody knows what's going on."

Levy looked up to the sky and shook her head in slow motion. "It's way, way too complicated for you."

"Oh god." Conrad gave up and sank his head. "I bet you're totally forgetting at that girls school."

"No I'm not."

"Yeah sure. So how is Saint Emily's anyway?"

Levy held her stomach and gurgled. "Ugh. I hate it. I want to go back."

"Back to sixth grade?"

"No I mean to Dad's. Days like this I want to swim *so bad*."

"Well yeah!" Conrad punched her in the shoulder. "I was just there in my head and you ruined it." He sank into a grumble. "God I hate this place so much. I'll never get why Mom dragged us out here."

"Well why don't you ask her? I'm sure she'll tell you every detail."

"Don't make me laugh."

"Yeah well anyway it's all cold there now so whatever."

"How can you just say that?"

"Well it's not like we can jump back on the plane."

"But it's like you get here and you're like, *whoo-hoo, oh yeah*, like you don't even care."

"Sure I care, but what am I supposed to do, pour a bucket of glue all over my head? There's fun stuff here you know. Just different stuff..." Levy stopped to scrunch her face between her knees. "For swimming though, forget it. Mom's like, *I'll take you to the pool*."

"Ugh. It's gross. People here have no idea. And Joey just laughs at me like we go live in bear skins all summer and eat chipmunks for dinner."

Levy snickered. "That would be pretty cool actually."

"I guess... But Dad would make it all tough and hard to chew. Mom though, *Mom* would make the best chipmunk."

"Eew!" Levy's mouth stretched from disgust to a grin. "Yeah it would be like, fennel chipmunk pâté, on crackers." She pretended to spread it with a knife.

"Yeah, or maybe chipmunk liverwurst. Though I guess you'd need like fifty chipmunks per serving..."

"Mom asked me if I want to streak my hair."

"What?"

"Yep, not kidding. She just asked me today."

"But-" Conrad paused. "Wait, that's backwards. It's *your* job to ask for streaks, and then *she's* supposed to say that you're not old enough, or that streaks are low class or something, and then *you* get all upset. That's how it works."

"Nope! She said they're in style." Levy fattened her lips and batted her eyes. "Her friend's daughters all did it."

"Ohhh, I get it. So what did you say?"

"I told her I want to get a green Mohawk with sparkly tips, and shave my head on the sides." Levy used her wiggly fingers to illustrate each detail — the hair, the sides, the sparkles. "I begged and begged like I was serious, and then she said that she would *think about it*. As if!"

"Ha!"

They sank again into the warm breeze, serene in a way they didn't feel anywhere else in Los Angeles — except up in the hills. It felt stolen, as if the minutes they spent under the light pole had slipped out of their regular twenty-four hour day.

# Mid-October

# 4

Wattles park was a fantasy of sprinkler-fed green on a slope shaded by wide-topped palms, hemmed in on both sides by old cracking walls. But at the top of the hill was an archway leading out to untended territory. Conrad leaned there while his sisters gorged on water down at the fountain.

"OK, we're ready!" Beth huffed as she came running up with Levy behind her. Conrad always found it amusing that little Beth – calm, serious Beth – would move so quickly when it came time to run, her arms and legs flurrying the air. She could stay out in front of Levy, and Levy was fast.

Through the archway they ran under trees that shaded the path like a tunnel. From now on they would use gestures only, like a wolf-pack would, like jungle people would. These were the Hollywood Hills after all, home to imaginary enemies and very real freaks. They padded soft and fast — to avoid being followed to the *secret areas* that no other person in the entire city of Los Angeles had yet discovered — and escaped up a side path without a word.

As the hills opened up the kids quickened their pace, emerging from the shade onto a loose dry trail that snaked upwards in the direct line of the afternoon sun. At the top of the first slope they dashed along a rusty metal fence that ran along its crest. A large swath of the land beyond this was black from a brush fire, right up to the burned fence where presumably firefighters had stopped it.

Really there was nothing to love in this landscape for Conrad. The parched, sandy trail filled his nostrils with scorched dust, and the plants had a hang-dog look as if the nourishment their roots required was being siphoned away by the city down below. But as the joy of bounding from footfall to footfall took hold, this was still freedom, still the outdoors. The kids pushed faster for its own sake, for the adrenaline of scrambling up toward the sun and feeling even this soil under their feet and hands.

Descending into a narrow valley, the kids came to a place with no sight-line to anything man-made: a thousand miles from civilization. At the bottom they scrambled up a rain-washed crevice, Conrad poking a stick at the front in case of rattlesnakes. Twenty feet higher was a hideout, a kind of hole off to the side under a ridge that blocked the sun. They couldn't be seen here but they kept quiet anyway, with their eyes closed and their hands pressed into the cool dirt, releasing the heat from their lungs with deep breaths. But Conrad soon heard a scratching and looked up to see Levy attempting to wallpaper the side of the hole with her body.

"You guys ever told Mom about this?" she asked, sideways.

"About what? Coming up here?" Conrad asked. Levy nodded. "No," he said. "No way. Have you?"

"Are you kidding? But do you think she guesses? I mean, we're always coming back dirty."

"Kids get dirty at the park," Conrad said with a shrug. He turned to Beth. "What about you? You always follow the rules. Did you say anything?"

"No." Beth held up her chin. "If we simply don't tell her, there won't be rules about it."

Levy and Conrad began to laugh.

"Shhh!" Beth warned. "Someone's coming."

They leaned back into the shadows as the crunching sound of shoes came closer. Levy raised one finger, then a second. They listened again, then Conrad raised three fingers. Levy nodded. The voices came clearer: definitely teenagers, and at least one was a girl. At the bottom of the crevice the voices became suddenly loud.

"I can't believe he would say something like that to her!" a girl said.

"I know, right? That's just so self-involved," another girl said. So there were two girls.

"That guy's a dumb-ass," said the third person, male. "If I don't kick his ass, somebody else will."

Conrad found a rock and threw it as hard as he could. It landed with a thump on the other side of the ravine.

"What was that?" one of the girls said. Their footfalls stopped. Conrad and his sisters froze themselves mid-smirk.

"Must've been a rabbit," the boy said.

"Rabbits, up here?" the second girl asked. "Wouldn't the coyotes eat them?"

"That's why they *breed like rabbits*, duh!" the boy said to giggles.

Conrad grabbed another large stone and chucked it farther ahead where it tore through a bush.

"The hell was that?" the first girl said.

"This place is freaking me out," the other hissed. "We should go back."

"Aw come on!" the boy said. "There's nobody up here but us. You'll miss the lookout."

"But this is boring," the first girl said. "And I'm all sweaty. Let's go down to Melrose for a juice."

The boy grumbled, but soon they could be heard going back the way they came. Conrad pumped a silent fist. Levy and Beth made a show of diabolical hand-wringing. In a few minutes the invaders had retreated over the hill and out of earshot.

"Hey," came a voice from above, a deep male voice. Conrad saw Beth's eyes bulge in alarm. He shuffled out in front of her and looked up to see a man with scraggly gray hair and deeply sunned skin standing at the edge of the crevice. The man's clothes were stained and worn, yet his shirt was neatly tucked into his jeans. Neither did much to hide his wiry, powerful build. He peered down at Conrad and his sisters, then squatted above them and crossed his arms. This made him less immediately threatening, but the kids were still cornered.

"Uh, hi," said Conrad, furtively looking the man over for any sign of a weapon. "How's it going?"

"Look," said the man, "a big enough rock to the temple can kill a person." He locked onto Conrad's eyes as he spoke. "Imagine if you screwed up and hit one of them in the head. Now I've seen you kids running around up here before not bothering anybody, so I know you were just messing around this time, but I don't want to see you doing that kind of thing again, got me?"

Conrad stared back as he tried to sort out what kind of person this was. But meanwhile he had to respond. "Yes sir, we get it," he said with sudden shame, imagining blood seeping through a girl's long hair. "We're sorry," he added.

"Good, then see you around." The man stood up and walked away.

"Whoah," Levy breathed out.

Beth peeked out of the crevice. "Where'd he go?" she whispered.

Conrad stood and scanned in a circle. The man was nowhere in sight. "Wow. He just up and vanished."

"Do you think he works here?" Beth asked.

"Looked more like a homeless dude to me," Levy said.

Conrad sat back down. "Yeah," he said, "could be."

The kids kept still for a while to let their heartbeats subside.

"So now what, do we still go up?" Levy asked, looking to Beth and Conrad for a vote.

Beth shrugged. "Let's keep going."

"Yeah," Levy said, slowly grinning. "The man of the mountain will protect us."

A sun-baked, dirty man slinking around the hills was not usually a hallmark of safety, but in this case Conrad's instinct was to agree. The kids crawled out of the hole, slid on their shoes to the bottom of the crevice and continued up the trail, this time with their eyes darting from side to side as they wound around the hills. But when the trail began to climb straight up they let loose again and began to run. Beth arrived first at the top and danced a victory hula.

"Bearw bearw bearw!" she sang, approximating a ukulele and waving her hands over rotating hips. Levy and Conrad stopped to witness this rare display before it dissolved into giggles.

"That was most excellent!" Conrad declared officially.

"Why yes!" said Levy, snapping herself to full height, "I must say, good show!"

The kids sat down in a line to stare out at the late-afternoon view. Warm winds still breathed up the hills, but now they were calmer in the heat, part of it, a feeling that seemed to have bronzed every detail of the city spread out below them. Conrad let his gaze wander from neighborhood to neighborhood. *Why do they do the things they do,* he thought to himself, picturing all the bustling little people. But soon it occurred to him that if he could actually know the answer for every person, his head would grow bigger and hotter than the star currently heating his face.

"You know what's weird?" said Levy.

"What?"

"We talk about Mom knowing what we're doing, but not Dad. But if he were down there we'd be all scared he'd find out."

"Yeah," Conrad said, considering for a moment. "It's like he's on another planet."

Beth sat up. "No, *we're* on the other planet."

"Yeah I bet that's what *he* would say."

Levy held her arms wide. "Welcome to Planet Freakazoiko! Don't drink the water."

"Ha ha ha!"

Conrad pulled a half-melted Baby Ruth from his pocket. The girls did the same. It was their ritual snack since their first time up there, and conversely it was forbidden to consume a Baby Ruth anywhere else. They scanned their eyes over the city and chewed, not speaking, each holding a hand under their chins to catch the falling pieces of chocolate shell. This was the silent end time, the peace of having arrived and the sadness of having to leave again, familiar feelings that made these hikes more than just playing.

○ ○ ○

"Where have you kids been?!"

Sueanna had rushed to the front door at the first click of the bolt.

"Oh my god Mom we had the best time at the park!" Levy enthused, trying to get ahead of her mother's tone.

"Do you kids realize that it's seven forty-five? Dinner is getting cold and I've been here freaking out that you were in trouble!"

"We're sorry to make you worry Mom," Beth said.

"Yeah, sorry Mom," Conrad murmured.

"Really Conrad, you were in charge. You should be keeping track of the time."

"Yeah, sorry, you're right, we just got carried away," he said, avoiding any made-up explanations that might lead to questions.

"Oh well then," Sueanna said, relief gaining, "go dust yourselves off I guess. I've got ribs and yams."

Beth cheered and ran up the stairs with Levy, but Conrad moved slower and caught a glimpse of Sueanna's worn-down bearing as she turned back toward the kitchen.

At dinner Sueanna didn't talk much. Conrad also kept still while Levy and Beth bubbled. The guinea pigs were breeding again.

"I say we name the first one Cheesy" Levy said. "Its fur is cheese-colored."

"Maybe we should name all the babies after cheeses," Beth suggested.

"Yeah! Cheddar, Swiss, Gouda..." Levy paused, her memory of cheeses running out.

"Gorgonzola?" Conrad suggested.

"Yeah!"

"Manchego," their mother mumbled, as if the word had come out on its own. She stared at her fork pushing her yams around.

"Oh I remember that one," Levy said. "Yummy."

"That's that hard white one we kept stealing, right?" said Beth. "It's perfect! We'll use that name for the boy baby with the light hair, number five."

"Ha! *Man*-chego, hee hee!" Levy patted Beth on the head for her wit.

The girls pulled out their guinea pig chart and laid it on the table. Second column: gender. Third column: hair color and style. Fourth column: personality (according to them). Now in the first column they filled in the cheese names. Normally this kind of activity at the dinner table would invite scolding from their mother, but tonight Sueanna wasn't entirely present to begin with. Conrad peeked at her face but couldn't pin down what it expressed. She wasn't only angry with her naughty children. That would have passed.

Doonie, the dog, ran panting through the dining room.

"Oh no," Beth whined, "not again!"

Doonie's solution to the problem of happiness was to get it over with all at once. Most days the morose little terrier could be found sulking in a closet, but every once in a while it got up to sprint from room to room in a never-ending circle, possessed by a desperate joy.

"Could somebody catch the dog before it explodes?" Sueanna sighed. Doonie came around again and Levy jumped up to follow.

After dinner Levy and Beth went out to the garage to hold a 'naming ceremony.' Conrad refused to participate, instead crawling upstairs to plant himself face-down on his bed. The sun had set outside but still glowed warm in his skin, while scenes from the day flashed through his mind. He pictured the man blocking the sun over the hole, the skin on his neck weathered and cracked like dirt. He followed the shapes of the hills, curving into each other, offering refuge in their creases. He jumped up again to pull his largest sketch pad from under the bed and began to drag long bending lines across the paper.

At midnight Conrad was still shaking his softest pencil like a seismograph to darken the shadows in a sea of rolling hills. A circle that was either the moon or the sun glowed above them. He stepped back to look at his work: something was unbalanced about it he decided, but he would keep it. He stood to pin the paper to the wall, then slipped downstairs and crept across the dark kitchen.

"Hello young raccoon," came his mother's voice.

Conrad's hand froze on the refrigerator door. Sueanna was sitting at the kitchen table lit only by the blue-tinted streetlight through the window.

"I'm hungry again," he mumbled.

"Well then I think it's honey toast time," said Sueanna. "Can you make me some?"

Conrad turned to assemble the ingredients: seed-covered oat bread from the bakery down the street, fresh butter, and dark avocado tree honey from the farmer's market. He dropped the bread into the toaster and waited without moving. After an awkward half-minute he glanced in his mother's direction. She gave him a little smile, but the toast popped up. Conrad laid it on a plate and carefully pressed butter into every pore all the way to the crust, then dripped on the honey in a lattice pattern. He gave both slices to his mom, because she ate a lot slower than he did, then repeated the process for himself.

"There's hot water on the stove," Sueanna said. "You can make some bedtime tea if you want. I've already got mine."

Sitting down at the table with his mug, Conrad looked at his mother again. She was quiet, not eager to pounce on any particular subject like she so often did. Conrad could relax into the warm bready scents and the tea steam floating up to his face. He lifted a piece of toast and took a slow-motion bite: a sense-tingling marvel, one that he and his mother had been sharing since he was a little boy.

"It's *so* good," his mother said. "You always make it perfectly."

"I think this is the best version yet," Conrad said.

"Well I think it's a tie with that maple tree honey on

sourdough."

"Oh yeah," Conrad said, remembering the previous year's favorite toast. But after that they munched and sipped without speaking. Sueanna's gaze drifted between the kitchen and somewhere else.

"So... Mom," Conrad eventually ventured to murmur, "what's up with you?"

"Oh, I'm fine, I'm good," she said with a smile that pushed aside the sadness that had been plainly visible a moment before.

"But you seem, um, down about something." It was new for Conrad to speak like this, and it felt that way. "I'm sorry about today," he added under his breath.

"Oh it's not that. It's nothing really," she said. "I just get this way sometimes. This toast will make me all better."

Conrad didn't know how to push, so he didn't. *She's a spy for the Russians,* he thought.

"So how's school going?" Sueanna asked. "Is high school different?"

Conrad stared at the wall for a moment, but then raised his eyebrows and shrugged. "It's the same school, and mostly the same people," he said. "So yeah, it's the same I guess."

○ ○ ○

"Hmm, yes. Mmph," Mr. Sebastien grunted, hinting that his eyeballs were nearly finished with the essay laid square in front of him and would soon turn to the nervous leg-shifter in his office. Conrad struggled to ignore the teacher's endless details: stubble spreading down a thick neck, fat-stretched-khaki-trunk legs, aggressive hair-thatches on the arms, waxy ear holes. And all around him the walls flapped in a non-existent wind, pinned as they were with posters and papers at odd angles. One match, Conrad imagined, and everything would burst into flames, including the teacher.

"Mmm, right! OK." Mr. Sebastien put the paper aside and pulled out Conrad's proposal folder. Just then a knock sounded from the cracked-open door, but Mr. Sebastien put off the visitor with a gesture and turned back to Conrad.

"You know, it would have been normal course for me to just fail the pile you turned in," he said, meeting Conrad's eyes with the word 'pile.' Conrad nodded. "But then I saw what you were up to. Really it's quite ambitious."

With that he paused to give Conrad a chance to speak, but Conrad didn't take it — instead the pendulum of his imagination swung to the rafters, picturing the teacher sending him out the door with a hearty congratulations and an A-plus.

"I've never had anybody explore this area," Mr. Sebastien continued. "But what I see in your proposal itself is, mmph, another one of your volcanoes."

Conrad blinked. Had the volcano become a joke among the teachers? Still, he wasn't sure what that had to do with anything. Mr. Sebastien could sense as much.

"OK, let's say you're making cookies," he said. "Do you reinvent flour? Do you formulate your own baking soda?"

"Well, no," Conrad said.

"Well then look at all these crossed-out paragraphs for instance." Mr. Sebastien flipped to a page covered in hashed-over ideas. "You're trying to pull conclusions out of thin air. And you're agonizing about it because you want it to be good, right?"

"Yeah."

"Look, you're mixed up about something here. This was supposed to be a *proposal,* for a months-long project, not the finished product. I'm not asking you to know all about it yet. That's the whole point — you're supposed to go out and do research, gather lots of interesting tidbits. You don't know where it will lead. Only then can you can have an opinion. But this here is backwards. You're trying to paint a balloon before you inflate it."

"So what would the proposal say, then?" Conrad asked.

"Did you read the handout I gave you? The one called *Constructing a Proposal*?"

Conrad remembered the pink sheet in his binder.

"Well there you go," Mr. Sebastien said, shaking his head. "A word to the wise, Conrad. *Read the instructions.*"

"OK, yes, I will, sorry about that," Conrad said, slumping further.

"OK good. Now as for your idea, good on you. However if you don't want a failing grade on the proposal part, you'll need to do it again, and don't forget the first research check-in is coming up soon."

"Yes, thank you," Conrad said, taking his cue to leave.

"You're welcome. Say, on your way out could you call miss Helms in here? She's been waiting."

Miss Helms. *Anise Helms.*

Conrad pushed the door open wider. Sure enough, Anise was sitting just outside where she could hear everything. Maybe he would slip away sideways. Maybe she wouldn't notice.

"Hi Conrad!"

Conrad stopped and swiveled and blood rushed to his ears.

Eyes and teeth. Soft hair reflecting the light. Fuzzy peach sweater.

"He's ready for you now," Conrad's mouth said.

"Oh, uh, OK, thanks," said Anise, her smile turning to puzzlement as Conrad slipped away.

"What is *with* you anyway?" Stacy said, throwing her braided head back in exasperation, but Miss Lanto swooped in before Conrad could answer.

"What happened here you two?"

Stacy thumbed at Conrad. "Space monkey here was time traveling again."

It was true. Conrad's hands had dumped all the sugar into the beaker while his mind was parsecs away dive-bombing a dark planet.

Miss Lanto shook her head. "Well I would say start over again, but time's nearly up so how about you two go watch Robb and Todd. They nearly have it."

Stacy leaned closer to Conrad and narrowed her eyes to slits.

"Great. Just great."

"Sorry."

It was much the same at lunch, up on the bench where Conrad mostly swung his legs while Joey made fun of anyone who passed at a distance. Conrad, if he spoke at all, either mangled or mumbled his words, failing in his role as Joey's audience. Joey turned to him finally.

"Dude it's like you're high, except you're not nearly cool enough to be high. The hell's wrong with you?"

Conrad shrugged. "I don't know."

But Conrad did know. Everything was wrong with him, and everything was wrong with everything else! He soon found himself shooting down the alley by himself, propelled by the pressure of all the wrong things. The fact that everything he did there was wrong was the natural consequence of a bigger-sized fact, one that formed a cage around his every thought: that he wasn't supposed to be there in the first place. His real life had been stolen from him, and here in this smoggy concrete-covered replacement life he was constantly on the run, from words like *loser* and *reject* and *nerd*.

Mrs. Parkins, the English teacher, was also on the run it seemed, or she would have been, but for now she paced the room in her flower-patterned dress like a flightless bird at the zoo while the ring of students stared.

"OK people," she said, her voice already shaded by the knowledge of certain defeat, "today we'll discuss Cat's Cradle. I trust you finished it." Her trust was misplaced. "Everybody pull out the worksheet I gave you last week. Oh and while you're at it I've got your essays!" With an unexpected burst of speed she circled the room returning the papers. Conrad grabbed his and quickly pulled it down under his desk, as it was marked in red all over the margins. Still, when he paged to the end, it said "B" with a note underneath saying 'please see me after class.'

"Let's get to it now," Mrs. Parkins picked up again. "So this novel, has been described as, *allegorical*. Who can give me an example? I mean, what in the story could be called allegory?"

Robb Cott cleared his throat. "Well the ice part's kinda gory... sort of." Muffled chuckles broke out.

"Robb I want serious answers only," the teacher said.

A girl next to Conrad whispered to her friend. "Why couldn't she just give us something normal to read?"

When the time was up, Conrad waited for the others to leave so nobody would see him approach Mrs. Parkins. But she came straight over and sat next to him.

"Conrad let's go over your paper," she said, flipping through it. "Look, in many ways this is a D paper, it's just a mess, and look, here at the end it just stops like you never finished."

Conrad nodded.

"But then again, I can *see* when someone's actually there. It's obvious you read the book and you really thought about it, too. There's some good stuff in here! But it's all mixed up, just like your first one. Makes me think you can't figure out how to finish."

Conrad nodded again.

"Look I'll tell you a secret. Perfectionists are always ending up like this, and do you know why that is? It's because they want it to be perfect right away. But it never works. And it's painful, too. I should know."

Conrad was piqued now: he wanted to know why she should know. But she stuck to the topic.

"This is what you do Conrad. You let it be bad, and you finish it. Then you go back and make it better, changing this, cutting that, little by little. That's the only way anybody does it. You got me?"

"Yeah" was all he said. Something about all this talk was making him inexplicably sad.

"Another thing Conrad." Mrs. Parkins leaned a tiny bit closer. "I see you back here every class, keeping to yourself. Is everything OK with you? Anything you want to talk about?"

"No, I'm fine." He shook his head and smiled to reassure her. "I'm good."

○ ○ ○

Conrad's eyes drooped shut. Then SMACK, his head hit the next seat as the bus squealed to a halt. He groaned and stared longingly through the window. It wasn't fair. The air outside was a breezy sixty-eight degrees, as cool as one could hope for in October, but inside the ventilation had failed and the plastic bubble windows weren't designed to open. *I'll just get out and walk*, he thought again, but he was too far from home, and anyway the bus was stuck in traffic between stops. Lava could be melting the wheels, but if he begged to get out the driver would bark "stand behind the yellow line!"

*Lava.*

It was so clearly idiotic now, his bid for glory in eighth-grade science gone wrong: plywood, chicken wire, papier-mâché and poster paint, then garden dirt and freshly-pulled weeds — Mount Saint Helens, with a removable peak! The result was impressive, he'd thought when he transported it to school, but there the real dirt, still damp, began to mold and filled the lab with the fusty odor of a bog. "Your mountain stinks, Conrad!" random students scolded as they passed him in the halls. But never mind, eruption day soon arrived, and — just to be sure — Joey would assist. Struggling, they carried the volcano to the basketball court. There the sight of two boys stretching wires and tubes from a not-so-miniature mountain soon attracted a hooting crowd. Conrad's job was to trigger the six model rocket engines affixed below the peak, while Joey's was to pump the murky contents of a hidden reservoir over the top to simulate mudslides. It was time! Conrad remembered Mr. Clarkson, the science teacher this was supposed to impress, standing with crossed arms looking decidedly skeptical. Conrad touched the wires for the first two engines. Instantly the paper mountaintop flew up and away like a frisbee from the force of ridiculously vertical flames. But there was more! Conrad ignited the next pair of engines. The hissing fire doubled in size while a cloud of noxious smoke spread through the onlookers. For the finale Conrad set off the last pair of engines, at the same time signaling to Joey, who came down furiously on the pump. Just as planned, dark mud began to drool down the paper mountainside, however it also disgorged onto the rocket engines, blasting specks of stinking black liquid across the watching faces.

That last part was not the actual reason Mr. Parks gave Conrad a D on the project. "Where is the *science*?" he had asked. But the worst part was seeing Anise standing in the front row getting it full in the face.

Conrad played the scene backwards: Anise's horrified expression reverting to cheerful expectation, the mud lifting from her cheeks.

*Stop!*

Conrad tried to hold this picture of her in his mind. But she appeared only a piece at a time: the long dark silky hair, the open eyes, the shy expression breaking into a laugh... The way she held her hands at the ends of her sweater sleeves, the graspy fingers with neatly-trimmed, glossy nails... Her compact curvy figure, her light-blue jeans, the Charlie Chaplin way she walked with her friends. As one formed, another vanished. Then the bus driver slammed on the brakes.

# 5

# Early November

Conrad sat wedged in a crook high up in the back yard's lone tree, watching branches loaded with unripe oranges sway in the wind. After a balmy Halloween, November was doing what October should have — that is, going gray and wet and blowy, this weekend anyway. He listened to the wind picking up, to the leaves reacting then quieting: a whispering mother's language, incomprehensible but soothing nonetheless. If the branches were not so flimsy he would climb higher, to lift his head farther above his deep dark well for air.

A surge — hail began to fall. Conrad monkeyed down and squatted under a fat sideways branch. The hailstorm rushed louder, covering the yard in a layer of white beads, then abruptly halted. Conrad crawled out and rolled his palms over the freshly-minted ice, reveling in the concept that each little ball had been flying thousands of feet high just seconds before. Then he jumped up and ran to the front to find the whole neighborhood decorated like a cake. He quick-shuffled from yard to yard, cutting a zig-zag pattern in the hail as if it were snow.

Mr. Onter was leaning at his door. "Nature's Priest," he said.

Conrad swayed with a demented smile and pointed. "Duhhh, look! It's hail!"

"Is *that* what that is? And here I was worried the stars were falling. Say, would you like to hear something?"

Conrad followed Mr. Onter back to his usual spot on the sofa and accepted a steaming cup of greenish Oolong tea. The contrast with the hail could not have been more perfect.

"Mmm, smells good," Conrad murmured. "I think I get this

now." He could say this today, after many indifferent tries.

Mr. Onter twiddled his fingers in triumph. "It's a good one. Just got it. High grade Tie Guan Yin. Cost me a fortune." He laid an LP on the record player. "OK, now for the main event. Make yourself still." He let the needle fall and sank into his easy chair.

Conrad closed his eyes as a double-clang of piano chords crystallized the air: blue-green shivering cold, and liquid welling up from a lifetime, and bells. When it was over he found himself breathing deeply, and his eyes were hot. The reflecting sounds had become the lake — how it felt to watch it, out floating on it alone, and how it felt to miss it.

Mr. Onter sat up. "That's called *Carillon Nocturne*. It's by George Enescu."

"What year?" Conrad asked, mostly to cover himself.

"Before 1920 I think. He was Romanian." Mr. Onter looked at the album sleeve. "Yes, 1912. Isn't that remarkable?"

"Yeah, it's like two different places at the same time, or a double-exposure, or something…" This felt incoherent but Mr. Onter nodded in perfect agreement.

"Yes. A carillon is a set of many bells, you know, in a bell tower. Here I'll show you." He jumped up to pull a volume from his shelf and flipped through the pages. "See, it's the craziest thing. Some even had keyboards connected to them. Enescu must have heard them as a boy. It's like the bells are sounding far away in this piece." Mr. Onter looked away through his bookshelves. "You know it's also like bells, when the past echoes inside of us, in the present, but we can't grab hold of it, can't escape back to it. It's there, but it's not. It hurts. Sometimes it hurts a lot, even if the memory is beautiful, or I guess especially if it is…"

"Huh" is all Conrad said, as if he were pondering, but really he was unable to express the overlap with his own feelings, or was unwilling to, which amounted to the same thing. Mr. Onter kept talking.

"Did I ever play any late Fauré for you? No? Well I got to hear Paul Crossley play one time. He started one of Fauré's preludes and I remember having the most surprising reaction. The piece had this jabbing, and a chord change. It stripped my defenses. I just wanted to curl up on the floor in a ball holding my stomach, like I wanted to say *no, no, stop doing that, I don't want to talk about that*. All in a few seconds."

"But you're smiling about it."

"Yeah, it was great."

Conrad didn't want to go home so he walked east. It would have made more sense to head west, toward things fancier and safer, not to mention expensive-er, but east it was. The sun had come out bright on the hail, melting it but leaving strangers more willing to make eye contact, as if to say 'did you see that?' But that was only temporary.

At the back of 7-11, behind the rolling hot dogs in a nook somewhat protected from the comings and goings of customers buying cigarettes and condoms, Dig-Dug was gone, replaced by something new and noisy called Dragon's Lair which cost double. A swarm of younger kids ignored it, instead making a ruckus around Frogger and Joust. Conrad gave up and left. He was getting old. He continued down Sunset Boulevard, at every corner resisting a persistent grade-school urge to shake the newspaper boxes — especially the old dented ones with sleazy triple-X papers inside, since those were more likely to drop loose coins onto the probing fingers of the local boys.

A delicious sense of escape pushed Conrad onward as if he had sails, floating free on foot past window after window. But soon he found himself perceptibly sinking. Now the pointlessness of this walking grew apparent. He had no destination, yet returning would be a defeat. It made no sense. He could call it fatigue, except it was more than that, as if he had accidentally swallowed a black hole and now it was sucking in his face.

He slowed.

He stopped.

Cars and people flowed past him in the corners of his vision.

A church stood to his left. He knew this one — he had sneaked through it with his sisters the first week they had lived there. It would be calm inside, a hypnosis of richly-polished wood and colored glass, but today the windows were dark and large sloppy chains had been strung through the door-handles. Conrad folded up on the front steps, breathing in and breathing out as the street blurred before him.

After a while Conrad roused himself to examine the outside of the building: old beige stucco pocked with grimy street dust, lacking any sort of border where its walls unceremoniously met the sidewalk. It bothered him.

*A gateway to heaven should stand apart from the ground,* he thought. *It should iridesce like a pearl.*

A passing form stopped and yelled.

"Conrad!"

It was Sal Montejo, from sixth grade, except now he looked more like a senior. Conrad lurched up and reached out a hand. "Sal!"

Sal ignored the hand and pulled Conrad in for a hug and a slap on the back. "My man! What's up? What are you doing here?"

"Just out looking for food. I wanted to peek inside." He pointed his thumb at the chains.

"Yeah this place got shut down. Something about money. My mom was totally going off."

Now an entire world Conrad had once been a part of snapped back into his head. He could picture it: Sal's normally quiet mother launching into a surprise tirade in Spanish about some matter out of her control, then Sal pretending to scream *take cover!* But here Conrad found it difficult to meet Sal's eyes.

"Do you ever see the guys anymore?" Conrad asked.

"Hell yeah! Well, mostly. Carson moved up north somewhere. His mom got a job. But Satish is still around, and Farid and Rodrigo. We were just talking about you! Remember that haunted house we did at your place?"

"Yeah."

"That was the best! We actually made one girl cry, remember that? We were nuts, all that stuff we did. Now everybody's so serious."

"Yeah, everything's a big deal."

"I tell you man, high school's bullshit. I can't wait to get out of there."

"Yeah. I hate it."

"Well I'd talk more but I gotta meet somebody." Sal shook his eyebrows to mean *girl*. "Miss you man! Look me up."

"I will," Conrad said, shaking Sal's hand and watching him saunter away. Then he turned toward home.

Conrad had gone straight to his room, but he was followed. Now he sat on his bed watching Levy folding her limbs on the floor in a series of slow-motion angles, like a mobile that had fallen from the ceiling yet still moved.

*Here we have a most unusual specimen of the Earth creature commonly known as 'sister.'*

*Bleep.*

*The other they call 'Beth' is also a sister, however this 'Levy' shows behaviors we haven't seen elsewhere on the planet.*

*Bleep.*

It was clear now. Sal was the closest Conrad had ever come to 'brother' — Sal the welcomer, the instigator, the belly-laugher. Conrad could still picture it: when he'd arrived at the local grade school fresh from the move, so shy and lost. Right away Sal and the other guys had pulled him in, without question making him a part of their 'new rules' basketball games and goofball pranks. And when Sueanna bought Conrad one of the new wide-deck skateboards, a huge Alva, he and Sal rode it together, yelling and hooting down Sunset. One day they cruised the streets testing the tacos at six different trucks until they were stuffed, then headed up to Hollywood Boulevard to watch *Airplane*, after which they tried riding the skateboard back down again but cracked up all over the sidewalk repeating the gags out loud. "Brothers forever," Sal had said to him, "best day ever for all time!"

But then came the long sunny months, and the glittering lake and the leaves whispering sixth grade right out of Conrad's head. Meanwhile Sueanna decided that she wanted something better for her son than the local school with its local kids. Come September Conrad went straight from the plane to Divergent like an exchange student from the same country — or so it had seemed. In the shock of it he went mute: he dared approach no one, and no one approached him.

*But actually...*

Actually there was a party that first semester. Robb Cott had gone around handing out invitations to anybody in the seventh grade. Conrad remembered it now: an enormous house, a chlorinated pool with polished red-brick edges ringed by neatly-trimmed eucalyptus trees, boys debating which ski resorts were the best, girls shiny-wet in their swimsuits... and Conrad, desperately quiet in the corner of the pool: his eyes bobbing just above the surface and his mouth sealed tight below it.

But *what if*, he wondered, what if Sal had gone in his place? Sal might have made friends with everybody, belly-laughing his way to popularity. In any case, now there was only shame.

*I left my brothers behind.*

"Talked to Dad today," said Levy off-handed, still rotating.

"Yeah, what did he say?"

"It's so funny, he always says the same stuff."

Conrad made his voice deeper. "*Doing OK in school?*"

"*You be nice to your sister,*" Levy grumbled.

"It's not like he knows what we're doing."

Levy stopped moving. "Yeah I hear Mom talking to him on the phone. She makes it like everything's perfect."

"Yeah, but even if she didn't he couldn't do anything anyway. When we're here, it's like he's not even our dad. Then when we're there, Mom's not our mom... kinda."

"I want to go to your school."

"What? But you already started at Saint Emily's."

"I don't care. I don't want to go to a girl's school anymore. Your school's cool."

"Did you say that to Mom?"

"Uh huh. She got all fussy. Says I *already started*, and I should *at least wait until high school*."

"Bet she thinks you'll change your mind."

Levy switched to pleading. "But would it be weird if I went to your school?"

"It's already weird. Maybe two weirds would fix it. Except if you go and get a boyfriend. That would be *weird*."

Levy rolled onto her back, pooched up her stomach to caress it and spoke in a baby-doll voice. "I'm going to have fifteen boyfriends," she said, "and then I'll have quintuplets. Mommy will love them."

"Oh gross!" Conrad laughed face-first onto the bed. Then he sat up. "Wait, that's actually possible. You better watch out. Mom would lose her mind."

"Yeah at first, but then we'd have baby clothes catalogs all over the house."

"Ha! Yeah, it'll be like, *Hey Levy, do you like the white tutu or the pink tutu?*"

"So you won't be mad if I go to your school?"

It was surprising to Conrad how worried Levy was about this, as if she needed his permission. Usually she did whatever she wanted.

"I don't mind," he said. "Maybe you should go instead of me. I want to go back to Dad's."

"No way *that's* happening. Plus we wouldn't be at the same school! I want to be at the same school. Then I'd have a big brother there."

"Why would you want that? It's not like I'm popular or anything."

"I'll make you popular. Then when Beth shows up we'll take over the place. Hie-ya!" Levy karate-chopped the air.

○ ○ ○

Sueanna's voice grew louder as it neared the back door. "Levy I told you to stop doing that! It's gross!" The door slid open and her head popped out. "Conrad, come down from there! You'll get yourself all dirty."

Conrad climbed down as good as new. The tree had never touched his clothes. He grabbed his backpack and went around to the front to watch Levy and Beth run out to their carpool as if the house would detonate behind them. Sueanna locked the door and headed for the car.

"I have to work just to *go* to work," she grumbled as she started the engine. "At least today I'm seeing your school first for a change." She turned to squint at Conrad. "That's not going to be work, is it?" Conrad shook his head.

It was 'Activity Week' at Divergent, a kind of festival in which no one relaxed. Besides performances and competitions relating to every academic subject simultaneously, and daily assemblies where 'people' were told to quiet down, every student was assigned a schedule of mandatory conferences. Parents strolled in and out, in some cases torturing their offspring by touring the campus, such as it was. Conrad was not among those unlucky ones, as his mother had requested the earliest possible sessions and would rush away to work straight after.

"Make yourself comfortable!" said the cheery counselor, Mr. Frunkle, who went to pull out Conrad's file. Sueanna and Conrad sat facing the desk like a couple applying for a bank loan. Mr. Frunkle laid the file on the desk and slid a worksheet to the middle. "OK, today we're going to talk about your college plan." Conrad wasn't aware of such a plan but nodded. Mr. Frunkle pointed at a list of keywords with the tip of his pen. "Math, science, English, foreign language, history. If you want to get into a good school you have to excel in all of these. And you should be in honors classes for at least one of those subjects. Plus you need extracurricular activities to show."

"Is there honors art?" Conrad asked.

"No, that's an elective. Anyway, looking at your record so far I have to warn you, Conrad. Your grades are all over the place." Sueanna stiffened as Mr. Frunkle pulled another paper from the file. "Math, nearly failing. Says here you're missing assignments. Science, A-minus, one of the best in class. English, B-minus.

History, C."

Sueanna felt the need to triangulate. "Really Conrad, you can do better than this."

"It has no pattern," said the counselor. "Bad at math, but good at science? Shows me he's only focusing on things he likes."

"Do you think a tutor would help?" Sueanna asked.

"Perhaps, but he simply has to do the work."

"Are you listening, Conrad?"

Joey sat gnawing on his burrito, the largest kind the truck sold. "Have you been Frunkled yet?" he asked Conrad.

"Yes."

"Did it feel good?"

"No."

"Did it hurt?"

"They made me pick a language for like, the rest of high school. It's so dumb."

"What did you pick?"

"Latin."

Joey stared aghast. "Why?"

"I don't know, it was different. The only other choices were French, German or Italian."

"Oh man, you are *so* clueless. Dude let's say you go for a year abroad in college, right? And you meet, you know, *hot girls?* I promise you, none of them will be speaking Latin."

"I want to learn one of those clicking languages."

"Uh, yeah, good luck with that. This place is bogus. I thought high school would be more like... I don't know..."

"It's like we're guinea pigs in a tunnel. There's lettuce at the end, they say."

Joey laughed and pointed at him. "Yeah! You're a total freak, but sure, guinea pigs, in a tunnel. That's *exactly* what I was trying to express. And what if I get to the end and it turns out I like carrots instead?"

Conrad made himself serious. "Then you go find another tunnel that leads to carrots, and you start all over again."

"Yeah but then I'll starve before I ever get to the carrots."

"So you eat the lettuce, even though you don't like it, because that's what mature guinea pigs do, *then* you go look for carrots."

"Screw that. You know what? I'll just take a steaming dump on that lettuce, and I'll run backward through the tunnel, and if I meet any other guinea pigs they'll have to join me or I'll eat the motherfuckers! Then I'll have a *massive* guinea pig army, and we'll rush out and attack the jerks who built the tunnel in the first place and bleed them to death with itty, bitty, tiny, little bites." Joey writhed to imitate his army's victims.

Conrad shook his head. "No way. They would just stomp on you. Better to take over the tunnel, see? Then we could dig even more tunnels. They'd never find us. We'd run out at night and steal their food."

"Whoah, I think you just figured out how mice evolved. Way to go, Conrad!" Joey pressed the leftover foil wrapper from his burrito into a crinkly disk. "And here is your Nobel Prize, sir."

"Why thank you, young man." Conrad bowed.

Joey sat up, but then he appeared to check himself and sat back. "Hey, uh, there's this old samurai movie in West L.A. on Sunday." He shrugged his shoulders. "You can come if you want."

Conrad wanted his wallet to be heavier. Mr. Onter wouldn't pay him until the end of the month. "Sure," he said.

o o o

Conrad needed jeans, but that meant shopping with his mother.

"Oh look Conrad! The suits are on sale. They have such nice ones here. How about you try one on?"

"I only need jeans."

"But you would look so good in navy blue."

"No. And look at the price tag. And I'll never wear it anyway."

"Sure you will. You never know, we might get invited to another wedding."

"So we'll come get it *after* the invitation shows up. Can't we just look at jeans now?"

"Oh it doesn't hurt to try it on. Sir? Sir!" She waved to a man waddling across the store with a measuring tape hanging around his neck. "My son is interested in this suit."

"No I'm not."

"Yes you are."

The man flashed Sueanna a genial smile and proceeded to slip the suit onto Conrad's arms from behind like a straitjacket.

"See? Look at that," said Sueanna. "My handsome son."

"Nice, very nice," said the man. "Needs a bit of alteration of course."

"How long will that take?"

"Mom!"

"A week, though we do have express service. Hold your arms straight." The man began measuring and marking with wax.

"We're not in a hurry," said Sueanna. "Can we try on the trousers, too?"

"Oh god."

"Of course."

The store didn't have pre-shrunk jeans in Conrad's size, so after more fussing they left with the regular kind: very blue and very hard. He wouldn't be able to wear them in public for decades. They drove away: mother self-satisfied, son deflated.

"Have you chosen a team yet?" Sueanna asked.

"What team."

"You know, sports. I think you should be on a team. You need friends."

"I don't need a team to have friends. I have friends."

"Like who?"

"Like Joey."

"I'll believe this Joey exists when I actually meet him. Why don't you have him over sometime?"

"Ugh."

"Well you can't just hole up in your room all year with your fishing posters. You've been back for months now and it's the same thing all over."

"I'm fine."

"You don't seem fine. It's like I'm dragging you to a monastery every day. There's no vow of silence at Divergent you know."

"I hate it here."

"Oh you'd like it just fine if you stopped hating it. Don't be so negative. And you just said you're fine. Which is it?"

"I'm fine."

It was an impasse of sorts. But then Sueanna turned her attention to the Beverly Cinema passing on the left.

"Oh look! They're playing *Foreign Correspondent*. That's a good one."

Conrad followed the marquee with his gaze until a red light brought the car to a halt. Saying something would betray the resistance, so he didn't. But then Sueanna turned to him with a dastardly grin, as if planning to cheat some higher authority other than herself.

"The girls will be at the dance rehearsal until at least three," she cackled, rubbing her hands. "The matinee starts in thirty minutes, but there's a Russian pastry shop right over there I've been wanting to try. Hee hee!"

Conrad nodded and she turned the corner to park.

○ ○ ○

Conrad lulled on a bus that had already rumbled a good half-mile from West L.A., but then his last five dollars found their purpose passing outside. He yelled to the driver and bolted out the back door.

The false promise of the previous week's hailstorm had given way to eighty-degree stickiness, but Conrad soon escaped into Kakuyasu Sushi, formerly Dusty's Donuts, its long glass cases now lined with clear-plastic take-out containers. Conrad scanned these breathlessly, not having eaten in hours. For more than five dollars he could have nigiri sushi with actual fish, or rolls with actual fish, or both. For $4.25 plus tax, the lowest price, he could get a Futomaki and Inari combo: more like snacks, with no actual fish, but close enough. If someone asked him if he liked sushi he could still have an opinion.

Sitting alone by the window, Conrad watched the passing cars through the windshields of the parked cars. He ate slowly with chopsticks, though he could use his fingers, for the practice. Meanwhile a scene replayed in his head: just after the Samurai movie when he'd asked Joey to hang out. "Some other time," Joey had said, waving off toward the horizon, "got places to be." It was just like Joey: there at his leisure, then sayonara! Not like Sal. Joey would never do anything that he didn't think of himself. He only hung out with Conrad in cool, discrete allotments: *hey man*, *see ya man*.

In the movie, samurais had defended a town from bandits, running and slashing through scene after bloody scene, but it was the ending that struck Conrad the most: after all that fighting, the surviving samurais couldn't stay in the town they had saved so they drifted on, defeated even in winning. *It's like that all the time here*, Conrad thought. No matter what it was he did, it would end, and then he would be going somewhere else by himself and the *thing* would be disassembled to fit in his head, or digested. That's how he felt now, the movie entertainment being over, and the eating entertainment, too. He could wander the city to locate another entertainment, and another, until he could no longer stay awake.

Conrad dropped his container into the trash and fell back out onto the street under a blazing haze. On the next block a bus was rushing away.

"Well hello," said Sueanna as her son shuffled into the kitchen. "What have *you* been up to all day?"

"Saw an old Japanese movie with Joey. It was amazing!"

"Another movie? The same weekend? Have you even started your homework?"

"I'm starting now."

Sueanna eyed him, unimpressed. "Well let's make sure that

happens, OK? Your counselor got me worried."

"OK," he said, but then he sat down to watch Sueanna roll some sort of dough.

"Here, I need these real small." Sueanna pushed across a cutting board with a bunch of green onions.

Conrad lined up the shoots and set to mincing them. "Levy wants to go to Divergent," he said.

"Yes I know. We'll just have to see about that."

"Maybe she could go instead of me."

"Instead of you? Then what'll you do?"

"Maybe I could try the school at Dad's, for tenth grade."

Sueanna stopped and looked hard at Conrad. "Try? What does that mean? You don't *try* tenth grade. You only get one tenth grade."

"So? If I don't like it I'll come back."

"No, you won't come back. You'll get stuck there with those people."

"But why can't I spend some of the time there? I miss it."

"Sure, you miss the summer. But what do you think it'll be like after that? I went to that school you know. Kids there don't go to college half the time. It's just beer in the woods..."

"But I'll still go to college."

"It's not the same! You keep talking like everything's fair. You just don't get it. Kids at Divergent go to the best colleges. You have a chance here, for *that*. I'm spending the inheritance money, for *that*. I could have bought a nicer house, you know. You don't appreciate that at all."

Conrad folded into a sulk. "It's what *you* want, not what I want."

Sueanna turned to the back counter to press the dough into a pie tin. "Oh, it's what you want, you just don't know it yet."

"You don't know that."

Sueanna let out a sigh. "Conrad, you can't just leave and come back in the middle of high school. I'm sorry but it's simply not on the table. You live *here* now. You're just going to have to accept that."

The green onions were all in a pile, so Conrad escaped the kitchen while his mother's back was turned and went into the living room, where he found Beth scowling on the sofa with her arms crossed. Conrad plopped down next to her.

"What's up with you?" he asked.

"Nothing."

"Doesn't look like nothing."

Beth squinted at him sideways. "You're in high school but you can't even do math."

"The heck are you talking about?"

"Boob," she huffed and got up to walk toward the stairs.

"Why are you so grumpy all the time?" he called after her.

# Early December

# 6

Lightless, airtight, nonexistent between inhale and exhale: Conrad was a pupa in silk, the silk being his thick wool blanket. But the more he blocked out, the more immediate his own heart and breath became. As a compromise he let his face emerge, though still covered by his yellow cotton sheet: an insect immobilized in resin, able to peer out but not to move. A million years would pass before him. He would forget how to breathe. In fact he wasn't breathing.

A shock of adrenaline sent Conrad stumbling down the stairs and out the front door where the warm air felt cold and the light made him squint. Soon he had traveled many blocks, peeking up only to navigate, each step lighter as the distance from his bed increased.

He glanced at the stores along Melrose Avenue — the overpriced used clothes, the trendy juice bars, the cookies he couldn't afford — but didn't linger anywhere this time, instead continuing to La Brea Avenue and turning south.

Crusty old shops were the best, on the lower-rent blocks. He often hunted the disheveled aisles of these places for the strange and unidentifiable. 'What's Mang-Da?' he might ask at the front counter, or 'what do you do with pomegranate molasses?' The owners were often brusque. Conrad rarely had much cash after all, but today he could spare fifty cents for a tantalizing patty of Vietnamese sesame nougat — a genuine find. *Oh yes*, he thought, ripping off a seedy, peanutty chunk with his teeth, *Levy will love this one.*

Refueled, he shot back outside, the sidewalk squares rushing faster and faster under his feet as he wove around slow people and newspaper boxes and light poles like a fish in a dirty river. The shadows behind him would swirl and congeal in his wake. He would blur the whole city!

Wilshire Boulevard appeared with its taller buildings, then a few blocks later, Olympic. Conrad remembered something: if he turned left here, he would eventually come to a library. And he still needed books for his history project.

The library was cool but wasn't quiet: a circle of grade-school students sitting by the door were giggling, and the librarian had come out to scold them. Conrad found a table at the opposite end and sat facing the interior. Apart from the students, the place was nearly empty: an elderly man at a table peered down at a large volume of botanical illustrations, and at the far corner a girl on the floor sat hunched over a book with her wavy hair hanging around it like a theater curtain.

Conrad kept still and watched the room. With each exhale, his insides began to sink. His evasions had failed. Once again he was a ghost that could only view the world through a blurry halo. Nearby was a giggling planet, but he could only observe it from orbit. The only sensations remaining to him were the tips of his fingers touching the table — all he had to do was lift his hands and he would fade into deep space.

"Can I help you with something?" came a quiet voice. It was the librarian. Conrad started, then stood up.

"Yes can I borrow a pen and a piece of paper?" he blurted, checking his volume too late.

The librarian put a finger to her lips and beckoned him closer.

"You can borrow the pen, but keep the paper," she quipped as he stepped up. "Here you go."

Conrad took the pen and paper from her hands, which he noticed were smooth and beautifully formed, just like her arms, and looking further, her face. He wanted those hands to grab hold of him, to tether him to the warm Earth. But he thanked her and floated back to his table. There he aligned the paper squarely in front of him where it glowed pure white in the light streaming through the windows. Upon closer inspection he could see tiny filaments dancing in all directions within its texture. The ball of the pen now appeared large and destructive as it pressed onto the paper's surface.

Dear Anise,

Conrad hadn't planned to write this, but there it was. *OK I'll practice.*

I'm sure you think I'm weird and could never like a person like me, but

He stopped. This was exactly what he felt. He crossed it out.

I can tell that you're not into me, but I wanted to let you know that I like you, and have for a long time.

Now that he could see the words "I like you" awkwardly printed on the paper, they looked suspicious.

*I like you.*
*I like you.*
*I like you.*

Had Anise reached some sort of qualifying round in his head? It felt like a lie, as if the words covered for something. He wanted to kiss her, but he had never kissed anybody, so where did all that wanting come from? He imagined sitting next to her on the grass at Wattles Park — wrapping his arms and legs around her, rolling around in a tangled state of bliss.

*I'm out of my mind!*
*She'll never like me back!*

Conrad crumpled up the note. He propped his elbows on the table and pressed his face into his hands. He counted long moments in breaths drawn in through his fingers, then out through his fingers. Finally he stood up and walked to the librarian. She had been slyly watching him the whole time.

"Do you have any books on German Expressionist painters?" he asked.

The librarian's eyes widened. "Well yes, sure!" she said, sitting up straighter. "I'll come around. Just a sec." She led Conrad toward the stacks at the far corner, near the wavy-haired girl who was still heads-down over her reading.

"We have a few," the librarian said, quickly pulling out books to peek at them. "The main library will have more of course, but this one covers just the Blue Rider group, and this one here is more of a general overview."

Conrad thanked her, sat on the floor under the stacks and fell fully into the Blue Rider. He'd seen many of these paintings before, but this book had better prints. He flipped through the pages, skipping the words but stopping at the pictures. He wasn't sure why the paintings depicted what they did, but that only added to their mystery. The intense colors resonated through his senses like sounds, especially the pictures by Franz Marc: abstracted forests thrashing with pure color along crossed lines, populated by animals that were only partially separate, shaped instead by the surrounding patterns as if only briefly existing.

Conrad turned to 'Forest with Squirrel' and slowly traced his finger along the places in the picture that were black. He liked this black. It was delicious and clean, not frightening — the source of all the other colors. He thought back to pictures he had pored over as a boy in his mother's old volume of Swedish fairy tales: in the foreground a small child might glow innocently while the surrounding forest turned dim with the shuddery suggestion of trolls or wolves. The darkness of those forests was dank and creepy, but this squirrel's forest was the scene of a private magic.

He lingered again on 'Deer In The Forest II' — it wasn't his favorite, but he found it so odd: a deer slept in a secluded dell while a dark tree trunk crossed in front of the entire picture. What did it mean?

*Maybe the trunk is a barrier*, he thought.

*Maybe it says I can't go in there, that people can't be like the deer...*

*But I've been there, haven't I?*

"Conrad!"

The book jolted from his hands across the aisle.

"Ha-ha-ha!" came a familiar laugh from behind the wavy hair.

Conrad had completely forgotten the girl in his absorption. She straightened up to reveal her face: it was Stacy Branden, of the braids, except the braids were undone. Now her hair cascaded to the sides and re-framed her face in a way that sent electric shocks all through him.

"Jerk-face," she said. "You just sit there and don't say hello?"

"I didn't know it was you!" Conrad said, finding himself surprisingly defensive. "Why did you have to give me a heart attack?"

Stacy giggled some more at the sight of Conrad so discombobulated. "To make you talk," she said, "instead of going around all silent and grumpy."

"I don't do that."

"Oh yeah you do," she said, going mock-serious. "You're a grumpy jerk-face. You go around all day just pooping on people's heads like the giant dodo bird you are."

"What are you talking about?"

"We'll just call you Dodo Pooper from now on."

"What? Who's *we*?"

"The Royal We," said Stacy, holding up her chin.

"I never did anything to you," Conrad said, though a vague recollection of being curt with Stacy in the lab did flicker through his thoughts.

"D.P. for short," Stacy said, ignoring his defense. "That's your nickname now. I'll make sure to tell everyone."

"Who's everyone? You don't even have any friends to begin with."

Stacy's face dropped. Conrad avoided her eyes, and his stomach clenched, but that only slowed the apology forming in the back of his mind. Stacy meanwhile gathered her things and stood up.

"See what did I tell you," she said, and walked away.

Conrad traced the squiggles in the library carpet with the tip of his finger, but when he got up to go find Stacy she had already left the building.

○ ○ ○

"Psst Conrad!" said Mr Onter's head poking from his front door. "Just a reminder. This is hedge week, in case you forgot."

Conrad stopped and looked up, weary after failing to out-walk himself. "Oh yeah," he said. "I'll be right back."

*Perfect.* If his mother wanted something he could turn tail. But letting himself into the house he found it empty, and he couldn't remember why. In any case he was hungry so he cut a square from a mysterious cheesy casserole in the fridge and forked it down, barely stopping to register its flavors, then hurried back out.

Mr. Onter had a lot of hedges, and today they were decidedly ratty. Conrad retrieved the trimmers from the shed, walked to the end of the yard and began to chop at any little branch sticking out. Each violent thrust of his arms felt more like revenge.

Chop.

*I'll get you little branches for what you did.*

Chop chop.

*I see you.*

Chop chop chop.

*I'll get you, all of you!*

Forty-five minutes later, Mr. Onter emerged to find Conrad in a violent trance. But he only needed one word.

"Lemonade."

Conrad became aware of himself: aching arms, dry throat, body decorated head to toe with orphaned leaves and twigs. He dropped the clippers and wobbled toward the porch. Ever observant, Mr. Onter had a damp towel at the ready.

"Don't you dare come in here until you clean yourself off," he said. "It's like you stood too close to a wood chipper."

Mr. Onter kept his kitchen austere: bare counters, stainless-steel pans hanging on hooks, and fine Japanese knives lined along a magnetic strip. But one exception stood out: an industrial-sized electric citrus press, gleaming alone on the counter like the latest model of a middle-ages execution apparatus. This had one purpose: to make lemonade that could peel paint.

Today's refreshment was presented as usual in two tall glasses on a silver tray, with a full decanter behind them glowing yellow with hope for seconds. Conrad knew the secret recipe: besides the juice from heaps of local lemons, Mr. Onter mixed in eucalyptus tree honey, burdock root bitters and a dash of salt. To serve he placed a single mint leaf at the bottom of each glass before adding ice cubes and finally the lemonade itself. Then he sipped slowly, painfully slowly, forcing Conrad to follow suit out of politeness despite wanting to drain the glass as soon as it met his lips. Having tasted this, every other lemonade in the world had become undrinkable.

Mr. Onter waited for Conrad to sit before raising his glass in a silent cheer. The first sip met Conrad's senses as a shock-wave that rippled through his every nerve. He closed his eyes. He was a superhero regaining his powers: bolts of lightning shooting from his fingers and toes! But he failed to regain the power of speech.

"I saw you trying to murder my hedges out there," Mr. Onter said.

Conrad nodded.

"What did they ever do to you?"

"Nothing."

Mr. Onter watched for a moment and raised his eyebrows. "You seem out of sorts," he pressed again.

Conrad breathed for a few moments and looked at the floor. "My life just pretty much sucks right now, that's all," he said, thinking this would cover the subject.

"Hmm… you know, I always feel that 'sucks' is one of those lazy words that doesn't actually say anything, like 'amazing', or 'weird.' Why don't you tell me what specifically isn't going your way."

At this Conrad's mind salad-tossed, like when people say their lives flashed in front of their eyes but without a glorious realization at the end. "It's hard to explain," he said. "I don't think you'll understand."

"That may very well be so," Mr. Onter said. "After all it's well-known that I'm a dinosaur, hatched from an egg." He said no more and let Conrad shift in his chair. Time passed.

"I just," Conrad began to say. "I mean..." He stopped again.

"I just, therefore I mean," Mr. Onter said. "Has a nice ring to it." He sipped his lemonade.

"I don't belong here," Conrad blurted out, then sank into his chair. "I mean, I don't feel like I belong here, in L.A. I want to go back to the woods, to the lake."

Mr. Onter nodded toward the window. "Interesting that you don't also say, *to my dad*."

"Well yeah," Conrad said with a shrug, "to my dad, of course."

"Are you sure the symptoms and the prescription go together?"

"What?"

"You don't feel like you belong here, that's the symptom. And not being here, being back in the woods, that's the cure, right?"

"Yeah."

"Are you sure about that?"

"Well, of course, it's obvious. My mother dragged us out here. I want to go back." For once Conrad felt confident in a statement.

"But how about we do an experiment. We'll take away the obvious cure. You feel like you don't belong, because... *fill in the blank*."

"There isn't anything else," Conrad said.

"Well think of it this way: perhaps you're not belonging because you're doing it wrong. Belonging is tough. I certainly don't blame you for having trouble with it. Though come to think of it you *could* take a short-cut and join a gang, or a religion, or better yet a cult! Those are surefire ways to belong, as I hear it."

"Hardy har har," said Conrad. He looked up to the antique clock on the kitchen wall. "Oh shoot it's late!" he said, standing up. "I better finish and go home so I don't get killed. Thanks for the lemonade." He drained the last drops from his glass and hurried back out to the hedges, leaving Mr. Onter with the still-full decanter.

"What happened to you?" Sucanna asked as Conrad swept through the kitchen.

"Yard work. I'll go change." He continued at a question-resistant pace, but Beth's voice stopped him at the stairs.

"Dad's on the phone!" she yelled from the sun room. She handed over the receiver and ran toward the back door, presumably toward the garage where Levy was setting up a new cage.

"Hi Dad," Conrad said. "How are you?"

"Good! You should see the lake. It froze over real early and we got early snow, too, not like the last few years."

"Huh."

"Business will be better this year. Lots of winter tourists."

"That's good. Not like last year."

"Sure hope not. Last year a bunch of folks went out of business. Too bad they couldn't stick it out. So how's school?"

"Good. I'm doing a big project on German painters."

"Keeping your grades up? No more D's in science, right?"

"Right, no more of that," Conrad said, though he wasn't actually sure.

"I hope not. Now listen, you're going on fifteen, so it's time you had a summer job. We talked about this before, remember?"

"Yeah," Conrad said, though he had pushed it out of his mind.

"I've been talking to the owner of the Alder House and he said they would take you this summer."

"Oh, uh, that's good," Conrad mumbled. The Alder House: the place with pine paneling that made their staff wear German outfits and served burgers and fish&chips on fancy plates.

"You can't just play forever you know," Henry pressed. "We talked about this. The Alder House is a great place, good people. A chance for you to get your foot in the door, you know? You'll work your way up in no time. Then when you're a server you'll make lots of tip money."

"But what'll they have me do to start?" Conrad asked, alarm about this distant-future employment already palpable.

"Oh, help out in the kitchen I expect. You'll see. They'll teach ya. All right? Got it?"

"Yeah. But what will Levy and Beth do when I'm not around?"

"I'll figure it out. But do me a favor and let your mother think about that on her own, if you catch my drift."

"Roger that," Conrad said. "I wish I could be there now, Dad."

"I know you do. So do I. You study hard, OK?"

"OK."

○ ○ ○

Dinner was another square of the same cheesy casserole with added greens. But again Conrad didn't taste anything. Instead he slouched through a boisterous discussion about the day's adventure at the stables and which horses his mother and sisters had liked best.

Then he was back on his bed, feeling what he imagined to be a photo negative of how he had felt in the morning: no worse, no better, his thoughts still swirling like tie-dye. He laid his head sideways on his arms across the windowsill and let the cool night breeze pull away what it would.

A woman walked into view and stopped at the corner. From a distance she resembled a linebacker in the wrong uniform: stocky legs in lacy leggings stuffed into extra-high heels, stiff wig-like hair, and a dainty purse on a thick gold chain. *Maybe a plant from the police*, Conrad thought. He had watched their sting operations before.

A car pulled up. The woman leaned to the open window — a discussion. But then she looked sideways and backed away. The car sped off and the woman ran toward the house, clomping her heels into the parking lot just below. Conrad crouched down so she wouldn't spot him in the window overhead. At the edge of the lot she pulled something from her purse and shoved it deep into the bushes, then pulled off her heels and carried them as she jumped out of sight over the far wall. Just then a police car turned into the lot and drove through to the next street.

Now Conrad became aware of the windowsill: its hardness, the angle of its edge creasing his arms. He could feel the floor under his feet, the mattress under his bottom. He looked up to the ceiling cast with long shadows from the streetlights. He sensed himself alone in the room, breathing. There was nothing more, and it was time to sleep.

# Early January

Head down, torso curved forward like the letter C: Conrad's doodling form was perfect. The spirits of geometry steadily filled his notepaper to its edges. Sitting at the back provided the illusion of anonymity, but Mrs. Parkins could see him quite plainly. Joey wasn't much better, reclining in the next chair as if he were stoned, gazing over the classroom in cool, calm bemusement.

"O.K. people!" said Mrs. Parkins, her voice thin rather than commanding. "I assume you've read the story I assigned, *The Upper Berth.*" Here she spoke in a spooky hush, for drama. This failed. Bored murmurs trickled away. "That's great!" she said. "Our discussion today will start out with a question: what about this story is frightening?"

Moving would be volunteering, so nobody moved. Mrs. Parkins scanned the room with eager eyes, but the bone-cold awkwardness was already setting in. Finally a girl spoke.

"It's just because it's just so weird," she said, sounding both confused and dismissive. "All these weird things happen, you know? And it just gets weirder." The girl relaxed, participation accomplished.

"OK, good," cooed the teacher, "but how does it being weird make it frightening?"

Now Theo Benton spoke up, if barely. "It's all the old-fashioned words," he said, shy and soft. "The words are, you know, creepy."

Joey shifted in his chair — his eyes were squintier now. But Robb Cott decided to help out. "It has a deeply disturbing theme," Robb said in a husky voice.

"OK, but what *is* the theme, and how is that *frightening*?" Mrs. Parkins was holding fast to the word 'frightening'. Conrad wondered why she avoided 'scary'.

"It's the monster," Robb answered. "People are always afraid of monsters, you know, like the monster in the closet, it's gunna getcha!" Giggles rewarded this bit of dash at the end.

A subtle desperation moved behind Mrs. Parkins' eyeballs. She paced the room and hummed as if Robb's contribution required further pondering. Meanwhile Joey held onto his hair.

*Joey the stoner.*

*Joey the take-nothing-seriously guy.*

*Joey the cool cat.*

Conrad had been to Joey's house, where you couldn't see the walls for the books lined up by his scientist parents. Conrad knew the real Joey: *Joey the secret achiever*. But no matter. In class, only the prospect of being dinged for non-participation could make Joey open his mouth.

Mrs. Parkins was starting to rake the peanut gallery. Conrad jammed his pencil into Joey's back.

"Joe Mackal!" Mrs. Parkins called out. "What say you?"

Joey slumped back down and half-smiled — just foolin', just one of the boys. "Well, you know, I was just thinking..." he paused. "You know, maybe it has to do with what, mmm, people don't know?"

The teacher brightened. "That's very interesting! Go on."

"Well, it seems like, at the beginning, you know, the narrator is skeptical, he's just like us, we don't take supernatural things seriously." Joey paused to screw down his tone.

"Yes?" said Mrs. Parkins.

"Well," Joey continued more loosely, "the narrator dude is so confident that people are, like, being superstitious or something, but then things keep happening that he doesn't expect..." Joey slowed again, evidently hoping that somebody would take over, but the class only stared. "...and then he's trapped himself in there, and even when he looks straight at the *thing* he still can't tell what it looks like, it's just all slimy and cold... or something like that." He shrugged at the end, noncommittal.

"Those are excellent observations, Joe!" said Mrs. Parkins.

"You son of an asswipe," Joey hissed as they emerged from class.

"Hey, that was really good in there!" Conrad protested. "You saved poor Mrs. Parkins."

"You could have helped at least."

Conrad made like a Neanderthal. "Well maybe I just, you know, didn't maybe, uh, you know, have any ideas of my own, guh, today?"

"Yeah, well next time it's your turn."

FLUMP

Face on the floor, arms sprawled out, books sliding down the hallway — something had tripped Conrad at the ankles.

"Oh, I'm sorry D.P.! Are you OK?"

Conrad stood up dazed to see Stacy crouching at the end of the lockers, her hair wound back up into braids and her leg retracted. Still visible however was the shapeliness of her face, now that he knew about it.

"Why did you call him D.P.?" Joey asked her.

"Oh don't you know?" she whispered as if revealing an embarrassing secret. "Those are his middle initials."

"Initials? Conrad? You have two middle names?"

"Shhh!" Stacy covered her mouth. "He doesn't want anybody to know."

Conrad had gone over various apology scenarios since before winter break, but now they all evaporated.

"You're OK then?" Stacy asked with innocent concern but not stopping. "Phew I'm so glad. But you should really watch where you're going."

"Thanks for the advice," Conrad said, then picked up his books and continued down the hall. Joey followed but peeked back at Stacy more than once. When they were out of sight outside he pulled at Conrad's shirt.

"Uh, hey man... is there like, something going on with you and her that I don't know about?"

"No," Conrad grumbled. "She just keeps getting on my case. I wasn't nice to her like one time and now she won't stop."

"Oh good..." Joey paused, looking back in Stacy's direction as if he could see her through the walls. Conrad eyed him, incredulous.

"What... really?"

"Yeah, she's *so* cute, can't you see it? I've been crushing on her for so long."

"I *cannot* believe what I'm hearing."

"Why not?"

"You ask me why not? All you ever do is talk about *hot chicks*. What ever happened to Angela, or Lacey? I know all about them because of you. But *Stacy Branden*? You've never said anything about Stacy."

"Man, I'll tell you what. Stacy can wipe the floor with these other girls here. She's got a hundred times more going on in her head. And talking to her is a laugh riot."

Conrad stood staring. In general he trusted Joey's powers of observation so much that he doubted his own, but in this case he already agreed.

"I think I'm going to ask her out," Joey said, talking faster now, more like himself. "I have to! I mean, I'm running out of time. All these other jerk-wads around here will start noticing how hot she is and beat me to it."

"Oh, well, yeah then..."

Conrad went quiet. This was revolutionary. Up to this day their routine had been to stare at girls from afar like birds on a wire. Now one of them wanted to fly down.

Joey turned to Conrad directly and pointed. "You should ask Anise out," he said.

Conrad's eyes bugged a little. "Oh, I don't know..."

"Don't know what? Don't know whether you've been goo-goo about her since forever?"

"I don't know, I mean, I don't think she even likes me."

"Who gives a flying shit?" Joey squeaked. "Say she says no. I bet she'll be impressed you asked. It might even freak her out. She's in the same grade as us, after all. It's not like she's a college girl." Now Joey was rolling. "Just suppose," he continued, professorial, "suppose a girl you never talked to suddenly came up to you and said, *hey Conrad, I think you're cute, wanna go to a movie?* You would shit your pants right there."

Conrad laughed. "Yeah and my nose would spurt blood," he added, chortling. "And sweat would squirt out, and then I'd be gagging on my own barf. Then I'd fart huge gas-clouds, and my crotch would soak, and diarrhea would ooze out around my shoes. Poor girl would run screaming."

Joey held his sides. "Hey Conrad," he cooed, "I've liked you for oh so long and  — thththththththth — oh no!" He wiggled his hands in the air in mock distress.

"Hey, don't laugh," Conrad said, standing up straight. "It's my superpower. Girls wanna crush on me, they better watch out."

"What's that smell? It's Shy Man!" Joey pointed one heroic hand to the skies — the other held his nose.

"Fags," called a boy across the alley, who, along with his pack of friends, continued smirk-walking past. Joey dropped his arm and blinked.

"Who was that?" Joey asked. "Do we know that guy?"

"He's new," Conrad said. "I think his name's Patrick." Being new hadn't stopped Patrick from being handsome or taking point in the popular herd, which included Robb and Todd.

"Well anyway..." Joey picked up again grumpily as he began sliding away, "think about it. I'm not kidding this time."

○ ○ ○

"What are you doing in there?" came Levy's voice through the door.

"Nothing!" Conrad called back. "I'll be out soon!" Putting off sisters from inside the bathroom was a time-worn habit. Showered and fully dressed, yet still facing the mirror, he combed

and re-combed to make his hair perfect, though knowing it never
had been only fanned his frustration. His baby-fine locks sprang
up in the front like the Fountains of Rome but fell dead and limp
to the sides. An experiment with Levy's hair gel had failed (too
shiny), so he had rinsed his head in the sink and was trying again
with his mother's brand.

"I have to pee!" came Levy's voice again, more desperate.

"Go pee in the pooptangle!" Conrad yelled, causing his hair to
slide forward again.

There was a tiny second bathroom downstairs, but the toilet
was acting up, and anyway Doonie was in heat and refused to let
anyone in. Conrad was suggesting that Levy go outside to the
rectangle of grass at the back of the yard where the dog did its
business.

"Please! I'm dying!" she pleaded. If it were Beth there would
be insistent pounding on the door, but Levy used sympathy.
"Please," she said again, her voice weaker. "I just need to pee."

"OK, fine, but I'm not done." Conrad cracked open the door.
Levy was a pitiful clam on the floor, not only her legs but also her
arms squeezed tight to prevent leakage. Conrad stepped over her,
only then noticing that her hands were clutching something —
clothes! In a few swift monkey-movements, Levy rolled into the
bathroom, slammed the door and flipped the lock.

"Thanks buddy-o!"

"I wasn't done!" Conrad yelled. Then came the squeak of
faucet handles and the rush of water. "Levy!"

Her voice echoed from the shower. "You looked very
handsome to me!"

"Conrad, stop yelling at your sister and come to breakfast,"
said Sueanna's head poking around the bottom of the stairs.
"Wow, you look so nice and trim today!" she said as he dropped
down into the kitchen. Beth was already set to go and munching
on toast. Her head swiveled like an owl's, following Conrad with
her eyes as he moved through the room, as he fell into his chair in
the corner, as he scooped his scrambled eggs, as he chewed. He
peered back at her. She batted her eyelashes.

"What," he grumbled.

"Oh nothing," Beth said. More eye blinking.

"Stop it!"

Beth lifted herself into a languorous ballet posture, then, with long swoops of her finger, drew the letter A in the air. "Somebody has a sweetie," she said.

"No I don't!"

"Really, Conrad?" his mother asked, smiling but not with surprise.

"Bet I know who it is," said Beth. "Starts with an 'A', right?"

"How would you know anything about it?" he said, but a note of alarm gave him away.

"You put her name into every doodle last year, hee hee!" Beth giggled. "I'm a big fan of your work you know."

Levy was squatting in the hallway, her damp hair swinging as she stuffed her backpack. "Come eat!" Sueanna called to her. Most days Sueanna dropped Conrad at school, extending her commute, however she also helped carpool the girls and their friends in an even less convenient direction. Today was her turn. "Levy, hurry and eat!" she called again.

Levy scampered in, lowered her face to the waiting plate and began shoveling eggs into her gaping, gnashing, smacking mouth. But Conrad and Beth watched Sueanna. Predictably, a conflict crept into her face.

"Can't you eat quickly like a lady?" she peeped, and her children laughed at her.

"Have a great day!" Sueanna called. Conrad nodded and merged into a rush of students, conscious of the skinny angles of his limbs, his hair out of place, his collar pulling back from his neck, and a voice whispering *it's all for nothing*.

There would be no model today in art class. A week of preparatory drafting was done, and now it was time to begin their 'personal paintings.' Conrad sat himself in a corner away from everybody, especially Stacy. He had already sketched out his canvas in pencil, so now he began to squeeze paint onto his palette. Mrs. Pelora swept close in a cloud of vanilla.

"Remember Conrad, remember what I said before. Painterly, OK? No big gobs of oil. This time I want to see layers, a building up, a history, a little at a time."

"OK."

Conrad mixed a blob of Phthalo Green with spirits, tested it, then thinned it more, then again. His first small stroke spread transparent into the bumpy texture of the canvas, barely a wash, lovely. Still, he wasn't sure why he had done that, and he couldn't take it back. He would have to work in the green somehow, or cover it later. He busied himself with thinning more colors and applying them as transparently as possible.

Conrad drifted from the studio in a state of delicious, colored concentration. But then the world turned blinding white: Anise was strolling in the alley, flanked by her friends.

Conrad turned and followed just behind — for him the wrong direction. For some reason Anise was the focus, all her friends leaning in as if to advise on some urgent subject. But Anise herself stayed mostly silent, responding only with "mmm-hmm." One by one her friends peeled away into classrooms until Anise was alone, reaching for a door handle. He would dare! Passing the doorway, Conrad turned his head, met her gaze, held it... and smiled. Anise paused, then, with a sideways squint of her eyes, slipped behind the door.

That was progress, anyway.

Late for chemistry.

"Hey D.P.!"

He had already seen Stacy through the little window in the lab door, and she knew it, but that didn't stop her.

"Over here D.P.!" she stage-whispered across the room.

"Would you cut that out?" he implored under his breath as he took his station. "It's not funny."

"It's nothing to be ashamed of you know."

It would only get worse, so he shut up. Miss Lanto began to call out instructions for the day's lab assignment — a special challenge with many convoluted steps. But Conrad and Stacy had boiled down their lab strategy: Stacy read out each instruction, then Conrad repeated it with words as different as possible, then, if they both agreed that they really understood, one carried out the step as the other stood guard against mistakes, ready to blurt out with comic seriousness, 'abort!' This lasted to the end of the period when, with hoots of triumph, Stacy and Conrad were the only pair to finish with a valid result. Every other team had gone off the rails somewhere in the middle and now stood dejected watching the 'winners.'

"Nice job you two!" Miss Lanto called from the board.

High five!

Stacy's hand was strong and warm. Really Conrad couldn't hate her. She was everything Joey had said — still kind of a brat, but at least he was visible to this brat. It was powerful, that she saw him. Or he could say that she welcomed him. Of course she did so by teasing him mercilessly, but that only went to show that they came from the same planet. So he didn't hate her, in fact...

In fact, he liked her.

*Oh no,* he thought.

*I like Stacy.*

But what kind of *like* was this? He couldn't make sense of it. It wasn't how he liked Anise, was it? How could it be, without the trance, without the paralysis? Little by little he had gotten to know Stacy before feeling a thing. But if he really liked her, maybe that train would hit him later. And if it did, he would simply have to stand there and take it in the face, because of Joey. It was useless really, this new liking or whatever it was, because nothing in his mind had changed about Anise, and now his head would spin even faster until his brains dribbled out of his ears.

"Bye Stacy."

"See you later D.P.!"

Anise sat between her friends as usual, but she did more than simply exist: she positively glowed in her trademark fuzzy sweater (in a new color), sporting something on both her lips and eyelids that gave a slight sparkle. How could Conrad get anywhere near such a being? Scenes of approach stuttered across his imagination, words that would gelatinize in his mouth. *Impossible*, he thought. And for her, completely random. He would appear out of nowhere, and say what?

Actually he already knew what. Joey was now the self-appointed expert, ever since first talking to Stacy, and Joey had told him what to say:

'Hey Anise, do you wanna hang out some time?'

This was as good a plan as any: cool, casual, light. No pressure. Except walking up to Anise and saying only that would be deeply strange.

Mr. Sebastian was in a heat about cannons. The antique pictures from the overhead projector — the sponge, the rammer, the touch hole — distracted Conrad for a good while, but then he went back to peeking at the side of Anise's head. If he didn't do something, *anything*, Joey would ask 'did you talk to her yet?' for the hundred-millionth time.

One minute remained and Mr. Sebastien was not slowing down.

"The flintlock, you see, allowed the person firing the cannon to look straight down its barrel and therefore take better aim..." He used his stubby arms to semaphore a cannon into existence and pretended to peer along its length. "This was an advantage over standing to the side, since the ship would be rolling in the water." Finally Mr. Sebastien looked at his watch and shouted out reminders as a wave of students rose up toward the door with Anise at the front. By the time Conrad had stuffed his bag and run outside she was nowhere to be seen.

*Here we go again, then.*

Conrad set out on a zigzagging course through the campus.

Gym: no.

Offices: no.

Theater hallways: no.

Basketball court: no.

She had to turn up somewhere, but this couldn't be called hope, not if it was dread.

Science building... *so hungry.*

Food Truck Man was smiling. For the first time ever, Conrad saw his teeth: over-sized and sheet-white as if he had bleached them. And the smile was for Anise, smiling back as she paid for a burrito. In his amazement Conrad failed to slow as he approached. Would Food Truck Man smile at him, too? Had the man won the lottery or something? No: as soon as Conrad arrived, the smile vanished into an expression furtive then stony again. Conrad stood directly behind Anise, her fuzzy sweater just inches away. But she didn't turn. She would walk away soon! He darted for a sandwich then jumped back, this time to the side so she could not fail to see him.

She saw him. "You like those?" she asked.

Conrad looked down to see a cucumber sandwich in his hands. "Well, yeah," he said, "they're um, you know, cool as a cucumber..."

Anise squinted. "So that's how you got that way, huh." Humor crept across her face.

"Anise! Anise!"

Carrie and Amy arrived to sweep Anise away, their faces lit with some exciting secret. Conrad watched them go but saw only the smallest of peeks back.

"You payin' for that?" said Food Truck Man.

At first Conrad didn't move.

"Yeah, here." He slapped bills into the man's hand, deep-stared the evasive tooth-hiding face, grabbed the change and walked to the benches. Joey looked down at him, grave like a judge.

"Did you talk to her yet?"

"Yes I did," Conrad whispered.

Joey gaped as Conrad slid up next to him. "Bullshit."

Conrad shook his head.

"So you asked her out?"

"We had a conversation."

"About what?"

Conrad paused. "About my sandwich."

Joey burst out laughing. "Your - ha! And the heck are you eating? Ha ha!"

"I like these now. Well, I'm going to like them, I've decided."

"So that's it, your sandwich?"

"So it was a short conversation. Give me a break."

"OK, sorry, heh-heh-heh." Joey tried to be serious. But then came mumbles, 'hey baby, wanna bite my sandwich?', then chuckles, then 'hey girl, my sandwich has a lotta meat on it,' then chortles.

"Would you quit it?"

"Hey sweet thing, I've got some ham and cheese here for ya."

"Stop."


Conrad accelerated through the halls. After sitting near the door in his last class he had bolted at the bell. Now he hurried out to the curb and paced its length to be sure Anise wasn't somewhere out of sight at either end.

There!

Anise appeared near the main entrance, but she stopped at the elevator, orange paper in hand.

Of course! *All students are to turn in their health forms directly to the office.* Conrad had this same paper in his binder, signed by his mother. He dashed over just in time to squeeze in among a crush of students as the elevator doors opened, directly behind Anise. He could say something! But no, everyone would hear. And now he could smell her: a faint sense of some perfumed cosmetic, and bubblegum, and especially her hair — the remnants of shampoo giving way to a delicious muskiness that shocked him awake, that made his blood run dizzy. Everything about her was suddenly an unknown quantity. The doors opened.

"One at a time please!"

The office secretary had to double-check each form, so the offloading rush of students formed a line that pushed Anise toward the front and Conrad to the end. Anise was soon back waiting at the elevator. He could ride down with her! But no again: he was still holding his form. *Too obvious.*

Anise swiveled to survey the line. When her eyes arrived at Conrad she gave a little start and a quizzical cock of her head, but just as quickly she collected herself and popped through the opening doors.

Now Conrad became aware of himself: he hadn't spoken, or acknowledged her, or smiled. He had only stood there like a mute and charmless post.

The secretary took his form and checked off his name.

"By the way Conrad," she whispered, motioning to lean into her window. "A bunch of kids have come asking about your middle names. Of course I wouldn't say, but actually your file doesn't list any. Can you tell me what they are?"

"I'm not sure," Conrad said. "I'll have to ask my mother." With that he shot down the back stairs and ran all the way around to the front. Anise was still there but surrounded by her friends. Amy turned to peer at Conrad, while Anise herself dropped into a waiting car and was gone.

○ ○ ○

"Look what I *just* got this summer," Mr. Onter said. He went to the shelf and pulled out one of the new books Conrad had seen months before. Mr. Onter's sense of time was geologic. "I finished the series I've been reading, and now I'm starting these. I had to order them from England." He handed Conrad a heavy volume, beautifully hard-bound with pages of fine, thick paper. "Here, let me show you something." Mr. Onter took it back and leafed through the pages. "Yes, here they are," he said. "I just love these." He spread the book open on the table so Conrad could see a series of maps. In the first, almost the entire picture was obscured by dark clouds, however a small break in the middle allowed a few countries to be seen. In the next map, the hole in the clouds was larger, revealing more territory, and so on.

"Huh…" was all Conrad said. He read the caption: 'Historical Atlas by Edward Quin, 1830.'

"Isn't that clever?" said Mr. Onter. He pointed from one picture to the next. "See, each one represents a different time, as people's knowledge of the world increased."

Conrad's nerves hadn't yet come down from the day's high pitch, and he felt somehow impatient with these pictures.

"They're cool-looking I guess," he said, "but kinda dumb too."

"Oh? How so?"

"I mean... the places you can see right at the edges of the holes, of course they knew about the places next to them, even though the clouds cover them. And those hidden places knew about the next hidden places, right?"

"Oh, undoubtedly they did in reality, but this was meant as a sort of metaphor, you know, from the point of view of somebody or some group in particular."

"Yeah, but who? And couldn't they just ask the people at the edges, *hey you, what's over there?* Or go look themselves?"

"Well yes, but like I said, it's metaphorical."

"I guess. Still seems dumb."

Mr. Onter's face hid shock and amusement. This wasn't Conrad's usual mode, and he was bouncing on the sofa.

"I suppose I see your point," Mr. Onter said, "but in any case it's still a nice stroke of imagination." He sidled back to his shelves for another volume, then added, "by the way, you seem pretty keyed up today."

The urge to cover himself, but then an opposing flash of annoyance — "Uhhh!" Conrad threw himself backward onto the upholstery. Then he lurched up again and held his head between his hands. "I'm so sick of myself," he said.

Mr. Onter's first response to this sudden violence was to stand perfectly still next to his books. But then he seated himself at the other side of the coffee table, at an angle to Conrad, and sipped his tea with more apparent interest in the potted plant. "Is that so?" he asked. "Pray tell me what your *self* is doing to bother you. I will have a word with him."

"I just can't figure anything out. I'm such an idiot!"

"I wouldn't let you in here if that were the case, so why the hair shirt?"

From long exposure to Mr. Onter, Conrad had a vague understanding of phrases like 'hair shirt' and 'mortification of the flesh', or at least the comic use of them. "My friend Joey is making me talk to this girl," he muttered.

Mr. Onter nodded. "A repulsive, pustule-ridden hussy, I take it?"

"No, I mean, Joey knows I like her so he's making me ask her out."

"And you don't want to?"

"Well I don't know, I guess, yeah, I want to, but there's no way she likes me. She's totally amazing! And anyway I keep screwing it up." He pounded his fists on the sofa cushions.

"So actually you like her, a lot, and, *actually*, you want to ask her out. Is that right?"

Conrad didn't respond, so Mr. Onter turned his head to squint directly. Conrad nodded at the floor.

"When did you first like her?"

"A year or so ago, I guess..." It was longer.

"Oh, a year or so? So tell me about her."

"Like what?"

"Like, how many brothers and sisters does she have?"

"I don't know."

"Where does she live?"

"I'm not sure. Why does that matter?"

"OK, how about this. What is she interested in? Does she do art like you? Does she have favorite books? Is she outdoorsy?"

Conrad felt a kind of panic. He had to know something, but little came to mind. He shrugged at the floor.

"Hmm..." Mr. Onter raised his chin. "So according to your testimony, you've been watching this girl for countless ages, thought about her, *longed for her* I'm guessing, yet you know nothing about her whatsoever. Don't you find that a bit odd?"

"Wouldn't I learn all that stuff later anyway?"

"You mean you haven't spoken to her, she's not a friend?" Mr. Onter waited. "A friend of a friend?"

"I spoke to her a couple times... sort of."

"Oh, then you're using the wrong word. You don't like her. You want her. Those aren't the same. It'll make you feel better to call things by their right names."

Conrad only grew hotter. "Doesn't feel better."

Mr. Onter repositioned himself at the end of the sofa to pour fresh cups of Dianhong tea. A comforting steam rose as Conrad sipped the copper liquid and the flush receded from his face. Mr. Onter spoke more gently.

"Maybe you feel like I'm criticizing you, Conrad, but really I'm not. I've been just the same. I wasn't always this ancient husk."

Conrad peeked doubtfully at the eternally cool and collected person opposite the sofa. "What, so you were a gang member or something?"

"I just mean there's a girl out there in the world, and there's a girl in your head. You don't really know if you like her. So maybe Joey's right. Maybe you should ask her out. At the very least you could mingle with her at school, see how she ticks. In any case you have to talk."

Conrad folded up his legs, wrapped his arms around them and squeezed his nose in between his knees so his voice came out muffled by his jeans.

"But everyone's doing that stuff like it's all so easy and I just flop around like a dope."

Mr. Onter sat straighter at this. "Oh, so they're all perfectly confident, and know exactly what they're doing, is that right? And I take it that you go around telling people how afraid you are, that you don't really know anything? I bet you go up to your fellow students every day and shake them and say, *I feel so vulnerable today! I am so bewildered by this world! Please tell me what to do!* That's what you say, right?"

"What? Of course not."

"So what *do* you do?"

"I don't know, nothing really."

"Nothing, yes, exactly, but how do you imagine you look to other people, when you're doing nothing?"

"Like a spazz."

"Oh I doubt that. And really, hardly anybody is watching you in the first place. That's your first mistake right there. And even if they do... well I bet if you saw a movie of yourself, like if someone secretly followed you around all day with a camera, you wouldn't even look like *you* to yourself."

"I'd look pretty weird."

"I'll tell you what I think other people see. I bet they just see a fast-walking kid with intense eyes. And since you're quite hard to read by the way, those other people are free to assume whatever they want about you, for instance that you know exactly what you're doing, thank you very much."

"But I don't."

"Sure, but how could anyone tell? And it's the same for them, all walking around as if to say 'I'm doing just fine! Nothing to see here!' and smiling. So much smiling." Mr. Onter emphasized this last point with a grin that showed more of his gums than Conrad had ever wanted to see.

○ ○ ○

He would take one bite. An unsullied sandwich wouldn't be casual.

*Ick...*

It was especially bad today. If Sueanna were to make one of these, Conrad was sure, she would make it with country bread maybe, and an herbal spread to complement the crispy cucumber cuts — not like this cold slimy sponge turning to paste in his mouth. But he needed this sandwich. It was his talking point.

From high up on the bench he could already see Anise through the trees, at the truck pulling a juice from the ice, all by herself. He knew something of her habits by now. Soon she would dash through the picnic area right under him, to the edge of the campus where she often huddled with her friends at the 'wall garden,' the remains of a demolished brick wall just long enough for an entire clique to perch. The spot offered privacy and flowering vines up the back fence, but also a sideways view to the gate that older students used to go off campus.

Anise was paying, the smiles again... and moving his way!

She *had* to see him. Maybe when she passed he would swing his legs a little. If she didn't say anything, he would. Just this morning he had said 'Hi Anise' and she had said 'Hi Conrad' back. It hadn't been just plain 'Hi.' It was *his* name, in *her* voice: it made this thing possible! He would invite her to climb up and eat lunch with him, and ask her lots of questions like Mr. Onter had suggested. He would do it today or go down in glorious flames.

Closer, closer... *NO!*

Carrie and Amy rushed out to Anise from the lab building, hooking their arms with hers. Before thinking, which might have told him to remain upright, Conrad laid himself flat on the bench out of sight from the ground. Now he could only hear the girls approach.

"But you said he was cute," said Amy in a whisper.

"I did," said Anise. "But that doesn't mean anything."

"Yes it does! It means you like him."

"No it doesn't. Really I'm not into him at all. He acts like *such* a jerk. And I wish he would stop trying to talk to me all the time."

The whispers trailed off as they rounded a corner, but Conrad kept still on his back and stared up at the trails left by jets taking luckier people away.

# 8

# Mid-February

Knocks on the door again.

"Conrad?" came Beth's voice.

Conrad wasn't asleep, but he was still under his covers. Being under covers allowed him not to respond, as if he were asleep, as if the person on the outside should know that, despite it being noon.

"Conrad, are you just going to stay in there all day again?"

Conrad had every intention of staying in there all day again. He had many excuses, one even legitimate. He didn't offer any however. Beth kept talking.

"Levy wants to graze the herd but I want to go up the hills, too. If you don't come I'll have to sit on the grass the whole time. Don't you want to go?"

"No."

"Please?"

"No."

He listened to Beth harrumphing down the stairs. An urge came to stop her — it was a perfect California winter day after all. But he was stuck, drawn into his mattress if he lived on a planet more massive than Earth.

Sounds of activity came from downstairs, then from out back — laughing words, complaining words, metal clanging, then hard wheels rolling: the old red wagon, loaded up with twenty or so guinea pigs in their cages watching wide-eyed behind the bars, chewing and calling out 'weet! weet!' at the bumps while being pulled first along rushing city streets then up past increasingly fine homes, all the way up to the park. Conrad waited until the sounds had faded then slunk down to the kitchen. Soon he was back in his room with a basket of food. He locked the door, despite the house being empty, then pulled out the book Mr. Onter had loaned him for his history project: *The Apocalyptic Vision - The Art Of Franz Marc as German Expressionism*, by Frederick S. Levine. Its black and white illustrations were indistinct, but no matter. He would look at the words this time.

When his concentration flagged, Conrad reached his hand into the basket. He read for hours this way. Bars of light and shadow glaciated across the bedroom floor, their hues gradually warming until it was dark. He folded himself up under his lamp with the book open on his crossed legs, reading in a wakeful trance.

"Conrad, don't make me come up here again. It's time to come out of there and come down to dinner."

"I'm not hungry!" It was almost true — he had eaten everything in the basket. But he was going on fifteen.

"Conrad, you come to dinner, and that's final." Sueanna spoke through the thin part of the door so her voice sounded inside the room. This was not the first weekend her son had shut himself up, and it was still Saturday. A double-helix of worry and irritation shaped her response. "You know what?!" she said, giving in to exasperation, "I'm not even going to tell you what we cooked today!" She tramped down the stairs.

"Hi Conrad," Beth whispered. Her brother had appeared under the dining-room archway like a visiting ghost. Now his body slumped into the chair next to Levy. Sueanna pretended not to notice. A foil-covered object glittered at the center of the table.

"We're having African food for dinner tonight," Levy said and slapped him hard on the back. "Aren't you excited?"

It stung. He could try to hit her back, but he would miss — she was too fast. If he actually attacked her she would strangle him with her arms and legs like Rubber Girl, like that one time... And he wouldn't attack her with words because he didn't really feel like hurting her feelings.

"Brat," he mumbled.

"I hope you can handle exotic cuisine," Beth said. She stood up to reach and pull off the foil.

"Ta-dah!" Levy stretched out her palm. "Leopard pie!" It was SPSP, but with three kinds of sweet potato: white, purple, and orange, carefully dolloped to resemble a leopard pelt.

The food didn't last long, as everyone was hungry, especially Conrad. The starch warmed his insides, but his thoughts paced in the space between the voices sounding around him. The book had been short but hard to read, packed as it was with references not only to art but to poetry, music, literature, philosophy, politics — the entire cultural universe that Franz Marc had been born into. Conrad was proud at having understood some of it, but also it made him uneasy. Of course Franz Marc had been a real person, but reading about his messy real life threatened to rob the paintings of their magic. And due to missing records, the outline of Marc's life skipped from his birth to his seventeenth year. That was more years than Conrad had been alive. Wouldn't those years matter for someone like that? Conrad felt a twinge of injustice for the young Marc. But what bothered him most was reading about Marc being depressed and reclusive, obsessed with death and escape. This wasn't what he'd expected at all, not the artist-seer of mystic forests. He felt reluctant to mention this in his report.

"Sorry for not going today," he said all of a sudden, interrupting his sisters. He hadn't spoken the whole dinner.

Beth gave him a little smile. "That's OK," she said.

"We made a corral out of sticks," said Levy. "It even worked!"

"I can go tomorrow if you want," Conrad offered.

"Nope! Tomorrow's a horsey day!" Levy made coconut-hoof sounds with her tongue in case he hadn't understood.

Now Sueanna sat forward, obviously hopeful that her hermetic son might let in some air. "Would you like to come with us?" she asked.

Conrad considered. He liked horses, but didn't like riding

them — the controlling leather and metal, constantly stopping the animals from doing what they wanted.

"No thanks," he said. "I'm going to the art museum with my friend."

○ ○ ○

*Bodies sliding into clothing.*
*Bodies zooming around in cars.*
*Bodies scooting in and out of buildings.*
*Bodies hiding away in little rooms.*
*Bodies always seeking their shells and their boxes, their cases and*
*containers and compartments...*

Conrad was rolling in such a thing: a bus. He looked down at his feet, absurdly tied into thick material and rubber. He wiggled his toes to make sure they were still there. He followed the lines of his enclosing pants up to the folds of his enclosing shirt, then visualized his layers of skin and muscle around the squishy containers within. He pictured his brain sloshing around in the dark inside his skull — but wait! Maybe it wasn't fully closed-in after all. If eyes were part of the brain like some teacher had said, then his brain was actually peeking out of his skull.

*Peeking left.*
*Peeking right.*
*Our shiny wet eyes, just like our shiny wet brains.*

For the briefest moment Conrad experienced the faces enclosed around him as an extraterrestrial might — the glistening eyeball surfaces, the odd hairs, the creases and lips and folds — all meaningless for just a moment. Then the meaning came back, and Conrad saw it, or thought he did. Mostly the faces were grumpy.

The bus was heading downtown and Conrad was going it alone, Joey having begged off once again. It made him want to slouch, but if he didn't stretch up to peer through the standing bodies he would miss his stop and end up on a suspect corner. Of course he couldn't know just by looking if a particular spot was dangerous or simply devoid of humanity. These easterly places weren't so much threatening as suggestive, as if the danger was also contained — behind the crusting walls, or in the shadows behind the structures visible from the bus. Really the worst thing he could see outdoors was a dusty sun-bleached hopelessness, but he wasn't going to take any chances. Plus he had only enough money to reach downtown, pay for the art gallery, maybe have lunch, and get back, so he couldn't waste a dollar backtracking.

"Art museum, get off here!" came the driver's voice from up front. Conrad thanked the eyes in the mirror and squeezed his way out.

The Temporary Contemporary was the warehouse kind of container and still looked like one, but inside it felt more like being outside than the real thing, at least in that part of town. Each space opened to another space, with ramps at odd angles to join them and high-hung spotlights that lent meaning even to the empty corners. Conrad paid for his ticket and launched himself along the guide-rails with giddy expectation.

He stopped first at a painting: rectangles of oranges, apparently simple shapes that shifted and dissolved as he stared. He could see them but not see them. The word 'miasma' came to mind, like in *A Wrinkle In Time* — the part when the children face the horrible IT — but this was a good and gorgeous miasma. He leaned over to read the label: Mark Rothko. *Oh yeah!* He'd heard something about that guy...

Two men passed by, glancing at the painting but not stopping. "What do people see in shit like that?" one of them asked. Conrad turned to follow them down the ramp. The men barely paused to take in each painting, pointing and shaking their heads at one work after another, until the ramp ended at a large corner space entirely occupied by a life-sized papier-maché subway car. "Just look at that garbage!" the man said again. The two continued away laughing, but Conrad stayed behind, indignant. He would see what they could not!

A step on the side allowed him to board. Painted paper riders sat along the benches inside, stiff like the pyroclastic agony of

Pompeii but here absurdly bulbous. One of the paper figures had nodded off onto the shoulder of a mortified fellow passenger. Conrad scanned the interior as he waited for deep and artistically-informed thoughts to surface.

A woman boarded, her husband behind her. "Oh this is so cool!" she said and pointed.

"Aw look, he's dozing off," her husband chuckled. "That's so cute."

*I should go pee in the corner to make it more realistic*, Conrad thought. Then he hurried out, picturing the sappy figures drooping as they burned. Looking up he saw a line snaking away from a brightly-lit space on the second tier, so he leapt up the steps to join at the end behind a little elderly woman wrapped in knits.

"What's this we're waiting for?" he asked her.

"We're waiting to see nothing," she said and turned away with a witty lift of her chin.

Conrad bobbed on his feet in the barely-moving line. Well-lit objects downstairs tried to lure him away. The woman turned again to whisper, "almost there kid."

An attendant was sending people in one at a time. Now it was Conrad's turn. "Shoes off please," she said. "Toes to the line." Conrad stepped to a faint mark on the floor, then looked forward.

Nothing. A bright white nothing.

The space in front of him had no corners, no shadows, no up, no down, just white.

But *not* nothing. His eyes would not stop moving, though the world in front of them was gone. Shapes swam at the edges, and wisps danced behind his eyes like ghosts hiding from the light. His eyes soon rebelled against the illusion. He began to make out where the walls actually were, the slight imperfections in the paint.

"Time's up," said the attendant.

Conrad stepped out into a darkly-colored world. The old woman was standing there still, waiting for his reaction.

"Did you see nothing?" she asked.

"Kind of. My brain wouldn't shut up."

"Ha! Your brain will never shut up. Better get used to it." The woman began to walk away, but then stopped to add, "hey if you liked that, you should try the dark room they have downstairs."

The dark room had its own line, but worse: Conrad had to wait just to get into the actual waiting area, which was dimmer than the brightly-lit galleries in order for people's eyes to adjust. Once there he fidgeted for fifteen more minutes before his group was called in.

"Please do not lean on the walls," said this attendant. The walls were actually thick paper hung from the ceiling, starting narrow like a hallway but widening into a black void. The walls gave as Conrad drew his hand along beside him, his only sensation as he left all light behind. The attendant led them to sitting spots by the sides and told them to wait. "Your eyes will adjust in ten or so minutes," she said, and left.

Now like before but the reverse, his eyes refused to accept the darkness. No amount of blinking or calm staring would clear the non-existent forms dancing in his vision. He wanted to swat away whatever these things were, spinning in the dark like bats. But time passed, and he began to sense real forms around him, though much delayed, just blurry after-impressions. Then more time passed and he could make out an indistinct shape: somebody was pacing slowly in the space, a shadowy being, visible then not, reappearing farther away like a spirit against the barely-glowing walls.

"OK everyone," came the attendant's voice. "Time for the next group." Ghostly shapes rose and moved toward the exit, but Conrad remained still. As he guessed, the attendant couldn't actually see him since her eyes had just been exposed to the waiting area. New people soon groped their way in, but now Conrad was the ghost, creeping to avoid them, his quiet movements masked by the air conditioning. When the new people were settled along the paper walls he spider-crawled across the carpet to listen to their whispers at close quarters.

"This is so creepy," one woman said.

"Yeah, but is it art?" whispered her friend. "Kind of pretentious, don't you think, making us just sit here in the dark?"

"Yeah but aren't we supposed to see something?"

Conrad moved to a young couple. He could tell who they were from the voices he had heard earlier in line.

"I can't see anything!" the girl whispered, though Conrad was squatting directly in front of them listening to the dry sounds of her boyfriend's hand stroking the material around her chest.

Conrad leaned closer, exhaled a cloud of hot breath onto their faces, then leaned back onto his hands.

"That's gross would you stop?" the girl hissed at her boyfriend, who didn't answer but instead flailed out his hands. Conrad could feel the air move and perceived hand shapes, like snapshots of hands in his mind instead of moving hands, but he had already crept safely out of range.

That group eventually moved out, then another came in, then another. Conrad continued to move among them until his breathing was the only part of himself remaining, as if all of his wrappers and boxes and enclosures had dissolved. It should have been freedom, but instead he found himself inhaling and exhaling faster and faster toward a heaving despair. With nothing to contain them, tears began streaming from his eyes. He felt himself draining away into a subterranean river, whisked along helpless. *But why?* He opened his mouth wider so nobody would hear his sobs.

In time the rapids leveled out to a slowly-swirling eddy. Conrad dried his face and looked around again to find that his night-sight had reached a new level: now he could make out people's distinct outlines and even the stripes on their shirts. Finally, and not without a kind of awe, Conrad perceived the color red: just red, without the other colors. Anything red on a person stood out as a bloodstain on a gray-black form. Would more colors appear? His stomach was growling. Before giving up he let a new group settle in, then laid on his back, lifted the paper wall and slid his head under to see the truth: the paper was hanging inside a normal square room, and lights were hung along the real walls behind thick damping material. And if this was God, a lot of extension cords were involved.

The dark room exited to the same dim waiting area, where after so long in the dark Conrad had to sit with his eyes clamped shut. Even then the gallery lights were so blinding that he stumbled toward the cafe squinting tightly.

A blessed truth: every museum cafe served tomato soup and grilled cheese sandwiches. Conrad consumed the heavenly substances as Mr. Onter would: savoring each savory soup sip, each rough and cheesy bite, each cool stream of water down his throat. He stared down at the clear bright reality of his arms moving the food to his mouth, the hairs fading onto the back of his hands, the veins and wrinkles. He was just this person holding a shiny stainless-steel spoon, while so many other things were only in his head, not in the world of hand hairs and red-colored soup. He pictured the lake, and the trails in the woods, things he once touched and felt and loved, now only copied in his mind. He pointed his head at the couple he had pranked, sitting sullen and silent at a booth nearby. He closed his eyelids like a camera shutter, then turned away to view his mental capture, then looked back again to compare.

∘ ∘ ∘

"If it isn't Sir Mopes-a-lot," Joey called.

"It isn't," said Conrad, walking up to Joey and Stacy in front of the school.

"Oh no?"

"Nope. It's Cal Worthington," Conrad said, pointing at Peter Fronton who happened to be arriving, "and his dog Spot." Peter sportingly barked as he zipped past.

Stacy stroked a nonexistent beard. "He shouldn't have barked actually."

"Oh yeah!" Joey laughed and trumpeted like an elephant. Stacy roared. Joey made like a monkey. This went on.

Conrad didn't usually see Joey until lunchtime, but lately Stacy had been meeting Joey out front before school where she conspicuously looked up to his face and he conspicuously looked down into hers. In this circumstance she was shy, or glowing, or something, and in any case she didn't tease Conrad. He missed it. He also missed Joey, who hadn't been showing up at the bench.

When the animal sounds ran out, Conrad described the Temporary Contemporary show in a stream of enthusiasm to polite murmurs of 'oh, really?' and 'that sounds cool' from faces obviously mystified by his raving about a white room and a dark room and soup. Joey and Stacy switched the subject to their weekend adventures about town, something about Westwood and a new cookie store and a cute park and a blue dog. Then it was time for class.

Conrad's painting was still mostly a sketch. Now he had a vision of what it could be: both a forest and not a forest, a reflection of itself, a memory of a forest. He could see it half-resolved in his mind. It was impossible! Or at least beyond his ability, the kind of thing a long-experienced painter might pull off. But maybe if he did it fast and light he could come close. He set to mixing and thinning paint at a frantic pace, until he had assembled a great many colors in little cups. Then he spent the rest of the period applying thin washes and laboriously cleaning his few brushes in between. In the end his hands were color-stained and his face was striped where he had absentmindedly itched.

"My goodness Conrad!" said Mrs. Pelora. That's all she said, then helped him hang the canvas high on the wall to dry.

Miss Lanto was lecturing in chemistry today, so Conrad sat copying her diagrams while imagining what his painting could be. When it was time for history he hadn't understood much of what was now so neatly etched in his notes.

Pacing the classroom, Mr. Sebastien slowed at the sight of Conrad's colorful skin and harrumphed like a passing steamboat. Conrad peeked across to the familiar waterfall of lustrous dark hair that hid a face that hid a person he didn't really know. Maybe she was no more to him than the wisps in the corner of his eyes. *But it's real that she's beautiful anyway.*

Mr. Sebastien regained his attention, returning to a central battle of World War One — the death, the gas, the machines — but adding a new angle today: the way the war was reflected in the papers and in people's letters. "Remember," he said, "there was no TV, and normal people didn't have radios yet. Sure they had trains, and some richer people had cars, but for the most part people still used horses or walked long distances."

Conrad had known all this, but today the idea gripped him: it was the opposite of the containers and compartments but somehow just as confining, a negative space as strong as epoxy. Packing up for lunch he imagined a farm somewhere far off, the only news coming slowly over land in the form of hand-written letters or from the loose mouths of passersby, otherwise just wind passing through the trees, day after day. Students were crowding the food truck. Conrad waited to get close.

*So when people left home for the war, that was it: no contact for weeks, or months, or even years...*

He gingerly pulled his bean and cheese burrito from the little microwave on the food truck and tossed it in the air so it wouldn't burn his fingers.

*Father and mother, alone on the farm, fretting and imagining, no pictures, just waiting for ages to know if their son is even alive, having to work without him, then in the end... just getting an envelope.*

Conrad crossed to the picnic area picturing all this through the asphalt. As he rounded the corner he noted shoes dangling and climbed up the bench.

"Hi Conrad."

He froze before the top. This wasn't Joey. This was Anise.

"Oh, uh, sorry," he said, "this is where I usually, uh... never mind, sorry." He looked down to place his feet in the rungs, intending to retreat.

"No, it's OK," said Anise. "You can eat here."

Conrad looked back up at her: feet and legs aligned neatly

together, eyes darting, arms folded over her stomach.

"I mean, why don't you just eat lunch here?" she said quickly, then added, "we've never actually talked you know." She looked at the part of his face visible above the bench, then looked away.

Conrad was sitting next to Anise. Instinct had apparently moved his limbs for him. He turned to look again. *Yes, that's her all right.* His eyesight could resolve the individual hairs on her head.

"Where's your cucumber sandwich?" she asked.

"Um, I traded it for this," he said, showing her his burrito.

"So it's a cucumber burrito, then?"

"Yeah, it's a tortilla, with melted cucumbers inside. And margarine. Lots of margarine, all blended together." He made a show of squishing the burrito with his fingers.

"That's disgusting," Anise said, but she smiled. "You always say stuff like that. You almost made me bust out laughing in history once, saying Germans like sausages."

He blinked, and then he found himself speaking. "Yeah, well I guess I'm used to it, from telling my little sisters all kinds of lies." Conrad was struck by having said this, it being true, and never having thought about it before. "Like, once I told them that oatmeal is made from oats and meal-worms."

Anise laughed.

"They're immune now, though," he added.

"So you've done your job as a big brother then."

"Yeah, toughened them up."

"By lying to them every day."

"That's right."

∘ ∘ ∘

"Wanna hang out some time?!"

Conrad shook Levy by the shoulders, which joggled her head. She stared back at his wild-boy face. "Uhhh, I guess?" she answered.

Beth arrived at the kitchen door. Conrad ran to her and

grabbed her shoulders the same way. "Wanna hang out some time?!"

"Not if you're going to murder us," Beth said. "I don't have time to be murdered right now."

"Hey Mom! Wanna hang out some time?!"

Conrad didn't wait for her answer and dashed up the stairs to his room. There he flopped onto his bed from an exultant height. But lying still wasn't an option. The gears of the world were turning, nearing a long-hoped-for alignment. It was time to leap through the portal at last, to join those select men standing tall in the mists on the other side: the ones with girlfriends.

It was an hour-long pause as he remembered it, after hearing Anise say, "hey, uh, do you wanna hang out some time?" — a pause of utter disbelief, thinking of Shy Man, almost laughing, not being able to form thoughts or move his lips, then saying something garbled but appropriate, like "yeah, that would be great."

Conrad sprang from the bed and began ripping apart his room. Never mind the unlikeliness of Anise coming over any time soon. Everything had to come off of the floor. The shelves would be stripped of their dusty childhood clutter! He heaped it all onto the bed and began to sort it into piles: *keep*, *give to sisters*, *toss*. After a frenzied hour, a large trash bag was nearly full and two loads of laundry were ready to be carried to the basement. Then he started on the walls, first taking down all the half-finished sketches and putting back up only his very best work. And those posters had to go, especially the stubbly old man holding up a smallmouth bass.

Night.

Anise was lying next to him, close and warm, or at least a facsimile of her was. Conrad drew his hand along the side of his pillow to clear her hairs, which kept falling in front of her smiling imaginary face. The pillow was too short — he couldn't simulate wrapping a leg around her body. Instead his knees bent into empty space, now emptier since so much had been cleared from his room.

*I had such a good time today*, Pillow Anise whispered.

Conrad held her closer and laid affectionate kisses on her face, which smelled annoyingly of fabric softener. The moon shone down upon their quilt-wrapped forms, cradled snugly in the bottom of a canoe, gently bobbing on the current pulling them downriver. Ages passed on the water, ages and eons of caressing and affectionate staring. Then a bump: the canoe had run aground. They peeked out to see an island, far from anything, their very own. Out onto a sandy beach, water seeping into the imprints from their bare feet as they moved up into the dark trees, up and up the path, even less light here. A clearing, a shelter, a circle of stones. Fire and warmth. Alone, but always together.

# 9

# Late February

"You're acting weird, Conrad."

Stacy had seen it right away, while Joey was too used to Conrad's nervous spells to notice. There were six or seven Conrads at the moment, occupying the same body but causing his limbs and facial features to act independently.

"It's the ludes, man, the ludes!" Conrad squealed as he hurried into the building.

*They'll see. They won't believe it.*

Conrad again grabbed a corner spot in art class, ignoring Stacy's suspicious glances, and proceeded to spend more time than usual setting up his easel, his colors, his palette, linseed oil, thinner... but then he sat and stared at his painting. He couldn't steady his hands, and if he did anything rash now he might destroy the carefully built-up effect. All he could see in the layers of thin overlaid colors was hair, Anise's hair flowing down. He picked up his smallest brush and began to apply thin edging lines. Mrs. Pelora squatted down at his face level to watch.

"Conrad," she said, "are you sure you're not going perfectionist again?"

Conrad pulled his brush away and looked at her.

"You know," she mused, "if you over-define something, it's no longer a suggestion. You lose the forest for the trees."

"Hardy har har."

Mrs. Pelora smirked and moved on. But she was right. Conrad hung the painting back on the wall. Instead he pulled his unfinished life drawing off the shelf. He could be perfectionist on this, the mincing lines and careful shading. He focused down to the texture of the paper, but the tip of his pencil would not be still.

"What is the *deal* with you?" Stacy complained in chemistry. Conrad had lost track of the steps.

"I told you."

"Yeah sure. If you ever really did that I'd clonk you on the head."

Stacy ordered Conrad around for the rest of the period while he bounced on his toes next to her.

Slipping into history class, Conrad pulled out his binder and opened it businesslike onto his desk. He lined up his new note-taking pens: black, blue, red, green. He wrote the date at the top of his paper. Only then did he peek across the room. Anise was sitting between Carrie and Amy, listening to them exchange skateboarding opinions by proxy.

"My brother's at Pipeline like *constantly*," said Carrie.

"Yeah?" said Amy. "Mine says there's too many beaners and posers out there. He likes Del Mar better."

"What kind of board does he ride? Jerry has an Alva."

"Frank says Dogtown's better, but I think he just likes the name."

Anise leaned back and flashed Conrad a secret smile.

The clear eyes and the clear him...

But now Amy's eyes flitted in his direction, so he snapped his focus to Mr. Sebastian, who was busy making marks on the chalkboard. Conrad wasn't sure what the marks were for, but he copied them anyway. And also for some reason the teacher was making sounds with his mouth. Conrad found that he was able to convert the sounds into little shapes on his paper. Where had he learned this amazing skill? Then a bell rang.

Now something important would happen, but he wasn't sure what. Anise stood up with her friends. Once again a conspiracy was brewing — the sneaking whispers. But Conrad jumped out into the hallway first. Anise motioned toward the picnic area with her eyes and scooted away,

Food laid out, Conrad leaned back with one knee up and the other leg dangling, just casual. He stared intently at a page from *Farewell To Manzanar*, expecting Anise to show up any second. But she didn't. Twenty minutes passed. He was hungry, so he nibbled. Soon half of his sandwich was gone. Then all of it. In a few minutes he would have to give up and run to English class. Now it all made queasy sense: Anise had seen him up close and had changed her mind. He pulled up his other knee to bury his face and block out the future.

"Psst!" Anise was standing directly below. "You OK up there?"

Conrad leaned over. "Uh, yeah, just napping." He smiled but didn't move. Anise looked back for a moment, then motioned for him to come down already. Conrad shimmied to the ground and stood wobbly, unsure how close to stand.

Anise whispered to him. "I tried to come earlier but my friends are like  *completely* nuts." Conrad nodded. "So anyway," she said, "this weekend, like... tomorrow?" Conrad nodded again. "What do you want to do?"

*Run around the hills.*

*Fly up to the lookout place and sit next to you.*

But that was crazy. It was dangerous up there, and she wouldn't want to get all dusty.

"Maybe we could go to Westwood?" he offered. "I heard something about a new cookie place."

○ ○ ○

"Conrad!" Sueanna called up the stairs. "Conrad!" Her son had been flying wordlessly through doors since the wee hours, avoiding eye contact. This increase in speed suggested that something positive might be occurring, but that didn't stop her from worrying. Maybe he was hurrying himself toward a cliff, or to meetings with a cult. Cults were all in the news, stories of teenagers disappearing from home.

"Conrad!"

"What?" he said, dropping down into the kitchen.

"It's your tangle turn."

"No it's not. And don't change it. We say Pooptangle Turn."

"That's not polite."

"What, *poop* isn't polite? What are we supposed to say then?"

Levy was listening at the table. "Feces tangle turn?" she suggested.

"Eww," said Conrad. "That's worse."

"Ex-cre-ment... tangle... turn."

Conrad blinked and thought for a second. "No, how about... Canine Bowel Movement Tangle Turn."

Levy burst out laughing.

"That's quite enough!" Sueanna said. "In any case, it's *your turn*, Conrad. The grass back there is practically covered, and they're good and crusty, so get to it."

In terms of this particular chore, poops that had dried in the sun to innocuous husks were preferable to the fresh product, especially if the dog had been sick. But Conrad still protested.

"I just got cleaned up and I have to go! I'll do it tonight, promise."

"Wait, where are you going? I thought you would stay with your sisters today. I have to go down to Anaheim."

"No! I can't stay!"

"Why not?"

"It's important."

"That's not an answer. I need your help sometimes you know. It's not like I actually want to spend my whole Saturday sitting in a stupid meeting."

"Mom, please, I can't stay here."

"It can't be that important if you won't tell me what it is. I don't want the girls running around alone all day."

Conrad had actually backed against the wall. Then a word struck him: *Anaheim.*

"Here!" he said, and fished a bill out of his pocket. "I found twenty bucks on the sidewalk. Drop them off at Disneyland. That'll pay for two kids tickets, right?"

"Yeah!" Levy gumby-jumped up and down. "Yeah yeah yeah!"

Sueanna stared as if stunned. "Actually that's not a bad idea," she murmured.

"Beth!" Levy yelled up the stairs. "Put on your clothes! We're going to Disneyland!"

A pause, then the sound of a stampede pounded through the ceiling.

Pulling forward on his collar, smoothing his shirt-front: Conrad was no longer a fourteen-year-old whose poop-scooping turn it was. He was a man, or would be soon, and his driver would soon arrive, at the bus stop, driving the bus. Actually he could afford a taxi, but it wasn't every day that treasure appeared in the bushes. Casual investigation after the police chase had turned up $240 and a vial of white powder. Conrad dared not even touch his fingers to the vial, but the roll of bills had come straight home to be individually windexed and dried, dirty money no more.

Conrad boarded a bus and stood at the front, not risking what might be sticking to the seats. Leaning toward the front windshield he levitated over the onrushing street, sailing toward that which was gloriously fated to him: the fuzzy sweater arms wrapped around his waist, the agate-brown eyes staring into his own, the satin hair tingling his face. Except that as the bus moved closer to Westwood the knot in his stomach grew tighter and his vision contracted. Now he was all too aware of his own breathing — that, and the pattern on the floor of the bus, and the bumps on the metal girders as he stepped off.

He walked: a block along bushes, a block along bricks, then glass fronts.

A shoe store, a bank, a jewelry store, a cookie shop — *the cookie shop*.

Conrad looked at his watch: against the odds of public transportation, he was fifteen minutes early. Then when he leaned to peer through the window his heart jumped: Anise was already inside! But wait — was that really her? The person in there inspecting the cookie case was a different Anise. That Anise wore a black motorcycle jacket, not a fuzzy sweater. Neatly-combed hair bent past little silver earrings over leather shoulders. Below she wore dark-blue jeans rolled up at the cuffs and orange pastel sneakers.

Jewelry store, bank, shoe store.

Bricks, bushes.

Conrad stood in the shade of a hedge as if it hid him from view while Leather Anise turned at the back of his retinas like a glossy hod-rod on a dais at a car show. He wasn't allowed anywhere near such a model of show-room perfection. *Please step back, sir.*

The day had started warm and now it was hot — if he stood there any longer he would sweat. He turned his eyes to the bush, to its leaves, to the layers of street dust that dulled their shine.

Bricks, shoe store, bank, jewelry store, cookie shop.

"Hi," Conrad said.

Anise turned and smiled. "Oh hi!"

Conrad smiled, too, but his lips refused to part. They stayed that way until Anise turned back to the case. "Just look at all these!" she said. "What kind do you like?"

There were indeed many kinds. Conrad peered at the labels. Sweet goat-cheese cookie with white truffle oil? Basil-cashew-banana with coconut crumbles? Anise waited for him to speak. She seemed really strong on taking turns.

"What are those dark ones?" Conrad asked the clerk, pointing to a tray that had just shown up from the kitchen.

"Those? Oh, molasses-ginger with dried orange rind," said the clerk. "Still hot."

"I'll have one of those."

"Me too!" said Anise.

"I got this," Conrad said, slapping down a twenty. But then his mind ran riot — he'd made a mistake! He knew better than to do that, he knew from sex-ed what it meant to pay for a girl and he'd planned to go Dutch but he'd forgotten and really he hadn't a clue how to even propose it and anyway it was too late and he had paid for her cookie with the hooker money!

Anise showed a note of concern at Conrad not picking up his change. "Um, thanks," she said. "I'll get the next one."

They took their cookies to a four-top by the window where Conrad bent himself into the corner. Anise sat across, but her eyes followed the teenagers passing outside in the latest fashions: for the males, jackets with popped collars; for the females, cleaned-up, store-bought Madonna.

Conrad bit into his cookie: burned-sugar ginger-biting orange-scented euphoria. "Mmmm," he hummed. But the tingling sensations only served to make him more aware of his face, of his lips and eyelids in contact with the air separating him from the girl directly across the table, telescoping away even as she sat there still. He was supposed to be asking questions, he remembered. He waited until she took another nibble. "It's good, right?"

"I don't know," Anise said, picking at hers. "It's kind of weird. Maybe I'll get used to it."

Wrong. He had chosen wrong. *Strike two!* And every useful thought had fled. In the entire universe there was nothing left to say and he could only sit there and sort of breathe.

Anise shifted in her chair, her eyes darting from the window to the table to the shop clerks taking orders from the line of mostly young people that had grown all the way to the corner. At the end a tall older girl with long bare legs and golden hair looked down at them. She gestured to her two muscly male friends, who turned to smile at Anise, but they only squinted at Conrad for a moment before resuming their conversation about Boy George and whether he was really gay or just acting.

Now Conrad's heart was beating in his head where it didn't belong. Anise shifted again. It was possible she was desperately bored.

"Do you like it here?" Conrad asked.

Anise cocked her head. "Here? Where's here? You mean this shop?"

He didn't know what he meant. "Um, no, I mean Westwood. Do you like it?"

"Like it? Well I guess. It's just a bunch of stores, but yeah I guess I like it. Really I only come here because everybody else does."

"Oh yeah, me too," Conrad said and took a big enough bite from his cookie to keep him occupied chewing.

"Seen any good movies lately?" Anise asked.

Movies... movies... the answer was no, not if she meant new ones. Before the bushes he had been saving his extra dollars for tapes at Tower Records but mostly spending them on burritos because he was always hungry.

"I saw something good on TV last night," he said, forgetting what it was called but then desperately remembering. "It was called *The Thin Man*." Anise squinted. "It was funny," he added as a sort of defense.

"Is that new?"

"No, it's really old, black and white. A mystery. There's a dog named Asta."

"Huh... a funny mystery."

"I like those old mystery movies. Like there's a good one called *The 39 Steps*. Ever seen that one?"

Anise shook her head. Her voice went quieter. "No, I mean, maybe. I've seen old stuff on TV I guess, but I don't remember the names."

"I'd forget too but I write them in my movie book."

"Your what?"

*Oh no.*

Conrad glanced back at the burly guys now by the cookie case and felt that he had drifted very far in the wrong direction. But he had done it to himself, and anyway Anise would surely find out what kind of a dork he was — though he had hoped to put it off past the first date. He took a breath and faced his inevitable doom.

"You know those books with blank pages?" he said. "My aunt Babs gave me one when I was seven for drawing, but I've been using it to write down movies I like."

"Oh that's cool," Anise said, perking up. "Since you were

seven?"

"Yeah. The first page says 'Best Movies Ever' in big crayon letters."

Anise chuckled. "So what was your favorite movie when you were seven?" she asked, her face now primed for humor. Conrad went quiet. She waited. "Come on, say it." Her crystal-clear eyes vaporized any chance of him lying.

"OK, fine," he mumbled. "The Shaggy D.A."

"Ha ha! The Shaggy D.A., that's funny. Mine would have been Charlotte's Web."

"Oh yeah, my sisters love that."

Anise shut her mouth and nodded.

"What?" Conrad asked.

"Huh? Nothing." She shrugged, but looked out the window. "Want to get another cookie and walk around?"

"Sure."

○ ○ ○

Conrad heard shushing in the next room. His sisters were up to something but he couldn't be bothered. For once he was first to the dinner table, after being too keyed up to eat all afternoon then finding himself banned from the kitchen by Sueanna.

"Quiet!" came the whisper again. "Make them super wet."

Smacking sounds, then fast footsteps, and they were on him.

"Oh, you're the nicest brother ever!" said Levy, locking him to his chair with an iron hug and smooching his cheek with sloppy puckered lips.

"Thank you for Disneyland!" Beth squealed and nuzzled him on the other cheek with added drool.

Conrad struggled to escape. "Gross! Get off! You're welcome, OK? Let me go!"

They did so when Sueanna arrived with a bowl of something she called 'Mongolian Chicken'. It tasted nothing like what they had tried downtown but Conrad could still wolf it down.

"Chew your food Conrad," Sueanna said.

"I'll count your chews for you, super-cool brother," said Beth.

"No thanks," he said and shoveled more into his mouth. Beth counted anyway.

"One, two, three, four, five, six, seven, eight, nine…"

"Stop!" Really he had wanted to swallow at four. "What rides did you go on?"

"Oh lots. You know, the good ones. Haunted house, pirates. And Mr. Toad's Wild Ride so many times! We totally memorized the whole thing, and then Levy invented the *pre-scream*. See, we always sat at the back, and we screamed really loud *before* each scary thing happened, then we shut up when it really happened."

"It was *so* great," Levy said with an evil snicker. "People kept turning to look at us all funny."

"I can't believe Mom got you two to come out without calling security."

Sueanna sat up with pride in her dutiful daughters. "They were very good and were standing at the gate at the appointed time," she said. Conrad looked from Beth's calculating eyes to Levy's calculating eyes. Clearly they were anticipating the next meeting in Anaheim. Sueanna had to know that.

"OK let's start at the beginning," Beth said. "So Mom bought us our tickets and she totally lied to the ticket lady like she already had hers."

"Yeah then she just up and left," said Levy.

"We were like abandoned children. We pretended to cry but then a guard was staring so we ran in."

"Mommy left us!" Levy groaned, head back, to demonstrate her acting.

"Yeah then we ran to Tom Sawyer's cave as fast as we could."

Beth went on while Conrad pictured himself following Anise through a doorway, into a dim jewelry store lit by spotlights reflecting on her hair like on record grooves as she paced from case to case and pointed. *What do you think of this one?* she had asked. *That's nice*, he'd answered. *How about this one?* She pointed at a necklace that cost thousands. *That's nice, too.* Actually he didn't like any of them: too thick and showy. Then the pretending clogged his brain. Why had he pretended?

"Levy almost peed her pants!"

Walking like a butler at Anise's side, each glance from her eyes tripping his steps and sealing his mouth. She wanted him to talk it seemed, but he only smiled.

"No way! That water ride at Magic Mountain is so much better."

But — there *was* that one time he made Anise burst out laughing, about a man wearing a striped shirt: *circus must be in town*, he'd said, his dad's line. And later Anise stood still and looked right at his face. That had to mean something... didn't it? And she'd squeezed his hand just before she left and said *see you soon!* So maybe the day hadn't been a crushing failure after all.

"It's still your turn Conrad."

"What?"

○ ○ ○

*I had such a great time with you today.*

*So did I*, Pillow Anise whispered. *It's so fun hanging out with you.*

Conrad pushed the hair away from her face. She seemed shy about something.

*What is it?* he asked.

*I really like you.*

*I like you too.*

*But what's going to happen this summer?*

*You can come with me! We'll stay on the island together.*

She smiled and pulled him closer. *Conrad?*

*Yes?*

*Can I kiss you?*

*Of course.*

# 10

# Early March

A morning clear and bright even by California standards stretched out over Conrad's upturned face all the way to outer space, jet trails cutting the pure gradients of blue. Underfoot the sidewalk was surely full of diverting cracks, but this time he stood calmly watching the cars arriving in front of the school. It was March now, a new month and a new world.

"You're not acting weird," said Stacy. "It's freaking me out."

"Oh don't worry," said Joey. "The weird's in there. It can't hide forever."

Conrad only smiled. Then a car stopped and Anise jumped out.

"Hi Conrad!"

"Hi Anise."

Anise popped over to face him. "That was fun on Saturday," she said, quiet but not unhappy it seemed.

Conrad nodded. "Yeah, it was."

"Hey Anise!" came a voice from down the block. It was Amy, peering from afar. "Hey!"

"So maybe I'll see you at lunch?" Anise whispered.

"Yeah." Conrad nodded again. He watched her pivot and scurry away, then remembered he wasn't alone. He couldn't have planned it better if he had tried: Joey and Stacy stood as if blasted by a shock wave.

"No... way..." Stacy breathed.

"Dude..." was all Joey could say. "Dude!"

"Yes?"

"Dude!"

Stacy slapped Conrad on the shoulder. "You forgot to introduce us, dummy."

"Oh yeah, sorry. How does that work again?"

"You just ask, like, *have you met Stacy, and her pet monkey?*" She gestured at Joey. "Or you can say it straight, like, *this is Stacy, and her pet monkey.*"

"Ooh ooh ooh!" said Joey as the monkey.

"But doesn't she know you already?"

"Well, yeah, sort of," Stacy said, "but we're not exactly in the cool crowd, in case you haven't noticed. And you know, politeness, duh!"

A slipstream, a quick-moving river reflecting the light — Conrad flowed with his fellow students down the halls, his painting all-of-a-sudden before him. Its colors had woken up without him adding anything. Now they moved up the canvas with vivid clarity, as if all they had needed was sleep. And it was obvious to him, right in this moment, where some darkening was needed: trickles and pools of black. He combined Alizarin Crimson and Prussian Blue, like magic turning deeper than black itself, a trick he'd learned from a letter by Van Gogh Mrs. Pelora had read aloud one day. With a small brush he pushed this ooze around the feet of the trees. But then he came to a little thin patch of green: his first stroke on the canvas, still showing a little. He avoided covering it, letting the dark paint flow around it then down to the corner. Finally he took out his tube of Phthalo Green and painted a little 'C' in the opposite corner and it was done. He pulled a table to the wall and climbed up to hang the canvas as high as possible. Mrs. Pelora stepped under him and peered up.

"See?" said Conrad, pointing at the patch of green. "See? You can still see it."

Mrs. Pelora squinted at the thin place at the end of his finger and guffawed. "Good one Conrad. But seriously, that's nice work. Let's put that in the art show." Conrad climbed down, but Mrs. Pelora was still looking up. "You know," she said, "I'd love to see what would happen if you tried painting it again from scratch, you know, a few more times. But anyway, *now* you can come back to reality, and work on that still life you haven't done. I want to see some skills, sir."

Conrad was real and present. The jars and the gourds and the dried sunflower were real and present. He cut sharp dark lines into the paper, to the edges. The paper wouldn't be able to hold all this reality, he decided. It would try to escape the paper into the air.

"I can't freaking believe you," said Stacy under her breath as Miss Lanto lectured.

"Believe what?"

"You didn't tell Joey."

"If I told him it would've blown up."

"Why's that? He wouldn't have done anything. He's your friend you know."

"No, I mean telling him would have jinxed it."

"What?" Stacy squinted at him sideways. "That's insane," she said more hushed. "Didn't you think she could maybe, you know, like you back?"

Conrad shook his head. Miss Lanto, in the middle of a forceful point, stopped to stare in the direction of the whispering sounds. Stacy and Conrad stared back.

Anise was real and present. The lights in history class seemed brighter. As usual, Anise took notes for dear life in perfectly-straight rows of tiny letters. Conrad surveyed her friends. They weren't really like her, it seemed to him now. Neither of them sat at attention or bothered to take down everything — they only slumped and peeked at each other as if class time was no more than a bothersome interruption of their incessant communication.

*Please Anise, please look over.*

It didn't make sense to admire her focus while hoping to steal it. But he wanted it, wanted more and more voltage to course from her eyes between them, to keep him fully charged with hope.

She could lose interest. Or give him that funny look, the look that stole across the faces of so many people when he spoke. He hated it — when they changed the subject like he was a crazy person. If Anise were to do the same thing his universe would implode.

Mr. Sebastien grunted his final instructions, and finally came a look, the subtlest eyeball-point: *to the benches* said her eyes. His universe would expand a little longer anyway.

Two legs dangling. Anise had beaten him.

"Hi Conrad," she said as he appeared at her level. But her smile was tense.

"Hi," Conrad said and sat next to her. Nothing happened, then he remembered Stacy ribbing him. "I should have introduced you to my friends," he added.

"Oh that's all right," she said, brightening. "I should have said hi or something, too, but I felt shy. They're so smart."

"How did you know Joey's smart? It's his big secret."

"Oh everybody knows. I bet he's never gotten a B even once. He gets on all the lists you know."

"Oh."

Conrad didn't know. He wasn't sure what lists she was referring to.

Anise fidgeted some more. "I um... same here. I haven't introduced you. To my friends I mean."

Conrad shrugged like it was no big deal, but inwardly he pictured Amy's confident rich eyes staring him down.

"Actually, to be honest..." Anise went on, "I didn't tell my friends we were going for cookies, and then they got all pissy about it."

"Really?"

"Yeah like I'm supposed to tell them every single thing I ever do. Plus they've been pestering me nonstop about the new guy. They made up this big drama like we're destined to be married and have a house and six kids, just because I said he was cute."

"You mean Patrick?"

"Yeah."

"Well... he is pretty handsome."

"Yeah like a movie star..."

Anise went quiet and stared at her feet. Conrad paused to let the awkwardness sink in before he spoke again.

"Do your legs get all rubbery when you look at him?"

"Stop it!" she scolded. Then she wiggled her legs and they laughed.

○ ○ ○

"Hey Mom, can you drop me off at the Nuart?"

Sueanna's elbow went round and round, stirring a thick brown substance in a ceramic bowl. "What, tonight? That's all the way over in West L.A. Why not see a movie near here? Plus it's a school night. Can't you just wait for the weekend?"

"No, it's not playing over here, only there, just one time, 8 o'clock."

"But then I'll have to go all the way back out there to pick you up late at night. I have to get up early tomorrow you know. And what's this movie that's such a big deal anyway?"

Panic crept up Conrad's neck. It would be humiliating to phone Anise and make excuses. Of course he could use his bushes money for a taxi, but Sueanna would want to know where he had gotten it, and anyway she would say the taxi was too dangerous.

"Strangers On A Train," he mumbled.

Sueanna stopped stirring. "Oh," she said, blinking. "That's a good one. Hey, maybe I could go with you."

"No, you can't!"

"I can't go to a movie?" Sueanna stood taller, then leaned closer to her son's evasive face. "Who are you going with, might I ask?"

"A friend."

"And what's his name?" Sueanna turned to the innocent

chopping of cucumbers. "Maybe I'll take you if you tell me who you're going with."

He was trapped. "It's my friend Anise," he said softly in case of lurking sisters. His mother's eyes bugged then un-bugged and the chopping continued.

"OK, but you better get ready now so I can take you right after dinner or you'll be late."

The lights of the Nuart dappled Anise's hair and jacket — a different jacket, soft white suede. They had seen one like that in Westwood, he could swear, one that cost as much as a used car. In any case the sight of her smiling as he approached sent his head spinning.

"How did you get here?" she asked.

"Got a ride." He pointed a thumb toward the adjacent block where he had insisted on jumping out. "How about you?"

"Oh, our housekeeper..." she looked to a car parked a few yards away, an old black Mercedes like the one in Octopussy that jumped onto the train tracks. An older woman sat at the wheel, watching. Conrad gave a little wave. The woman nodded and pointed at him, then drove away. "She's like my auntie," Anise said. "You better watch out."

Conrad stood mute next to Anise in the ticket line. This, after an entire day rehearsing in his head. Now again he had nothing to say, only quick glances and tight-lipped smiles, his heart rate and temperature spiking as they passed inside.

"Just a sec the restroom," he blurted. Rushing into the bathroom he found an empty stall and locked himself in. He stood with his face smushed against the cold metal door, holding his hair. Seconds ticked by. Then he went to the sink and looked at himself in the mirror. He splashed his face, and dried himself. He took more time making sure, with a new paper towel, to get every bead of moisture off his face, his neck, inside his ears, behind his ears. He straightened himself and moved toward the door, but then he stopped, and turned to the wall and stared down at the marble floor. His insides gurgled, and now he really needed to use the toilet, so he headed back to the stall to repeat the entire process.

"Ready?" said Anise.

"Yeah!"

They found good center seats and looked up at the interior.

It was happening.

It was real.

She was sitting right next to him and it wasn't accidental. It was a wonderful non-accidental pre-planned perfect dream, but it was also happening underwater where the sonar from a hundred U-boats pinged his brain and vibrated his hands.

"This place is cool," Anise said. "I've never seen an old movie in a theater like this one."

Now Conrad had something to say, but it all came out in a flood. "Oh it's great but I go to the matinees on the weekend, it's cheaper. My god you should have seen The Seven Samurai last year, it's Japanese, it's three hours long but it was so amazing! They fight and fight and fight, and then Joey and I came out and we forgot it was still daytime and we were all blinded and confused."

Anise giggled. "But you said you've already seen this one. Won't you be bored?"

"No way. It's so good, and anyway I only saw it on a little TV at my dad's house, and the commercials kept coming on during the good parts, even right at the end. Made me so mad."

The lights went down. Conrad was glad he had already seen the movie, because that meant he could turn his head without losing the story. Anise's face, lit by the dancing silvery light and clearly enthralled by the film, was beautiful again and again. And again. But she began to notice, and waved him away and pointed at the movie. *She's focused*, he thought, *just like in class*. But at the end of the story, as the merry-go-round span faster and faster, Anise grabbed his shirt and yanked, her eyes remaining glued to the screen.

"Oh my god that was so fun!" Anise bounced up and down as

they spilled out onto the street. "That thing spinning, and that little boy helping punch, hee hee!"

Conrad had never seen Anise grin so wide, and she was *so* beautiful and he was *so* uncomfortable and his arms had no idea what to do. They certainly couldn't wrap themselves around her like they *so* wanted to.

A car honked.

"Oh! She's here. Will you be OK?"

"Yeah." Conrad smiled and nodded.

"Well thanks! See you tomorrow!"

Conrad waved as the car pulled away from the curb. Then he leaned against the wall under the theater lights, aching. It really had been real, but now she had gone away and the entire evening was already shifting at the far end of a kaleidoscope in his head.

"Did you have a good time?" asked Sueanna at the wheel.

"Yeah." The city whisked past Conrad's face.

"Did she like the movie?"

"Yeah."

"Well, that's a good sign anyway. Did you see her mother?"

"No, just her housekeeper."

"Really? No freaked out parents looking you over?"

"No. Though the housekeeper did give me the evil eye."

"Oh, well I guess if you're rich you can do that. Still seems sad though. I mean, what if it was her first date?"

"It wasn't."

"Oh no?"

"We went out already."

"What?" Sueanna goggled at him then looked back at the road.

"It was just for cookies," Conrad said. "On a Saturday morning. Not sure if that counts."

"Oh now I get it. My son, the playboy. And here I was all excited that I was taking you to your first date."

"Close enough."

# 11

# Mid-March

Amy and Carrie stood talking up to Patrick's crestfallen face — or at least it looked crestfallen from a distance. Amy reached out and gave his thick arm a shake, then the girls scooted away in close confidence, leaving Patrick casting a long shadow in front of the science building. He noticed Conrad approaching.

*Never mind him,* Conrad thought. *Just act natural.*

But the smallest flick of his eye was enough.

"Faggot!" Patrick barked, flexing his large shoulders. "Don't you *even* look at me, artsy pinko fudge-packer."

Conrad continued into the building growing hot in the face. People had seen.

"What a dumb-ass," Stacy whispered as Conrad sat down, burning and breathing. "Don't worry about it," she said, leaning closer. "He's just jealous, ha!"

Conrad looked up from his slouch. "You know what's nuts? I've never actually talked to that guy, but there he was, calling me names."

Stacy made herself horsey again. "Welcome to high school, same as middle school."

"College better be better," Conrad grumbled.

*All the name callers.*

*I'm 'artsy' which makes me a 'fag.'*

*And Stacy's a 'brainiac', meaning 'not pretty.'*

"Today is hard!" Miss Lanto called out. "Hard!"

*I hate them, all the name-calling, posturing, macho bullying shit-for-brains jerks!*

Pieces of Patrick splattered onto the concrete in all directions:

curled intestines, gloppy brains, bloody shards of bone. Then gasoline, and a match, and fire! But Stacy punched Conrad in the arm, so he sat up and got down to taking notes. Miss Lanto was a really good teacher, he decided. Just as good as Mr. Sebastien, yet so many other kids went around calling her 'the bossy Asian lady.'

Mr. Sebastien wasn't losing his trophy to Miss Lanto just yet. Today he roamed the room, symphony-conducting long arcs of the semester's main themes in preparation for Friday's test, a fifth of their final grade.

"The chain!" Mr. Sebastian called out. "Industrialization. Militarism. Alliances. Nationalism. What else?"

Anise raised her hand and recited from her notes. "Class conflict, fear of socialism."

Mr. Sebastien nodded. "Yes, thank you miss Helms. And now I see the time's up." The class began rustling but the teacher held up a hand. "Wait! Do not forget, that next week... is the last - research - milestone."

Four dangling legs.

"Check this out," said Conrad. He pulled two lunch bags from his backpack and gave one to Anise. "I dared my mom to make the ultimate cucumber sandwich." He had admitted to hating the ones from the food truck, so this was funny.

"Mmm, wow," Anise murmured as she chewed. "This is edible."

"Oh great, thanks, I'll tell my mom you said that."

He could just sit and chat with her now, familiar: a triumph in itself! But then again, he only grew less sure who it was sitting next to him. Sure, he could still see her hair and her eyes, and the endearing quirks of her movement he had watched from afar, now almost as close as he could ever want. But the details only multiplied, crowding in all kinds of things he hadn't had a crush on to begin with, like the odd way her hair grew fuzzy up the back of her neck, and tones of her voice he'd only just heard for the first time, and her tendency to trail off mid-sentence with the word 'yeah...' All these extra things weighted his nervousness, sinking it down under the acid leftover from old nervousness still pooling in his stomach. But he would have a crush on all those things, too, he decided.

"Want to study for history after school?" Anise asked.

"Sure," Conrad said, but speaking so casually felt like a lie. What he really meant was, *I will float here next to you as long as you allow.*

"OK, then we'll pick you up."

"Wait, what? To go where? Who's we?"

"To my house. The housekeeper, remember her?"

*Her house.* Conrad stopped breathing and nodded.

"We'll pick you up at that bus stop you stand at."

"Why not just go with you from the front?"

Anise shook her head. "Mmm-mmm. Drama."

"Oh. OK."


The old black Mercedes pulled up to the bus stop, but Conrad only stood gazing past it as cars leaving the school zipped by. When the coast was clear he scooted through the back door.

"This is Yolanda," said Anise from the front seat. The housekeeper turned her head to nod once, then put her foot on the gas.

Rather than bending around to talk, Anise stared out of her window without speaking, so Conrad did the same. At first the car zipped past the same places he saw every day from the bus, but then Yolanda made an abrupt turn north, toward Bel Air. After blocks of faceless apartments, the scene quick-changed to the kind of fine little homes inhabited by the entry-level rich. The car didn't stop here however, instead winding higher while the manicured trees along the street grew more numerous, the street-facing garden walls growing taller to match the homes set back behind them.

Still Anise didn't move — not dozing, just watching. Conrad followed a lock of hair curving past her ear. In that ear was a hole leading into her head. What was going on in there? Whatever it was, she had included him, rushing up into the hills with spotty tree light and wind through the windows, flying...

The car slowed at an automatic gate. Conrad saw a spiked fence and immense hedges, then beyond these a steep driveway, then a wall. This turned out to be the front face of the house: smooth and undulating, woven with thick vines around irregularly-shaped windows. If there was a roof Conrad couldn't see it. This was modern art. He stood by the car looking up.

"Come inside!" Anise called. Conrad followed into a circular entrance hall. From there, interior chambers divided out like sections of a seed pod, none on the same level as another. Straight ahead but down a ramp, an expansive pillowed living room bent around out of sight. Wide windows followed the curve of this room to reveal bushes blooming up a terraced hillside. And to the left, wide stone steps rose to a sort of cafe area with little tables and a bar for parties, then a brick-lined arch led to a kitchen gleaming white with bleached stone and stainless steel. These were just the rooms he could see. In any case, the whole place was dim and silent like a museum after hours.

"My room's over here," said Anise.

"Door *open*," said Yolanda, her face and tone both hard.

Anise nodded then dashed up a corkscrew stairway on the right, to a walkway high over the living room that ended at more stairs leading up to who knows where. She opened the last of three doors. When Conrad passed through behind her he couldn't remember having followed. The walls of this room rose tall and wavy like a cavern worn through limestone, washed with light streaming down from artificial skylights high above. Anise plopped into an immense white-leather chair.

"You can relax now," she said. "Like, really."

Conrad had stopped at the door to ponder what material the walls were made of.

*Maybe this is an alien spaceship and I'm being abducted. So be it!*
*Oh my god that's Anise sitting there.*
*Oh my god I'm in her room.*
*Oh my god.*

Conrad laid his backpack upside-down against the wall to hide its tatters and sat cross-legged near the chair, not looking at Anise directly. He scanned his eyes around the room: at the tall white-stained oak bed, at the woven rugs covering rustic floor planks, at the little nick-knack nooks spaced randomly up the walls, and, most incredibly, at a long fish tank built into the far wall that ended at a fairy-painted door in the corner.

"Where does that go?" he asked, gesturing at the door.

"Oh, that's just my bathroom."

"Oh. So you can see through the fish tank in there?"

"No they put blurry glass down the middle."

Conrad could see this now, and little mountains and houses on stilts like the Hollywood Hills but submerged.

"Anyway, you're not allowed to pee in there."

"Oh."

"I'm just kidding!"

Conrad stared at the fish swimming in and out of caves while the quiet of the house seeped back into the room.

*Keep talking.*

"Where are your sisters?" he asked. At lunch he had gotten Anise to say that she had three sisters, but that was all.

Yolanda appeared at the door. She peered first at Conrad on the floor, then at Anise in the chair. Anise kept still for a moment but then burst up and shook the woman's shoulders.

"Can you make us pacalla?" she begged. "Please?"

Yolanda shook her head. "No. All gone." She walked away toward the kitchen.

"She's from El Salvador," said Anise in a whisper when Yolanda was far enough away.

"Is that in Mexico?"

"No dummy, it's a country. She had to run away because they killed her family. They actually hung her mother, and shot her grandmother. Isn't that awful?"

"Who's they?"

"Bad people, the military or rebels or something. I made her tell me."

Anise pulled out her books and laid them in a neat line on the rug.

"So where are your sisters again?" Conrad pressed.

Anise shook her head. "Study time."

"OK fine. But how should we start?"

"Let's use that chain he keeps going on about."

They began laying out their papers in columns, and hunted for matches in their notes. Conrad had thought his notes were good — they were good-looking anyway, with lots of bubbles and arrows. But Anise's were thorough: tightly-packed lines of little letters. In fact Conrad's notes covered all the big blurry ideas while Anise's were a jumble of details, so combining them felt like solving a puzzle. When Yolanda appeared again much later she found Anise and Conrad creeping like monkeys around their papers.

"I make you pupusas, OK? There." Yolanda put down a plate heaped with mottled, dumpy-looking patties and left. Conrad lifted one off the top and bit into it.

"Oh," he said, looking down into its warm, aromatic filling. "Oh wow, this is so good."

Anise smacked her lips. "Ooh yeah, extra tasty," she said, then yelled into the hallway, "Thanks Yolanda!"

It was dark outside the room now. The skylights seemed brighter, and the food warming Conrad's insides made Anise appear more vivid: her waist curving around her jean-stretched hips to her legs to her sock-covered toes, her arms curving around her shoulders to her satiny-smooth neck to her ears. Her hands... he had watched her hands as she clambered around and pointed at the papers: the perfect graspy hands. He wondered why they were so strong-looking. He wanted those hands to hold him, to press against his face.

"You're such a good student," he said, biting into a second patty.

Anise shrugged. "Nah, it just looks that way."

"But look at your notes! And you pay attention the whole time."

"Yeah but if I don't I'll go flush! Down the tubes. Seriously, my grades were *bad* before... but it's not like I don't get it! I mean I do, but then it gets all scrambled. Then I freeze on the test and forget half of it."

"Huh." Conrad might have said the same thing happened to him but Anise kept talking.

"It sucks! I actually like school. I want to be smart. I just don't feel like I'm very good at anything, not like you, or you know, Stacy."

"What am *I* good at?"

"Art, duh! Though I guess I'm good at horses. That's something anyway. I miss my horse!" She threw back her arms.

"You have a horse? Your own horse? Oh my god, I better not tell my sisters. They'll die. They're completely horse-bonkers these days."

Anise's eyes widened like she was cornered. Conrad squinted at her for a moment then pointed at her face.

"You know my sisters!" he whispered.

Anise crumpled her lips into a guilty smile and curled up behind her legs. "Yeah, well, I help the riding teachers with their lessons. Your sisters are so cute! They ask me a zillion questions."

She stopped but Conrad watched her face: sewn up tight with only her eyes looking out over her knees. He would venture to ask.

"Did they, uh... say anything about me?"

Anise flushed distinctly. "Maybe?" she peeped.

He wanted to know! Maybe later he would torture Beth for the truth.

"So when do I get to see *your* sisters?" he asked.

"Oh god." Anise threw her head back.

"What's the big deal?"

"I just get all stressed out talking about them."

"Why's that?"

"Oh I don't know... it's like I'll say oh yeah, Greta lives here and Patty lives there, and stuff like that, and then I smile. But I can't *even* explain the real stuff. It's too much. So I don't tell people."

"I'm not people. You can tell me." Conrad didn't know what this meant but it sounded funny.

"Yeah I don't know what you are," Anise said. But then she sat up and drew a breath. "OK, fine. So the deal is, my sisters are all older, so they don't live here anymore. I miss them so much!" She paused to frump. "But really when they did live here, like especially when they were in high school, it was *completely* nuts."

"Isn't that normal?"

"You have *no* idea. I was little but I remember everything. Let's see... so, Greta's boyfriend in 11th grade forced her to you know, *do it*, and then she got pregnant and didn't want to keep the baby but my mom made her keep it, and my mom and dad fought about it, like *screaming*. This was Greta's room by the way. And Patty ran around with all the cool guys, but she got caught with cocaine and was kicked out of school, and she went to rehab a bunch of times. And then Lisa was always *so* depressed and tried to kill herself twice and was in the hospital, and then right after high school she ran off with a guy to South America." Conrad's eyes were extra open now. "She's better now though," Anise added hastily, "starting college finally." She looked at the floor.

"So you're the youngest then."

"Yeah I'm pretty sure I was a mistake. I mean, do the math. Nobody plans it that way."

"Oh, yeah, heh." Conrad went along with the joke, in case it was one.

"So now I'm in high school, and Patty always goes wink-wink and laughs like it's my turn, like I'm a bomb ready to go off like they all did, you know like it's no big deal that she's a basket case. And then my mom sees my grades and says I'm going to be just like them. Makes me *so* mad." Anise's face was flushing hot.

"Won't your mom be home soon?" Conrad asked, sensing the need for a diversion.

"Oh, she's abroad right now. It was Greece last week when she called, but she said something about Crete. She's always somewhere or other, selling houses. She's so cool. She'll be back soon, next week for sure." Anise smiled with this last part.

"What about your dad?"

Anise looked at the floor and her face tightened again. "My dad is *dead*," she said.

"Oh, I'm sorry. Shoot. Sorry, sorry." Conrad reached out to squeeze the side of her arm.

"Your friend need a ride?" came Yolanda's voice in the doorway.

Conrad sat back. "I can stay," he said. "I mean, if you want to study some more."

Anise looked up pink in the face, first at Yolanda then back at Conrad. "It's supposed to be her night off," she said, "so I guess it's better if, uh, yeah..."

"I go get the car," said Yolanda.

Sitting on his knees, Conrad stacked his books and papers into neat piles and placed them into his bag one by one — carefully, slowly. He peeked up: Anise was sitting cross-legged in front of him, looking blankly toward the other end of the room. Conrad put another book into his bag. Then he leaned forward onto his hands and pressed his lips onto hers. Hers were scratchy and didn't move, so he leaned back to see her eyes open wide. Then a horn honked from the front and he jumped up.

"Um, sorry," he said.

"It's OK," Anise whispered, but she looked at the floor.

Conrad retreated out the door and moved to the car. After a pause Anise followed him. Again she stared out the front window while Conrad kept silent in the back as they sank back down the hills.

"You can just let me out on Santa Monica," Conrad said to Yolanda.

"You sure?"

"Yeah. The bus to my house goes right through here all the time."

The car pulled up to a bus stop and Conrad climbed out. Then he sat for twenty minutes wondering what the strain in Anise's eyes had meant when she waved back to him from the window.

○ ○ ○

Pillow Anise was still wrapped in Conrad's arms when he woke, but her back was snapped horribly backward. Conrad stayed under his covers, cryogenically still. Emerging into the light would restart time. He wasn't ready for time. Maybe he would sleep in reverse and shoot out the other end of a possibility tube. He would follow his past self and sneak a note into his bag: DO NOT TRY TO KISS HER. When his past self read the note, his stupid present self would explode in a hail of guts.

But was it actually so bad? It was entirely possible that Anise had been so thrilled by the kiss that she wasn't able to move. Maybe... but his churning stomach disagreed.

"Conrad?" came Sueanna's voice up the stairs. "Girls?"

"Coming!" Conrad yelled from under the blanket. But he dawdled, letting his sisters take the bathroom so they would arrive first to the breakfast table. He found them there debating the merits of getting a rabbit, despite Sueanna having clearly vetoed another species. At the cupboard he dug a gob of honey onto a spoon, then spread half of it over his lips.

It made sense to go for Levy first. Standing behind her he leaned down and planted a good smooch on her cheek, then moved toward Beth.

"What the hell!" Levy yelled, wiping her hand across her cheek. "Eww gross!"

Conrad squished more honey onto his mouth and leaned under the table where Beth had fled. "Stay away from me!" she squealed.

"Conrad *don't* waste the honey," Sueanna said with enough finality to end the scene right there. Conrad licked his lips and sat down.

Beth cautiously climbed back into her seat. "What is *up* with you?" she asked.

"He's a weirdo," said Levy. "A freak." She wet a napkin to clean her face. "Factory reject."

"You know me," Sueanna sighed, "can't pass up a discount."

She put down a steaming pot of oat-fig-nut porridge, a favorite. The kids got busy scooping it into their bowls and adding brown sugar and milk.

"Did you get a lot of studying done with Anise yesterday?" Sueanna asked. Levy and Beth inhaled.

"Mom!" Conrad protested.

"What? Didn't she tell you we met her at the stables?"

"Yeah." Conrad squinted at his blinking, smirking sisters.

"She's really good with the kids, like a real teacher. I met her mother once at a parent meeting. So put together. Oh and that suit thing she had on! Didn't see her dad, though."

"She said her dad's dead."

"Really? No no, her dad's not dead. He just ran off with some floozy. It was in all the papers."

Conrad watched Sueanna stacking clean pots back onto the shelf. "Why would it be in the papers?" he murmured.

"His company's on the stock exchange you know. He's super-rich."

"Oh."

Joey stood on the curb in sunglasses with his arms crossed, a picture of magazine cool save for his jeans being a tad too short.

"Where's Stacy?" Conrad asked.

"No idea. She better not be not sick. We got plans. But hey man, what about you?" He gave Conrad a conspiratorial nod. "I hear you two went off into the sunset yesterday. Yeah?"

"Where did you hear that?"

"Oh I hear things, got my thumb on the pulse. Come on, man, tell me."

Conrad shrugged and spoke facing away. "We studied. It was good. Really I don't know what's going on with her."

"Really? Dude you gotta be more aggressive."

"Yeah I guess."

Conrad pinned a fresh sheet of white paper to his easel. Today they would draw with charcoal. A mannequin held a broom at the center of the room.

"The light is already there," Mrs. Pelora said to the class, "but we create the illusion of adding *more* light by taking some away."

That sounded nice, but Conrad still hated charcoal: imprecise, and dirty, smearing by accident, getting all over his hands and clothes. Stacy however was already at it, forcefully darkening a shadow. She hadn't looked toward Conrad nor said a word.

"You OK Stacy?"

Stacy's eyes reddened as she scraped at her paper with jagged strokes. She only stopped to wipe away tears and kept working, her face now pitifully coal-streaked.

Conrad packed up before Stacy, then walked beside her from the studio to the lab without speaking. After setting up their experiment, Conrad did all the talking while Stacy only nodded through each step until again they were the first to succeed. Conrad patted Stacy on the back, but only the briefest of smiles showed on her face. Then she gathered her things and left.

*Don't forget your face...*

The narrow hallway filled with moving heads: brown hair, black hair, short hair, curly hair... but nowhere was Anise's hair. Conrad stopped to peek into his locker on the off chance that a note had been pushed through the grate. Not that she had ever done that.

The door to history was just ahead. Opening it might tell him something, maybe the truth. He stopped and stared at the handle, but Peter Fronton came up from behind and smacked him on the back.

"Buck up buddy!"

Conrad stepped through, and he pointed his eyes to Anise's usual place, and there she was: still existing, a beautiful relief.

But not a relief. It was the anti-relief, to see her unmoved as he appeared, to see her eyes glued to her desk. He moved to sit, struggling to breathe the air that didn't belong to him anymore. Then the room went silent. Mr. Sebastien pulled out a stack of tests and sent it on its way around the circle.

Peter handed Conrad the stack. "Don't die!" he whispered.

The test: three double-sided pages, with room for eight short-paragraph answers and one essay-type answer. *Merciless.*

"Before you start!" Mr. Sebastien shouted. Pencils that were already scribbling stopped. "Before you start, take a minute to read and understand all the questions."

Writing, erasing, writing, shaking, panicking, writing faster — Conrad had lived! And now he would die, if not for the burrito turning in the food truck's little microwave. He dug his sore fingers into the ice and left them there as he waited.

No dangling legs. Conrad climbed up the bench and sat in a heap.

*Please come, Anise. Sit next to me again.*

*Please.*

Time passed and he was still alone and the burrito was gone, but its calories had recharged his frustration. Of course! He should scour the campus!

Conrad climbed down and peeked around the corner toward the wall garden. Carrie and Amy were there with some older girls, but also Patrick, and Robb and Todd. Conrad hesitated long enough for Patrick to notice.

"Hey look folks, it's the fagmeister!" Patrick yelled.

Any other day Conrad would keep walking, but this time his inner gears propelled him straight at the group. Their eyes widened as he approached.

"Have you seen Anise?" he asked Amy.

"Uh..."

"He's confused," Patrick interrupted. "He thinks he likes girls." One of the older girls punched Patrick in the shoulder.

"Yes or no?" said Conrad, still looking directly at Amy.

"No." She smiled like it wasn't true.

"Have you?" he asked Carrie, who shook her head, but in her case without defiance, with an expression more like shame. Conrad turned and walked away.

Mrs. Parkins was already writing on the board as Conrad sat down. Joey hadn't yet arrived.

"You made it man!" said Peter Fronton in the next seat.

Conrad nodded with a weary smile. It occurred to him now that Peter was always hovering at the corner of his vision. Of course he and Peter were still on familiar terms, having run around together in the seventh grade until it simply faded. Conrad could hardly explain it to himself, except maybe to say that they were tuned to different channels, and that the only show on Peter's channel was a goofy comedy.

"Check it out," Peter whispered, holding open his backpack to reveal a flat wooden case. Conrad recognized it immediately.

"You've got to be kidding me," he whispered back. "You're still doing that?"

"Took it out of retirement. New guy's going down."

"Oh. Well then, carry on."

Conrad had a similar box hidden in his closet. Inside was a narrow aluminum tube, a vial of vegetable oil, pipe cleaners for applying the oil to the inside of the tube, and a little glass jar to store gloppy, darkening, overripe banana meat, all of which added up to the worst kind of blowgun. He hadn't taken it to school since the seventh grade but still trotted it out on occasion — his sisters knew it was him but didn't know how.

Joey slipped through the door and sat in his chair board-straight. When the teacher faced away he turned to Conrad.

"Was Stacy in class today?" he whispered, nearly imperceptible.

"Yeah, but she was really upset."

"About what?"

"No idea."

Between classes they stood out of earshot, Joey's eyes flitting to each student appearing between the buildings as he spoke.

"Dude after lunch I saw her, and for *sure* she saw me too, but then she just marched away to class."

"What did you do?"

"What do you mean what did I do? Yesterday we were totally cool I swear."

"You didn't, like, try something... or something?"

"No! Man if you find out anything you gotta tell me."

"Of course." Conrad had never seen Joey like this, so he let Joey be the person having a crisis. The pit in his own stomach was too large to come out anyway.

After school Conrad again balanced on the curb, hands folded behind his back, periodically looking around, just casual — the queasy waves passing through his body being invisible to the other students streaming out around him.

The black Mercedes pulled up. Conrad ambled over and leaned down to the window.

"Hi Yolanda," he said. She gave one nod. "The pupusas were amazing. I forgot to say." She nodded again, the tiniest bit softer. He stood up again to wait.

*Can I talk to you?* he would say. Anise would stand aside with him and listen. *I'm sorry for surprising you.* Maybe then her eyes would warm. *I don't want anything to come between us.* He had learned these words from Guiding Light when he had the flu, but anyway she might agree, maybe even take his hand. But what if she didn't? *If you stop seeing me now I'll cry so hard I'll suffer brain damage and spontaneously combust and they'll find nothing but a burnt crust in the road.*

Amy came at the front, with Anise between her and Carrie in the back. Conrad watched from the car's headlight. He hadn't planned it this way. Amy opened the front door and stood looking at Conrad as Anise reached for the back door.

"Anise?" Conrad said at the last second.

"Hi!" she said with a sunny wave, then climbed across the back seat to make room for Carrie. The doors slammed and the car pulled away with Anise looking out the opposite window.

Conrad watched his shoes taking step after step up the sidewalk toward his house. Tunnel vision had gotten him from school to the bus stop, but on the bus he had passed out, curled up tight on the seat. How had he known to get off? It was wonderful how the walking just happened. *This is why zombies are possible.*

"Joey's on the phone!" Levy called as Conrad ghosted through the doorway. "Whoah, what's with your face?" she asked and handed him the receiver. He shrugged.

"Hi Joey."

"Dude where have you been? You gotta help me. She won't take the phone. Can you go to her house for me?"

"Her house? Me? Where's that?"

"She's only like six or eight blocks from you. You didn't know that? My dad won't let me go. Please, man. I'm dying." Joey lived closer to the ocean so it would take eons to get across town on a Friday evening even if he could drive himself.

"OK, give me her address." Conrad grabbed a pen and scratch paper to write it down. "Uh, I'm pretty sure that's more than eight blocks. What should I say?"

"Just make her call me, or say why she won't."

Conrad went to the front door and opened it slowly. It creaked. Chopping sounds in the kitchen halted. "Going-on-an-errand-be-back-soon!" he yelled and ran.

Stacy's house was small but cute and private, a short ways above Hollywood Boulevard where the elevation and mortgages both climbed. He found a button on the outside wall and pushed it.

"Yes?" came a tinny voice.

"I'm here to see Stacy? My name's Conrad."

Nothing happened. Conrad pushed the button again and waited. Then he heard flip-flops and the gate opened.

"What," said Stacy, wrapped in a thick robe with her hair down, miserable and pretty.

Conrad nodded. "That's right. I'm here to find out what."

"Why? Did *he* send you?"

"Yeah, he's freaking out."

At this Stacy looked at Conrad more intently. Then she turned and let him follow her to a little cafe table by the garden where she sat down in a terry cloth heap and scowled.

A woman's voice came from an upstairs window. "You all right Stacy?"

"Yeah, this is Conrad."

"Oh yes! Nice to meet you," the waving shadow said and receded.

They sat but Stacy didn't talk. Conrad thought of Mr. Onter, except now the roles were reversed.

"Joey has no clue what's going on," he said.

"Jerk-ass."

"What did he do?"

Stacy didn't answer, so Conrad began to search for imperfections in the ornate die-cast table legs while looping the scene of Anise's escape in his mind: the black car speeding away, the back of Anise's head just visible through the window. "You should answer the phone," he grumbled, still staring at the table legs. "Maybe he did something, but you should at least say what it was." He began to feel hot in the eyes. "It's not nice to do that, to just shut off like that. It's terrible."

Stacy was watching him. "OK... but why are *you* so upset about it?"

Now it was Conrad's turn to go quiet. Stacy shook her head. "There he goes."

"Anise stopped talking to me."

"Oh! Huh. I'm sorry. Oh I get it! You don't know why?"

"Not sure. Probably my fault." He paused again. "I mean, I tried to kiss her."

Stacy began to laugh. "Oh the poor thing!" she said and dropped her face onto her folded arms on the table. "You monster! How could you do such a terrible thing?" She laughed into her arms.

"Oh thanks Stacy. Thanks a lot."

She sat up again. "Seriously though, that can't be the only thing, unless you were, like, forcing yourself on her. You weren't forcing her, were you?"

Conrad shook his head, though he wasn't a hundred percent sure.

"Hmm." Stacy thought for a moment. "Really there's so much gossip going on. Those friends of hers never stop I swear. Plus Robb and Todd have been following her around since forever, and then there's *Patrick*." She spoke this last name with utter disdain. "I'm pretty sure they're talking every genus and species of shit."

"About me?"

"Who do you think? About me, too. I heard it." She went scowly again. "OK I'll tell you. So this morning I was trying to sneak up on Joey. I was going to jump out from behind a car but then Robb and Todd showed up. They were like, *hey Joey, you banged Stacy yet?* then Joey said something like *dude, a man doesn't talk about what goes on in the bedroom*, but you could see on his face, I mean he was totally acting like we'd done it, and those dumb-asses were laughing."

"Oh man. He hates those guys."

"I can't believe he would do that."

"Well I can," Conrad said, but then he paused to figure out why he wasn't surprised. "Well you know, it's like he has to be ultra-cool, all the time. He never acts like himself. Except around me. And you, actually."

"It's so stupid."

"Yeah. Maybe if you tell him that he'll cut it out."

Stacy didn't respond to this, just sat with her chin stuck out.

"My mom's going to kill me," Conrad said. He got up to leave with a little wave, but Stacy followed him to the gate.

"You're such a good friend," she said, and hugged him. Conrad put his arms around her, and sank into the soft robe and felt the strength of her back under his hands and breathed in her hair, and it was the best thing he had ever felt in his life.

# 12

# Early April

A line of little cups were filled with shades of the same gray from dark to light. A new canvas sat on Conrad's easel, traced with the identical forest from his previous painting, but this time he had decided the trees would only be barely perceptible when he was done. The paintings would be displayed side-by-side, a riot of color on the left and blind night on the right.

Mrs. Pelora squatted next to him looking doubtful. "I like your idea, Conrad, but I want to put a bug in your ear."

"OK."

"Put it this way. Things are never really opposite. You have darkness in your first painting, see?" She pointed at the dark pools at the bottom of his first painting on the wall. "So in this one, you can still have color. Gray is color but with less saturation, less light. You can have a cool gray from the blue side, or brown gray, or whatever. It can be super-subtle, but it still has an effect. You'll want to think about that, if you want this painting to be as successful as the first. That's what I think anyway."

"OK, thanks." Conrad stared at the trees in the first painting, and imagined them darkening and losing their color. He remembered standing in the woods with only filtered moonlight to see by, straining his eyes to make out the colors of the things around him, like in the dark room. Maybe he wouldn't start today. He put the canvas aside and clipped a sheet of thick paper onto the easel, then set to experimenting with colored grays.

The good part of the day was over, but Stacy didn't know that and followed Conrad to chemistry making goofy faces. Now that she had run Joey over white-hot coals they were back to looking at each other conspicuously every morning. Conrad had to watch this and be happy for them.

When he had taken his place next to her in the lab, Stacy turned to him. "You still haven't said anything?" she whispered.

Conrad shook his head.

"You shouldn't just let her get away with it! Go tell her she hurt your feelings."

"I don't know... she never promised me anything."

"You're too nice! She can't just do that. I mean really, what a bitch."

"Don't say that."

"Why are you defending her?"

Conrad marched to history class and took his seat. He pulled out his notebook and waited to write letters on it. He would be a good student in this class, then the next one and the next, and when there were no more classes he would calmly escort his body outside to the bus. Eventually the school days would run out and he would fly back to the woods where he belonged.

"You may be pleased to hear," announced Mr. Sebastien, "that today I have the test results." The class went breathless. "And as per usual I will name the person with the highest score. That person, I am very proud to say, is Anise Helms."

All eyes turned to see Anise agog. She reached out to accept her test and paged through to the end to look at the score.

"Oh my god!" Amy squealed. She pulled on Anise's arm to get a look. "Holy crap! Ninety-six!"

"Who's number two?" asked Peter. The rest of the class murmured the same.

Mr. Sebastien shook his head. "Now now, you know I won't say. You'll want number two, then top five, then top ten. I might as well post everybody's score. The rest of you will get your tests after class."

Everyone groaned except Conrad, because his eyes were still locked onto Anise's face. Maybe now she would crack. Maybe now she would look at him, even warm to him again.

But she didn't.

When the time was up Conrad slipped out first. Outside in the shadow of the building he unfolded his test: 93%. Mr. Sebastien had scrawled notes in the margins. 'Good point!' said one. Nothing this wonderful had ever felt so bad.

Joey wouldn't be on the bench at lunch and neither would anyone else, so Conrad heated up an extra-large burrito and took it on tour. Really there were so many places he rarely went. How about the drama building? A group of drama-cools were leaning against a wall behind the stage. Conrad approached them.

"Hey man, what's up?" said Jake, a long-haired senior who acted in all the plays, onstage a prince but offstage greasy and limp. Two glassy-eyed girls flanking him smiled as if they were extensions of his personality.

"Want a bite?" Conrad asked, offering the partially-eaten burrito.

Jake grinned as if this was not the first time. "No thanks man! Much appreciated!"

Conrad shrugged and went to the next building where he found the musicians sitting together. He had a vague idea that they were exchange students, as all spoke halting English at most, and that the school had brought them in to play Bach on strings with discomforting intensity at school assemblies. But now they all watched him instead of the reverse. *It's infinite*, he thought: the possible expressions that could ripple across their eyes. But never mind that — all he wanted to know was, how did they stand on the *belonging* question? Perhaps he would find out. "Want a bite?" he asked, lifting the burrito.

Nobody moved, only stared. One girl scowled as if they were all being insulted again. *She's beautiful*, Conrad realized. "Oh well," he said and walked away.

At the end of the alley behind the last building, Conrad found the legendary junior George kissing Lacey Flanigan against the wall. Conrad closed in and held the burrito up to their faces.

"Want a bite?"

The kissing slowed. Their eyes slowly opened, then George pulled away and Lacey broke out laughing. "Want a bite of my fist?" George yelled. Conrad retreated.

Nobody anywhere wanted a bite. *Fine then.* One foot in front of the other, Conrad traced the center-line of the alley all the way back to its end where he finally looked up to see Patrick standing face-to-face. Again the shoulders flexed. "Want a bite?" Conrad said, lifting the burrito under Patrick's nose in one last act of suicidal generosity. But Patrick blinked, and his shoulders relaxed. Now instead of staring Conrad down, his eyes focused on the burrito. And he might have said something, maybe even taken a bite, but then he flinched and grabbed at his neck, then looked at his hand, then spun around to see where the slimy yellow-brown substance had come from. Then he ran off.

Conrad dropped the remainder of his burrito into the trash and hurried indoors toward his locker. Inside, a group of students saw him coming and scurried away giggling. On the wall was a hand-written poster:

### Conrad's Middle Names. Vote here!

A chart had columns for the letters 'D' and 'P', and most of the rows were already filled in with clever entries including "Dildo Poker," "Douche Pumper," and, with the most votes, "Dick Pussy." Conrad tore the paper off the wall, crumpled it into a ball and compressed it inside his fist.

Mrs. Parkins was already getting going but Conrad only stared straight ahead after sitting down late.

"Dude, just forget about it." Joey whispered. Conrad hadn't said anything but Joey assumed anyway.

"What, like it didn't matter? Like *you* forgot about it?"

Joey shook his head. "It's not the same. We have a *relationship*. You hadn't gotten anywhere with her yet."

Conrad was still squeezing the paper in his hand. Soon it would be pure diamond.

○ ○ ○

It was a clear line from the door to the stairs, but Beth was waiting just inside, bug-eyed.

"Levy and Mom were yelling," she whispered. "Watch out."

"Conrad is that you?" came Sueanna's voice, not soft. "I need some help in here!"

"I'm busy!" he called back.

"No you're not, you just got home. Come help me."

Conrad appeared in the kitchen where his mother was again surrounded by animal, vegetable and flour.

"Here, chop the chicken," she said, and pushed over a cutting board piled with raw meat. "Wash your hands first."

He did as he was told. The chicken was rubbery and the knife not sharp enough.

"Not so small," said Sueanna. Conrad obeyed but didn't speak. "How was school," she said, more demand than question.

"Fine," he said. He continued cutting without looking up.

"That's all, just fine?"

He wouldn't mention the test. She would use that cooing voice of hers. And celebrating the test would mean letting go of something. He would hold on tight to whatever it was.

"Why can't you ever talk, Conrad?"

"Why do you always get on my case when I'm in a bad mood?"

"Oh you're just making yourself feel that way. You don't have to spread it around."

Conrad and Beth sat at the table. Sueanna came in with a large bowl and set it down, then turned toward the hallway and yelled "Levy! Come to dinner!" but no response came from above. She left the room and soon it sounded like an oversize cat was upstairs.

Levy stomped into the dining room and fell hard into her chair, arms crossed, face scrunched tight. Sueanna followed and began scooping food onto the kids' plates: some sort of gloppy chicken-vegetable stir fry. It had a particular smell Conrad didn't recognize so he picked at it with his fork to see what was in it. Beth did the same.

"Oh go ahead, dig in," Sueanna sighed.

Levy frowned at the mound on her plate. "Chunks," she muttered.

"Eeew!" Beth whined, leaning back and putting down her fork as if it were contaminated. "Why did you have to say that?"

"That wasn't nice, Levy," Sueanna said. "I worked hard on this."

"She ruined it," said Beth.

"No she didn't," said Sueanna. "Just try it."

But now the food was tainted even for Conrad. He forced himself to ingest a fork-full of the shiny mass, gross even as it tasted good. Sueanna watched her son not inhale his meal and sat back.

"What, you too, Conrad?"

"I can't help it."

Sueanna fumed. "I can't believe you kids. I try to give you everything but all you do is complain and ask for something else."

"What did I ever do?" Beth cried out. "It's you guys who go all grumpy all the time!" She slid down in her chair.

"OK fine then!" Sueanna said and slammed down her utensils. "Eat whatever you want!" She stood up and retreated to the kitchen. At this Levy bolted upstairs. That left Conrad and Beth both staring through the table. Tears dripped down Beth's face.

"It's not fair," she said.

"What's not fair?"

"You know."

They were still hungry, so after a few minutes they sat up and ate together in silence. Now Conrad felt like talking, but Beth was still sniffling so he spoke in a whisper.

"What's Levy like at school?"

Beth whispered back. "She's the same, but it's different there."

"What do you mean?"

"I mean, here she's normal, sort of, but not there. The other girls act all prissy *all* the time, and they talk about Levy like she's a gang member or something. And then the teachers are always scolding her, you know, like Mom. *Be more ladylike!* It's like a hundred Moms at school."

"Oh man, no wonder. But do you hang out with her there?"

"No, we're in different buildings. But we go in together and leave together, which is good. Nobody messes with me, not after that one time. But if she goes to your school it'll be just me there."

"Oh yeah, I didn't think about that."

"Figures. You never think about anything. But I do. I made a chart. In three years you'll go off to college, right? So for me, for *all* of high school you won't be here. Then Levy will leave and it'll be just me and Mom for two whole years."

"Oh... whoah. That's weird to think about."

"Yeah, but you don't have to care. You get everything. You're the first."

o o o

Conrad rolled out of bed and crawled to his desk. He could sort of imagine but wanted to see it on paper. He drew columns for himself, Levy, and Beth, filled out with their years in school through college. None of this had ever occurred to him yet his fifth-grade sister had already worked it out, and she was right. Even more, Conrad would graduate college the same year Beth graduated high school, meaning that when Beth started college, he would already be out in the world, whatever that meant. On paper the numbers were already alarming, but the worst number of all was *three* — just three more summers with his sisters, as kids anyway.

At breakfast all sat chastened, quietly spooning and chewing, but Sueanna's fancy porridge was too satisfying to allow such a mood to last.

"How's Anise doing?" asked Sueanna.

Conrad didn't look up. "I don't know. She won't talk to me now."

Levy and Beth sat forward to watch him.

"Oh I'm sorry," said Sueanna. "Did you have an argument?"

"No. Don't know why."

"Oh well, those are the breaks. Don't worry, there'll be somebody else." She continued ladling porridge, then added, "what I want to know is, who names their kid Anise? It's such an odd name."

BANG! The bowls and silverware jumped — Levy's fists had pounded hard on the table. "Who!" she yelled out.

Sueanna stared at her daughter. "Levy?"

Levy's arms remained stiff, her face contorted, huffing. "Who... names... their kid... Levinia!?"

Sueanna relaxed and lifted another spoonful. "Mothers with a sense of style, that's who," she said, and slurped. "Mothers with a sense of history."

Conrad hadn't planned to laugh, but once it started he doubled over. "Yeah," he gasped, "ancient history!"

Warm stomach, warm face: both cooled as the car neared the school. Conrad stepped out but remained standing on the curb while Sueanna sped away. He would keep apart until the last second. He had nothing to gain or lose.

Something!

Anise stood at the end of the block, looking up at a tall figure and smiling. It was Patrick, talking at her and gesturing with his arms. Conrad hurried indoors.

The dark version of his painting was almost done. He sat glaring at it, resisting the urge to cover it all in an inch-thick layer of Mars Black. But then a thought came: if at the tops of the trees a bit of night sky showed through the leaves, just a hint lighter and a bit more saturated, it would make the woods seem even darker. He mixed a dark blue-gray, thinned it, and used a small brush to carefully fill in little gaps at the top right of the picture. It worked. He used the same color to sign his initials, then hung the painting high on the wall next to the other one. He couldn't really see his paintings up there reflecting in the fluorescent lights, but no matter. He cleaned his hands and left without a word.

And of course it was *that* day, the first day of history presentations, and Conrad already knew that he was fourth on the list. In chemistry he found himself alone in a fog-filled valley somewhere just beyond fear. Stacy was missing, so he sat and listened but didn't hear. When he took his seat in history he did the same.

*Three more summers.*

"Very nice!" came Mr. Sebastien's voice as the third presenter sat down. "Next up we have Conrad with an unusual topic."

Conrad gathered his materials and went to the front where he stood looking at the door across the room. But by some reverse-miracle, he was as stiff and cold as a steel girder. "People didn't know what the war would be like before it happened," he said to the door, "including the artists."

He went on to explain all the things he had planned to explain, in what afterward became a half-remembered monotone mouth-moving blur, with frequent glances down to the index cards in his hands, the room becoming rounder and fuzzier the longer he spoke. He passed around black-and-white photocopies of pre-war pictures by Marc, Meidner and Kandinsky as he outlined their themes of pure nature and the cleansing away of a corrupt urban world. He read quotes to demonstrate how those themes overlapped in the artists' imaginations with the oncoming war, making the war something they nearly welcomed as if a better world would follow. He told the story of Franz Marc being shot dead on patrol. He showed nightmarish paintings by Dix, Grosz and Beckmann from during and after the war. Then he sat down at his desk.

A poke on his shoulder — Conrad glanced over to see Peter's upturned thumb. *That's nice*, Conrad thought and nodded, but then he went back to tracing the imitation wood grain on his desk's laminate surface.

*Three more summers.*

Conrad carried his lunch to the end of the campus and sat against a wall looking out to the road — no more tall bench for him, no more sitting and hoping. But at least he had plenty to eat. Sueanna, on a tear from something she had read about nutrition, had begun forcing her children to take lunches to school. Conrad's brown paper lunch bag was packed to ripping at the corners. He pulled out the appetizer: cucumber sushi rolls.

Shouts — words echoing 'fight!'

Conrad ran to the scene. Nearby students stood rooted in place with their eyes wide open, save for Rob and Todd who pumped their fists and hooted at the action. The action was Patrick, thrusting at somebody who had fallen onto his back. With a queasy shudder Conrad saw that it was Peter Fronton, blowgun lying nearby, hands waving to fend off the punches. But it was futile — Patrick landed every blow and hard, crouching red in the face and out of control. When Peter's arms went limp the onlookers began to murmur in alarm. "Stop it Patrick!" a girl yelled, but the thumping sounds went on.

*Three more summers.*

Conrad dropped the lunch-bag, sprinted onto Patrick's back and grabbed the hair on both sides of his head, sending Patrick toppling face-first onto the asphalt with Conrad riding on top. But Patrick twisted to bone-pound him with an elbow, flipping him stunned onto his back. Patrick stood up with blood streaming from his forehead. "I'll fucking kill you!" he screamed, looming closer. But Conrad's body acted for him, kicking out his legs, just like he had practiced so many times on his dad's dirt driveway — his useless ninja skill of springing up without hands — but this time his feet met Patrick's face, sending Conrad rolling away while Patrick collapsed into gurgling wails.

○ ○ ○

"I still can't believe you would get into a fight," said Sueanna, both hands squeezing the steering wheel. "It's not like you!"

"I wasn't fighting."

"You broke his jaw! How's that not fighting?"

"I didn't mean to."

"Oh that's easy to say, but they'll have to wire his jaw shut you know, for a long time! Did you ever think of that?"

Conrad stared down at his guilty shoes. "He was hurting Peter."

"Next time just let the teachers handle it, OK?"

"But nobody was around."

Sueanna wasn't hearing it. "This could jeopardize everything!" she said. "You're suspended now, but what if they don't let you come back? This kind of thing could follow you around you know."

"I don't care."

"You should care!"

Conrad headed straight to his room and locked the door. When his sisters arrived later he didn't let them in, and refused to come down each of the countless times that Joey rang the phone. Under his wool blanket, all light sealed out, he fell into a deep sleep.

At dinner-time the door-pounding came again, an exasperated Sueanna.

"You can't just hide in there every time you have a problem!" she yelled.

Later Beth came to the door. "Are you OK?" she asked through the wood. Then a pause. "Should I bring you a plate?"

Accepting a plate would mean opening the door. He refused. His stomach was tied in knots anyway. He closed his eyes again.

Something different.

Somebody below had knocked at the front door when he was asleep but he knew it. Now a familiar voice was speaking, then Sueanna's voice, then the front door closing. He tumbled off his bed and ran down the stairs.

"Who was that?" he asked, wild-eyed, hair bent sideways.

"Oh that was your friend Stacy," said Sueanna. "I told her you're not talking."

"Why did you do that!?" he yelled.

"How am I supposed to know who you'll talk to?"

"God dammit Mom!" he yelled louder and pounded his fists on the banister. "You don't know a god damn thing!"

"Don't yell at me like that! And don't swear!"

Conrad dashed out onto the front lawn, but Stacy had come with her mother in a car that was already turning the corner. He reversed back into the house and shot up the stairs, ignoring his mother's demand that he come back down this minute.

Now Conrad could never sleep. Stacy had been there and he had missed it! He paced his room. "Dammit!" he yelled and sat down hard at the edge of the bed holding his hair.

Another knock on his door. "Dad's on the phone," came Levy's voice.

Conrad stopped breathing. Then he opened the door and followed Levy downstairs.

"Hi Dad," he said into the receiver, his voice at half-volume.

"What do you have to say for yourself?" came the deep voice at the other end.

"I'm... sorry."

"For what?"

"I don't know."

"Why not?"

"I don't know. I was just trying to help somebody, now I'm the one in trouble."

"Still, you hurt him."

"I wasn't trying to. I didn't think I could."

"Well, now you know. So you just tell the truth, OK? Things will work out. Got me?"

"Yeah."

"And I *don't* want to hear about you yelling at your mother."

"OK."

○ ○ ○

*Indefinite Probation.*

The words sounded like action, an administrative choke-hold of sorts, and though they only meant that Conrad wasn't allowed back at school until a decision was made, they hung heavily on his head.

While he waited Conrad flipped back and forth between two modes: watching the street from his bedroom window, or sitting on the floor playing his tapes. He had eight tapes. He wanted more tapes. Come to think of it, nobody was home and he still had bushes-money hidden behind his desk. He could stroll the scenic miles along Sunset Boulevard to Tower Records... Or he could stay in his room and blast the Black Flag tape Joey had given him, mirror cracked by a fist on its cover — just the thing. But another music pulled at him. He'd almost memorized it now. Its sneaky humor made him chuckle. He lifted up the tape to admire Mr. Onter's calligraphic printing on its sleeve:

Beethoven
Piano Sonata no. 18, Opus 31 no. 3
Bella Davidovich, piano

Conrad went to get Levy's tape player. He set it up playing the Beethoven at one end of his room, then sat his boom box on an opposite shelf playing Black Flag, both at high volume. Then he flopped onto his bed in between and stared at the ceiling.

He remembered something from math class, about how many different pairs you can make from a group. There was a formula, he vaguely recalled, with exclamation marks that made the numbers louder. He jumped down to dig out his notebooks and flipped through page after page but couldn't find it, so he gave up and drew a chart with all the combinations of his eight titles, laboriously crossing off the duplicates. That left twenty-eight total, twenty-seven left to try! He started by placing *A Flock Of Seagulls* flat on the floor, and *The Best Of Basie* next to it.

On the second day of this Joey called again.

"Dude they had a whole assembly and everything!"

"What did they say?" Conrad asked with a morbid sense of having missed out.

"They were like, *we don't stand for violence in this school*, and stuff like that. They were super serious, man. They talked forever."

"Did they say anything about me?"

"No it was so stupid. They didn't use any names even though everyone knows. It'll be so bogus if they kick you out."

"They would do that?"

"I don't know. Sounds bad though. You should talk to them."

When Conrad put down the receiver he had forgotten how to inhale and had to make himself do it.

That night Conrad left his bedroom windows wide open to let in the night air, such as it was, so he could curl deep under his covers. Pillow Anise wasn't meeting his eyes. He reached again to smooth back her hair.

*Stop it.*

*What are you so mad about?*

*Nothing.*

He couldn't think of a legitimate way to continue the exchange, so he held her close and drifted into a fitful sleep.

The next morning Sueanna called in sick to work. Buildings blurred past as she drove. They parked. They walked. Students stopped to whisper as they neared the administration building. They rode the elevator without talking.

"Thank you for coming," said Mr. Frunkle. His face was unreadable, as was that of the principal sitting cross-legged in a corner chair. Sueanna would normally start talking but this doubling of authority made her shy.

"So then..." said the counselor, exhaling, "we've got *two* kids in the hospital. Mr. Fronton's in pretty bad shape, but thankfully it's nothing permanent. As for Patrick, you did quite a number on his jaw, Conrad. In fact his dad was in here threatening to sue the school."

Conrad glanced up to Mr. Frunkle, then to the principal, then back at the floor.

"But never mind that." Mr. Frunkle waved a hand. "We take fighting seriously here, or we say we do, since we don't usually *have* fights, at least not the kind that end with ambulances."

The principal nodded. "More blood and screaming than we're used to. In the chaos we took you as one of the instigators."

"Yes," said Mr. Frunkle, "however since the assembly we've had quite a few students pounding on our doors, you know, demanding justice. They all say you came later, that you jumped on Patrick to make him stop. But can you tell us about the jaw-breaking part, Conrad, in your own words?"

Conrad sat up a little. "Peter..." He stopped, but then he spoke in a rush. "It sounded like a piece of meat so I didn't care if Patrick killed me and I wasn't thinking, but then he knocked me on my back and he came at me, and then I did care so I had to get away."

Sueanna sat up to interject. "He was def-"

The principal held up a hand. "We would prefer to hear Conrad's point of view, thank you."

Sueanna sat back, but Conrad's attention had returned to the floor. Mr. Frunkle leaned forward.

"So is it fair to say that you karate-kicked Patrick to get away?"

"Karate? No. I was flipping off the ground and kicked him by accident, I think. It was like my body did everything, then later it was all mixed up. I was so mad but really I was sorry for doing that and then I almost wanted to throw up. It's always like that. I'm so sick of it! I never know what I feel about stuff until way later."

"Oh that's all perfectly normal," said Mr. Frunkle. "Listen, we've heard about Patrick's aggressive behavior, but you can imagine the pickle we're in because of his injury. We'll do things by the book, but we should be able to have you back at school on Monday, OK?"

"Oh... OK." Conrad sat up. The tone of the entire conversation was just now dawning on him.

On the drive home Sueanna didn't speak, not until they stopped at the farmer's market. Then she talked about the produce.

"Have you ever tried blood oranges?"

"No."

"Do you want some? They're really good."

"No."

"I'll get some anyway. You'll change your mind later."

Conrad continued at a distance.

"Oh look at this strange honey, Conrad!" she called, holding up a jar filled with what looked like an orange paste.

"That one's from pepper trees," said the seller. "Tastes like kumquats."

"Oh my son and I are crazy about honey. We'll take it."


Levy and Beth stormed the front door and ran straight up to Conrad's room. He had forgotten to lock his door.

"Did they kick you out?" Levy asked.

"No, they found out I was helping."

"Who told them?"

"A bunch of kids came to the office. That's what they said."

"Ha!" said Beth. "You boob. You talk like nobody there likes you."

"No I don't."

"Yes you do!"


Suspending his self-imposed exile, Conrad came down to recline on the living room sofa where he paged through recent copies of Newsweek. One cover said 'Saving Our Schools' in large type over a roomful of scowly high school students. On another was a picture of Richard Gere, one of 'Hollywood's New Sex Symbols.' Conrad was pretty sure that if he went outside right then and walked around Hollywood he wouldn't find any sex symbols drifting along the grimy streets, at least not that kind.

In the sun room Sueanna was talking to somebody on the

phone. "I'll tell him," she said and hung up. Walking out she noticed her son sitting out in the open and came to stand facing him. Conrad ignored her and continued turning pages.

"That was Peter's mother," said Sueanna. "She called to thank you. The doctor told her that with any more punches it might have been much worse."

"Mmm." Conrad nodded but didn't look up.

"Conrad," Sueanna said, "I wanted to say…"

Conrad stood up to leave.

"No, please Conrad, sit back down. I want to talk to you."

"There's nothing to talk about."

"Yes there is," she said, but Conrad only stood with his arms folded tight. "Listen," she pressed, "I was upset. I shouldn't have assumed."

"I want to go live at Dad's."

"What? Why are you bringing that up again? We've talked about this."

"It's what I want."

"But it doesn't make any sense. Can we not talk about that now?"

"It's what I want."

"You can't just go backwards!"

"It's what I want!"

In the corner of their eyes a shape moved into the living room. It was Levy, practicing her special skill: walking front-up on her hands and feet like a spider. She had become so good at this that she could scuttle feet-first up a flight of stairs.

"Levy I've told you not to do that!" Sueanna yelled. But Levy advanced on her. "Levy you stop that right now." Levy began pumping her hips, defiance clear in her eyes. "Levy it's not nice to expose your vulva like that!"

A siren-scream sliced the room: now it was Beth, at the archway, her face contorted in terror. "It's the tarantu-vulva!" she squealed.

This was the tipping point. Conrad had seen it before: Sueanna went blank as her internal gears shifted, then her face began to fold into exaggerated pity. "Oh no!" she whimpered, wringing her hands. "Look what's become of my daughter! She was such a nice girl. Somebody call the professor."

"It's too late," said Beth. "Out spider!" She swatted at Levy with a sweatshirt to herd her away.

Sueanna turned back to Conrad, humor still bright in her eyes. But Conrad hadn't moved. "I want to live at Dad's," he said again.

Sueanna's mouth sank. Then she turned and sighed "maybe you're right" as she left the room.

Later Conrad passed the kitchen and saw Sueanna sitting by herself in the corner holding her face in her hands. He thought maybe he should say something but wasn't sure what, so he went back up to his room, where he sat thinking about going downstairs to console her.

# 13

# Mid-May

Six dangling legs.

Luring Conrad back to the high bench wasn't difficult: Stacy cajoled him just once. Now she sat on one side and Joey on the other, all three swinging their feet with a palpable sense of counting down to the end of the semester. After such an eventful year, sitting together felt like the end of a story. They spoke wistfully about this or that episode as if about a bye-gone era.

Conrad sat up. "Today's the day!"

"What day?"

"OK, so a while back you guys were talking and said something, and I heard it, but I just said *yeah, uh huh*. Then, that same night, I woke up, I swear it was three in the morning, and I was like... *blue dog?*"

Stacy began to giggle.

"Oh sure, you can laugh, but then every day I was planning to ask what the heck you guys meant but I forgot every time."

Joey gave an evil chortle. "I don't think we can tell you."

Stacy shook her smirking face in agreement.

"Aw come on!"

"We'll let you think about it over the summer," she said.

"But then I might never find out."

"Why? It's only a few months."

"Well actually..." Conrad stopped. Talking about it would make it real. "Actually, um, I'm thinking of staying with my dad..." He paused, then added, "after the summer."

At first they only stared. "You serious?" Joey said finally. "You mean, go to school there? Do they even have schools there?"

"Well yeah, of course they do."

"But why?"

"Well... I miss it there all the time. And I guess I just don't feel like I belong here in L.A., at this school."

Stacy stared down at the ground. "But you're our friend," she said. "Don't you belong here with us?"

Conrad had pictured a soaring flight to freedom, not this hurt in his stomach. "But think about my dad," he said. "Wouldn't it be sad if I never live with him again, not even for a year, and then I grow up, and it's too late?" It was a strong argument, which didn't explain the nagging tug of guilt he felt in using it.

"I guess I can see that." Stacy murmured. "But we'll really miss you."

"Yeah, dude, that'll suck. Come on, you sure?"

Conrad nodded, but it didn't feel like sure.

∘ ∘ ∘

Sueanna picked up Conrad after school to take him shoe shopping.

"I've been thinking," said Sueanna. "St. Emily's is kind of old-fashioned. How would you feel if Levy went to your school?"

"I already told her I don't care. Doesn't matter anyway. I won't be there."

"But you might change your mind." She spoke more softly now. "And she'd have her big brother around to protect her."

"What good would that do? I don't even mess with her myself."

"But it's different in high school. You know how it is."

"I don't care."

"You don't care about your sister?"

"Don't guilt me. I already told you."

"I'm not guilting you, I just want you to think more about it."

"I did."

○ ○ ○

Mr. Onter lifted his glass of lemonade into a beam of sunlight from the window where it glowed like a crown jewel.

"So," he said, "I blink my eyes, and a whole multi-chapter drama unfolds in your life. I feel like Rip Van Winkle."

On a break from mowing the lawn, Conrad had, in a stream of words free of audible punctuation, related what had happened with Anise, and with the fight, and with arguments at home, while Mr. Onter nodded attentively.

"So, if you don't mind me asking, why haven't you spoken to Anise?"

Conrad shrugged. "Oh I don't know. She won't even look at me. Anyway my mom says it's only practice in high school."

"Oh yes! And I take it you're having practice feelings? How's that going?"

Conrad only crossed his arms. "My mom doesn't get me at all."

"Seems you're pretty hard on her."

"Well it's only about what *she* wants, like we're a bunch of wind-up robots."

"Hmm." Mr. Onter contemplated for a moment. "That *is* pretty bad. It makes me wonder, did your mother ever go to parenting college?"

"What's that?"

"You know, where they make future mothers and fathers go through two years of classes about developmental psychology, domestic finance and such? And training courses for pubescent conversation? Temper Tantrum Management 101?"

"Oh god, you're always kidding aren't you."

"Am I?"

"It's like you always mean something else."

Mr. Onter paused to take a big sip. "Well I guess what I'm really saying is your mom's just a person. Kids always imagine a big gap, like there's some sort of border between the time you're a kid and when you get married and so on. Sure we have rituals, but there's no border. You're a kid, and you get a little bit older, and then a little more, then a little more, then boop! *You're* the one having kids, and you're in way over your head."

"But how would *you* know? You don't even like women."

Only silence — Mr. Onter failed to laugh on cue. Instead he stared fiercely back at Conrad. But then he took a breath.

"OK I appreciate your openness with someone you thought was gay, but in fact I'm not." He paused, then added quieter, "I even had a family once."

"Oh I'm sorry," said Conrad, taken off guard. "Wait, once?"

Mr. Onter nodded. "I had a wife and three kids, then one day I didn't. They didn't make it home."

The old clock ticked on the wall. Ripples traveled down Conrad's skin.

"That's why I moved here," Mr. Onter continued. "Though on the face of it, it doesn't make any sense. I swear this whole city's a demented paradise for cars. But I might have gone mad if I'd stayed in Boston."

Conrad felt sick now. "I'm sorry Mr. Onter," he said.

"That's OK. Here, have some more lemonade." He filled Conrad's glass to the top.

"Thanks." Conrad sipped, and again his senses communed with whatever universe lemons came from. But then Mr. Onter swiveled to face him.

"Look Conrad, it's like I've been saying. People get stuck, doing what they think they should. Sure, she's the mother, but she's just a person. Nobody ever told her how to do it, not really. And I'll tell you what, it's terrifying, the idea that you'll screw it up and then you won't be able to take it back *ever*. Just look at me, I can't take anything back!"

Mr. Onter stopped to breathe until he could speak calmly again.

"What I'm trying to say is, if you dig yourself in, acting all put upon, that leaves *her* stuck in the mom role. It doesn't always have to be that way."

"I understand what you mean I guess," said Conrad, scrambled now, "but I don't understand how it would be, what *you* mean, I mean..."

"That's all right, just keep it in your head. You'll figure it out sooner or later."

○ ○ ○

Finals were only beginning but already the campus felt like an emptying place, where thoughts were turned out toward the brightening sun with less concern for other people's business. This mood had lately taken Conrad drifting through the hallways. After feeling like a ghost for so long he was actually going to be one. In fact he had become *more* visible since the jaw-breaking incident: passing kids glanced at him, maybe nodding or saying 'hey.' Conrad had no illusions about the so-called fight but he basked anyway. It was a fitting end: the valiant giant-slayer, fading over the horizon.

*But what if I stay?*

The thought ran up his blood pressure like a panic. A feeling was there, but not its meaning. It was the future — he couldn't know what it meant. Staying would be losing and gaining, and going would be gaining and losing.

Conrad stopped to peek at Mr. Sebastien hunched over a pile of papers in his office. The teacher looked up.

"Well if it isn't Conrad. Join me for a minute?"

Conrad slid into the hot seat, now just cool vinyl. Mr. Sebastien believed in 'work, not finals,' so there was nothing left for Conrad to worry about here anyway.

"I know it's been a while, but I never got a chance to personally congratulate you on your project," said the teacher.

"Thanks. I actually did spend a long time on it."

"Oh surely you did. I can tell you know. On that note, I wanted to say you've qualified to be in my specialty class next year, an alternative to tenth-grade history, on just one subject, a deep dive if you will. Interested?"

"Yeah, that sounds great," said Conrad. There was no point in saying he might not be there at all.

"Good, well then I'll put you on the list. And also if I may, let me suggest the speech elective? On paper your presentation was good, but you hardly took a breath. You can say all the words without people hearing, if you know what I mean. Give it a thought, will you?"

"I will. Thanks!"

Conrad saluted as he left and swelled with pride. He had succeeded in history while so many others had sizzled as they died. He bounced down the back stairs, but then he stopped half-way. Anise was stomping her way up toward him, her face flushed with apparent anger. But then she also stopped and looked up.

"Oh! Um, hi Conrad."

"Hi."

Anise didn't move. Her eyes searched the steps in front of her. "I, uh." She paused, then looked at Conrad. "I wanted to tell you..." She stepped up into the stairwell light. Now everything she had ever been to him was there again, and he could only listen. "I wanted to say," she said, "I really like your paintings. And uh, yeah..." She nodded and looked away.

"Thanks," Conrad said. Anise glanced once more at his face and scooted past.

The school gallery had spotlights like in a real museum, and pedestals for the sculptures. Conrad walked the perimeter. Most of the art was laughable, but here and there something stood out. He especially liked the triptych by his classmate Gabby. In the first panel a strong wind bent trees and fluttered people's clothes as they struggled to take refuge in buildings which also appeared to sway. The second panel showed a suited man impaled on a giant spike, his blood pooling around its base. The third showed a woman's breast in closeup detail, complete with nipple bumps. Conrad didn't know what it was all about, but the pictures were elegantly drawn and forced his eyes to stutter from one to the other as if most of the story was missing between them. He had never once spoken to Gabby, though she had sat across from him the entire year.

Now Conrad arrived at his own paintings. This was his fifth visit that week, but again he couldn't help fussing: the spotlights reflected on the oil surfaces, and there were unintentional lumps in the paint, and the splotchy sides of the canvases weren't covered. But he tried to put all that aside, in the hope that for at least one blissfully unwrapped moment he could experience his pictures as someone other than himself.

It didn't work. He was himself, so he grabbed his backpack and left for the bus stop.

14

# Early June

Shhhhhhhhhhhhithead.

That was all the jet engines had to offer this time, no summer wind and water, only an unceasing accusation in Conrad's ears without the relief of window views from where he and his sisters sat fussing in the worst possible middle seats. The girls had bickered since before the flight but now they were bored even with that. Stranger still, Beth was fidgeting. Conrad watched her: yes, today she was definitely taller, and less calm.

Sueanna hadn't been calm either, in sending them off — not like the other years. This time she had shown up unannounced in doorways, repeating how lonely the house would be all summer without her kids. Instead of bouncing around gleefully as they packed, the kids had gone cautious — and it stuck.

"What should we do this summer?" asked Levy, moping rather than excited.

"I don't know," said Conrad, "but it has to be big, like something we'll always remember."

Beth sat up. "OK then, how about we make an underwater house?"

"Yeah," said Levy, "way out at the bottommost bottom, and we'll make a submarine to go down there."

"We'll have lots of fishy friends."

Conrad shook his head. "No, I mean something real."

"You're bonkers," Levy said. "It's all just fooling around, you know that."

Beth wasn't giving up. "I saw on TV they put a plastic dome thing underwater, and connected it to the air with a tube! That's not impossible, is it?"

"Where are we supposed to get a dome?" Levy asked.

"I don't know..."

Conrad would normally have loads of ideas for a dome but today he could not summon a single one. Sueanna had been tearful at the airport. He could still feel the impression of her shirt sleeves around him, her short breaths in his ears.

Minutes passed. Levy squirmed again.

"There's a whole summer course at the stables and we're missing it."

"There's a horse place near dad's," said Beth. "Maybe he'll take us there."

"Yeah right."

Now Anise rode across Conrad's thoughts. Though he'd never actually seen for himself, Beth had described it: Anise's perfect cantering form, her antique riding clothes, her fancy leather saddle — all on a well-kept, well-bred, shiny spotted chestnut mare. He had no doubt it was a beautiful sight, the long manes of horse and rider both flowing in elegant curves. Anise was a rich girl, with a horse and a fantasy house and a maid driving her around in James Bond's leftover Mercedes, but he couldn't hold any of it against her because now he knew her, a little bit anyway, and she was just a person, one he liked. It was worse than never knowing her in the first place, that she had shown a part of herself then turned away. But he couldn't complain that he hadn't seen more, because he had revealed so little of himself. Of course he'd imagined saying more later on, when he was absolutely perfectly one-hundred-percent sure that she liked him for real, but now the plane had taken off and all the possibility tubes were pinched shut and it was so obviously stupid that he had said and done so little.

"I can't wait to jump in the lake," he mumbled.

"Oh yeah... yeah, yeah..." Beth breathed out her words as if gazing toward heaven.

"Oh my god," Levy groaned. "That's going to feel so good."

Now the plane was landing and their gloom lifted.

Henry was waiting at the gate, big and awkward, the lights reflecting off his glasses and obscuring his eyes. "There you are!" he called out when he saw his kids.

It was always a shock to Conrad when his father took physical form again, like an oversize character loose from a dream. Now once again the real Henry had big rough hands, and a bit too much fat around the middle that his tucked-in business shirt struggled to compress. And the real Henry's voice boomed too loud — the voice, the body, the arms, the hands: every gesture larger than Conrad had ever been comfortable with. And yet, it was Dad.

"Hi Dad!"

"Hello city kids! Ready to be country kids again?"

"Yeah!"

They retrieved their bags and pulled them out to the old sedan, freshly washed for the occasion.

"You kids hungry?"

Beth snapped back to form. "They fed us on the plane," she reported, "so we won't be hungry till we get to the truck stop. We're stopping at the truck stop, right?"

Conrad nodded along, though his stomach was growling.

Henry was skeptical. "It'll be the middle of the night when we pass through there."

"That's OK, we always go there!" Beth insisted.

"Yeah!" said Levy. "We have to. Anyway they serve twenty-four hours. Conrad wants a hot dog, right?"

Conrad nodded again. He sure did.

As if propelled by months of yearning, the kids were finally shooting toward summer, asphalt and plastic giving way to rolling farms. They drank it all in with faces close to the windows, re-memorizing all the passing places they had memorized the last time. Levy and Beth played by announcing what would appear next then disagreeing until reality appeared to settle the matter.

Conrad only stared, feeling clearly this time that these were more than window images — these were places real people lived. He knew what living at his dad's was, and in Los Angeles, but he found it mystifying that people also lived in these middle places passing one after the other. They were middle for him anyway.

The light outside gradually dimmed, and the landscape hadn't appreciably changed in a while — the trees wouldn't come on thicker until after the truck stop — so the kids began to drift off. Soon they were curled up on the seats. When their father shook them, the sky was deep black and a row of parked eighteen-wheelers towered over the car. Other kids less used to travel might wake bewildered to this, but these kids only sat up and trudged bleary-eyed inside.

An old waitress they remembered took their orders while the kids sucked on ice cubes to perk themselves up.

"Don't much like these roads at night," said Henry. "Not many lights, then these big trucks fly by. The worst are those long straight stretches."

"Why's that?" Conrad asked.

"Because there's nothing to do, just drive straight. Pretty soon you're asleep, then *wham* you're dead. You hear about it all the time. People need change to stay awake."

The food arrived, dwarfed by heaps of french fries. Conrad's hot dog was just as he remembered: red and wrinkled and double-sliced lengthwise, in a bun that had been grease-fried on the griddle. He squeezed mustard into the cracks and took his first bite with a show of religious fervor. He remembered being very small, waiting in the back seat for this hot dog with the pure desperation that only children can feel, looking to the silhouette of his mother in the front cooing *we'll be there soon honey*.

Henry paid and they piled back into the car. For the last stretch nobody would sleep. The road was unlit now, but there was just enough sky light to shape the treetops. The kids picked out a landmark here and there and peered up to the stars. Then the forest came on thick and closer to the road. As he stared out the window, Conrad only barely joined the quiet chatting in the dim interior of the car — the school year, the horses, their dad's old stories. They were far from everything now. A bigfoot might appear at the edge of the woods, or a U.F.O. might dart overhead. And the next morning's light would start the clock on the first of three more summers.

The car slowed, then turned off the highway onto a narrow road that wound through the dark woods in long arcs, flashing the oncoming trees with its headlights. The kids went quiet. They watched through the front windshield as the car turned up the long gravel driveway and illuminated the approaching house. The engine stopped, and Conrad stepped out into the still night and breathed in the damp earthy leafy air and was home again.

○ ○ ○

A summer bird sang high outside, repeating its two-note song, both a whistle and a sigh. Conrad pushed aside the covers and rolled out into his shorts, then crept out from his closet-room into the beams of sunlight streaming through the windows to see how joyfully little the house had changed. On his bare feet he padded softly out the back, down the old stone steps and out to the very end of the dock. There he squatted with his toes curled over the edge, looking first down into the clear greenish water where little fish hovered by the piles, then out to survey the shoreline all round in a big circle. The lake's surface glittered in the slanted morning sun. A breeze sent promising shivers up his back. He took a deep breath to pull it all in, then jumped up and ran.

He would make the rounds before anyone noticed. Pine needles and sticks crinkled under his city-softened feet as he skirted the sides of the house to visit each of its window wells, where all manner of toads, frogs and salamanders tended to fall in and become trapped — then dry up into sad dead husks. Being saved by Conrad meant immediate freedom for all except toads, which had to endure a brief incarceration due to being loved more. He was fifteen now, but it had always been his job to save them. He couldn't just stop, could he? In any case there were none today. He dashed to the other regular spots: the boards behind the shed, the log pile, the flat rock under the gutter drain... no luck. But it was early in the season, they would come. He snuck back into the house.

It was like any summer morning from any year: dust-motes floating in the window light, a bowl of cereal, and the little black-and-white TV showing 'Land Of The Lost.' Today's episode was the one where Holly gets stuck in a pylon that skips all over the universe. When it opens to a park on Earth she doesn't get out because that would mean leaving her brother and dad behind.

"You're still watching that show?"

It was Levy, emerging squinty-eyed from the girls' room. Conrad only nodded and slurped another spoonful. Then Beth came out and saw the screen. "Oh god," she groaned and followed Levy to the kitchen. From the sounds Conrad pictured their actions: bowls clunking onto the table, corn flakes hitting the bowls, pauses between flakes for sugar to be layered on before more flakes, then milk, then more sprinkling to replace the sugar washed off by the milk. It was a very complicated process. Then the show went to commercial and a familiar tune began to play.

"It's on! It's on!" Conrad called. The girls raced back and stood side-by-side next to the TV: their longtime routine for this ad, in which a local Chevrolet dealer had his two daughters stand next to him in fluffy dresses while he waved his arms about all the great deals. But today his daughters were no longer cute toddlers, more like middle-schoolers, and had become detectably uncomfortable in their roles. Levy and Beth mocked them by staring drooly into space.

Henry came out wearing the long pajamas he only wore when his kids were around. "It's not nice to make fun of those poor girls," he said.

"I can't believe he's still making them do that!" said Levy.

Henry shook his head as he headed to the kitchen. "Nobody can tell that guy anything."

The kids took seats around the kitchen table with their father. It was too early in the summer to just run off into the woods and leave him.

"Can you makc dog stew tonight?" said Beth.

"What, already? You kids really want the same stuff?"

"Yeah!"

"I don't have the meat."

"Aw!"

"I'll be going up to town tomorrow though." Henry sat up into a more official posture and faced Conrad. "Speaking of tomorrow, I'll take you down to the Alder House to meet the owner."

"Already?"

"Yes sir, summer's here and that means tourists. They need you trained right away."

"Oh OK." Conrad nodded to make his dad happy. But this *thing*, this not-the-same-summer mystery occupation just ahead, made him want to run.


Conrad peeked out from the wall then turned back to whisper at Beth and Levy crouching behind him.

"You two cause a distraction and I'll jump from the side."

Beth stood up and screeched. "Why did you pull my hair?!"

"I did no such thing!" Levy yelled, her face extra mad. They tussled.

Conrad had already crawled fast to the left. Now he made a desperate dash from an angle and leapt through The Gate onto his face.

"I saw you pull it you brat!" said Beth, still in character.

Conrad got up and poked the correct sequence of numbers into the birch-bark. "It won't hold for long!" he yelled. The girls dropped their act and sprinted through to glide behind him up the trail, remembering every root and turn of the path, feet grabbing at the dirt, flying and howling through the trees to welcome themselves back.

"Right! Go right!" Beth called from the rear.

Conrad veered at a fork, along a crest that began at the tip of a long trough descending below them. It was dimmer down in there, and murky. They called it The Valley Of Shadows, and having named it such they rarely visited, but today they had an errand. Soon they dropped down a deer trail through close grabbing branches into a sunken clearing. In the middle was a circle of seeping black mud: Abigail's Pit. Their first time here, Conrad had told the story of the little girl named Abigail who once lived nearby, whose doll had vanished from her house. Abigail cried to her mother all day, and cried into the night from her bed, but then, through her window, a faint mechanical voice called from the woods. 'Mommy!' it said. 'Mommy!' Abigail snuck out and followed the sound along moon-lit deer paths to this very place. And there in the middle, sitting up and looking back at her, was her doll. 'Mommy!' it said again, and when Abigail walked into the mud to retrieve it a hundred bony hands pulled her down.

"We got you a present from L.A.!" Beth yelled at the mud. She turned to Conrad and whispered, "get a stick." Conrad found a long stick with a fork at the end while Beth reached into his bag to pull out the thrift-store doll she had found while Halloween shopping with Sueanna. Conrad balanced the doll on the fork and extended it out onto the mud, right to the middle. But instead of sinking it sat unclaimed on the surface.

"She'll never reach it up there," Levy whispered.

Conrad used the stick to push the doll down. Mud squished around its plastic body until it was completely under. The kids stood quietly in observance, but then Levy croaked "Mommy!" and shivers went up their backs and Beth screamed and they all ran laughing back up the hill.

That was enough to fuel another sprint, along a roller-coastery path through abundant ferns, an area they considered prehistoric. This dropped thrillingly down into Bigfoot Alley, but they didn't stop here nor at The Church and instead pushed faster toward The Belly, a round outcropping with excellent views of the lake. It was a perfect spot, far from any house and having a treacherous approach from the water, making it less likely that locals would show up in their boats. Conrad ran straight to the shoreline, dropped to his knees and sunk his face into the water. His sisters did the same. Then they rolled back onto the pine needles and breathed. After listening to the leaves above their wet faces and just knowing that nobody should speak, they sat up and pulled their lunches from Conrad's backpack: liverwurst and mayonnaise on white bread, and Nutter Butter cookies.

"These are too new," said Levy when she got to her cookies. The others nodded. The cookies were perfectly dry and crunchy, but the kids liked them better when the package had sat open on top of the fridge for a few days, after the summer humidity had made the cookies good and soft.

Beth stood up and screamed into the woods. "Levy's cookies are too hard!" Nothing happened, so Beth sat back down. "Sorry sis," she said and shrugged.

"I can't believe we haven't gone swimming yet," Levy groaned. "We could have jumped right in this morning."

"It's more fun to wait and get all sticky first," said Conrad.

Levy sat up with big-idea eyes. "We're sticky now! Let's swim back!"

"Are you kidding? It's too far. We'll either drown or get run over by a boat."

"Not if we stick close to shore."

She was right. In fact they weren't wearing shoes, and all they had on were t-shirts and shorts with empty pockets. Conrad climbed a tree and tied his backpack to a branch. Then they walked a little ways down the shore to a little hidden beach where they could tiptoe into the lake.

"Agh! It's so cold!" Levy yelled. But they flopped in anyway. The bright sunlight didn't make the early-summer water any warmer but promised an easy escape. They frog-swam near the shoreline where it was just deep enough not to touch bottom, only going out farther to make their way around the numerous fallen trees. They knew better than to try going over or under any of these. But when they came to the bay that marked the halfway point, they had been in the water for a long while and Conrad could see that Beth was tiring.

"Oh no," he murmured.

"What?" said Beth.

"I saw a fin."

"A fin?"

"I think we should get out."

When girls turned toward shore, Conrad dipped below the surface and dove under Beth to draw the edge of his hand along her ankle. Right away her legs thrashed, but Conrad was already shooting back an innocent distance behind her.

"What's wrong?" he called. Beth was splashing toward the beach.

"There it is Levy!" she screamed and pointed at him. "The Boob Shark!"

When they reached the shore they didn't stop even to drip and took off running up the trail with gleeful hoots, sailing through The Gate and down to the dock where they jumped right back into the water.

They spent the afternoon in and out of the lake, lying stretched-out on the bare wood of the dock between times to re-experience the sun and wind drying their shivering bodies. The sunlight glancing off the water made them squint as they stared out to distant shorelines, and flashed though their eyelids as they napped. But this was only the first day, too early to fully relax. Like every year when they arrived, they felt a deep-rooted ache for this place like the clench before tears.

When the sunlight was slanting from the other direction, and the beaded water on their skin didn't immediately evaporate, and they were cold, the kids were forced to admit that it was time to get up from the dock and go to dinner. They ran into the house to put on clothes that would block as many mosquitoes as possible, then came back out to sit damp-haired at the picnic table by their dad. Burgers were already sizzling on the grill and the orange glow of the coals showed how much the day had faded.

"These are gunna be good!" Henry said with his familiar, half-

serious show of boasting. "I always make the best burgers, don't
I!"

"Yeah!" the girls cheered. But Conrad wondered if they meant
it. He distinctly remembered their *oohs* and *ahhs* at Dilettante
Burger on Pico Boulevard, the only place Sueanna had ever taken
them for hamburgers — let alone spoken the word — for its
impressive variety of spiced patties and artful garnishes.

Their dad's burgers on the other hand were elegant in their
simplicity: hamburger patty, sliced onion, sliced tomato, ketchup,
bun. But the meat was overcooked and flavorless, and the tomato
was under-ripe, and the onions were raw, and the bun was plain
and dry.

"Pass the ketchup," Conrad grunted. Levy handed it across the
table, then yanked back her arm to smack a mosquito on her
neck. Conrad smacked out a liberal coating of ketchup and put
the bun back on.

"Pretty darn good, huh?" said Henry.

"Mmm hmmm!"

Henry really wanted them to enjoy it, and they were hungry,
so they did. Meanwhile Conrad watched his dad. There were
creases on Henry's neck he didn't recognize, and a mole below his
ear. They had to have always been there, right? But those were just
the beginning. Henry was mostly strange details, it seemed now,
with extra fat under hairy skin that never tanned. It made Conrad
uneasy to see this stranger stirring the coals, and while he could
hardly imagine the place without all the things they did there
together, who was this man really?

"Dad? What do you do when we're not here?"

Henry looked sideways at Conrad. "Oh, well you know I work
a lot," he said, facing back to the lake, "so I have my favorite shows
and go to bed, but I have some buddies I hang around with, you
know, they come here or I go there to watch the games, and I go
to play cards at Babs' place on Thursdays. And you know I'm
always tinkering."

"Oh."

Now Henry was Dad again, and it was the kind of answer

Conrad was expecting, but something was still missing. Maybe Henry was a spy for the Russians, too.

A lazy evening followed, of *Bonanza* reruns and the local news on the little TV and everyone lying on the floor or the couch. Then the girls went to the porch and snuggled under blankets with their books. They had packed an extra supply of paperbacks this time, mostly about animals. For the summer's first read, Beth chose *Where The Red Fern Grows* ('A story of two dogs and a boy'), while Levy picked *Animal Farm.* Conrad knew that one from eighth grade and he was sure that Levy had only chosen it for the title, but he decided to keep quiet and see what she said.

Henry fell asleep on the sofa watching the late show, so Conrad went down to the basement. He had taken one canvas with him on the plane, exactly as large as his suitcase. This he screwed into his old homemade easel, then he sat under the yellow basement light staring at the little canvas bumps. He didn't need the memory of a forest this time — the forest was right outside. And he certainly didn't need the memory of Los Angeles. Nothing came to him, so he gave up and carried his fishing gear down to the dock.

His tackle box stank when he opened it, but all of his lures were still in their slots. After clipping on his trusty spinner-bait he switched off his flashlight, cast out over the water and reeled. He could barely see but his arms remembered the motions and his lungs remembered the cool night air. As the lake began to resolve in his vision, he thought of the dark room, and just like then he couldn't clear his head. He cast and reeled some more, and made his breathing quiet so he could listen to the hushing breeze. But then he thought of Joey and Stacy, and Anise too. Anything else he would swat from his mind, but not them. A new thought came to him: that he wanted them to be there, to run through the woods with him and leap into the lake, and the fact that they never had, and probably never would, meant that they didn't know him at all.

○ ○ ○

Morning light warmed the lake, but Henry's car pointed away from it with Conrad strapped in the passenger seat. A ways down the highway Conrad saw something new, a little round building between the trees and the road, like a pimple where before there had been nothing for miles. A sign said 'Photo Hut' and under it 'Don't Forget Your Pictures!' in red letters.

"What's that thing doing there?" Conrad asked.

"Oh that's a story. You know that photo place in town? Well, there's lots of resorts between here and there, but home is south for most tourists. So they'd go up to drop off their film then forget all about it when they drove home, and the photo shop kept developing pictures and not getting paid. So what they did was, they stuck that hut there, and gave people the option to pick up their pictures on the way out of town."

"Did it work?"

Henry shrugged. "Jury's still out. But people here'll try anything these days."

"I don't get why the tourists don't just take their film back where they came from and have it developed there."

"Most do I guess, but there's always somebody who wants to see if he got the money shot. Anyway funny thing is, I heard the hut's already selling tons of film to people on their way in."

"Huh."

Henry slowed and turned at a sign saying 'Alder House' in Old German letters. A narrow forest road dead-ended at a rectangular building with a log cabin facade and views to a lake. Henry drove behind and parked by the dumpsters where a dirty back door led into the office.

"Roy! This is my son Conrad!" said Henry with the big-chested cadence of a Norse chieftain announcing his progeny.

Roy was an older man with trim gray hair, but he crushed Conrad's hand and peered as he shook. "Good to meet you, Conrad" he said, but turned back to Henry. "We'll have him trained in no time. Actually we're short, so you can just leave him here now."

"Hear that Conrad? They need you already!"

Roy walked Henry out. "You can pick him up after the lunch shift, say, three. I'll let you know his schedule when it all shakes out."

"I can't get back here till after five, so he'll just have to hang around I guess." Henry turned back toward Conrad. "Got that?" Conrad nodded. "Don't worry," Henry added as he left. "There's food here. You won't starve."

Roy led Conrad to a closet for a smock and then into the kitchen. None of the walls were visible in the place, packed as it was with grimy aluminum equipment and storage shelves loaded to the ceiling.

"This here's Conrad," said Roy as the two cooks stepped over to look him over. "This is John." Roy motioned to the head cook. "He's not very nice. Just letting you know now."

"Oh thanks a lot boss." John gave Conrad's hand a warm shake. John was chubby and wise-eyed.

"And this here's J.J. He's nice." Conrad shook the other hand, attached to a wiry, pock-marked little man with an expression somewhere between surly and facetious. Then Roy led Conrad to the back. "This is Glenda. She's the nicest of them all."

Glenda didn't shake Conrad's hand, however being a woman had nothing to do with it. There stood a figure that caused words from horror tales to speak themselves in his mind, words like *vile*, *ghastly*, and *hideous*. It wasn't that she was old and wrinkled — her wrinkles might have been endearing, except they were all in the wrong places.

"What's crackin' Conrad?" Glenda said, cigarette bouncing in her lips. Conrad had no words now. "Don't worry," she said. "Glenda'll take care-a-ya!" This wasn't comforting, coming from someone who looked like she had spent her entire life doing one terrible thing after another and taking smoke breaks in between.

"I think he's remembering something," said J.J. "You've seen the Wizard Of Oz, right?" Conrad nodded. J.J. pointed at Glenda. "She used to be the good witch. See the resemblance?"

"Aw yeah you go on," Glenda threatened with her chin out. "I'll drop a house on your ass." J.J. scuffled back into the cook station snickering.

Roy motioned at the cigarette. "I've told you not to do that in here, Glenda. People will taste it in the food."

A mumble came from the grills. "Wouldn't want the fish to smell like Glenda would we."

"Aw shit," Glenda grumbled. She dropped the butt into a sink and Roy left them to it. Glenda motioned for Conrad to follow her.

"So this is how it works," she said. "The bus-boys bring in the dishes, to your side, and you pound the food off 'em through that rubber hole there, and spray 'em, and then you load 'em up! Then they go in the machine. Wait till it shuts off and the light turns green, and I've pulled out the cleans, then you just slide in the dirties and shut the door and push this button."

Conrad had been nodding through all this. "So I'm washing dishes?" he asked.

"Bwa ha ha ha!" Glenda laughed and coughed.

"Well nobody said."

Glenda laugh-wheezed some more. "That's right kid. You don't get to hang around with the tight-titties out there till you've done your time with Glenda. But don't you worry. Glenda'll take care-a-ya."

As the lunch shift heated up Conrad grew more curious about who the 'tight-titties' might be. Luckily the bus-boys didn't come at lunchtime so it was up to the waitstaff to bring in the dishes. It would have been simple enough to have Conrad go out on the floor and cart them back, but he wasn't in uniform and Roy was strict about appearances. Today there were two waitresses, older teens, seniors maybe: sweet to the customers (Conrad peeked at them through the door) but robotic otherwise. One of the girls burst in and dropped a tub of 'dirties' next to Conrad.

"Who's this?" she yelled to the cooks, though Conrad was a foot away.

"That's Conrad," said Glenda. "Ain't he sweet?"

"I've never seen you," the girl said to Conrad.

"I used to live here."

"Oh yeah? Where do you live now?"

"Los Angeles." At this she stared at him. "Planning to stay here though," he added.

"You could be in Los Angeles, and you came here?" Conrad nodded. She pointed her thumb at him but looked back to the cooks. "Something wrong with him?" John shrugged. "Fucking shit," she spat and hurried back out.

John noticed Conrad standing out of sorts. "That was Jenny," he said. "She's even nicer than Glenda."

The job was easy enough, if gross. But at the height of lunch the tubs came faster.

"Hurry it up!" Glenda barked. Conrad was attempting to spray every speck of food off the dishes before putting them in the trays. Glenda shoved him aside. "Look I'll show ya." She grabbed a mashed-potato-encrusted dish and slammed it onto the rubber hole, then quick-blasted it with the sprayer, leaving a still-dirty dish, then banged it into the tray. She pointed at the machine. "There's a reason for that you know!" Then she went back to her place. She continued to pressure him as the tubs accumulated. "Just wait till dinner," she grumbled. "This is nuthin', you'll see."

For Glenda's part, she racked up the 'cleans' with impressive force, stacking them back on the shelves without a care for noise. The entire kitchen was like that, less like the studio of persnickety gourmands that Conrad had imagined and more like the World War One gunnery teams he'd read about in class. Pots and pans and cooler doors slammed, the washing machine convulsed, the cooks yelled 'order up!' like a canon was set to go off, and everyone cursed, all in close quarters with Top 40 radio eating up any remaining calm. It surprised Conrad at first that he knew all the songs, but then he remembered that Top 40 came from Los Angeles in the first place.

After learning how to punch out, Conrad had two hours to spare, so he sat out by the bar watching the servers reset the tables for dinner. It was probable their titties were indeed tight, but he couldn't see much as they were covered by German-patterned aprons, inauthentically high at the bodice. For their part the girls didn't speak a word, then bolted and left him alone. Apparently the cooks never went home — they were still in the cooler rearranging trays of food.

Conrad walked out to the parking lot and noticed a little sign saying 'Nature Trail.' He followed where it pointed, to an asphalt-covered path along the side of the lake. At its end, only twenty yards or so, was a picnic table by the water where lily-pads floated at the edge of a middling view. The lake was small and murky, and thick with underwater weeds that were good for fishing but creepy for swimming. Under the lily pads Conrad spied cigarette butts decorating the bottom.

○ ○ ○

Henry leaned over when Conrad let himself into the car.

"So how was your first day at work?"

"Good."

"Teaching you the ropes?"

"Yeah."

"Well you just learn everything you can, OK? The sooner you do, the sooner they'll promote you."

"OK."

They passed the photo hut again. Conrad wished he owned a bazooka.

By the time the car came to a stop in the driveway Conrad was wound up for action.

"Don't run off now," said Henry. "We're goin' to Babs in half an hour. Go take a shower."

"Oh man! I was going fishing."

"Don't worry, there's plenty of summer left."

Babs had once lived in a house just down the road, always like an aunt to the family, but now she lived on another lake in a

much larger house left by her third husband when he died. *Goin'
to Babs* was a big to-do for his sisters, but Conrad was ambivalent.
Of course there was fun to be had around her property, but he
had plenty to do around his dad's thank you very much, and Babs
would force him to talk.

Babs paid every year to have her deep-black driveway sealed
against ice, so it came on smooth as silk when the car turned in.
The house itself was a glorified cabin, every interlocking log
lacquered to a shine inside and out. A strip of green lawn
surrounded the place like a moat, set apart from the surrounding
woods with large white stones, and a French flag greeted visitors
above the entrance (next to an American one to appease the
patriotic) because Babs was French and never let you forget it.
Her real name was Babette Latrue, and though she was only
French by blood she emphasized her Frenchness throughout the
interior by way of imported nick-knacks and yet another flag over
the mantle.

As usual the table was being laid out, but Babs knew what the
kids wanted first.

"Bonjour, mes poussins!" she chirped in her highest social
voice as the girls hugged her. "Would you like some croissants?"

"Yeah!" Beth and Levy cheered and ran to the trays of what
were actually freezer-section rolls with imitation butter flavor.
Every visit, Henry scolded them for eating too many, but that was
the drill so Conrad rushed to grab his share.

Babs herself was the same: big and frilly like a man in drag. The
only difference between this year and the last was that Conrad
had seen Monty Python.

"You kids go fool around," she said. "Your dad and I need a
cocktail."

"Damn straight," said Henry. Ice was already plinking into
tumblers.

The kids ran down to copper-colored Lake Bean. They rarely
liked another lake as much as their own, and this lake was no
exception. It just seemed scraggly, and there were too many
houses crowded close, one dock after another. But Babs had lots

of grandchildren, so entertainments were scattered all over the
property, among them pedal-boats, a pontoon raft anchored a
ways from the dock, a metal lazy-swing on the shore, and a thick
rope hanging from a tree-branch over the lake. This last had a
board at the end, for swinging or leaping into the water. A pole
with a hook was used to pull the swing back to shore and also to
retrieve any squealers who didn't want to get wet. This was
enough to keep the kids busy until it was time to eat.

"I've got all your favorites!" said Babs when they had tramped
back in around the table. "And look Henry, your Stroganoff's
here too."

Stroganoff was something their mother used to make: egg
noodles, canned mushroom soup and ground beef baked as a
casserole — long before she graduated to the level of Figs In
Savory Sauce — but Conrad didn't bring that up. Also on the
table was a tray of 'lunchmeat' and cheese slices for sandwiches, a
plate of deviled eggs covered in paprika, another incoherent
casserole, green jello with suspended cherry slices, and a bowl of
potato chips. Conrad scanned the table in vain for chip dip.

Whatever Babs and Henry were drinking, it wasn't the first.

"Henry tells me you're thinking about staying here," said Babs
to Conrad.

"Mmm-hmm."

"Why's that?"

Conrad said the first thing that came to mind. "I just don't
like the city. I feel like I belong in the wilderness."

Babs nearly choked on her drink and sat back laughing until
tears came to her eyes. "Wait, is he serious?" she asked Henry.

"Be nice, Babs," Henry murmured.

"But it's funny. I'll tell you what Conrad, this is a *small town*
you're in. If it were really the wilderness you'd be having quite a,
hee hee, a different experience." She tried to take another sip of
her drink but succumbed to hysterical fits. "Wilderness, ha ha
ha!" She noticed Henry's face and sat taller. "Well it's not like half
this place wasn't logged a hundred years ago!"

"Just be nice."

"OK, fine." She let her guffaws subside. "How about you girls, what have you been doing this year?"

Levy kept quiet, having learned from Conrad's example, but Beth did her job.

"Levy and I were both in the top ten percent in our school, all A's and B's. And we've been learning how to ride horses and take care of them, and I'm still dancing, level five now."

Conrad noted Beth's diplomacy, using grades as a firewall.

"Oh, top ten, good!" Babs said. "So you really are serious about dancing then. That's nice. You've been doing it since before you were born I remember. Ha!"

The kids went still at this reference to Sueanna, but Henry laughed along. "Ooh!" he said, making his eyes suddenly shocked and holding his belly. "That's just what you were like," he said to Beth.

"Aw dad!"

Babs turned back to Conrad. "How about you? You still want to be an artist?"

Conrad nodded, sure that more derision would follow.

Henry leaned toward Babs. "I'm hoping a little taste of the real world will cure him," he said, smiling for laughs.

Babs only shrugged. "How's he any different from you?"

"What do you mean?"

"Oh I've seen you. Like I saw that canoe-motor-mount contraption you made. You ever seen one of those before?"

"But that's useful. Maybe I could even patent it and sell it."

"Sure sure, at the *end* of the story. But what do you think started the whole thing?"

Henry elbowed Beth. "Your dad's really smart, that's what."

"No no," said Babs. "What I'm saying is, you've got that habit. Anybody else would've thought, *stick a motor on a canoe? You're crazy!* or poked around a store for something factory-made and given up day one. But you were tossing in your sleep trying to figure it out, right? And the next morning you were down in your basement half-finished already. You told me all about it you know. So proud."

Henry jiggled his ice in the air as if to suggest Babs was running at the mouth. "You know how hard it is Babs. He has to learn something people will pay for."

She waved. "Oh that's just short-sighted. You're not hearing me. You take some kid who doesn't have that habit and you put him through business school and diddly-squat comes out the other end. The ones with the habit make the money."

"Oh there's lots of ways to make money. You just gotta work."

"Yeah sure, go do what everyone else does, you're just working for somebody else, I don't care what you call it. I've seen it my whole life. Just look at these yahoos around here wanting to open fast food chains right in the middle of our cute little town. Those people don't know art, I'll tell you that much."

Henry was shaking his head. "I don't like it either, Babs, but people have to make a living somehow."

"Sure but it's aiming so low. Oh! Speaking of art, when I was in Paris this winter..."

"Here we go," Henry mumbled.

"...I saw a whole room of Monet haystacks. You would have loved it Conrad! In books they're so soft but in person, well, I'll never be the same woman. Eat your vegetables, Levy." Babs pointed at the other casserole dish, then looked down to twizzle her drink. "I think I need a topper-upper. Oh and I have surprises for you kids!" She stood up and waddled to the other room, returning with a cardboard box.

"That swimsuit store in town went out of business already and I got these for cheap." She handed a small pile of swimsuits to the girls. "Maybe they'll fit you, I don't know. Whatever you don't like just give back. There's kids I know whose folks couldn't afford winter coats this year. And for you Conrad — now don't think it's not fair, girls, I'm only lending it to him — my oldest sent this but it's too fancy for me." She handed Conrad a brand-new Canon AE-1. "It has so many knobs and dials. I tried reading the manual but it's like rocket science. Maybe you can make sense of it and teach me some time?"

"Sure, thanks!" Conrad turned the precious object around in

his hands. He had drooled over ads for this in magazines despite having zero interest in photography.

"Don't have any film though," Babs added. "You'll need to go buy some."

○ ○ ○

It was ten-thirty a.m. but Henry found his son down on the dock.

"Do you know what time it is Conrad?" he called.

"Dad I saw three smallmouths swim by! They were huge!"

"I said do you know what time it is?"

Conrad dashed up into the house and slipped on his work clothes (pants instead of shorts, shoes instead of none). He was soon in the car, but Henry wasn't happy.

"I have to leave work to pick you up so when it's time to go you be standing there got me?"

"OK."

Henry started up the car and turned out onto the road. He drove for a while but he wasn't finished.

"You promise to be somewhere on time, it's your word."

Conrad nodded. They turned onto the highway.

"In the real world you show up late enough times, they don't put up with that, you're out the door, got it?"

"Uh-huh."

"Uh-huh is all you can say? Did you know I fired a guy for doing that? Showed up late all the time, full of excuses. I don't stand for that, neither does anybody else."

"OK I get it."

"You better get it. And I don't need that attitude either. I swear I worry what you're learning out there. Or not."

"I'm sorry. I'll be on time." The photo hut came up ahead. "Hey can we get some film?"

Henry pulled over and dug out his wallet. "I'll pay this time, but next time it comes out of your wages, understand me? You *work* for your spending money now."

Conrad took the cash and his bag to the window. It was dark inside the hut, but when his eyes adjusted they saw something exceptional: a panther turning in its cage, in the form of a girl. She came to the window and peeked out sideways.

"You're with Henry's Electric?"

"I'm his son."

She looked hard at him. "Why haven't I seen you then?"

"I moved away." He didn't add any more about Los Angeles. Now he looked at her more directly, but this was a mistake. Her beauty immobilized him.

"You just going to stand there? Or maybe you're going to say it, too?"

"Say what?"

"The big joke. Ha ha, so funny, I laugh, you laugh." She wasn't laughing.

"Uh, I don't know what you mean. I just need film."

"Sure you do. What kind?"

"I don't know. It's for this." He pulled the AE-1 from his bag and laid it on the counter.

"Jesus. You have one of these and you don't know what film?"

"I'm just borrowing it."

"OK, well, you need thirty-five millimeter. You want one-hundred or four-hundred?"

"What's that?"

"ISO. It means how sensitive. One-hundred for daylight, four-hundred for less light. Higher number's more sensitive. It's like people. I bet you're a four-thousand. Just look at that baby face. Better cover up or you'll get burned."

Conrad blinked a few times. "Um, can I have one of each?"

She produced two little boxes and he paid. "Thanks baby face," she said and turned away.

Conrad went back to the car.

"Got what you need?" asked Henry.

"Yeah. Who was that girl?"

"Oh they've got their daughter in there. She's your age, or maybe a bit older. She's a looker. There's this joke going around."

"What's that?"

Henry paused. "Oh never mind," he said, "I shouldn't repeat it."

"Aw come on."

"OK, they're saying, *something else is developing at the photo hut.*"

Conrad laughed, but then he remembered the girl's expression and checked himself. It was like Food Truck Man, except this was a girl, one of panic-inducing attractiveness. He wouldn't have to wait to have his heart broken this time — it had already exploded into four-thousand pieces.

o o o

"Hurry it up!"

Glenda had started out in a bad mood and wasn't improving. It didn't help that Conrad periodically paused to stare through the wall down the road.

*I never learn a damn thing. Stand there like an idiot. What was her name? I should ask her questions next time. God she was amazing. No that's not enough. Spellbinding. Mesmerizing... Splendiferous?*

"Order up!" Bang.

The songs repeating on the radio had begun to form grooves in his consciousness. Pretty soon the hits would start again from the bottom, and today the cooks had a new routine: every time 'She Works Hard For The Money!' came on, one of them came out to say "Your song's on Glenda" in a humdrum voice.

"Aw you go on!" she grated this time. "At least I know how to work, not like you two ass-scratchers."

J.J. stood with his hands on his hips and yelled "that's not nice Glenda!" — also part of the routine.

Besides eating whatever was at hand, Conrad spent his break times studying the camera manual. Roy had scheduled him for lunch, then kitchen cleaning, then an hour break, then dishwashing again through most of the night shift until his dad picked him up at nine, Thursday through Sunday. Child-labor laws allowed that much, and though he could legally do one more day Henry had been magnanimous, saying 'next year'.

The schedule also meant that Henry had to come away from work to drive Conrad on Thursday and Friday mornings, and that his sisters needed a place to stay those same days. That place was Babs' house. After work Henry would pick up the girls and make them dinner, then come out to the Alder House at nine. Henry was liking this last part, as it gave him an excuse to order a cocktail at the bar and bellow "this is my son!" to people Conrad didn't recognize when he was limp from pounding plates and stank of steamed leftovers.

"Gotcha workin' hard?" said one of these people, this time the high school principal. Conrad nodded. "Well Roy'll make a man outta ya if your dad doesn't!" Both men belly-laughed. Conrad stretched his lips into a smile.

If Conrad wanted to cheer himself up at the Alder House he could go look at the wall fountains. All individually hand-made and for sale, these were both the worst and the best art objects he had ever seen. Each was a sort of diorama, with carved plants or a bird or a jumping fish, set behind a scrim of vertical strings. But it wasn't art until you plugged it in: a pump circulated oil to the top, where it fell as beads down the strings like raindrops — or like tears on a cage of sorrow — illuminated by hidden model-train lights. Conrad decided that each drop should be called a 'plight', his new definition. *Plight, plight,* they came down one after another, *plight plight plight,* bringing on hypnosis. He gave each fountain a name: 'Plight Of The Loon', 'Plight Of The Weasel', etc.

Come Sunday night Conrad could not get the stink out of his hands. Leftovers seemed to have taken root under his nails where soap couldn't reach. He lay in bed, sinking deep into the dark and hoping Pillow Anise wouldn't notice the smell.

*Will you take me to the island tomorrow?* she asked.

*Yeah sure... We'll get up before sunrise...*

# 15

# Mid-June

Beth pounded on the door. "Conrad are you ever getting up?"

Conrad emerged to a blinding blur and fell onto the sofa face-down.

"It's halfway to lunch already," Beth scolded, but then switched to pitiful. "I thought we were going to Other Beach."

"We're going, we're going. Just let me eat first."

Two weeks of getting home late then fishing even later had misaligned his rhythms. A bowl of corn flakes had no effect, but he brightened after remembering that the 100 ISO film was all used up, which meant today he could hunt dimmer subjects with the 400. And soon he could return to the photo hut.

Levy was yelling somewhere outside, an echo of "toad." Conrad grabbed the camera and ran.

"Check it out!" Levy said, at a window well on the side of the house. "It's Franken-Toad!"

It was indeed large, one of the ancients that had survived innumerable seasons of snakes, owls, raccoons and oncoming car tires.

"What should we do?" asked Beth, looking to Conrad and rubbing her hands.

"I want a picture."

"Oh god."

Conrad knew the perfect flat rock. He propped the camera near it and focused on a pine cone, then replaced it with the toad. But it wouldn't sit still.

"Dammit!" Conrad yelled the seventh time the toad jumped away. "Hey Levy can you do the cupped hands thing?"

Conrad stood ready while Levy pressed her hands over the toad to make it crouch down. She waited a moment, then lifted her hands. The toad opened its eyes first, then when it perked up Conrad got a good shot from the side. They repeated the process for every other angle.

"Can we go already?" Beth whined.

Though tempted to keep it, Conrad let the toad crawl under the wood pile. Then the kids strung on their bags and squeaked toward the road on their bikes. None of these were big enough anymore, but Henry had at least oiled the chains and filled the tires.

Going to Other Beach meant pedaling almost all the way out to the highway — up a hill, down a hill, repeat — but then turning south onto a wide dirt road, dusty-hot under the sun. Here the kids noted the state of the blackberry vines in the gullies, far from ripe at the moment. After a half-mile they came to the entrance to a dark side track, blocked by a rusty chain hung with a PRIVATE PROPERTY sign. Bypassing this they bumped down through especially dark forest, hid their bikes in a patch of ferns, then crept low to the lake in case the landowners, whom they had never actually seen, were present that day.

They weren't. The beach welcomed the kids with sand-colored sand and dramatic views to nearby islands. After a few rounds of rolling the lengths of their bodies on the warm beach and jumping into the sun-heated shallows, they sat on their towels to read. Beth and Levy soon fell deep into their books. As for Conrad, the cover of 'Call It Courage' looked exciting, but this time he was the one who could not sit still. Instead he looked toward the islands and pictured himself out there with Anise as he had so often imagined. How silly it seemed in the light of day, if only because it was impossible.

*They can't be here, but I can send pictures.*

The plan came fully-formed: to his friends he would send one photo at a time, mounted neatly, unlabeled: mystery pictures showing up in the mail, ready to pin to their walls. They would love it! He jumped up and tramped into the woods behind the beach.

"Where are you going?" Beth called. "Can't you just calm down and read with us?"

No he couldn't. There was a marshy area in the woods where strange little flowers poked up in the dim light at its edge. Lying face-down he fiddled with the camera dials and checked the light meter as nearby mosquitoes woke up to discover his skin. He liked the shutter sound, its satisfying *kuh-shunk*, but he had to choose his shots wisely or run out of film.

When after a long while he went back, the girls were still reading. Even Levy hadn't stirred the whole time. But at the sight of Conrad they began packing up. It was well past lunch and they hadn't brought food.

"My book is nuts!" Levy said to Beth. "You should read it when I'm done. It's on a farm but it's just like school."

○ ○ ○

Henry arrived home in clouds of car dust and weariness, mumbling something about the *god damn clients and their god damn mansion* and stomping straight to the fridge for a can of beer. After a few sips he went to the sofa to lay face-up. Henry had the ability to nap in an instant, but was liable to stay that way. After a while the kids switched on reruns, but really they were hungry. They could make dinner themselves but didn't want to start without asking the sleeping hulk.

"Oh, I passed out," Henry murmured, eyes still closed. "You kids want Dog Stew?"

"Yeah!"

Henry rolled off the couch and headed for the bathroom. When he came out he was fully awake.

"I've *told* you kids to pick up after yourselves," he said, loud and red-faced. Henry hadn't parented for a long while, so when the spigot turned, the parenting came out full pressure. "There's towels and underwear all over the place! Is this how you live in L.A.?"

Beth was cowering but she spoke first anyway. "Sorry, we were in a hurry this morning."

"That's no excuse. I have to re-train you kids every year I swear."

"What, like we're a bunch of animals?" Levy muttered.

Henry stood over her. "I don't want to hear you talking back to me like that, hear me?" At this Levy nodded with a frump. Henry headed for the kitchen. "I really don't know what your mother's been teaching you out there." The kids went back to watching Bonanza.

Dog Stew was a bachelor meal, or a divorcee one, consisting of ground beef, shell noodles and tomato paste, plus every spice from the cupboard in equal amounts whether they matched or not. It tasted terrible and the kids loved it — or they had.

Once, back in the 'middle time' after the divorce but before the move when Henry had picked them up for a weekend, they passed a dead dog by the road. Later that night Henry made a pot of stew, and as the kids sat slurping, Beth asked what was in it. Conrad explained that people of the woods never waste a perfectly-good animal, dog or no, to which Beth spat her mouthful onto the table and burst into screaming tears. Sueanna heard about it later — midway through scolding Conrad for being insensitive she had broken out laughing instead. *My poor little girl.*

Conrad sat chewing. "This would be good with those little cherry tomatoes, chopped in half," he said.

"Yeah, we could try it with Parmesan grated on top," said Beth.

"What, don't like your dad's cooking anymore?" Henry grumbled.

"Yeah we do, we're just suggesting," said Conrad.

"That's what living in a place like that does to you, makes you want everything all fancy."

The kids canned their ideas and dinner went quiet.

Everyone was in a mood, including Conrad, so he drifted

down to the basement to stare at his canvas. Something was moving now behind his vision: a shadow, or a reflection of something that was already finished in the future. He would just have to find his way toward it. It was a contrast, or an opposition... there was the water, and the trees. The water and the trees. One pooled flat, hiding its depths, while the other shot up — or reached up, or grabbed up — toward outer space. That was a start anyway. He began dragging the tip of his pencil across the canvas.

○ ○ ○

"Be quick," said Henry as he pulled over by the photo hut.

Conrad ran over to the window. "Hi!" he said, and smiled.

The girl came out from the shadows, but she didn't say anything, just stood in the window light like the severe daughter of royalty in a painting.

"What's your name?" Conrad asked.

"My name's The-Fuck-Do-You-Want."

Conrad struggled to process. "I have some film to develop." He fished it out and placed it on the counter.

"I take it you want to pick it up here?"

He nodded. "And can I have two more, the same?"

Two more little boxes appeared and he paid, but then he stood staring slightly to the right.

"Anything else?" the girl asked.

"So what's your name?"

"You really want to know my name?"

"Yeah."

"Why?"

"Well... I'll be coming here a lot." He paused and added "plus I just want to know."

"OK, it's Helen. Any more questions?"

"Do you have any brothers or sisters?"

Helen's eyes went big and she blinked. "No!" is all she said, and disappeared to the back. Henry tapped on the horn.

"What's with that girl?" Conrad said as he climbed back into the car.

Henry smiled. "Did she give you a hard time?"

"She just seems so mean."

"Yeah, well one thing is her dad's your classic son-of-a-bitch. But you ever hear about that kid they found floating in Lake Lucy about four-five years ago? That was her big brother."

"Whoah... oh yeah, I remember seeing that on TV. What happened again?"

"You know, teenagers drinking."

"Oh yeah."

*What if Helen's actually nice inside?*
*So beautiful.*
*I'll keep trying.*
*So, sooooo beautiful.*
*It doesn't matter if I never see her away from that hut. If it's all practice then I'll practice. After all, it's not like she can go anywhere.*

John came out of the cook station. "Your song's on Glenda."

"Yeah that's right, I work it hard all night long, not like you two limp dicks."

"That's not nice Glenda!"

Conrad laughed along. At least the people here were funny. Roy even pinned cartoons to the bulletin board. But Glenda turned her eye to Conrad next.

"Hey why're you so slow? I'll never get a smoke if we don't catch up."

A busboy named Pete came in and slammed down another tub. Conrad hadn't spoken much to Pete yet, though they were close in age. Being from out of town plus doing dishes made Conrad a foreign leper, or so it seemed. And it wasn't true that busboys had to do time with Glenda first — Pete hadn't. Conrad wasn't clear yet how the whole thing worked.

"Keep 'em coming," Glenda urged. Conrad pounded and sprayed and racked at a more-frantic pace.

Jenny came in to slide a ticket above the cooks, then stood

behind Conrad with her arms crossed. He glanced over his shoulder while he pulled over another tub.

"You don't talk much do you," she said, but she rushed back out while he was considering what to say. A few minutes later she came back with another server named Angie.

"You see those folks in my section?" Angie said to Jenny, peeking through the doors. "Where do they think they are?"

Jenny also peeked, and whistled. "Jeez. Nobody told *me* we work at a fancy restaurant."

"You girls get a move on," came Roy's voice from the back. The girls scooted out and Roy followed them.

Conrad stepped to the door to see what the fuss was about. A family was sitting around the best corner table by the window, dressed as if the captain of a ship was scheduled to join them: the father in a tie and jacket, the mother in a flowered silk dress, a little girl matching her even to the shoes, and two boys in preppy plaid shirts, khaki trousers and penny-loafers — the perfect clones of Robb and Todd. Conrad also saw two more tubs heading his way.

# 16

# Early July

Pipsqueak was two trees conjoined at the base, surrounded by a beach barely wide enough to stand on. When she was only six years old, Beth had declared that it would henceforth be called 'Pipsqueak' instead of 'Pipsqueak Island' because it was too small to fit the word 'island', and also that one tree was named 'Pip' and the other 'Squeak' — an early inkling of her clockwork mind. In summers past both girls begged Henry to take them there, because it was cute, and because a picnic on Pipsqueak meant bottoms on the beach and feet in the water.

For Conrad it was all about the fishing: the lake floor dropped almost vertically nearby, a perfect hideout for *the big one*. On a calm day in his boat Conrad could see the depth-darkening from above, but really he had long-since memorized the contour map and never lost his place.

Staying put was another thing. If the wind would allow, he could cast sideways along the length of the drop-off, letting his lure sink halfway then reeling it back with lunker-tantalizing jerks. But the wind would not allow. His anchor rope was all out of the boat, and the moment he cast the wind changed its mind.

"Dammit!" he yelled to nobody as fickle gusts swiveled the boat again. He put down his pole and slumped between the oars. He couldn't keep calm. Time felt different now, *ruined*. He remembered every past summer as a stream of nameless days, carrying his ever-grander schemes bubbling along — until he was bodily ripped away of course. But now he always knew the day and date, and it was already July. As soon as he woke to each Monday, the coming Thursday added a note of frantic futility to any activity — made it all just silly goofing after all.

At least he had his camera to record it. He took a good shot of Pipsqueak, and of the bow pointing to a distant shore.

*But there's so much more to it.*

There was the wind always combing him, and the boat swaying... and how it felt to drop his hand over the side into the water when he was feeling too sunned, to let the water cool his blood.

He could get a picture of his hand in the water anyway.

Levy and Beth were waiting on the dock when Conrad returned. He was rowing hard, having felt the air turn.

"There's a storm warning!" Levy called when he was within earshot, as if he might not make it the remaining fifteen yards back to the dock if he didn't row faster. Clouds were indeed dimming the lake, from the far side, but the kids knew how fast it could come on and how gloriously bad it could get. After Conrad tied up they sat at the edge of the dock to enjoy the cool advance winds as an immense cloud-bank towered closer. A muted light flashed within it, and the kids began to count: one-one-thousand, two-one-thousand, three-one-

Crack-BOOM!

"Hurray!"

Only when storm made its final advance, changing the lake's surface from glossy to matte, and only after Conrad got a picture, did the kids run up into the house. The rain came on with a whoosh on the roof and with louder reports that rattled the foundation. Peanut-butter-and-honey sandwiches by the kitchen window with the lights off, and tall glasses of milk, and watching rivulets of water snake as if alive along the ground outside, were the perfect things for this time.

"How's it at Babs?" Conrad asked.

"It's OK I guess," said Levy. "There's all that stuff outside. But we can only swim right next to the dock, and she won't let us go far from the house, and then we always have to go in for some reason."

"Yeah," said Beth. "It's like, *do you girls want to do some knitting?*, but it means we have to knit whether we want to or not. She'll beg and beg till we give in. And she always has a cocktail and it smells funny."

"I hate knitting," said Levy.

"It's all girly stuff. The only girly thing I like is dancing."

"Boys do that, too."

"Oh yeah, so that means I don't like *any* girly things. So there! No girly things for me." Beth held up her chin.

"I expect you to act like a lady," said Conrad in their mother's voice.

"No!" Beth banged her fists on the table and thunder shook the house and they laughed.


The storm lifted as if to allow Henry's return. He came in to find Hee Haw on the TV and his kids at angles on the floor.

"You kids want fried chicken or fish sticks?"

"Fish sticks!"

Fish sticks it was, and peas and instant mashed-potatoes. Henry sipped a can of beer while he cooked, but drank water at the dinner table like his kids. He turned to Conrad.

"I saw all the leaves in the same places," he said, his voice grave.

"Yeah, I was going to sweep when I got back from fishing, but then that storm came."

"You do your work first thing and you won't have that problem. You can't say that kind of thing on the job, got it?"

Conrad nodded. "Hey Dad, I was thinking. How about if I ride my bike to work on Thursday and Friday, so you don't have to come all the way back? Then at night you can stick the bike in the trunk."

"That's a long way and I don't want you riding by the highway."

"But look," Conrad said and stood to point to the big map pinned to the kitchen wall. "There's this back road that goes behind it. I only have to cross the highway to get to it. I already measured. It's three times as long as the trip to Other Beach, and if I'm by myself I can go faster. It'll be fun."

Henry looked at Conrad for a while before speaking again. "You can't be late, you know." Conrad nodded. "And you gotta be super careful at the crossing." Conrad nodded again. "And maybe the first day you leave real early, and go at a normal pace so you'll know the right time to leave the next time."

"OK, I will. Thanks Dad!"

*Good idea.* He would figure out how long it took, plus time for Helen of course.

○ ○ ○

The back road was not fun: loose rocky dirt and more potholes than road, altogether slow-going and butt-hurting. Along its length, rattling around the holes, Conrad passed many crossroads, but he didn't know which one led out to the hut. On the first day he didn't dare try and stuck to the plan, but not turning was a torture that lasted through his whole shift. That night in the car he strained to see out the window, noting the signs and counting the crossings. At home he studied the map again.

The second morning he left at nine-fifteen — plenty of time, but he raced out anyway. After reaching the highway and crossing to the back road he paid no mind to the bumps, vibrating along in a cloud of dust. By his estimation, the turn should be Fern Way. Sure enough, after five minutes of rolling on creamy-smooth asphalt toward the highway, the hut appeared just to the left.

"Hi Helen!"

Helen came to the window as if a bug were in it. "Baby-face. Where's your daddy?"

"I'm cycling to work today."

"Oh, I see." She slid a packet of pictures across the counter and pointed at the total scrawled in the corner.

"Wait, I need two more, and here's some more to develop." He put his latest rolls on the counter, and Helen traded them for two more boxes. After paying he stood by the window but Helen had receded into the hut.

"I'm sorry about last time," he said.

"Sorry for what?" came Helen's voice.

"I mean, what I said. I didn't know about, you know... what happened."

Helen came closer and eyed him. "Oh so now you've heard the gossip, huh? Heard all about me? I bet you're a Helen expert now. Congratulations."

"No! I only know that one thing..." He stopped. "So what do you like to do?"

"What do I like to do? Oh, well, I like to sit around in a hut by the highway, with no air conditioning, all summer, doing *nothing*, that's what. Don't you have to go to work yourself?"

"You don't have any good books in there?"

At this Helen just stared. Conrad fished around in his bag. "Here, this is a good one." He slid his copy of 'Call It Courage' across the counter. He hadn't read it yet but he had it on good authority that it was a good one. Helen didn't touch it. Conrad kept talking.

"I mean when you're not here. What are you into?"

"Jesus, you don't give up. OK, you tell me first. What are *you* into, besides frogs I mean."

"Frogs? You looked at the pictures?" So far he'd kept ahead of his nerves, but now they caught up. "That's a toad," he mumbled.

"Oh! My mistake. Is that what you want to be when you grow up, a toadologist?"

"No."

"So what do *you* like to do? You started this remember."

The truth wouldn't save him. "Art," he said, then added lower, "painting."

Helen smirked. "Aw, there he is, the baby-faced artist. I bet your dick is painted on, too. We'll just call you Painty."

Conrad looked at the ground. 'You play to the end!' said the coach of the only team he had ever been on, when they were losing, which was every time. Conrad wiped the road dust off his digital watch: five-minutes out from the back road, plus five minutes back — that left ten minutes to spare.

"Your turn," he said.

Helen went silent for a few beats — a note of surprise. "OK, fine," she said. "I like geography. See you next time!" She backed away from the window, but before Conrad could press further a shiny new Mercedes pulled off the road and two pent-up children burst out with cash in their hands. Conrad mounted his bike and headed back to Fern Way.

Hunger came on fast from biking in the sun, but straight after lunch it was time for mat duty, which involved pulling up all the rubber mats from the kitchen floor, spraying the gunk out of their holes, then folding the mats onto trays to be blasted in the dishwasher, after which he stacked them at the end where they would wait until he had mopped the floor with a disinfecting solution and hosed it corner to corner.

By the time the mats were back in place Conrad was shaking and begged John for the biggest lunch possible. John obliged with a plate piled with a little of everything and Conrad wolfed it down. Then he felt queasy.

When his break was over Conrad felt like throwing up. Coming back inside to put on his apron he ran into Pete the busboy.

"Hey Conrad," Pete asked, "are they still having problems with the blackies in L.A.?"

"The what-ees?"

"You know, my dad says they were rioting and stuff."

"Uh, no? Not that I've seen."

*What kind of a question is that,* Conrad wondered, but another wave of nausea swept over him. He rushed to the bathroom to stand over the toilet, but nothing happened.

Tourists came early for dinner, and on time, and late. Orders came nonstop and so did the tubs. "Keep 'em coming!" Glenda yelled at Conrad as the waitresses rushed in and out of the kitchen. As for the cooks, no matter how many orders came in, food always cooked the same speed so everything else had to go faster. In the corner of his eye Conrad saw John and J.J. switching between freeze-frame and fast-motion like greasy superheroes. But even a night like this wasn't enough to stop their fun.

"Your song's on Glenda," said J.J., lugging a tray of potatoes from the cooler. Glenda was struggling to scrub a burned pot but stopped to face them.

"Yeah, your ma's song's on. Where do you think *you* came from?"

"That's not nice Glenda!"

Glenda didn't stop as usual and yelled over the dishwasher. "Well there's a reason you're an only child you know! I heard it. Old Mary's ass caught fire when you popped out, yeah they had to use a fire extinguisher! Twat burned to a crisp, ended her career right there."

John grabbed hold of J.J.'s shirt. "Now Glenda, we were just having fun with ya," he warned.

"Yeah everybody has their fun with Glenda," she growled, going back to vigorous scrubbing. "But what does Glenda get out of it? Jack shit that's what! And I'll tell you why. Because fuck this fucking pot!" She banged it up and down on the bare metal. "Fuck it to hell!" She shoved the pot in front of Conrad. "Here you do it. I'm goin' out for a smoke." She stomped toward the back door.

The kitchen went still until the door slammed, then work resumed at full speed.

"Better clean that fucking pot, Conrad," said John.

"Yeah, I fucking need that fucking pot," said J.J.

Conrad went at it, scrubbing with as much force as he had, but the black crust on the bottom was rock-hard. More tubs came in — a pileup! John saw and came over.

"Here, gimme that." He pulled away the pot and scrubber, then pulverized the crust with violent thrusts of his thick arm. Roy came in and saw.

"What are you doing? Where's Glenda?"

"There was an episode," said John, miming cigarette puffs as he returned to the cook station.

"Oh Christ." Roy went out to the back. Soon Glenda was back

racking cleans without a word. The kitchen stayed quiet for a long while, that is until Conrad decided to be the ice-breaker.

"Hey J.J., what's your real name?"

"John."

"Oh so you're both John. But what's the second 'J' for?"

"I know the story!" said Glenda.

"Don't you *even*," said J.J., but then Angie burst in between them with more order slips.

"He was drunk off his ass at a high school party..." Glenda cackled.

"Glenda!"

"...and he got up and yelled *I'll kiss Sueanna or my name isn't Juh-Juh-Juh* and then he puked and passed out cold, ha ha ha!"

J.J. stood with his fists clenched at the floor like he would murder it, then marched out the back door.

"Now you've done it Glenda," John scolded. But he couldn't leave the cook station with so many orders and gestured to Conrad. "Go get Roy!"

Conrad ran out among the noisy tables, conscious of his sticky steamed face and horrifying smock.

"What are you doing out here?" Roy hissed, but Conrad motioned for him to follow.

"Glenda told Conrad about J.J.'s name," John said when Roy came in.

"Oh lord." Roy shook his head with double the exasperation of last time. "Where is he?"

John pointed to the back door. "We're in trouble if he doesn't come back."

Roy went out. After a while J.J. reappeared looking stern with Roy behind him. Roy stood with his arms crossed watching Glenda as she racked and ignored him. Then he stepped to the middle of the kitchen and yelled.

"Hey!"

Everyone stopped what they were doing.

"No - more - bullshit," he growled, and returned to the floor.

Henry had gone to a dinner party, so after work Conrad stumbled out into the cool night air to wait, tempted to lay his face flat on the parking lot. But down by the lake he saw what looked like a lightning-bug glowing and fading in the dark. At the end of the nature trail he found J.J. smoking by himself with a flask and a little cup.

"Hey," J.J. grunted. He poured a small amount of a dark liquid into the cup and handed it to Conrad. "Have a swig."

Conrad sipped: sticky-sweet blackberry alcohol, awful but warming. "What's this?"

"Schnapps. Always cheers you up. And hey man, sorry about before."

"That's OK. You didn't do anything."

"I don't know, it's stupid. So long ago, you know? I have a kid now, a wife and everything. But that high school stuff never quits I swear."

"I'm in high school now."

"Oh yeah? Fun times. You have a girlfriend yet?"

"I did, almost, but then it just went poof."

"Yeah, that's how it goes." J.J. took a drag and blew a knowing stream of smoke toward the lake. "Life is a vale of tears my friend, life is a vale of tears."

Conrad wondered how tears could ever form a 'veil' when they come out one at a time, and at the corners, too. A veil of tears would be like the wall-fountains: *plight plight plight*. He imagined tears falling in a line from someone's eyebrows, after humans had evolved to cry better. In any case he did join J.J. in feeling sad, which seemed called-for at the moment, and sipped the schnapps.

"Did you always live here?" Conrad asked.

"Born and bred. Back in the day I never thought about going anywhere else. I get it more now though. Workin' here, payin' the bills, fixin' the house, and I see places on TV and think, *shit*, that might be nice. The older I get the smaller this place looks, but anyway it's home."

"Every minute I'm in L.A., I want to come back."

"Yeah? Well that makes you the opposite of your mom. Getting out of here was all she ever talked about back in school. Wouldn't shut up about it. Man I was so sure she'd shoot the moon. I couldn't believe it when she married your dad. I mean he's a great guy, don't get me wrong, it's just, you know, it made no sense, not to me anyway."

"Well look what happened." Conrad felt wiser about his mother now.

"You said it. People all over, pretending to be somebody they're not. Something's gotta give."

A familiar shape rolled under the lights behind the restaurant. "That's my dad," said Conrad. "Thanks for the drink."

"You got it. See ya man."

When Conrad climbed into the car Beth retracted. "Eww you stink!"

"How was your day at work?" asked Henry.

"It was nuts! I could hardly keep up."

"Well you just keep at it. Pretty soon it'll be second-nature."

Conrad arrived home too worked up to sleep but too weary to work on his painting, so instead he peered at his negatives over a lamp. He needed copies, since he only had one of each picture, but he wanted to start sending them now, so he set to making a chart to track them, with the pictures listed down the left and the recipients along the top: Mr. Onter, Joey, Stacy, Anise...

In a flash he felt it: Anise was the first reason he was doing this. But why was that? It made no sense. It was silly really, *he* was silly, still thinking of her. *That weirdo Conrad sent me weird pictures,* she would say to her friends. And if he didn't go back to L.A. he might never see her again, like never ever. But he would do it anyway, if for no other reason than to even the scales.

For each photo he cut a matching rectangle of medium-gray construction paper, a half-inch wider on each side, and used glue-stick to mount it. That was all — simple and neat. Into an envelope it went, numbered at the corner and recorded on his chart. It was important that the pictures arrive one at a time, every few days. He would start with a classic view of the lake from the dock, then progress to specific places and things, giving the envelopes to his dad to mail in town. For Anise, no return address.

○ ○ ○

Henry pulled over by the hut, but Conrad hesitated. His list of duplicates was ready but his limbs were not.

"You forget something?" Henry asked.

"No. I'll be right back."

Helen was already standing in the window, severe and disapproving — the most ravishing severe and disapproving he had ever seen.

"Hi Helen!"

"What are you doing here Painty? You know your pictures aren't ready."

"Yeah, but look…" he pulled out the sleeve of negatives and his list. "I need copies of these ones. Four of each. I'm sending them to friends."

"Oh! Painty has friends? Are they frogs, or toads?"

"They're people… back where I've been living."

"And where's that, Trailer Park County?"

"No, Los Angeles."

Helen paused. "Then what are you doing here?" she whispered.

"Why does everybody say that?"

"Jesus." Helen rotated her head in exaggerated disbelief. "Well Painty, you could be surfing, or going to movies in Hollywood, and I bet there's parties and pretty girls. You *like* pretty girls, right? Not to mention art museums and maybe even toad museums, just for you! Meanwhile, there's trees here."

"But I'm from here, and my dad's here. Plus I love it, the woods, the lake. Don't you ever do that stuff?"

"What stuff?"

"You know, like swimming in the lake, hiking in the woods?"

"When we were kids maybe. The only reason a girl *my* age goes into the woods is to get smashed or knocked up, with guys *your* age. But you must be some sort of retarded child, rolling around in the mud snapping pictures of the local weeds."

*OK I've seen her. It's done. So beautiful. Shouldn't be late. Dad's waiting.*

"Four of each, please," he repeated, not looking at her.

"Sure. Take your book back Painty." She slid it out, and he carried it with him to the car.

"All set?" said Henry.

"Yeah."

They drove away, Conrad frowning out the window. After a mile or so he looked down at the book. It was worn now, and the binding was cracked. Mr. Onter would call her a heathen for doing that.

# 17

# Mid-July

After a week Conrad needed more paper, so on Monday morning he got up early to ride into town with Henry. At the last minute of course, the girls stumbled out of their room, pajama-clad and bleary-eyed, begging pitifully to tag along. "Get a move on!" Henry was soon yelling at the bathroom door. "This isn't a play day for me you know!" Then after all the washing and dressing and combing, and hurrying out to the car, the girls returned to their slumbers across the back seat as soon as the car left the driveway.

Henry was the owner of Henry's Electric (named after his father, also Henry), a nondescript little shop on the edge of town that everyone knew. Henry typically arrived before his employees to do paperwork, but spent most of the daytime driving between installation projects in the area. Today was no different: he dropped the kids in town and headed north, taking his mood with him.

The town of Polecat Creek had one main drag: Lake Street. With the exception of bars, any establishment not on Lake Street risked vanishing before the next summer. But no matter where, most of the shops existed to tempt the steady stream of summer tourists. The locals hoped it was steady anyway — money not collected in the summer was money sorely missed through a long winter. As for Henry's Electric, a boom meant more resort cabins to wire, and more summer-home remodels for the well-to-do (homes that sat empty for most of the year), but it also brought competitors. That was fine in the good years, however this wasn't one of them.

Conrad followed his sisters into Grandma's Candy Castle, lined with lace, old-timey curtains and rows of wicker baskets filled with every type of wrapped sweet. Of course none of it was made locally, but buying the candies here in the heat of the summer rendered them twice as delicious. Levy ran to the clear watermelon hard candies and Beth went for the horehounds, but when their backs were turned Conrad snuck back out and headed toward a sign at the corner: Polecat Photo.

At first he passed by without looking, picturing Helen calling his name from the door — though he knew she would never do such a thing. He stepped into the next shop and looped around a t-shirt table before doubling back. Now he peeked through the photo shop's window-display to a dim interior. Still nothing happened, so he glided through the door.

It was a small shop: at the front was a single case displaying previous-generation cameras, and at the back was a long counter under a placard listing photo services. A tired-eyed woman watched over the premises.

"Can I help you with anything?" she asked.

"No I'm just looking thanks." Conrad pretended to inspect the cameras but snuck looks at the woman, Helen's mother no doubt: the same regal bearing, but otherwise deposed and banished.

A door-slam came from the back, and a deep voice: "I'm takin' Helen. Got anything?"

The woman nodded and pulled open a drawer, then handed a packet to a man behind her without meeting his eyes. The man was tall and burly, with a hard, know-everything glint in his eye. Conrad had seen that look before. Was it Patrick? No, it was Tony, that magic kid.

"Thanks!" Conrad said and shot out around the corner along the side of the building. Helen was standing by a pickup in the back parking area, facing away with her arms stubbornly crossed. But her father came out too fast. "Come on," he grunted, and Helen climbed in. Conrad watched her behind the glass: her dad handed her the packet and she looked down at it, but then as the truck turned out of the lot she glanced out and saw Conrad. For a second her eyes opened in surprise, but then they turned mean. She waved the packet in the window.

It was a trap, but the trap was in him. *God dammit.* Helen was a completely separate thing from himself, all curvy smoothness bending into the truck, movements suggesting elegant fitness, silken midnight hair swinging by gravity — *all of her out there, none of her in here.* But snap! The trap is sprung, and he's caught himself in a ridiculous tangle. And his heart calls out to her, *Help! Please!* Within that one second, Conrad could sense it. But then it was all a muddle, just blurry frustration. He needed paper.

Polecat Books was half magazines, and the books — bestsellers, romance, teen fiction — were themselves losing ground to souvenirs and candy. In the back corner was a small section of supplies.

"Do you have gray construction paper?" Conrad asked the clerk, a pimply teenage boy.

"No sorry. Down in Yort they might. We got this, though." The clerk pointed out a letter-sized pad with thick sheets of every color. Only five of the sheets were gray. At the art store in L.A. Conrad could buy huge sheets in any individual shade, with different grays to choose from. *Oh well.* He bought four pads.

The day's purpose accomplished, Conrad made the rounds, touring every store on every street to see what had changed. Not much had. He lingered as usual in the bait & tackle store, fingering the plugs designed to shimmy and shimmer like real minnows. He already had a number of these in his tackle box and they never caught anything, but look, here was a new kind: fat and wide, with dashing orange stripes and a long scooped lip for deep diving. He didn't have one of those.

Heading out with his purchase he stopped.

*Eyes looking left. Eyes looking right.*

To the left was the end of town, just a block south. To the right was the end of town the other way, two blocks north. The town had shrunk! It was compacting around him!

Narrowly avoiding being squished like a grape, Conrad scooted through the next door into the Feathered Fine Arts

Gallery, the only store in town with 'Do Not Touch' signs by the merchandise. Halogen spotlights dramatized each item in the otherwise dim interior, exquisitely-carved wooden ducks being the main attraction but all intended for the well-to-do mantle. Local wildlife, primarily of the flying type, adorned the walls in the form of large framed prints, 'signed by the artist'. Conrad walked around the store peering like an art collector, but in fact for most of his life he had dreamed of walking into this place with a baseball bat and smashing every last object to bits. Except the ducks. He kind of wanted a duck.

Conrad found Levy and Beth exactly where he expected: at the little park at the north end of Lake Street, swinging on sugar power. But they came running when he neared and followed him to O'Donovan's Cafe to order B.L.T.s and wait for their dad. But Henry was late, so when the sandwiches came they couldn't resist biting into them.

"This town's like part of Disneyland," said Beth.

Levy giggled. "Yeah, Polecat Land."

"But there's no rides."

"Yeah, needs rides. What do you think?"

"There could be a water-ski one I guess..."

"Yeah!" Conrad interrupted. "People would be strapped onto these chair things with hand-holds, and it would look like they're standing on skis, but really there'd be tracks under the water."

Henry came in flustered.

"What happened, Dad?"

"Oh that Carl," he said, speaking in a hush. "What a numbskull. We have this new contract up at the Big Fir resort, and the back wall faces downhill to Lake Patoosh, so they're converting half the basement into a dining hall, putting in big windows, real nice, so they can rent it out. They see these big companies coming up here for retreats and they want to get in on it. So anyway Carl goes and wires all the outlets with the wrong kind of wire."

"Whoah."

"So now we have to rip it all out and do it again, and I have to eat the cost. Half the wall panels were in already. Damn it all! Screw-ups like that make us look bad."

"Will you fire Carl?" Levy asked.

"Shhh! Not so loud." Henry shook his head. "What would I do then, train some other numbskull? No, Carl's a good guy. I chewed him out good. That's the name of the game, make mistakes till you don't, or till you die, whichever comes first."

After lunch they headed back toward the house. Conrad felt the photo hut approaching long before it came into view.

"Got any pictures there?" asked Henry.

*Stopping now, she wins.*

*Waiting until Thursday, she wins.*

"Yeah."

Henry pulled over and Conrad jumped out. Helen came to the window but waited for him to speak.

"Hi Helen," he said with a big warm smile. He would lose in style, which for reasons he could not explain meant being nice no matter what.

"Painty couldn't wait, could he."

"I've really gotta get those pictures in the mail."

Helen slid the packet across the counter and tapped at the charge. Conrad reached for his wallet and counted out bills.

"You like geography," he said, handing her the money. "So what's your favorite country?"

"Anywhere-but-here-land."

"Oh. I heard that's a fun place. When are you going?"

"Never at this rate."

"I like Japan. I like Japanese movies anyway. I want to go there so bad."

"Well you have fun. Maybe you can go paint Godzilla. That's sort of like a toad, just bigger. Anyway, see you!" She waved to indicate he should leave.

"Don't you want to go there, too?"

"I'm stuck here, you blind or what?"

"No I mean later, like in college. Like a study abroad program or something."

"You serious? My parents would never pay for that shit, let alone college."

Conrad heard the car door opening — Beth getting out! He scraped the change off the counter, said "thanks-Helen-see-you-next-time" and scurried to head off his sister. "OK I'm done let's go," he said and Beth retreated into the back seat.

Henry left the kids at home just after one p.m.

"Let's go on the expedition!" Levy said. On the kitchen map a tiny lake showed as a perfect circle of blue, far away in an area they hadn't yet breached. Especially enticing was its apparent lack of a name. Levy had won the die-throw but refused to say what name she had chosen, intending instead to yell it to the skies upon arrival.

Conrad tapped his watch. "No time. Look." He traced his finger across the map. "It'll take forever to get there, and then even if we come right back we'll be late for dinner and dad'll be pissed. That's no fun. I want to have time to explore the place."

"Aw man. Let's go tomorrow then."

"It's supposed to rain tomorrow," said Beth. "Like a lot."

"Oh god. Wednesday then."

"Maybe, but there's that dinner party in the evening and dad's coming home early and we'll have tons of chores, so yeah, maybe not."

"Ugh." Levy slumped like there was nothing left in the world to do.

"Want to take the boat to Frogville?" Conrad asked.

"Yeah!"

○ ○ ○

Henry came home tired but set to making a batch of spaghetti. Levy milled around the kitchen behind him dragging her finger along each wall in turn. She circled five times before she spoke.

"Dad?" she said in a whimpery voice. "Um, we've been

learning to ride, and take care of horses and stuff."

"I heard." He didn't sound impressed.

"Do you think we could do that here, too?"

"Here? You mean go on those trail rides, round and round?"

"No, like lessons."

"Oh that place is for tourists. And as far as I'm concerned horses are for rich kids. If your mother wants to pay for that kind of thing that's her prerogative but I'm certainly not encouraging it."

Levy moped back to the kitchen table and sat between Beth and Conrad. Henry came out with the spaghetti and they served themselves.

"Dad why aren't there any frogs?" asked Beth.

"What do you mean?"

"We went over to Frogville but there's hardly any there."

"Did you wear your life preservers?"

"Of course. We only saw two and they weren't very big. I wanted to see one of those big fatties."

"Yeah!" Conrad said, sitting forward. "And there aren't so many toads around either. I remember there being tons. And there were sunfish and crappies and perch I swear, by the dock when I was little. I used to catch them."

Henry nodded. "You're right. But then somebody had the bright idea to stock the lake with musky, you know, for tourists. Problem is this lake's really clear, not the weedy kind, so there's no place to hide. Muskies just gobble up anything that moves."

"There weren't muskies here before?"

"Not in this lake."

"God... no wonder I never catch anything."

"We'll take the channel sometime. It's better over there." Henry inhaled and sighed. "I just need a break."

After dinner Conrad sequestered himself to cut rectangles and paste pictures on them. When he stopped he had checked off many more lines on his recipient chart, and it was late, but he went down to fish anyway, casting his spinner over the shimmering black water with a flush of satisfaction. His project was off to a good start.

But then again, he couldn't be there to see his friends' faces when they opened the letters. It had a taste of the ridiculous: in trying to pull people closer, he had found a new way to feel distant. It was like this casting — nothing came back.

○ ○ ○

Beth wasn't mistaken about the rain. The happy morning light streaming through the windows dimmed well before lunch. But this wasn't the freshening charge of a summer squall. Instead the sky turned oily. On days like this the TV stayed on. Soon enough, a weather banner came across the bottom saying 'Tornado Watch' for the next county, then the same for theirs, then later the next county's banner switched to 'Tornado Warning'. Henry rang the phone.

"You see or hear anything even a little bit odd you go straight to the basement, got me?"

Henry had drilled the signs into them: sudden hail, or an eerie silence, or greenish skies, or a train sound. And along the road Henry had pointed out tornado alleys blasted through the forest. There were bad stories and Henry told them straight: houses pulverized, parents or children gone missing.

Wind-blown rain began to pelt the windows, which was ordinary enough, but the kids set to gathering food, flashlights, and books. Conrad noticed how many paperbacks from past summers sat mixed up together on the shelf: *The Martian Chronicles*, *Sing Down The Moon*, *Huckleberry Finn*, *A Wrinkle In Time*, *Great Expectations*, *My Side Of The Mountain*, *A Hitchhiker's Guide To The Galaxy*. Helen hadn't been nice, but she had read the book he'd given her, he was sure of it. Maybe he should give her more books, to see what would happen, like in science. Or maybe like his volcano.

A corner of the basement was fortified for the worst. If the house imploded, this spot would hold up, or so Henry promised.

Henry had taken Conrad through every detail more than once, pointing and scrawling diagrams in the hope that his impractical son would consume at least a crumb of practical knowledge. It was always cold down there, so the kids sat with pillows and blankets under a lamp, munching and reading. Conrad started on *The Restaurant at the End of the Universe*, but his chuckling bugged his sisters, so he stopped and took pictures of them reading, which bugged them even more. Then he farted. The girls threw down their books and attacked.

The weather did let up hours later, and the afternoon was ecstasy, swimming in water recharged by the storm under light filtered yellow through the surviving clouds. But Henry came home grim.

"Two touched down over there," he said, referring to the next county. "It's real bad."

"Anybody hurt?" Conrad asked.

Henry nodded. "Four dead, a bunch wounded, and a lot of damage. It's all over the national news."

It was. When the local news handed off to the national news they saw the same stories more slickly produced.

"Whoah..." Beth breathed, seeing images of house-confetti and stripped foundations. "I'm glad we stayed downstairs."

Henry spoke in a low voice. "It sounds selfish, but this is bad for us too. Tourists will be spooked for sure."

"But that makes no sense," said Beth. "It's all over now."

"Yeah, but people don't follow sense, they just get scared. Of course they'll forget, after a while, but summer's short."

The phone rang. It was Sueanna, jittery for her kids having heard the news.

"We're fine Mom," Conrad said. "Nothing came near here."

"I know, I just get nervous. I'm your mommy you know. So how's your job going?"

"It's OK."

"Are you meeting anybody your age?"

"Kind of."

"You know it's not normal to only run around the woods with your sisters. You need friends your own age."

"I don't care what's normal."

"Yes you do. So anyway I want to talk to you, Conrad." Her voice turned softer. "Are you still considering... I mean, do you still think you want to stay there, for tenth grade?"

"Yeah."

"Well, I want you to think hard, OK? You'll be cutting yourself off from so many things. I think you should reconsider."

"It's home here."

"It's home here, too. It's up to you what home is."

"But it's really home here."

Sueanna paused, her breathing audible. "Is it really so bad? I mean, living with your mother?"

"It's not that. I just never wanted to go there."

"But you did go there, I mean here, and you're doing good, can't you see that?"

"Doesn't feel good. It feels good here."

"But just think OK? You feel, and you think, not just one or the other. Don't lock yourself in, OK?"

"Mmm hmm."

"OK then, I love you very much. Can I talk to your sisters?"

He gave the phone to Levy and went down to the dock, but he didn't fish. He only sat in the dark listening to the water lap the piles, then he wandered back up. Levy and Beth were slumped on the sofa, still sniffling from talking to their mother. When they saw him they got up without speaking and all three went to read under their own lamps for the rest of the evening.

Later on in his room, Conrad woke to Henry's voice in the kitchen. It was Sueanna on the phone — there was no obvious clue but Conrad just knew, from the words and the tone. Both grew tense. Henry kept his voice down, but Conrad could hear something like 'have to let him decide' and the angry strains of his mother coming through the receiver. Words like 'you always' and 'stop saying that' preceded the clunk of the handset.

◠ ○ ○

*Chip dip.*
*Nothing else matters now!*
*Out of my way, all you blubbery cocktail-waving chatterers.*
Conrad swerved around a man's large behind to dig his chip into the bowl of creamy-salty-oniony bliss.

"Leave some for the guests," Henry grunted, turning Conrad by the shoulders and shoving him toward the door.

*Never ye mind.* His dad couldn't stand there forever. Levy and Beth were doing the same, swooping through like buzzards in turn. They too would take their reward for an entire morning of chores.

Conrad marched toward the picnic table with his dad close behind. Adults stood around holding cans of Schlitz, or gin martinis, or Scotch on the rocks. Babs was there with a few of her older moneyed friends, and Henry's long-time buddies sat with their wives, and Roy was there, too. Henry had chosen to hold the party on a Wednesday so the guests could see his kids all together, but after their usual poking questions the adults went back to joking among themselves.

"Hey Henry!" said Roy, "you hear about the Polack who crashed his helicopter?"

"No."

"He got cold, so he turned off the fan."

"Ha ha!" Belly laughs all round.

"What's a Polack?" Beth asked. "Is that like a polecat?"

"Bwa ha ha!" The adults had a good laugh at that one.

"No it just means a dummy," said Henry.

"No it means a Polish person," said Conrad.

"Yeah but people don't really mean it that way."

He had studied this! "Actually the Nazis started it when they wanted to invade Poland," Conrad said, feeling super-smart.

Roy shook his head. "No it's just for fun, kid. There's lots of Polish people around here, they don't care." He gave Henry an eye to mean 'just look at your smarty-pants'. But Conrad was rolling.

"No they spread the jokes on purpose to make Polish people look dumb so nobody would care if they invaded, then they killed off lots of educated Polish people so they could control the country easier." That was as much as he knew, but it sounded like there was more.

Roy just brushed this off. "That's a totally different thing kid."

It wasn't, but nobody was guarding the chip dip so Conrad slipped back inside. Babs was standing by the table now with a fresh cocktail and a paper plate full of pretzels.

"Young scavenger. How's that job?"

"It's dishes. Then more dishes. Then more dishes."

"Ha! So there it is, the real world. Feel like giving up art yet?"

"No."

"I bet. How about that camera? Figure it out?"

Conrad motioned for her to stay put and ran to his room, returning with a stack of mounted photos. "I'm sending these to my friends one at a time."

"Well I'll be!" she said as she flipped through them. "These are real nice. I like that you're going after the small things, too. Most people don't even look. Is that lichen?"

"Yeah. Small things look so cool in the camera. I guess I'm weird."

"Yes sir, don't do the same as other folks then *bam*, you're weird. That's how it works. I've been weird my whole life. Pretty sure I've had more fun though. Hee hee!" She shook her cocktail ice for emphasis. "I was talking to your mom last night," she added.

"Really?"

"Oh, surprised are you? It's not like we're enemies. I've known her since she was little you know. We talk."

"Huh. Uh, about what?"

"Oh, about you of course." Babs was having her fun. She watched Conrad squirming, and with nobody nearby she could speak freely. "She's very upset about you wanting to stay here."

"Yeah I know."

"I know you know. I'm still curious, though. You didn't say why you want to move back. And don't give me any of that wilderness stuff."

Conrad dipped another chip and stared at the table. He wasn't sure what else to say besides the wilderness stuff.

"Is it really so bad in L.A.?"

"No but it's all cement and cars and it's hot and it's all rich kids at school and I just don't belong there."

"Oh so it's all bad there? Not a single thing good? And you don't belong? You keep using that word, *belong*. So you feel like you belong here, is that it?"

"Yeah."

"Belong... hmmm." She eyed him for a few seconds. "Really somebody your age has no business using that word. It's one of those hidey-hole words people use when they want to cut and run, or for grandma and grandpa maybe, when it's time to retire. But you're a kid. You don't *belong*, you go out and explore, wouldn't you agree?"

"I guess." Actually it sounded like sense and took Conrad by surprise.

"It's all fear, everywhere I look, and people use all kinds of words, just like that one. Belong my ass. You're afraid of something Conrad, I guarantee it. You gotta get your words straight."

"So you don't think I should..." He stopped, feeling suddenly heavy.

"Oh don't you misunderstand me now. I love your dad. I'm not taking sides in this. Just listen to one thing, would you please?" She waited for Conrad to nod. "OK, here it is. You'll be afraid of the same things here as there. Got it?"

"Mm-hmm."

"Good, now take your hand away from that chip bowl."

After the guests had gone and the cleanup was done and the ten o'clock news was over and his lure had been cast from the dock enough times, it was no more clear to Conrad what he was afraid of. But Babs' words had stuck to him like the truth. His mind circled the idea but couldn't make out whatever it was directly. He circled and circled and couldn't sleep.

# 18

# Late July

Conrad stood on the dock after breakfast looking up in another circle: clouds maybe going, maybe coming, maybe both. His dad would return for him if it got worse, but he decided to risk it. He pedaled down the road feeling cool and breezy all the way — until the hut came within view that is. Like a freakshow tent at the circus, something inside made his stomach turn but he had to look again, just one more time.

"Hi Helen," he said.

Helen appeared in the opening as a celestial being, cruel halos encircling his consciousness.

"Here it comes again. Idiot bird, smack on the window. Does it hurt?"

Conrad nodded and smiled without parting his lips. Now as before, his going-in nerve was already going out, and his heart raced at the sight of her eyes — searing, always on the attack, but with a hardness just short of stable, hiding something. It was that last part that stirred his intuition, that made her still human. But her voice was granite-hard.

"What do you want."

"I have some more film. And I need copies." He piled his rolls and negatives and a new list on the counter. Helen took out a photo envelope and wrote 'Painty' in big letters on the front, with a flourish on the 'y' to make sure he noticed, and dropped everything into it. Then she waved goodbye.

"Plus I need two more, both kinds," he said.

She produced two boxes while he slid two bills across the counter. She slapped down the change.

"You cheated," said Conrad.

She peered at the change. "No, that's correct."

"You never told me your favorite country."

"Shit. Who says I have to have to have a favorite?"

"Like where do your eyes go when you look at a map? I always look at Japan, but it's weird. You think of it all by itself but there's all these other islands, like a chain going up to Russia. And I like Iceland. I want to go there *so* bad. I'm sure it's not but I always imagine everything's made of ice, like ice houses, ice castles..."

"Would you stop?"

He shook his head. It was the won't-stop-talking-until-you-answer move, Beth's specialty, and Mr. Onter's maps had armed him to the teeth. "You know it always amazes me that people live on those islands way out in the middle of nowhere, like in the Pacific. And have you ever heard of Madagascar? It's huge, but it got separated in dinosaur times so it's got all these weird animals..."

"Stop."

Conrad paused only to draw a breath. Helen interrupted.

"OK fine. Peru. Fucking hell. Now get out of here." She pointed out to the road.

"Why Peru?"

"Jesus."

"Would you go there if you could?"

"I told you! I'm going to sit in this hut for the rest of my life!"

She had yelled. She hadn't before, not like that. Conrad stopped to think of some new approach. "So you're not going to college?"

"Why should I?"

"Don't you want to?"

"You keep talking like it's all so easy. Everything's a joyride for you rich kids."

"I'm not rich."

"Don't make me laugh. I know all about your mom."

"But it's not like she's a millionaire. She used the money for a house, just a little one, and schools for us. Wouldn't you?"

"So you go to a private school, in Los Angeles, and you say you're not rich? What's the difference?"

"But my mom works. I take the bus home from school. Lots of kids there live in huge mansions and get BMWs for their 16th birthday. We're not like *that*."

"So let me get this straight. You wouldn't like it if your parents gave you a car? And let you drive around the city?"

"There's too many cars and traffic there and pollution. I hate it. I just want to be here."

"God you're a dumb-ass. You have to drive to get anywhere around here, haven't you noticed? Except *here* there's nowhere to go. Oh but wait, you don't care do you? You just want to crawl around the woods taking pictures, like those rich kids who show up here with their camouflage shirts tucked into their camouflage pants."

A patter of rain began to spot the ground. Helen faked a smile. "Oh no! Too bad *you* don't have a car!"

The rain came louder, then more. "When will it be done?" Conrad asked.

"When will what be done?"

"The film."

"When it's done."

"OK, see you tomorrow." Conrad ran for his bike and took off.

Soaked but also flecked head to toe with mud from the road, Conrad required a thorough going-over from Glenda with the dish sprayer before he could even towel off. But then lunch was slow. He stared through his hands repeating dish-to-tray motions. It was always the case, but it struck him today: no matter what he said, however innocuous, Helen counter-attacked like a jack-in-the-box. What could have made her that way? She acted so *sure* when she talked, but afterward it seemed... he couldn't think of a good word for it.

"Hey space cadet!" Glenda said. "I'm goin' for a smoke. You take over."

Glenda smoking was Conrad's chance to move up in the world

by racking cleans, which meant enduring the finger-scalding heat of industrially-washed plates and silverware. Like the rest of her, Glenda's hands were leather, but Conrad's were soft, especially after all the warm spraying. It wasn't clear if people ever used gloves for this task but he was reluctant to ask. The trick was to stack the plates fast — grasp and release — then scoot the stacks to the shelf and drop them before the searing at the tips of his fingers was too much to bear. He was getting more used to it but it was still torture. When Glenda reappeared it was a relief to go back to room-temperature plates covered in revolting leftovers.

"Did you always live here, Glenda?" Conrad found himself asking.

"Nah. I'm from Cleveland. But my parents moved here when we were little tykes so I don't remember nuthin'."

"Why'd they move?"

"Oh you know, niggers takin' over. My dad had some money, so they opened up a store in town, right on the main drag, but a few bad years in a row killed it. Then I was living down in Yort for a while with a fella, but he ran off after the baby, and that place is just ugly. At least it's pretty up here."

"Oh," Conrad said, and didn't ask any more questions.

Henry came for a cocktail and close conversation with Roy and some other men from town.

"Are people worried?" Conrad asked Henry on the way home.

"They're always worried, just more or less. Right now it's more."

"Seems like it's happened before. Glenda said her parents used to have a store."

"Well this town's all tourism. Goes up, goes down, never ends. It's different in places with more than one thing going on. Like some things might go down but others up, so it kind of balances out, know what I mean?"

"Yeah. But what else could people do here?"

"Well it's chicken and egg. It's not like anybody makes anything here, it's just selling nature really. And there aren't enough locals. Just look at that swimsuit store. You'd think with all the water it's a no-brainer, right? They stocked all the brands they thought tourists wanted. Turns out the only tourists who bought suits were the ones who forgot theirs at home, and even then they were picky. But the worst was the locals. You know what they said? *That place is too expensive*, they said. It wasn't that much more really, but instead of supporting a local they'd rather go down to Yort to those big chain stores, just to save a few bucks. Makes me sick."

"But that's like, an hour away. Wouldn't it cost gas just to go there?"

Henry smiled and punched Conrad in the shoulder. "Now you're thinking."

"Dad, why did grandma and grandpa move here in the first place? Didn't they live in New York City?"

"Yeah, but they didn't come straight here. I told you this before. They were just starting out, then the crash came and they nearly ended up in the streets. But your great-grandfather still had a farm, about four hours south of here. I drove you kids by there once, remember? So they worked that farm, just for a while they said, like they would go right back to New York, but meantime they had us kids. That's how they ended up here instead, always coming up in the summertime. I still remember it, your grandma always complaining, *all that Wilson ever wants to do is fish*. So my dad kept taking part-time jobs helping build resorts so he could stick around up here longer, until eventually he got the electrical supplies idea and the rest is history."

Conrad had the sensation of being at the receiving end of that history. The money that paid for school in Los Angeles came from an inheritance from the sale of a resort in the woods that his grandpa helped build after being poor on a farm after living in New York.

*Weird.*

○ ○ ○

"Hi Helen."

Today Helen wore a dark-gray soft-cotton buttoned shirt with black and white trim, unexpectedly fine, enhancing everything that it did and did not cover.

*That's odd,* Conrad thought. *She spends all day in there alone.*

Helen stood near the window with her arms crossed.

"What are you doing here Painty? You know they're not ready yet."

"Just checking."

"OK, you checked. Now it's over."

He should just leave, he was starting to feel. But then he would scurry away into the dust like a beetle, and she would sit in there all grumpy by herself: *lose-lose.* He thought of the hot plates. Maybe he would scoot just one more stack.

"So why don't you want to go to college?"

"Uhh! Who says I don't? It's just not happening, would you get that through your thick skull?"

"So you *do* want to go then."

"I just want to get out of here! And I want *you* to get out of here!" She thrust her finger at him out the window.

"OK, thanks, I'll check back again." He smiled, if only out of pride, but rode to work feeling sad.

Lunch was slow again, so Roy assigned Conrad to shelf-cleaning, leaving Glenda mumbling on her own. Between orders the cooks rummaged through the boxes that Conrad pulled down. Nobody told Glenda her song was on anymore, but the cooks were still having their fun.

A Duran Duran song came on the radio for the third time that shift. J.J. burst out yelling. "Yeah I got something you should know!"

"What's that?" asked John.

"This song is shit!"

"Yeah, what kind of person likes this song."

"It's all those eurofags," J.J. said, then added grumbling, "music was better back in Glenda's modeling days." At this Glenda only shook her head.

"You said it," said John. "Don't even know anymore if it's a woman singing or what."

"Yeah back then the tits were all real too. Not like now. There's all kinds of tricks. They'll take a hot body and stick any girl's head on it."

"Maybe you should go down to the hut and ask how they do it," said John. "I hear something else is developing there."

"Where's that?" Conrad interrupted.

"Oh that photo hut down the road near your place," said John. "You should stop there some day. There's a girl in there you'll find *real* interesting." He smiled. "Just don't get too close."

"Is she pretty?"

"Oh yeah," said J.J., "but we're not talkin' regular pretty, not even love-at-first-sight pretty. She's so pretty you have a heart attack and die right there on the spot. Worse than Medusa."

Glenda stepped out and pointed her chin at the cooks. "Yeah but I bet you two perverts would like a squeeze!" She made octopus motions with her hands.

"Oh no, not us," John said. "We're married."

"Yeah, plus she's way too young," said J.J., "...and soft," he added snickering.

Conrad played dumb again. "Is she nice?"

"No!" J.J. waved and shook his head. "She's the nastiest of the nasty. Too smart for her own good. She's in trouble all the time just for being mean. She makes Glenda here look like Mother Teresa."

"Yeah I'll bless you all to hell," Glenda mumbled.

"But aren't her parents worried, leaving her all alone out there?" Conrad asked.

J.J. smiled. "Sure they are, and they let everyone know about the shotgun, too."

"She has a gun in there?"

"Yes sir. Twelve gauge. Lose your head with that girl, you lose your head."

Glenda joined the cooks in laughing at that one.


It was time to go but Henry was gabbing at the bar. On his way out of the kitchen, Conrad noticed a new cartoon on the bulletin board. Rather than another Beetle Bailey or Hägar the Horrible from the Sunday funnies, this time it was a helpful diagram of a 'Black Bass', with labeled arrows pointing to the fish's distinguishing features, big lips being the main determinant.

Glenda was nearby. "Ha! That's a good one isn't it," she said, and went back to the dishes. Conrad didn't say anything.

"Order up!" yelled John, dropping two full plates under the warmers and facing Conrad at the bulletin board. He met Conrad's eyes and shrugged, then went back to work.

Henry was leaning at the bar with Roy and other business-owners from around town. Conrad sidled up nearby and sat down to wait. But Henry saw him and broke out of the conversation.

"You ready?" he asked.

"Yeah."

Henry talked all the way home about the slowdown, waving his hands around the steering wheel while Conrad only added the occasional 'hmm.' When they pulled up to the house Henry grabbed a stack of letters that was jammed in the seat between them. "Oh yeah, you got something," he said, handing Conrad an envelope. It was from Stacy. Conrad shoved it into his shirt so his sisters wouldn't see and headed straight to his room. Inside the envelope was a single picture: Stacy and Joey standing with horsey faces, brightly lit by the California sun, both pointing up at a palm tree behind them. Conrad stared and stared. Then he put the picture away. Then he took it out again.

From his first two rolls of film, all the good pictures had already been sent except for the toad photos. Conrad hesitated. It would be weird to send toads. But then again, he'd already sent lichen closeups.

Which angle then? Front, behind, top, or side: all were in

perfect focus, every bumpy detail. Masterpieces! Finally it came to him: use them all, but do it like a fold-out. He set to it, back-taping and stacking the pictures so they would pull out in a line, with a pull-tab on the top. The result made him laugh: the top photo was the toad's front, the last its behind.

*All you other weirdos take notice.*
*This is how it's done.*

○ ○ ○

Conrad heard only the dirt compressing under his bicycle's tires as they rolled. The tires would run straight, he decided, all the way to work. No way would he turn toward the hut this time, not after the yelling, not after the finger-pointing. *I'm such an idiot,* he thought, *going there to be sneered at.*

But the tires turned on their own.

"Hi Helen." Conrad only half-looked at the shape in the window.

"Well if it isn't Painty." Helen waited. Seconds ticked by.

"Um, I'm just here to check."

"Check on what?"

"My pictures."

"Oh did you have pictures?"

"Yeah."

"Well maybe, if you promise not to ask me any more stupid questions, I'll go look in the drawer."

Conrad met her eyes but they were too intense so he looked away and nodded. Helen turned to the drawer.

"Oh well lookee here it's your lucky day!" She slid out a packet and tapped her finger at the charge. Conrad pulled the pictures into his bag and reached for his wallet, but stopped.

"I uh... I remember now."

"Remember what?"

"About Peru."

"What did I say Painty!"

"But that wasn't a question. Peru's cool. It has a coast, then really tall mountains, then a jungle inside."

"I know god dammit. Give me the money and get out of here."

"My friend once showed me pictures of someplace there, with green farms on steps sort of, really steep in the mountains."

"Yeah dummy that's Machu Picchu. Rhymes with *beat you*. That's what's gunna happen if you don't pay up."

"I don't have the money today," he lied, jumping onto the seat of his bicycle and cranking the pedals. "I'll pay you tomorrow!"

Helen wouldn't really burst out the back of the hut to lay him flat with her twelve-gauge, but it sure felt like it.

Conrad arrived at the Alder House breathless like the pursued. But he was early, so he headed straight to the lakeside to cool off. Sticky end-of-July heat oozed into the shadows until he gave up. He found the kitchen even hotter, the busy faces flushed and beading. He went to stare at the cartoon, still the Black Bass.

*Here it is on the wall like it's all so normal, like ha ha ha.*

*But how can that still be normal?*

*It's 1984 for chrissakes. Civil rights was so long ago.*

Roy came through and patted Conrad on the shoulder. "Henry Junior! I hear you're getting better."

"Uh yeah, thanks."

"Well it's slow. What say you clean the far side of the cooler."

The cooler was deliciously cool, until it was cold. Conrad's fingers went numb as he hauled chilled metal trays between shelves, and then his hands ached in the hot bleach-water when he dipped his towel to wipe down the walls. An involuntary shaking traveled up his arms and down his torso. Then when the walls were clean, the icy cold trays had to go back exactly where they had come from. But finally it was over and he could escape out the door.

"Holy shit look at him!" Jenny pointed and bent over laughing. "He's like a lobster."

Conrad stood red and scowling, having flushed all over on contact with the broiling kitchen air. But Conrad found Jenny less intimidating now after so many rounds with Helen.

"Hey what grade are you in?" he asked.

"Oh he speaks! I'm a senior."

J.J. stepped over to whisper so Jenny could hear. "Don't get any ideas, Conrad. She's got a sweetie down in Yort."

"That's nobody's business but mine!" Jenny scolded. Glenda cackled at the back of the kitchen.

"What are you doing when you graduate?" Conrad asked.

Jenny was already walking away. "Getting the fuck out of this shit town, that's for sure."

No tubs were coming in so Glenda went smoking, while Roy stood out on the floor, grim and cross-armed as if to will more customers into his chairs. Conrad stared at the dish station and noticed the grime pounded into its cracks. He covered the metal in a layer of suds and began to scrub with a bristle-brush.

*No more shit.*

*No more shit.*

*No more shit.*

*No more shit.*

In seventh grade Robb and Todd had gone around asking random kids the same question: 'are you a sadist or a masochist?' Perhaps Conrad finally had his answer. But there was something else, something hiding behind Helen's angry hardness. In his mind's eye he saw her in the hut when nobody else was there, curled up tight like a ball on the floor. He felt it as a kind of hope, that if he pushed the right button she might uncurl.

Henry didn't come in for a cocktail and was sitting in the car. On the way home he spoke in quiet grunts.

"I've been talking to your mother you know."

"Mmm."

"She's not happy I'm sure you can imagine, but she agreed that it'll be up to you, if you know what I mean."

"Yeah."

"So you have to make up your mind. You in or out?"

"I'm staying, I told her that."

Henry breathed in and out a few times. "I'll take you down to see the high school next week. Course it'll be empty but you can talk to the principal."

"OK."

At home the girls were grumpy. They only sat reading under their lights but Conrad could tell, so instead of saying anything he went down to look at the night from the dock. He brought his camera, and a chair to support it, hoping to get a shot of the half-moon that would soon rise at the far side of the lake. He stretched himself out on the dock and closed his eyes to wait. But then a scraping sound startled him up again. Once before an enormous raccoon had cornered him there, come to steal his nightcrawlers, but this time it was only Beth. She came out to sit at the edge and dangled her feet but didn't speak.

"What's up with you guys?" Conrad asked.

"Dad was yelling at Levy again."

"What about?"

"Oh she was sloppy. You know. Towels or something. I hate it."

"You're no better."

"No I mean Dad yelling like that. Any little thing and he gets real mad like we murdered the dog."

"We don't have a dog here."

"Stop joking. You always joke."

"OK whatever."

"It's like bigfoot's loose in the house. He goes off like Mom's not teaching us right, and then we have to listen to a long speech about how life works."

"Yeah."

"Oh you can say *yeah*, but he doesn't do that to you."

"Sure he does."

"No it's not the same. Not the same way. You're not a girl, and you're not even *there* half the time."

○ ○ ○

A breeze came steady off the lake under a gentler morning sun. Float away the day, it said, but Conrad pedaled toward the kitchen. This time he turned intentionally. *Time to pay up.* And he had no doubt: Helen's beauty would hurt all the way through from the first glimpse, and then she would crush him.

"Hi Helen."

Helen stood in the window silent and livid, as though twenty-four hours hadn't gone by.

"I've got the money today," Conrad said. He put the cash on the counter and waited, but Helen didn't move. "I'm sorry about yesterday," he added. Helen pulled in the cash and slid out the change without looking at him. Conrad placed negatives and a list by her hand. "And I need copies again." She reached, still without looking. But this was good. He could watch her directly now. He openly stared, scanning every detail of her face while she stood as a statue for an entire heart-aching minute. Then she turned only her head, and locked her eyes onto his for another eternity. Hers weren't loving eyes — they aimed to beat him, but he was already beaten so he didn't care. He was her Icarus and she was his sun. But soon it all began to tickle, and he smiled. Helen did not.

"What's so funny, fuck-wad?"

Conrad pulled back a half-step and his smile evaporated. "You're funny," he grumbled. "You're like an anger robot. Hi Helen, nice day isn't it? Rawrrr! Hey Helen, what are you into? Rawrrr!"

"So? Why's it your business?"

"I just think you're smart. Why do you have to act so dumb?"

"Did you call me dumb?" Helen grabbed the sides of the window like she would launch herself through it and strangle him.

"No, I mean, you just sit around mad all the time."

"I can do *whatever - I - want.*"

"So do nothing? The rest of your life? Not even college?"

"Not that shit again!"

"There's scholarships you know. Just get good grades and apply."

"And then what?"

"Then just a get on a bus. If your grumpy dad doesn't like it, well you know, you'd be eighteen..."

"Don't you talk about my dad! You don't know anything about us. You show up here from L.A. all sure of yourself. Why don't you just *fuck* the *fuck* off once and for all? Clueless rich jerk."

Conrad's eyes grew hot. But he forced a mumble. "I've only ever been nice to you. Why don't you like me?" He wanted her to answer for herself, and for Anise, too. But Helen only seethed.

"I don't have to like you! And I don't have to be nice! And I don't have to smile, or dress pretty or act like a good girl! And I don't have to kiss up to bullshit people. And I don't have to get married to a nice man and have nice babies like God intended. And I don't have to go to college! All *I* have to do is sit here in this hut and listen to your stupid shit!"

Conrad met her eyes one more time, then nodded and climbed onto his bike.

Arriving at the kitchen Conrad went straight to work cleaning the other side of the cooler. Blurry kitchen movements ghosted across the foggy panes in the cooler's grill-access doors — movements too casual, none of the usual Sunday rush. That was fine with Conrad. The chilly air would slow him until he stopped feeling. The cooks would discover him blissfully frosted over in the corner.

But after his break Conrad had warmed again — too warm. He stood frowning at the Black Bass. John noticed and stepped close to his ear.

"Don't let that crap bother you," he whispered.

"It's wrong."

"Yeah but it doesn't hurt anybody. You see any black people around here?" He returned to the grills to shake the pans sizzling on it.

*No, I've never seen a single black person around here, not ever, as a matter of fact.*

Conrad removed a pin, then another.

"What are you doing?" John hissed. "Roy'll have a fit."

Conrad pulled out the last pin and held the cartoon in his hands. John waved a hand.

"Listen kid, you can't argue with a bunch of old hound dogs. They grew up that way. Just forget it."

Conrad ripped the paper in half, crumpled the pieces and threw them in the trash. John shook his head and went back to work, but Glenda and J.J. had seen.


That night Conrad stood on the dock but didn't cast, his thoughts projecting onto the water's silvery glancing, past and present. 'You'll get stuck with those people' his mom had said. Did that mean people like Glenda? Or was Roy included? Henry hung around people like Roy. And so did the school principal. When she was still in school Sueanna had told everybody she'd get out of Polecat Creek, but Conrad couldn't picture her swearing about it, not like Jenny, or Helen. Sueanna loved this lake, he knew that for a fact. Was there something she was trying to escape, or did she simply want to leave more than she wanted to stay? He'd never thought to ask. He'd asked Helen, in a way, but all he had gotten back was blind rage. Maybe that's all it was. In any case he was stupid, so stupid...

*But stupid is such a stupid word.*

Mr. Onter would make him find a better word — now Babs, too. Fine then, what did *stupid* stand for? He looked to the other end of the lake, visible now in the slanting moonlight as gray-black water beneath black-black trees against blue-black sky. It was just like that — a subtle difference.

He felt wrong, that was it. But what about? He couldn't see it straight on. 'I don't have to like you,' she had said, and he knew that it was true. But that also meant the opposite, that she didn't have to *not* like him. She didn't have to say either way, but he had shown up day after day to corner her, to force her. *Like me!*

*Please!* He was pathetic. At any rate she was an astral beauty. Not liking him was a rejection from the entire universe. Or that's how it had felt, but tonight... tonight the universe clearly stood apart.

Conrad lay on his chest and hung his arms from the dock, and slipped his hands into the cool water, and made circles, and watched the ripples move out across the star-speckled lake.

# 19

# Early August

"Expedition!"

Bang bang bang.

Conrad rolled out of bed and sprawled face-down on the floor.

"Expedition!" Levy screeched again from outside the door.

Bang bang bang.

Sandwiches were already under construction when Conrad stumbled into the kitchen, and Beth had set out his cereal and a spoon. "Eat!" she ordered. He was tasked to lead, but he wasn't in charge.

Conrad stowed his map as they set off. They would only need it for the second half. Luckily the nameless pond was near a stream they knew, just much farther up it. Their trekking mood was quiet, striding with purpose toward uncharted lands, the cool dew tickling their legs as they passed along the undergrowth. It was indeed a distance, but they didn't stop to rest until arriving in less familiar woods. Now they began to survey, marking the map with numbers and taking matching notes. If a place had a special *something* it might earn itself a name.

At one point they decided to turn, but it was too soon so they backtracked to keep their bearings, then later repeated the process again, and again, swearing each time, until the pond was near.

Their noses twitched first. Coming closer they saw a perfect circle just like on the map, but the water was dark gray and surrounded by a bog with no source other than rain. It was the least inviting pool they had ever seen, and it smelled like a sewer.

"Ha! Ha ha ha!" Levy jumped up and down and flapped her

arms.

"Yay!" Beth grinned and giggled "hee hee hee!"

"What the hell!" Conrad yelled. "Why are you so happy?"

"Dad was right," said Beth. "We pointed where we were going on the map and he was like, *that place stinks*. So we asked Aunt Babs to teach us some French."

"Oh man." He had been pranked. But it was funny.

Levy faced the pond and jabbed her hands up at the sky. "I pronounce you, Piscine de Merde!"

There was no solid ground around the pond, but a giant oak had fallen at the edge. The kids used this to shimmy out over the water with sticks. Insects swarmed to their faces.

"Eew," said Levy, not usually squeamish, as she poked in her stick. Unidentifiable substances gummed its tip beneath the brackish water.

"Gross! It's bubbling," said Beth. "Nobody fall."

They were famished but couldn't eat anywhere near the place, so they went back out to the stream and hiked a little further up it until discovering a large flat boulder to sit on. There they munched beside the trickling water.

"I think we should call this whole part of the map *France*," said Levy. "And we'll call this rock *The Cafe*." Beth nodded to both.

"Agreed," Conrad said and pointed back to the pool, "and the restroom's that way if you need it."

"Ha ha!"

The rock cooled them. "This is sooooo nice," said Levy, stretching her face up all the way back until the tips of her long hair danced in the stream with the water bugs. "It's weird thinking about my friends in L.A. when we're having so much fun here."

"Weird how?" asked Conrad.

"I mean they stay home all summer just the same."

"But that's normal."

"Yeah, but it's so boring. Just wait, I'll get back and they'll say *we went to Arizona*, but it was like, four days or something. The rest of the time they were watching TV or going to Melrose."

"They do other stuff!" Beth protested, but sank back. "Then they talk about it and I don't get it. But some do go to camp I guess."

"Yeah, the rich ones," said Conrad.

"I wonder if any of those kids are up here," said Levy. "There's all these camps on the map but you never see the kids."

"I saw camp kids once!" said Beth. "They came in a school bus to the movie theater. All girls in uniform."

"Uhh," Levy groaned. "I'd hate that. Saint Emily's all over again. They'd never let us poke a stick in a shit hole."

"Levy!" Conrad laughed.

"It's true! And they'd say, *swim like a lady!* "

"No they wouldn't..." he tried to protest but it was too funny.

"Are you really going to stay here?" Beth asked. A hush came over them.

"Yeah," Conrad said. It was easier to say on a day like this. But Beth just frumped.

"Then you won't be there with us in L.A. It'll be all girls."

"But I'll be here with Dad. Nobody ever talks about him."

"We all get to be with Dad part of the time, and Mom the other part."

"But I always want to be here. Don't you?"

"I don't know..." She looked down at the stream. "I just want us to be normal, Mom and Dad together. But if that were true we'd have been here the whole time. Actually that's weird to think about."

"Yeah," Levy said. "We wouldn't know what a burrito is. Or guacamole! I need it! Aaag!" She raised a feeble hand and went limp.

"Dammit Levy," Conrad scolded. "You're not supposed to say those words."

"Sorry."

They sat for a while hankering until Beth spoke again.

"Babs says there's nothing to do here all winter, and it's dark. All the people with money just go somewhere else."

"Yeah but she's old," said Conrad. "There's stuff to do. You know, cross-country-skiing, ice fishing..."

"You can't do those all the time."

"Don't you think I remember? I remember more than you."

"You don't have to be nasty about it."

"Then why do you have to bug me? It's just like Mom. Lots of people live here and so can I." He stood up and stuffed the empty sandwich bags into his backpack. The girls followed him home.

The kids were swimming when Henry returned early from work. They ran up in towels with their hair still dripping.

"What's news?" Henry asked, but he looked preoccupied.

Beth stood straight. "We got up early and traveled to France and visited the Piscine de Merde, then we ate lunch at a Cafe, but when we got back we were hungry again so we ate all the leftover potato salad, and since then we've been swimming, so now we're really hungry again."

Henry had nodded inattentively through this. "I've got some chicken legs and baked beans. Sound OK?"

"Yeah!"

The kids dried and dressed while Henry got the grill going. He came up to find the kids giggling at the TV.

"Hey Conrad," he grunted, "come down and help me a sec."

Conrad followed him out. Henry lifted the lid off the grill to shift the coals, then peeked up at the house to make sure the girls weren't in the window.

"Listen I wanted to talk to you first. I have some bad news." He lowered the lid and adjusted the vent. "I got a call today from the Alder House. Roy says the downturn's real bad, so he won't need you anymore this summer."

"Oh," Conrad said. His stomach lurched.

"You sure everything was OK there?"

"Yeah! I was getting good. Roy even said. Then it slowed down so I cleaned half the place."

"Hm. Well I'm sorry your first job had to go like that. Kind of rubs me the wrong way though."

"Why's that?"

"Well it's not like he'd go broke keeping you on. There's less than four weeks left at most, if we're just talking the summer. Though I was thinking it could be your part-time place, you know, during school. Now's a bad time to ask someplace else. Summer like this." He shook his head.

Conrad sat frowning. It did feel bad, shameful even, good reason or no. But why did he care? He shouldn't care. Actually... actually he didn't care. August was his!

"I have a bunch of stuff for you to do around here," Henry added.

○ ○ ○

It was late but Conrad sat awake under the basement light-bulb in quiet so pure he could hear the pilot light burning under the water heater. Every closed-in odor — the damp concrete, the greasy metal parts around the workbench, the laundry detergent — came distinctly to his nose. If only his feelings were so clear. But they weren't and it bugged him. Why did he have to be so blurry all the time? He'd never wanted the job in the first place! But he'd rearranged himself for it, because he had to. And now he would un-rearrange himself for a few short weeks — which wasn't bad in this case, but then he'd have to re-rearrange himself all over again in Los Angeles. He was a crazy mixed-up soup. He was Dog Stew.

His painting was looking like a stew, too. All he could see now was the surface of the paint, not what he'd meant for it to represent. The forest he'd seen only as a glimmer had taken shape in the form of smears up and down his canvas. Somehow forgetting everything Mrs. Pelora had taught him, he had globbed it on too thick. Maybe, if he stared and stared, he would see how he could rescue it. Maybe.

○ ○ ○

Conrad woke at the sound of a door closing and scrambled out to the window in time to see the car heading away. Slumping into a chair, he was conscious of wanting something, but as his head cleared it faded. He certainly didn't want to go to town.

It was still early. He could flop back into bed, but instead he spooned corn flakes into his mouth by the TV. Today the Marshalls could go home, but only if they caused their past selves to fall into The Land Of The Lost. Behind the TV all the old paperbacks still sat a-jumble on the shelves. Now he remembered! He wanted his dad to pick up his pictures. It was true he could go himself — really he ached to go — but his experiment had failed in the form of a mushroom cloud. Still, it made him itchy not to bring Helen the books like he had planned, like not finishing the story.

Conrad found a small cardboard box and packed some favorite books into it. But it wasn't full, so he added some of Levy's: *Island Of The Blue Dolphins, The Diary Of Anne Frank, The Witch Of Blackbird Pond*. He taped the box shut, wrote 'When finished return to Henry's Electric' on the top, stuffed it into his backpack and ran to his bike. He would be absolved from his stupidity or wrongness or whatever it was. He would even the scales. But time was ticking.

By the time Fern Way smoothed under his tires, Conrad was out of breath and covered in dust sticking to sweat. But now clouds had gathered and a sudden mist smeared the dust down his face. He stopped to flush droplets over himself and neaten his hair, just in case, then continued out to the hut.

Luckily the hut was still locked. He placed the box on the window-counter out of the rain and rode away. But nearing Fern Way he heard car tires crackling the gravel a distance behind him. He braked and turned his head: it was the truck, and Helen had stepped out of it. Seeing Conrad she stopped. Conrad returned her stare: a long expressionless pause, taking in as much of her as he could from a distance. Then he turned back to the road.

"Where did you go?" Levy asked when Conrad came into the kitchen, damp and dirty.

"I just felt like riding," he said. His escapade seemed so silly now. Good thing he hadn't actually talked to her. He would have been just like his mom.

*Hi Helen, would you like some books to read?*
*(Indistinct swearing and insults)*
*Oh great! Here's fifteen books. You'll like them.*

Beth sat down to eat. Now Conrad noticed that she and Levy were both wearing jeans and shoes.

"Why are you guys dressed?"

"Babs is taking us to Polecat Ranch."

"You're going on one of those rides?" Conrad asked, incredulous. Even the girls had mocked the tourists circling there.

"No, we're going on a trip to Midnight Lake."

"What?"

"They do private rides, like real ones, way far. Babs knows the owner."

Levy bounced in her chair like she was already riding. "Yeah, and guess what! When we're older we can work there for our summer jobs, taking care of the horses. Babs told them all about us." Both sisters grinned and rubbed their hands with glee at the prospect.

"Too bad you don't have the training," said Beth with a haughty lift of her head. "Otherwise you could go today, too."

Conrad frowned. Tromping through the woods on horseback sounded fun all of a sudden, plus Midnight Lake didn't have road access, so he had never seen it. Later when Babs drove the girls away, Conrad gave a droopy wave and drifted down to the dock to sit looking at the lake. He could go fishing, he supposed, or read. Or he could paint! But his painting was a flop, he had to admit in the light of day. And anyway he was hungry. He went back up to the kitchen to make a bologna sandwich. As he chewed he studied the map over the table. One place stood out: a bulge in a creek, as if forming a pond, a good distance away. He packed another sandwich and water, left a note with the coordinates, and set off into the woods.

It was different without his sisters, none of that bubbly tramping. Conrad glided swiftly through the spotty canopy-filtered light, the ground passing under him as a long unbroken shape. It was easy to find the creek but not to follow it, as it sat low under eroded banks and was blocked by thick underbrush at every turn. But he could hear it, so he used nearby deer trails to snake alongside from a distance.

When nearly an hour had passed he began to have doubts, but then he came to the widening part, and when he saw it he stood thrilled to his core. The pond wasn't large, but its surface rippled clear emerald-green over fine sand, illuminated by the midday sun. Conrad could hardly believe his eyes. Did his dad know about this place? Levy and Beth were going to flip.

Conrad walked ankle-deep around the edge to a more open stretch of woods at the other side — a great place for a shelter, he thought. Maybe he would build it in secret, a surprise. He set to work right away, clearing a flat spot and suspending a long branch between two trees.

When Conrad returned home he could hardly keep still and busied himself with raking leaves. Henry arrived home first and set to making dinner, then Babs arrived with the girls. They all sat outside at the picnic table, the adults with their cocktails. Every detail of the day's adventure to Midnight Lake bubbled out of his sisters, but soon Levy noticed her brother sitting with his eyes too bright.

"What are you hiding?" she asked, pointing.

Conrad broke into a guilty grin. "Nothing! Nothing at all!" Levy and Beth needled him the rest of the night but he didn't say.

# 20

# Mid-August

The car set to rolling, tires crackling the driveway gravel before rushing onto the road, Conrad listening at his open window. Henry had jostled him early to shower and look nice for the school principal, and now it was all just up ahead, whatever it was, what he had chosen. It made him go quiet, and Henry too.

Like most everything else there, the school was just a ways off the main highway. Henry turned and soon they came to a sign saying 'Fowler's High School' and another saying 'Home of the Polecats!' before two squat buildings with a square of concrete between them. Conrad strained to spot an opening in the woods, to another part of the campus perhaps, but saw only a solid line of trunks.

Henry led Conrad through an empty office, finding the principal at his desk in the back room.

"Jerry! This is my son Conrad!" Henry bellowed as if they hadn't already met at the bar. The principal stood to shake hands then sat back in his chair.

"Glad to have you aboard. What do you play?"

"Play?"

"Used to play baseball," Henry said, looking to Conrad now. "Back in grade school. You remember, right?" Conrad nodded.

"Well good," said the principal. "Our team's getting top-heavy with seniors. I'll let the coach know, sound good?" Conrad nodded again.

"Where do we sign!" Henry said and laughed.

"Actually you do sign," said the principal, standing up. "You know, forms." He motioned to wait and retrieved some papers from the front. Henry got straight to work. Meanwhile the principal sat back and peered at Conrad.

"Don't talk much do you?" he said.

"Um... do I choose classes now?"

"Yes. You choose math, science, geography and history." He looked at Henry and they both chuckled.

"What about art?"

"Not in your grade, but it's usually just girls anyway. Got some macaroni in the kitchen if you want."

"Oh."

Henry made a last signature and handed over the forms. "Well thanks Jerry." The two men shook hands and Conrad followed Henry out.

"Excited about the team?" Henry pushed on the way back after Conrad had stared out the window for a while.

Conrad only glanced and nodded.

"You like baseball, right?"

Conrad shook his head.

"What? Then why didn't you say anything?"

"I don't know."

"You've gotta start speaking up for yourself."

"OK."

A few more miles of road passed before Henry spoke again.

"Look, if you really care about the art stuff we'll figure something out. But you gotta start growing up, you know? You gotta figure out how to make it in the real world."

"Uh huh."

"You think I'm just making it all up? You need skills you know. That's what people pay for. I mean, just look at framers. That's an art too you know, but those guys are at least earning something for it. You see what I'm saying?"

"I guess."

Henry and Conrad returned just before lunch. The girls ran out of the house.

"Something's up with the toilet," said Levy.

Henry went into the house and soon the words 'god dammit' echoed inside. He stomped back out.

"Plunger didn't work. You kids haven't been putting anything down the toilet, have you?"

The kids shook their heads.

"Dammit," Henry said again. "I'll have to call the Chesters." He stood rubbing his chin, then headed for the car. "Hope it's not what I'm thinking. You can go pee in the woods for now, just not too close OK? Or use the outhouse."

The outhouse was a sagging, bug-infested horror shack that Henry kept around just in case. The kids made faces but Henry was already driving away.

"Can we go to Pipsqueak?" Levy asked Conrad.

"Why?"

"We want to start our new books."

"But you can do that anywhere."

"Starting's better there," Levy pleaded. "Please?"

Beth puppy-blinked. Soon they were all rowing away from the dock in life preservers. The girls had already packed a bag with three lunches and books.

"How's the school?" asked Levy.

"It's a school," said Conrad with a shrug.

It was a long row to Pipsqueak, especially with three in the boat, so the kids took turns. But not a bad idea, Conrad admitted to himself after they were sitting with their feet in the water under the shade of Pip and Squeak, books in one hand and liverwurst sandwiches in the other, the boat bobbing nearby at the end of its anchor rope, the words from their reading reflecting on the water when they paused.

When the boat reached the dock the kids heard unfamiliar sounds from the front of the house. They ran up and around to see a septic truck parked in the driveway and Henry standing with a pair of burly men. Henry was grim.

"They pumped out the septic tank but it's still blocked," he said to the kids. "Probably the inlet pipe." He pointed under his feet. "They'll have to dig it up. The whole thing's really old and deep, otherwise they'd be done by now."

One of the men came over. "It's too late now, but we can bring over the backhoe tomorrow. You have any records we could use? We don't want to damage it."

"Yeah, I got all that. My son'll be here," said Henry, frustration clouding his face.

Conrad noticed the oldest of the men eying Levy. Before leaving the man pulled Henry aside and whispered. After the septic truck had rumbled away Henry stood over the kids.

"Levy, have you been putting feminine things down the toilet?"

Levy looked at the ground and mumbled. "Well yeah I guess. Where else was I supposed to?"

"I told you, *only toilet paper*. I told you that a thousand times!"

"Isn't it like the same thing?"

"No it isn't. Why do you think I keep telling you? I tell you guys every year and you forget."

"But it's gross." Levy's face was red, but Henry's was redder.

"I swear you kids never get it. Don't you know how expensive this is going to be?"

"Dad, she didn't know," Beth mumbled.

"Yeah you kids never know what your mom doesn't teach you."

"Don't talk about Mom," Levy said, her face rumpling.

"And why shouldn't I? Shouldn't I care she's not teaching you any sense of responsibility?"

"You don't know that," Levy said.

"Sure I do, I can tell. Every time it's the same thing."

"You don't know!" Levy yelled and turned her face up at Henry and screamed. "You don't know! You don't know! You don't know!"

"Don't you ever yell at me like that!" Henry bellowed, towering over her.

"Dad?" Beth tried to say.

"You stay out of it," he said, pointing at her face.

"You don't know anything!" Levy yelled again. "You're never there! And all you do is boss us around!"

Henry turned back to Levy. "I know way more than you, and I won't have my daughter talking to me that way!"

"Dad," said Conrad, but Henry ignored him.

"It's all play time for you kids but things cost money I don't have! And now you're telling me I don't know?" Henry had leaned even closer down to Levy's face.

"Dad *stop*," Conrad said now, not in control of his own actions. He stepped up to Henry and pointed at his face. "*Stop - right - now*," he said again. With this Henry stood up and blinked at Conrad, then stomped up into the house.

Dinner was quiet, with only talk about the food and grunts from Henry, nobody looking at each other, then TV for Henry and books for the girls. Conrad slipped out, switched on the back light and headed down to the dock. The light beamed across the water near shore, allowing Conrad to see dimly into its dark-green depths. He decided to try his biggest lure, a double-jointed wooden pike minnow with enormous jangling hooks. If he was doomed to never again catch a bass or crappie or walleye because of the muskies, he might as well try for a musky. With a vigorous swoop of his arms he cast. The lure hit the water with a loud *ker-sploosh* and waggled heavily as he reeled, returning under the surface like a hyperactive robot fish. Conrad cast again and again until his mind had calmed, so at first he wasn't alarmed when a long dark shadow followed his lure back to the dock. But then he caught his breath and slowed his reeling to give the shadow a chance. When the lure neared, he caught a glimpse of an elongated face, its eye looking straight at him before its long striped body curved away into the murk. Conrad made a few more frantic casts where the musky had vanished until finally folding himself at the end of the dock in defeat. Then Henry came down, carrying his own pole.

"Aren't you fishing?" Henry mumbled.

"Yeah I guess," said Conrad and stood up again to cast.

○ ○ ○

The septic truck returned the next afternoon, towing an old backhoe. Conrad handed the men the papers Henry had left and watched as they methodically located the septic system and dug out the ground around it. Near the end of this step, when the inlet pipe and septic tank were exposed and heaps of dirt had grown nearby, the backhoe lurched with a metal snap.

"Aw fuckin' hell!" one of the men yelled. Both of them inspected the machine and came away shaking their heads.

"Old piece of crap," one grumbled.

In any case they got to work on the inlet pipe, deciding after dredging to replace it, which meant cutting it out of the ground. Through all this, the hellish gases emanating from the septic tank chased away any lingering curiosity on the part of Conrad, who retreated into the basement where he attempted to salvage his painting. But there was no fixing it, not really. He could only layer on more paint and make it worse.

When the men were done they asked to use the phone. Conrad led the older man into the kitchen where he called Henry at work to explain about the backhoe, saying it might take days to fix.

"Good news kid!" said the man to Conrad after hanging up. "Your dad says you're better than a backhoe."

After that the men drove away leaving the open trench and mountains of dirt.

○ ○ ○

"Girls? Girls!"

Babs stood large and frilly by her two-tone Oldsmobile waiting for Levy and Beth. Both had rolled out of bed just minutes before, so Conrad went down to stall for them.

"Sure you don't want to come along?" asked Babs. She was taking the girls for an 'assessment' at the ranch.

"No, can't," he said and thumbed at the mounds of dirt. It was true, but it was also true that he harbored a private envy — not about the horses, only that he had nothing so fitting for a summer job.

The girls came running down to pile into the car and it receded down the driveway.

"Buh-bye booby brother!" Beth yelled out the window.

*Alone.*

Conrad grabbed his bag and ran for the secret pond on legs already imprinted with every twist and turn. Over the entire distance the woods were dim and damp under persistent clouds, but he had a plan: eat lunch early, complete the lean-to, float in the pool, then dry off and run back home to get warm again.

Even under this day's dreary light the pool appeared mystically beautiful. Conrad came to a halt at its edge and stood to breathe in the mineralized air as the beating in his chest subsided. Then his stomach caught up with him. He sat to eat his sandwich, meanwhile staring through the pond's shifting surface to the rounded stones embedded in its sand. Noticing his hands were empty, he got up again to gather branches for the shelter walls. But before he could accomplish much he heard voices echoing just over a rise, so he scurried into a depression to hide.

The voices came suddenly close. Through the leaves Conrad saw two adults: a man and a woman, both in their late 30's and wearing vests with some sort of insignia. They headed straight for the lean-to.

"You can come out," said the woman. Conrad stood up where he was, ready to flee.

"What are you up to here?" said the man. Their insignias said 'D.N.R.'

"Making a shelter."

"Yes, but why?" The man was stern, but Conrad caught a twinkling in the eyes of the woman.

"It's a surprise... for my sisters."

"So no beer party, throwing cans into the pool, trampling the rare wildflowers, screaming all night, leaving trash all over the place?"

"No," said Conrad shaking his head. "No, we live down that way, on Lake Levinia." He pointed. "My dad does, I mean. My sisters and I come for the summer, we used to live here. But I'm coming back." He didn't know why he was saying so much.

"I see," said the man. "Look. I don't want you cutting live branches for this. Next time just bring a tent."

Conrad nodded, though he had no intention of bringing a tent. The man proceeded to inspect the lean-to and shook his head.

"In any case this isn't even going to work. First rain, you're soaked. You'd nearly have to bury it to seal it, but there isn't much around here for that, at least not if it's this big to begin with. Plus you're in this low area here. Water will puddle up in a storm. I'd call this a summer-day shelter at best."

It was all true, Conrad had to admit.

"Don't worry," said the woman, motioning for Conrad to come sit near them on a log. "We used to do the same thing when we were kids. I'm Shelly, by the way." She leaned over to shake his hand. What's your name?"

"Conrad. My dad owns Henry's Electric."

The man also shook his hand. "I'm Stan. Don't mean to scare you off, it's just we've had so many problems with teenagers. And we don't want them to find this pool in particular."

"It's our special place," said Shelly. "Stan proposed to me here."

"You don't have to tell him our whole life story," Stan grumbled.

"Oh pshh!" she waved him off. "It's our anniversary this week. We were hoping it would be nicer." She peeked up through the treetops at the clouds.

"You should have seen it a couple days ago," Conrad said. "The sun made the pool look like stained glass."

Shelly sat taller. "Did you hear that, Stan?" Stan blinked. "That's just what Stan said."

"So what were you planning?" asked Stan, pointing at the lean-to.

"Stay overnight I guess. My sisters will like it here. But I always think about that. You know, living in the woods. I want to stay out here."

Stan nodded and contemplated. "I know what you mean. Truth is it's darn hard, I mean if I understand you correctly, like to actually live off the land, that sort of thing. By yourself you need some serious skills, and serious knowledge. Luck, too. Even then you'd most likely end up dead eventually. There's a reason the natives lived in tribes you know. People need people, like it or not."

"Sometimes we don't like it," said Shelly, smiling. "But our jobs let us get away, so that's good."

"You're working today?" Conrad asked.

"Oh yeah, we do sweeps. Partly for our main job, monitoring the forest, especially protected areas like this one. All those resorts put pressure on things, plus there's off-season trapping and hunting we have to keep a lid on. And teenagers creating disaster areas."

"It's just sticks," Conrad mumbled.

"Oh we don't mean this. You should have seen a few weeks ago, over on Wicker Lake. Place looked like a dump truck came in the night."

"We'll let you keep the shelter for now," said Stan, "but take it down when you're done. And stay away from those little plants at the edge, they're rare. And don't leave a fire pit. Don't want to give anybody ideas. And keep this place a secret, would you please?"

"OK."

Shelly leaned forward between them. "So you said you're coming back to live here?" she asked. "Where you been?"

"Los Angeles."

"Oh well that's different! Why come back?"

"I like it better in the woods."

Shelly waited for Conrad to say more but he didn't. "Hmm. I know how you feel," she said. "I'm from here actually, but I was gone for a long time."

"To where?"

"College at first, in Oregon. Met Stan there, doing our masters, but he had a girlfriend then." She sneered at Stan to tease him. "Both of us studied high deserts, you know what those are? Like where it's arid but at a higher altitude. It's beautiful in all the opposite ways from here, and stars at night like you wouldn't believe. I was at the Oregon D.N.R. for years, but then my mom wasn't well, plus I felt so homesick for these woods."

Conrad sat up. "Wait, so how did Stan get here?"

"Oh that's the funny thing. He came to visit, and I told him some things, and he told me some things, and there was an open position here so he took it and stayed." Stan was looking shy by now but Shelly leaned over to smooch his cheek. "But anyway my mom passed last summer, so we're looking to move as soon as we can."

"What? You're going?"

"Yeah. Is that so shocking?"

"But you're from here. You said so."

"Oh sure, and the things I missed here, well... lots is the same, but it's not the same for me."

"What's not the same?"

Shelly crossed her arms and considered. "I guess you could say it's the memory versus the reality of the place. But it's impossible to say it in a way that feels fair. Makes it kind of a touchy subject for me. Just ask Stan."

"But I don't get it," said Conrad, "what's not fair?"

Shelly looked at Conrad for a moment, then out over the pool. "Well it was always small here, and hard for lots of folks, but we were kids, we didn't know any different. We were like animals, me and my brothers, outside adventuring all the time. When I was away I missed that, and places like this. I mean just look at it." She stopped for a moment to sigh at the water. "And there's good people here, people I care about. But then living here means living in Polecat Creek. You've got three TV stations with the same news, nearest library's in Yort. Sure I've got Stan, but we've got a little girl now. Took me a while to realize — Stan said this too — she doesn't need to have the same childhood that I did. Plus we really do miss the high desert. Oh there's some good ones in California! There's this place called Lone Pine we visited last year, near the High Sierras. We both applied there. So we'll see!"

Conrad stared at the ground. "I always want to be here," he murmured.

Stan spoke up now. "What happens with your sisters, if you stay?"

"They go back to L.A. ...with my mom."

"Without you."

Conrad nodded.

"Hmm. What about friends? You have friends there?"

"Yeah."

Stan looked Conrad in the eyes for a second, but then he changed gears and stood. "Well we should probably leave you to it."

"No!" Conrad said and jumped up, remembering that Shelly and Stan had come there to be alone. "I have to go. Sorry to mess up your date." He zipped his backpack and headed into the trees.

"Oh it's nothing!" Shelly called. "It was nice meeting you!"

When Conrad arrived at the house he remembered the trip back only as the forest floor passing underfoot. Now the long trench came into view, and the septic tank, and the heaps of dirt. It was a big job, but he still had the afternoon.

Shoveling dirt into the hole wasn't the hard part. The dirt went in fluffed with air, so he also had to jab the shovel down to compact it while taking care to avoid the pipe. After much scooping and jabbing, and aching and sweating, there was still a hole and large piles of dirt. Later when the hole was less deep it seemed there was more dirt than hole to fill. In the end there was, but he heaped it all on, making the trench overfull, then jumped up and down on top. He was already hot, but now a different heat grew inside him. He switched to whacking the dirt flat with his shovel, all along its length, enraged, hitting the ground harder and harder still. "God dammit!" he yelled. "Dammit! Dammit!"

He imagined the shovel's handle cracking, but it was too strong. "God fucking shit dammit!" he screamed and slammed the shovel again and again until his throat was hoarse and his hands were numb. Finally he thew down the shovel with a clatter and stomped into the basement where he saw his canvas on the easel. He wrenched it off and ran back out to the driveway and threw it paint-down onto the dirt. Then he went to get his dad's gas can and poured gasoline all over the painting, and struck a match and set it on fire. Then he picked up the shovel again and slammed it into the flames.

When the car pulled into the driveway, Conrad was nowhere to be seen, though he was actually within earshot up a tree. Through its leaves he watched Levy and Beth run up into the house in front of Henry. Then Beth came out again and ran the perimeter.

"Conrad? Conrad! Hey Conrad! Guess what!"

No answer came, so she circled back to the front. Henry was looking over the former trench.

"Look at this!" Conrad could hear him saying. "Did a real nice job, too. You find him?"

Beth shook her head so they went indoors. Conrad climbed higher up the tree.

A while later Levy came out and stood peering into the woods as if she might spy her brother returning along a trail, but she soon gave up and headed back. Conrad climbed down and followed her inside.

"There he is!" Henry boomed. "Boy you look worn out!"

"Yeah."

Conrad sat down to a plate of pork chops while Beth launched into her briefing.

"They said we know lots already! Our groundwork's good, but we need to study tons of horse care stuff."

"I want to learn to make horseshoes," said Levy, falling into a frump. "But they said it's not for kids."

Conrad's stomach gurgled at the smell of his dinner, but his hands were throbbing and he could barely hold his knife and fork. He breathed through his mouth to stay calm, but then he dropped his utensils and stared at his palms.

"You OK Conrad?" Beth asked.

He nodded, but hot tears streamed down his face.

"I think Conrad's losing his marbles," Levy whispered.

"No I'm not," he said. "I'm not!" he yelled now. "I'm not losing anything!"

"Whoah there Conrad," said Henry. "Girls, why don't you take your plates out to the picnic table."

"Aw Dad!" Beth whined, but one look from Henry sent them both out the door.

"What's going on Conrad?"

Conrad sat inhaling and exhaling, then looked at Henry for just a moment, but shook his head. "Nothing."

"Doesn't seem like nothing."

"My hands hurt," he managed to croak, "I think they're swelling. I was pounding the ground."

"Think you broke something?"

Conrad shook his head.

"And that's it?" Henry eyed him.

Conrad nodded.

"Poor baby. Here, I'll get some ice water." Henry rustled through the kitchen and came back with a bowl. Conrad dipped his hands into it. "Don't leave them in too long. That's not good either. Take them out for a while, then back in, repeat, got it?"

Conrad nodded, and Henry went down to the girls. After a while Conrad went to join them and heard more about the horses. The evening had turned blissfully warm, so Beth decided that after reading time they would all go night swimming, including Henry, so they did, and later Conrad took his boat out to fish under the smallest sliver of a moon.

○ ○ ○

Morning broke on the perfect day for the big reveal: bright, hot, and sticky. But Henry rang the phone before the kids could leave.

"Babs invited us to a party this afternoon," he told Conrad. "Be ready at two."

The boredom the kids would surely endure — sitting on the shore of an inferior lake, or bobbing on a glacial pontoon boat with elderly cocktail-handlers — propagated back in time. The day was smashed, and Beth fussed at Conrad's secret staying secret. The kids sat moping in the living room. But soon Conrad noticed there was still film in the camera, so they made do posing for 'lake portraits' on the dock before the sun got too high.

"You see that big tree?" Levy said, pointing down the shoreline. "The one with the two branches over the water? I always think it would be nice to read up there."

"You're crazy," Conrad said, immediately picturing boards between the branches. "Let's go look." They set off on the lake-side trail to assess the tree. By the time Henry picked them up later an idea had taken hold: The Reading Tree, like the high bench but better. Henry only grunted however, saying nails hurt trees. Plans for rope-attached parts began forming in Conrad's mind.

Babs stood cooing at her door and pointed to the 'croissants.' A surprising number of people were milling around the house and its lawn, with the sounds of clinking ice and storytelling and belly-laughs. Conrad wove among them, listening to the talk between raids of the hors d'oeuvres.

"They can just stay out of our business and we'll stay out of theirs," grumbled one man. The others nodded.

"Guess you don't need the highway re-paved," said Babs, standing behind them with her glass.

"Oh that's different."

"Is it? You think the tax base around here supports that, or the schools for that matter?"

"I'm sure we'd do just fine."

A woman Conrad vaguely recognized smiled at him. "Speaking of schools, your father tells me you're staying here this year. You excited?"

Conrad blinked at the woman and nodded his head. But then he looked up and found himself locked in Babs' gaze. Meanwhile the woman said something about her grandson being the same age, and Henry said something enthusiastic. Conrad smiled politely and slid away out the side door. But he didn't get far. Babs came around a corner to block him and pointed into the woods. Conrad didn't move, so she pointed more firmly. He walked. A little ways down a path was a clearing with a swing hanging from a tall tree. Babs stopped him there.

"There's something. Don't lie to me."

There *was* something. It couldn't have a name, or any words at all attached to it. He had hidden it way back behind his eyesight where it floated in circles.

Babs shook her head wearily. "Your mom and dad really taught you well," she sighed. "Listen, you can't go through your whole life this way. What is it?"

Conrad wanted to talk now but couldn't. Babs pushed.

"Around these parts you see it all the time: deer in the headlights. That was you just now. So what's the truth Conrad? Do you still want to stay?"

Conrad froze, so Babs reached over and poked his shoulder. That was enough.

"No," he said. "No, I don't. I don't. I don't." He shook his head and gulped for air.

"You need to tell him. And not later. Gather the courage and tell him today."

Conrad nodded, but his panic increased at the thought.

Babs spoke softer now. "Look I know how it is, believe me. The consequences seem too horrible, so you wait till you're cornered. Or even then you don't say, you just let yourself live cornered, to be nice. You're nice Conrad. Why do you think I like you so much?" She pulled him in close and hugged him. "But *not* saying things is worse. Sometimes it's not nice to be nice."

"But how? How do I say it?"

"The less *how* the better. Just pull him aside."

Conrad stared at the ground for a while. "Aunt Babs... why?"

"Why what?"

"Why aren't you making me stay?"

"Oh no." She wagged her finger. "I know how this game works. I give you *my* reasons, then you go use them to hide behind. Find your own words Conrad."

The party went on for hours longer, extended by boisterous pontoon tours of the lake. Henry drove the kids home in high spirits, waving his free hand too close to Conrad's face to illustrate stories from the party, not noticing that Conrad sat mute since that was normal. But Henry's enthusiasm rubbed off on the girls. Instead of heading off to read they sat on the yellow yeti rug playing Crazy Eights next to Henry as he watched the news.

For his part, Conrad emptied his tackle box onto the kitchen table, then proceeded to wash it out in the sink with soap. Then he scrubbed each of his lures with a toothbrush and lined them up on paper towels to dry. It was quieter in the living room now, but the job wasn't done. Next he sorted through his many boxes of hooks and sinkers. Some of these were rusting and had to go. And there were so many old folded papers and maps! Of course he had to inspect them all.

When all his gear had been placed back into the correct slots, Conrad closed the box and locked it. Then he returned to the living room. The girls were gone and Henry was lying face up, snoring.

"Dad?" said Conrad, shaking Henry's shoulder.

Henry opened his eyes halfway. "Oh! I was out. Time for bed." He stumbled up and disappeared into his room.

○ ○ ○

A door closing.

Conrad jolted out of bed and ran to the window expecting to see Henry walking down to the car. But the car was gone and the kitchen clock read eight-fifteen. Henry had left long before. Conrad went to check on the girls: still in bed. He went back to the kitchen and sat spooning cereal, confused. But soon Beth appeared in the door rubbing her eyes, and Levy behind her.

"Can you show us your secret today?" Beth creaked. Conrad shook his head but didn't look at her. "Why not?" she pressed. He shook again.

"You're acting really weird," Levy said, but she and Beth took their cereal to the TV to watch Reading Rainbow. They were too old they said, but liked it anyway. Conrad went outside and stood by an oak tree, tracing the hard ridged patterns of its bark with his fingertips until he had stood there long enough, then came back inside to stand by the phone. He reached for it, but then his heart and his legs took him to the basement. His hands lifted his fishing tackle and carried it down to the lake and loaded it into his boat and zipped up his life jacket, but then they fell paralyzed to his sides before he could untie the ropes. He stared at a little puddle on the boat's aluminum bottom, at the pine needles floating on its surface as if on liquid mercury. He climbed out and walked back up to the house.

"You going fishing?" asked Levy, seeing his life jacket. Conrad shook his head and Levy rolled her eyes. He continued to the phone and picked it up this time, and dialed.

"Dad?"

"That you Conrad?"

Conrad only breathed.

"Everything OK there?" Henry asked with immediate concern. "The girls OK?"

"Yeah. They're fine."

"What's going on?"

"Dad?" It was harder to breathe.

"You need something? I've got people here."

"I need to talk to you." Now he was breathing too fast.

"Can we talk later? I can call you when I'm finished with these clients."

"No. I need to talk to you."

There was a pause at the other end. "I'll come home at lunch, OK?"

"OK."

When Henry's car rolled up, Conrad had been pacing the property for sixty-thousand years, but now he cornered himself, watching out the kitchen window as Henry came closer. As usual his father came through the door frame like it was too small for his body. He scanned around to see if anything in the house was different.

"Where are the girls?" he asked.

"They found a new blackberry patch." Conrad pointed vaguely down the road. It was true. They had given up on him and taken their buckets with them. Conrad sat down at the table, so Henry sat, too.

"So you have something to you want to talk about?" Henry asked as if in a business meeting.

Conrad looked at the table. He would say it now.

"Conrad, you need to sit up and talk. Look at me." Conrad sat taller. Henry pressed. "What is it?"

"I don't want to stay." His heart raced.

"Stay? Stay where?"

"Here, after the summer."

Henry's eyes went wide and he loomed closer. "What? Why not?"

"I just don't."

"That's not a very good answer. What is it, not impressed with the school? Sure it's not fancy but there's good people there."

"That's not it."

"Then what then?"

"I want to stay with Levy and Beth."

"Oh, you're just getting cold feet." Henry's voice came deeper. "You stay a while, you'll be fine. It'll be fun. You'll make new friends, guys your own age."

"I don't want new friends. I already have friends."

"That's not what your mother says. Are you still bothered about the job thing?"

"That's not it. I don't care."

"Well then are you upset with me about something?"

"No, I just told you."

Henry poked the table with his finger. "Conrad we talked about this and you said you decided. You can't just go through life changing your mind every time things get tough."

"I know. I'm sorry."

"You're sorry? That's all you have to say? Don't I get a say in this?"

Conrad held his teeth tight and shook his head. "I'm sorry."

"I already bought the tickets for the girls you know. This'll be a major headache!" Henry stood up to leave.

"I'm sorry."

"Yeah, well I'm sorry too." Henry walked out, and soon Conrad heard the car rushing down the driveway.

Levy and Beth burst into the kitchen minutes afterward, but they stopped and stood with their buckets full of berries at the sight of Conrad's face. He kept his eyes pointed at the table as if he hadn't noticed their return. He wouldn't tell them anything yet, didn't want to hear their reactions, their probable cheers.

Beth moved to speak but Levy shushed her. She searched around in her bucket, then extended a palm under Conrad's nose. He looked down and saw two berries: one under-ripe, the other over-ripe. He opened his mouth, and Levy popped them in, and he chewed, and with the rush of bright tart sweetness he curled his face into his hands.

# 21

# Late August

Henry only drove while his kids debated.

"It looks all bulgy on the map," said Conrad. "Maybe we should call it *The Bulge*."

"That just makes it sound like dad," Levy said, batting her eyes.

"Hey now," Henry said.

"OK how about *The Emerald Pond*," said Levy.

"Nah," Conrad said. "That's too floofy."

Levy sat back and sighed. "Yeah you're right. It's real magic there, like there's no words that'll work for it."

The girls had finally seen the pool. But seeing was just the start: they had reacted with untamed love, waving their arms and thrashing the water and screeching every bad word as if the place were purging them of evil. But ever since they had struggled to name it.

"I guess we could just keep calling it *The Secret Place*," said Conrad.

Beth disagreed. "Then people will know it's a place. How about just... *Don't Know*. Because you didn't even know what it was going to be like there, and we don't want people to know about it, and we don't know when we'll go there again, and when we do, if anybody asks where we're going we can just say *Don't Know*."

Levy began to nod. "Yeah..." Conrad said. "That's perfect!"

When the sign for Polecat Creek zipped by Henry slowed onto the main street. He pulled up to the bait & tackle shop (open late to double as a liquor store) where Conrad jumped out to buy nightcrawlers. Coming back out he paused to look down

Lake Street, now dim and empty. The summer story was over for this place, its tourists mostly gone and the happy window products useless to those who remained. It could never be this lonely in the woods, he thought. The loneliness here was man-made, and it was partly his fault.

Conrad wedged the worms into a corner of the trunk and climbed back in. They continued north a good distance before turning onto a long dark road leading to the Big Fir Resort: fancy and expensive to be sure, but this would be the last fish fry of the year, for the kids anyway.

"Henry!" the owner said at the door but turned directly to the kids. "So here's what you've been talking about. Nice looking bunch you are! You want to see what your dad's been up to?"

"Yeah!"

The man led them downstairs to peek at the new dining hall. A long polished-wood table bisected the room, capped by a picture-postcard view of the sun setting on Lake Patoosh visible through large cut-glass windows. Henry paced around pointing and explaining, obviously proud of his role in creating such an opulent space. But after being seated at their table upstairs they all went quiet again. Conrad spied on his sisters: Levy sat at an angle sneaking peeks at boys across the room, struggling to be still so as not to invite another scolding, while Beth only looked down at her plate.

"Dad?" Beth asked after some time, almost in a whisper. "Why don't you ever visit us?"

Henry blinked at her. "You mean in Los Angeles?" Beth nodded. Henry let his eyes fall a little, then only grumbled. "Well you know," he said, "I have a business here, and business is tough. Plus L.A.'s not my kind of place."

"Yeah but *we're* there now, and it's so long. We don't see you the whole time."

Henry paused for longer this time. "Tell you the truth," he said lower now, "I never considered it. I guess I was so mad about it all. Guess I'm still mad."

"But we want you to come. You never saw us dance."

Henry sat up taller. "It's not polite to just show up without an invitation," he said.

"Aw Dad! Don't you get it? We're inviting you."

"Really?" he said, acting surprised.

"Yeah, please Dad?" said Levy. "Just don't come in September."

"Why's that?"

"It's like hell on earth."

○ ○ ○

A shoulder shaking.

*My shoulder.*

"Time to get up," came a rough whisper in Conrad's ear, then a shock of surprise through his arms and legs. He rose himself, and swayed, and tiptoed out with his eyes half-cracked. It was four a.m. and still dark except for the kitchen light, but cold milk and sugar on crunchy corn flakes soon perked him up. Within fifteen minutes he was heading out with Henry into the chilled air, lugging their bags and gear down to the dock. They didn't load the rowboat however. Instead they lifted the old canoe off its stand, and Henry bolted a tiny outboard motor onto his custom mount. After Conrad was seated in the bow, Henry wrapped a rope around the circular top of the engine and yanked. It only sputtered, so he tried again, and again, until finally the engine started with a rattling buzz that shattered the morning calm. Now the canoe glided out, its clip-on lights glowing in case of other boats. But there weren't any, and the water's surface skimmed by ancient and unbroken.

There was no speaking in this, never a word across the mystical pre-dawn eons, just occasional glances as foggy shorelines moved by at a distance. But eventually the far end of Lake Levinia came into view, and with it the entrance to a channel dredged out by loggers many decades before. Henry slowed to half-speed as they passed inside, where the rub-rub-rub sound of the engine echoed into the marshy fern-filled forest along the channel's banks. The rowboat might have fit here, but the channel eventually dead-ended at a steep wooded hill. Conrad jumped out to pull up the canoe, then hauled out the gear while Henry unscrewed the motor. Carrying these, they trudged three times over the hill and back again until finally lifting the canoe upside-down onto their shoulders and muscling it up and over to Hookbill Lake. Conrad was older now, so he had no excuse to let Henry do the brunt of the work.

Now on murkier water, they motored toward an adjoining bay, but Henry shut off the engine as they neared and passed Conrad a paddle. They would sneak up on the fish: not speaking, silent-dipping each stroke, no splashing allowed. Over the side Conrad watched weeds emerging from the cloudy depths like dirty-green Christmas wreaths under countless lily pads.

Conrad hadn't been alone with Henry since he'd *said*. Henry was all business however, getting his pole ready, clipping on his Hawaiian Wiggler. "We're gunna catch 'em today!" Henry whispered with an eager glint, casting his lure with a whiz as the line flew from his reel. Conrad liked his spinner bait best, but this was the perfect place for a bobber so he dug out a good fat nightcrawler and triple-pierced it on his hook. This was exactly how it worked: father and son, doing the same things together, talking only about those things, or not.

Luckily they did catch something: Henry hooked a medium-sized northern pike, which after all the excitement he threw back, while Conrad caught crappie after crappie. They were fat ones, too, and he chained the biggest of them over the side of the boat.

"Good so far!" said Henry, taking out the lunch sack and handing Conrad a sandwich. The sun was high now so both wore their fishing hats. "We'll go around that big island out there before we go back." He pointed to the middle of the lake. They had floated across the bay around a bluff into another bay with many of the fallen trees that fish loved, but they anchored to eat first. In his head Conrad tried to count how many previous times they had come here together. This was the only way he'd ever seen Hookbill lake, which made it seem like a males-only place.

"Dad, did Mom ever come over here, I mean, through the

channel?"

"Oh I expect she did. She went all over the place with your grandpa and grandma. Had her own fishing gear just like you. People called her a tomboy."

"Mom fished?"

"Oh yeah. But she liked night fishing for walleye the best. That's when I first met her you know. Or maybe you don't. I was eleven I think, out with my dad. We pulled up to their boat and there she was, casting like a champion, lantern shining on her face. Boy I never got over that. Ha! Of course she just looked at me like I was a bug. She quit fishing in high school though. You know how that goes."

Conrad sat stunned: Sueanna, walleye fishing. "I just don't get it," he mumbled.

"Get what?"

He met his dad's eyes for just a moment but pretended to look over the side of the boat. "I mean... why Mom left."

"Oh," said Henry. He rolled up the lunch sack and picked up his rod again, and with his face turned hard he cast his lure alongside a fallen tree. Conrad thought that was the end of it, and now again Henry appeared as someone other than Dad: a volume of resentful flesh at the other end of the canoe, a bit surly perhaps, sometimes irrationally mean, somebody Conrad didn't always like. "Doesn't she tell you all about it?" Henry blurted out as if to play the part.

"You kidding?" Conrad said. "We're just a bunch of suitcases. On the plane, off the plane." Now Conrad felt surly.

Henry glanced at him as his lure neared the boat, but he didn't cast it back out, just sat and thought. Eventually he spoke again, or grumbled.

"It's hard to say why. I mean I know my part, but I can't explain it all either. I mean I thought I could before, but now it's like too much has gone missing if I talk about it. Starts to feel like lying if you know what I mean."

"Yeah."

Henry cast again with a vigorous thrust of his arms. "She left twice, really. One she left me. Two she left here altogether. Can't say which was worse. I used to think of it separate but now it's like they're the same thing. Your mother was always wanting things to be different and I was just the opposite. I always had this idea we could build our own little castle on an island and just stay there and be happy. Turns out it was a peninsula and the road led straight away. And all I knew how to do was fight it. Pretty soon she was getting mad at me the same way she was mad at her mom and dad. Didn't help they always took my side. *This is good enough*, they told her, *this is as good as it gets*. We argued so bad about it." He paused for a while. "Seemed so simple then."

"Why do you say that?"

"I mean... so you have a castle, then what? Looking at everybody else I know, all I see is things falling apart and things getting rebuilt, over and over, and people pretending it's not happening, but when you're a kid you imagine you'll build it just once and that's it."

"So you're saying Mom was right?"

"Oh I wouldn't go that far. Maybe right for her. But even then I bet she had the same idea, like she'd go build her castle in California instead, make everything all nice and perfect. Wonder how that's going. You know more than I do."

Conrad smiled and cast by the tree. But as soon as his spinner hit the water a violent yank nearly ripped the pole from his hands. He yanked back to set the hook and reeled furiously. Whatever it was bent his pole past forty-five degrees and dragged his line from side to side under the boat. It rushed up and dove again, flashing its stripes: a smallmouth!

"Take it easy!" said Henry. "Don't let it break your line. Nice and slow now."

Conrad let off a little but still the fish fought with lightning changes of direction. When it swooped near the surface again they got a good look: a genuine lunker. But then with a snap Conrad's pole went limp.

"No!" he yelled. "No no no! Shit shit shit!" He reeled in his lure and saw that one of its hook's rusty barbs had snapped off.

"God dammit!" he yelled again at the water.

Henry laughed at him. "Would you have kept it anyway?"

"Well I don't know, but couldn't I have at least gotten it into the boat? I could have taken a picture!" He pounded his fist on the gunwale.

"But you didn't bring the camera."

"Oh yeah."

○ ○ ○

The next morning Henry drove Conrad to return the camera to Babs. "That was the deal," Henry reminded, and Conrad had forgotten. As soon as they arrived, Babs sent Henry outside to inspect her broken boat lift, then sat with Conrad on the sofa for a camera lesson. Conrad showed her how to focus, but she struggled to squint through the viewfinder, and then the light meter and aperture and shutter speed were simply too much.

"Tell you what Conrad," she said finally. "How about if you just keep the camera at your dad's. You can use it while you're here and if I need it I can come get it. Sound like a deal?"

"Yeah, thanks!"

"You're very welcome. You know I didn't get a chance to talk to you when the girls were here last week. So how did it go with your dad, you know, telling him?"

"He was mad."

"I can imagine it seemed that way. We had a good long talk. But I'm asking how it was for you."

Conrad frowned at the carpet. "I was really sick to my stomach. Like I was right and wrong at the same time."

Babs nodded. "I know that feeling. Terrible isn't it? It's like that when you care. And that's always the reality of it, feelings blurring at their edges. In any case Conrad, don't you worry, it's not the end of the world. You'll be back here next summer."

Henry stomped back inside with his report. "It's fine mechanically but the motor's burned out."

"Oh lord," said Babs, waving an arm as she went into the

kitchen. "I never get through a single summer without something or other. Those old cranks were better. Well anyway, come give this old crank a hug, Conrad." Conrad sank into her dress as her big arms squeezed him close. "You have a good year, hear me?"

He nodded into the frills. "Thank you aunt Babs."


On the way back home Conrad saw the words 'Don't Forget Your Pictures!' coming up ahead.

"Hey Dad, it worked! I've got another batch in there."

Of course Conrad hadn't really forgotten his pictures. He'd planned to have Henry pick them up, but then his imagination had taken over: Helen pulling out the packet every day, staring out from the hut wondering when Conrad would return, regretting her words. He knew it was ridiculous, but what a great story!

Henry pulled over by the side of the road. Once again Conrad hesitated.

"Make it quick," Henry urged. "I've got a lunch meeting."

Conrad stepped out. The gravel crunched under his shoes as he approached the hut, and sure enough, Helen came to the window, but this time her expression was oddly blank.

"Painty. Guess I didn't scare you off after all." Her voice was just as blank.

"Forgot I had more," Conrad said, glancing at her face just enough for his stomach to twist. He waited to pay and leave as fast as possible, but she didn't move.

"I'm surprised you're still around. I thought you had important Hollywood business."

"We're leaving tomorrow."

At this Helen stood looking at him. But after a pause she turned to find his pictures. "Well I hope you've had a good time touring our fair town," she said.

Conrad had run out of reasons to be patient. "I keep telling you. I'm *from* here. That's my dad over there."

She slid his packet of pictures toward him. "See you next time, Richy Rich."

"Would you stop saying that?"

"What else am I supposed to call you? You go to a fancy private school in California and come here to play on vacation."

"I did time with Glenda and you know it." He was burning now.

"Doesn't change a thing. You still get to leave, just like all the other dumb-ass tourists." She turned to write in the transaction log, then looked back at him. "Why so mad?" she asked, her tone back to normal now. "Somebody has to say the truth about you."

*Truth.*

Now — in the pulsing breathing present, not the pointless too-late future — fully-formed sentences wrestled free from their tangled roots. "OK fine, I admit it," Conrad huffed. "It's true. I'm an idiot! You know why? I come back here so many times because you're so beautiful, just completely amazing and I want to kiss you so bad! There! I said it! And that makes me an absolute, complete and total moron, because you're horrible! You're like a shiny shell with a nasty crab inside, and you'll say anything to bite me and it works every time, but do you know what's even worse? After all that, I like you anyway. *I like you!* I mean, shit. I must be a crazy person. If you were ever nice to me just once I'd forget it, but you know what? I curse you!" He pointed at her face.

"You curse me?"

"Yeah! I curse you to be stuck here forever! You'll have triplets in high school, even if you never have a boyfriend, because you won't! It'll be like triple virgin birth, that's how strong the curse is, except the babies will come out looking like the devil! And you'll never leave, and you'll never go to college and you'll never see Peru or anywhere else, and then you'll just turn into an old shriveled-up alcoholic hag smoking five packs a day. And you know what? There's an easy way to break the curse, but I'm not telling. And after I leave here tomorrow it'll be permanent! Bye!"

Conrad stomped back to the car and folded his arms tight. Then as the car moved away the after-wash came over him and he was ashamed.

Henry went to check in with the girls, finding them out on the dock sunning themselves one last time, but then he drove off again to his lunch meeting. Beth begged pitifully for Conrad to join them on the dock but he refused. His heart was still thumping in his chest. Instead he roamed the property. He would find a toad. He didn't know why, but it was desperately important that he find a toad. He couldn't leave there until he did. Once again he toured all the places: peeking in the window wells, looking under the steps, lifting piles of boards, moving the big flat rocks near the wall — finding nothing and growing more frantic. "God dammit where are you!" he screamed into the trees. Now he was running from place to place.

Finally, behind the outhouse, under some boards that Henry had piled there to fix it, sat a big fat perfect toad. It tried squeezing its eyes and body flat to match the dirt around its hole, but Conrad gently prodded it out with his fingers and lowered it onto the palm of his hand. Right away he felt calmer as he watched the toad shift and blink.

What was it about these creatures, that made him so happy when other people recoiled? Surely it was like being a little kid again, he understood that. He had squatted this way with some other toad when he was five, his hand tickling when the toad turned itself like a compass. So he was immature, *so what*. It was more than that. You had to look, to notice the muted browns and ochers and blacks flowing around a toad's bumps like silty river water around boulders, complete with a white streak like the foam, and it was always different from toad to toad. Catching toads was like collecting rocks, except the rocks moved. And if you watched you would see the toad's ridiculous confidence, standing proud on its front legs like a miniature body builder, taking action only after long deliberative pauses: a natural straight-man routine that always brought on the giggles. And when toads ate bugs or worms it happened as a hilarious spasm, as if surprised by their own biology. And their eyes: bottomless black, ringed by flaked gold, a window to the universe, or rather the reverse: a window the universe used to view the world, making toads seem only occasionally conscious.

*Hello universe. I still see you in there.*

A faint sound came from the road — creak, clink... creak, clink. The sound grew closer, until Conrad marked it as a bicycle, one in need of repair. He scooted the toad back under the boards, then walked halfway up the driveway to catch a glimpse of the rider from an unassuming distance. The rider it turned out was female, hunched and huffing as she cranked the rusty pedals into the driveway. He had known at first sight, but could hardly believe it until he saw her face. It was Helen. She had come to murder him no doubt, perhaps with her bare hands on his throat, but all he could do was stand and stare as she came to a halt, and dropped the bicycle to the ground, and stood near him holding a large canvas bag in her hands. She didn't look up however. She frowned and breathed at the driveway — partly from the effort, but also because she was near tears.

"If I..." she said, but stopped and scrunched her face — from rage or frustration or sorrow Conrad couldn't tell. She threw the bag between them on the ground and books spilled out. "If I say I'm sorry, um... will you lift the curse?"

Conrad's mouth was still hanging open, but now his intuition snapped into gear. "I cannot lift the curse," he said. "Nobody can do that but you. I can only show you where."

He walked toward The Gate and beckoned Helen to follow. After a doubtful pause she did. From down on the dock his sisters saw and came running. "Who's that Conrad?" they called, but Conrad held up a commanding hand. An entire childhood of made-up incantations paid off: his sisters froze in place. But their awe-struck expressions showed they had come close enough to get a good look at Helen. Conrad turned back to The Gate and, using silent brain-waves to hold it open, stepped through.

Helen looked unsure. "You're not going to try anything in there, are you?" she asked.

Conrad shook his head, put a finger to his lips and led her into the forest. He would figure out what he was doing at some point, he was sure of it.

Soon they were zigzagging along the deer trails, Conrad turning to beckon Helen further as the distance increased. Avoiding The Black Hole and The Dead Woods, he stopped first at Bigfoot Alley, motioning for Helen to sit on the slope next to him.

She fidgeted. "Uh, OK... now what?"

"This might be the place," he said. "We'll see."

They watched down through the immense shadow-casting tree trunks, and the ancient mood of the place sank in as they waited, but aside from time slowing nothing happened.

Conrad shrugged. "Guess not."

"Are you sure you know what you're doing?"

"Yes."

He stood and led her uphill into the Prehistoric District, where the ferns brushed along their bare legs, then far past The Valley Of Shadows along a long snaking path that ended at the sandy bank of a creek edged by rich satin moss to sit on. Shafts of light from the canopy spot-lit the water while the current burbled over their feet, and though it was all deeply calming, nothing happened here either. But Helen was softening, less apt to interrupt, and she followed Conrad further in.

Plants grew taller along the path, squeezing it narrow over their heads as they wound up a grade, up and up like it would never end until popping surprised into the light of Jingle Dell, an inexplicable clearing spotted white with late-summer flowers. Here they waited again, laying on their backs and taking in the sky while the air sat on them thick and warm, an occasional breeze tingling their faces as they watched a high-altitude jet trail silently lengthen. Conrad listened as Helen faintly hummed with each exhale: hmmm... hmmm... hmmm... But before she could doze he sprang up and led her back into the dark of the forest.

The trail turned low and muddy. Soon they came to a thrashing river, the only way across being a narrow fallen pine with rubbery branches for hand-holds. Conrad half-expected protests, but Helen clambered across behind him without a word. On the other side they climbed a steep incline to reach a rocky trench, The Hall Of Stone.

"Do what I do," Conrad whispered. Helen followed in the ritual: passing the tips of their left fingers along the chilled granite faces up one side and down the other, then in reverse with their right fingertips.

Unnamed gods successfully greeted, they sat between the rocks and for the first time were cold. Conrad peeked sideways at the long female form half-folded beside him, t-shirt and shorts leaving open expanses of smooth warm skin. He wanted to scooch over and wrap himself around that form. But he was calmer now and sensed the feeling coming on its own. Maybe he wasn't all that different from the toad and the universe. If he didn't choose to have the feeling, who was having it in the first place — was it really him? Maybe he was a body *and* a him, like Siamese twins getting on each other's nerves. Or maybe there were lots of hims, an onion of hims, and he could only see down through the first few layers. In any case he had led the form very far from anything, and one of his layers was growing nervous.

Helen had been quiet, but now she looked to him for direction. *Will the curse be lifted here?* asked her eyes. Conrad shook his head.

He decided to double back sideways. It was a long way, but at least it was sort of toward home. He stood and took off down to the river and shimmied across the log. On the other side his pace only increased. Helen would have to follow, would have to flow as swiftly up and down the trails as he did and feel the same joy in it that he did, and if she didn't then that was the answer right there. But she did follow, and kept up with athletic ease, and Conrad could see a thrill in her eye when he looked back.

After twenty uncounted minutes they arrived breathless at The Church. They found the place in especially fine form, its silken grass having grown long over the summer months. Helen laid face-down in it and stayed that way.

"Mmmm," she hummed again. Then she sat up cross-legged. Conrad sat down nearby. Being on a rise, they could see downhill a great distance through the woods, all the way down to the lakeshore where bright afternoon light glittered off the water in slices between the trees. That, and the high midday sun beamed green through the leaves above them and mottled the ground. It was more than a moment, sitting this way, blinking their eyes as they stared — a weightless pause. Helen breathed in deep, and breathed out.

"It's so beautiful here," she said.

Conrad jumped up. "Yes," he said, running a circle around her. "Yes!" he yelled up to the treetops and collapsed back down onto his back. "The curse is broken."

"That's all I had to say?"

"That's all you had to see. Now you're free."

Helen leaned back onto her hands and smiled. "Thank you Painty," she said.

# 22

# Early September

Stuck in the tunnel to the plane, passengers up ahead cramming in their carry-ons.

"Not so thin," Sueanna directed from the kitchen sink. "And do it sideways. It looks cuter."

Conrad chopped sideways. The carrot pieces were cuter.

"So have you thought about a team?"

Henry standing tall, smiling tight-lipped, his kids squeezing their arms around his scratchy jacket before tramping into the tunnel like everything was normal, but looking back to see their father walking away through the terminal keeping his feelings to himself.

"No," Conrad answered.

"It's not just my idea you know. I was talking Mr. Frunkle and he was saying that being on a team would be good for you."

They couldn't just be *away*, couldn't be instantly different. No, they had to stand there in a cold steel tube, breathing at the industrial carpet.

"I don't like football."

"They don't *have* a football team, Conrad. And besides, there's all kinds of teams. How about track? You like running. Ever thought about that?"

Conrad thought about running in circles on cracking asphalt under the burning-hot sun. "I guess," he said.

"Well, you bring me a paper and I'll sign it. I promise, you'll feel different if you join something. And by different I mean better, OK?"

At dinner Conrad had no cover — Beth was also sullen. Weetie had died in a plague that swept the herd that summer, and while seven total had tragically perished, Weetie had always been her favorite.

"At least you could have frozen the bodies!" she whimpered to Sueanna.

"I wasn't about to put diseased guinea pig corpses into the freezer next to the peas."

"Why not? That's what plastic bags are for." She moped further down in her chair. "Now how are we supposed to have the funeral?"

"You could burn effigies," Conrad murmured.

"What's an effigy?" Levy asked.

"It's like a paper model of a person, or in this case-"

"Oh that's a good idea! Can you help us?"

"Me?"

"Yeah, you're good at art stuff. Come on!"

"Oh god."

Exactly like every other teenage boy in Los Angeles, Conrad spent his Saturday evening building guinea pigs out of wire, cardboard, paper, and invisible tape. Each had to match a description recorded in one of the many charts his sisters had archived, so Conrad brought out all his old markers and watercolors. The finished products would be perfect, he decided, even though they would burn at midnight — they would call it midnight anyway, since Sueanna refused to attend any later than ten.

The event took place in the back yard with the lights turned off. Candles flickered on a stack of garden bricks over guinea-effigies laid side-by-side.

"Would you look at that!" said Sueanna. "Are you sure you want to burn them? Maybe I should get my camera at least."

"No!" Conrad said. "That would trap their souls..." He added in a mumble, "You know, they wouldn't be reincarnated for other kids."

"Oh can you be the shaman?" Beth begged.

"What, seriously?"

"Please?"

He had done it to himself. "OK fine. Just this once." He got up and kneeled between his sisters behind the 'altar', leaving Sueanna as the only attendee. He picked up the first effigy and laid it on the bricks, then took a deep breath.

"We gather here to consign our beloved Manchego to the elements. Would anyone like to say a few words?"

Beth made her face frumpy, somewhere between sincere and the stage. "Manchego was a good brave soul," she said. Conrad did his best to stay in character while picturing a guinea pig being brave.

"He was the manliest of the cheeses," said Levy.

Conrad struck a match and lit the end of the effigy. Earlier when his sisters weren't looking he had funneled gunpowder, from old ladyfingers hidden in his closet, into each of the models. Manchego burned slowly at first, but then his soul expanded with a flash of light.

"We bid thee farewell and safe journeys, Manchego!" Conrad called out, raising an arm toward the smog-orange night sky.

"Goodbye!" called his sisters.

Conrad brushed the ashes (burned paper, melted tape, blackened wire) into a grapefruit can, then began the process over again with Gorgonzola. He would save Weetie for last.

The fun of the funeral only served to expose Conrad's nerves to the air. Back at his bedroom window he found himself deep in the tunnel again.

*Here I am again.*

*This is my room.*

He peeked out to the street: eyes looking left, eyes looking right. It was all still there, the ever-changing, never-changing city. Not only had he pushed the button, but the bomb had dropped on the wrong place and nothing he did would ever take it back.

In bed he looked up at the ceiling instead of sleeping, not yet used to the unnatural light leaking in around the blinds. After an hour he got up and tiptoed downstairs to the sun room where he sat in the shadows and stared at the phone. He knew the number but didn't know what he was doing or why. Some minutes passed before he remembered that he never knew why anyway. He picked up the receiver and dialed.

"Hello?" came Henry's voice.

"Dad?" Conrad said. Right away he wanted to cry.

"Is that you Conrad?"

"Dad, are you... Dad! Are you OK?" Now he cried.

Henry waited on the other end. "I'm OK," he said, but he paused again. "Or no, I guess I oughta be straight with you. It's not easy. Maybe you're guessing that. But you didn't do anything wrong you know."

"I just... I feel so bad, about everything."

"You didn't do anything wrong, you hear me? None of this is fair in the first place. But you know when I think about it I'm proud of you. You made a choice when it was really hard. I know how much you love it here."

"But what about you?"

"Oh I'm still here. I'm a big boy. It's not your job to worry about me, got it?"

"Uh huh."

"But wait till I'm ninety-five and ask me again. I might change my mind."

"OK."

"You go do things. You won't have time to feel bad. Go do things, OK? I want to hear about it."

"OK."

Conrad ran out to the light pole and folded himself tight as if it were cold, and let the material near his knees absorb his tears until they ran out. He had come out there to be alone, but soon began to wish that Levy would show up uninvited. He wasn't disappointed. Grass-mashing sounds came from behind.

"What's up, buddy-o?" Levy whispered. Rather than launching

into a circus-wire routine she sat near him on the curb and watched his reddened eyes.

"I just talked to Dad," Conrad said.

"Yeah, I heard." Her eyes reddened, too.

Conrad breathed in and out to avoid crying again.

Levy lifted her chin. "Hey, uh, do you think Beth could join the club?"

"What club?"

"This club. The Street Light Club, or the Night Pole Club, or whatever. She's old enough, don't you think?"

Conrad thought for a moment. "The Night Light Club," he said. "And sure."

Levy motioned to the bushes. Beth scurried out and sat by Conrad's other side. He looked from one sneaky face to the other sneaky face and shook his head. "You guys are the worst."

The three of them sat for a while in the mild currents breathing down from the hills.

"I'm glad you came back," Beth whispered.

"Me too," said Levy.

○ ○ ○

*Hi Anise.*

*Oh hi Conrad! Thank you so much for the pictures.*

*You're welcome. Which one was your favorite?*

*Oh I loved that little island! I hung it right over my bed. Is that really a place you can go?*

*Yeah! And there's a really steep drop-off next to it. Good for fishing.*

*Wow, that's so cool. So, um, do you want to hang out sometime?*

○ ○ ○

From his bed Conrad heard a knock down at the front door. "Oh hello!" came Sueanna's voice, then some murmurs and the door closing again. Sueanna came up to Conrad's room.

"That was Mr. Onter," she said. Her tune about Mr. Onter had changed to *That Poor Man*, ever since Conrad had let loose a few choice tidbits about his past. "He says his lawn's getting long. Why don't you go down there?"

Conrad splashed his face, inhaled the oatmeal square his mother had left on a plate and headed out into the heat.

"Noble savage, looking the part!" said Mr. Onter at his door, seeing Conrad still bronzed and toned from the summer. Conrad followed Mr. Onter inside and sat on the sofa scanning the bookshelves. Much was different but he couldn't pinpoint exactly what.

"Did you get new books?" Conrad asked.

"I sure did! But then I ended up taking everything down and rearranging, and I sold a bunch, too."

Conrad nodded, but he was still finding it hard to smile. Mr. Onter sat opposite and looked him over.

"Well here you are again," Mr. Onter said after neither had spoken. "Guess you didn't have any fun this summer."

"I did."

"But you came back."

"Can I hear that piano piece again? The one that's like bells?"

Mr. Onter's eyes opened wide. "Asking to hear something again? Well I do believe my work on this earthly plane is complete." He went to his shelves to rifle through his records. "Bet you can't remember the composer's name."

"Skoo or something."

"No, but close! It's *Enescu*. Oh here it is." He laid the record on the player and peered to find the correct track before lowering the needle, then crept to his recliner. Conrad focused on the rug while the music's ringing sent ripples across the entire summer in his imagination.

"You seem sad," said Mr. Onter when it was over. "Did your mother force you to come back?"

"No, it was my decision."

"Oh, well then. Would you be willing to tell me why?"

Conrad went quiet, but Mr. Onter waited and sipped his tea as if he had nothing better to do than examine the wallpaper.

"It's all kinds of things," Conrad said. "Like, there's so many racist people there."

"Oh really? Well that's a pity. In that case I'd like to welcome you back to Los Angeles, where bigotry has been permanently eliminated."

"Hardy har har."

"In all seriousness Conrad, take it apart. Is that the only reason?"

"It's wrong."

"I wholeheartedly agree. Did you protest?"

"No. I mean, kind of. I ripped up a cartoon I guess."

"And then you came back here," said Mr. Onter. He pointed a finger in the air. "A new kind of tourism! But that's not really what I'm getting at. It's like I keep saying Conrad, call things by their right names, or try to anyway. It matters, at the very least for your own sanity."

Conrad curled his arms around himself. "It's like I don't belong there, and I don't belong here either. But my aunt Babs is just like you, says I shouldn't use that word."

"Belong? Hmm. It's worth thinking about. Or maybe it's not. Maybe there's something else underneath that word. Words are tricky, like weeds. You chop off a weed, and another grows in its place and there you are, chopping weeds your whole life. You have to go for the root."

Conrad felt a smile creep across his face. "Does that mean it's weeding day?"

"Why yes sir, but we'll talk more when you're done. I've changed my lemonade recipe by the way. Just you wait!"

○ ○ ○

*Conrad! Conrad! Oh my god it's you!*
*Anise! It's like a dream to see you again after so long.*
*Look at you! You're so tan and strong. Let me hold you.*
*Mmmm Anise, your hair smells like wildflowers.*
*I have something to tell you, Conrad.*
*What is it?*
*Your pictures inspired me, so I've decided to become a photographer. Let's take pictures together!*

○ ○ ○

Sueanna started the car but waited to put it in gear.

"Are you sure you don't want to try?" she asked, referring to the horses just beyond the window that Levy and Beth were already leading.

Conrad looked at his mother straight on. "Are you kidding?"

"Well I don't know! Just because you've refused five thousand times doesn't mean you won't change your mind today."

"No thanks."

"Well why did you ask to come along then?"

"Just wanted to see I guess." He looked out across the empty corral, to the hills rising beyond it. Riding a horse up those hills didn't seem like such a bad idea after all, though running on his own two feet was still better.

"Well now what?" Sueanna looked at him with sneaky eyes, as if she would soon begin scheming if he didn't beat her to it.

"Ice cream," he said.

Sueanna shifted and headed for the road. Los Angeles soon appeared below them, spread out to the horizon under a thin layer of haze. As always it was tempting to love the place from this vantage point, or to love the freedom the view suggested, however illusory for those who scratched out a living down in it. Winding down past exclusive million-dollar homes, even in this old dented car, made them feel inexplicably part of the place, or at least a part of its delirious story.

"Mom where are you going?"

"Pasadena."

"What? That'll take so long. What about the girls?"

"Oh they always whine when it's time to leave. There's this place I heard about."

Sueanna accelerated onto the freeway with eager eyes and both hands on the wheel as if reliving her glory days as a race-car driver. But it wasn't long before she lapsed into thought.

"I met your boyfriend," Conrad said.

"You what?"

"Drinks blackberry schnapps. Cool dude. I'm impressed."

"Who are you talking about?"

"J.J."

"Oh my god. He wasn't my boyfriend!"

"Don't worry Mom," Conrad said, dismissing her with a wave. "I know everything about your past now."

"Like what?"

"Like you were an expert walleye fisher-girl."

"Well yeah, I guess that part's true. Hee hee! I caught a twenty-nine incher once. I almost fell out of the boat."

"Whoah!"

"Got my picture in the paper."

"Why don't you ever tell me this stuff?"

"Oh I don't know, it's the past."

"No, it's like you're embarrassed."

"No I'm not," she said, but caught herself. "Well maybe, I don't know. And you're always wanting to run back there so... well how do I say it." She paused, but then she glanced over to Conrad as if just now noticing him. "Come to think of it, here you are," she said. "Do you want to talk about what happened?"

"No way. Not if you won't."

"Won't what?"

"Talk about it."

"Talk about what?"

"Why you left."

"Oh."

Sueanna went silent again and stayed that way until the outskirts of Pasadena, where she parked on the street in front of a little brick building with a swoopy hand-painted sign saying "Creamiest Cream." A line was snaking out the door, so they got out to bake in the sun at the end of it.

The ice cream, when it finally arrived at their lips, was glorious. They ate in stunned silence: sweet-corn flavor with pecan crumbles for Conrad and fig-caramel for Sueanna, spoon after spoon illuminated from within by heavenly lightness. When it was gone they threw away their cups and floated back to the car. But instead of starting the engine Sueanna sat looking at the steering wheel as if she had never seen one before. More than a moment passed like this, heavier by the second, as if she would say something. But then she only flashed Conrad a meek smile and turned her attention to the car key. Conrad's hand reached to open the door.

"Conrad?"

He found himself climbing out.

"Conrad get back in the car, we're late."

"Fuck this fucking car!" he yelled and slammed the door as a wave of nameless rage flooded over him. But just as quickly it receded and he felt silly, standing out on the asphalt like an anger clown in front of everybody. Then he felt annoyed at feeling silly, so he curled up his hands and marched away.

On the inside of the shop window a couple was standing up from a table. Conrad stomped inside to sit at it. In the corner of his eye he could see Sueanna in the car outside, looking through the steering wheel again. He squeezed his eyes shut and pounded his elbows onto the table and held his hair in his hands. Then he heard a rustling and looked up to see Sueanna sitting down opposite him.

"You don't have to get so mad," she said.

Conrad only stared back at first. "That's right," he said. "I don't have to."

Sueanna blinked, and stared at him, and blinked again. "Well I just don't like talking about all that stuff," she said. "I mean what's the use."

"Fine then," said Conrad, feeling clearly that he had her trapped — his slippery mother, actually backed into a corner. It might even be cruel, what he was doing, whatever it was. He felt an urge to relent, to just let it all slide, to be nice.

"Can't we just go now?" she asked.

"No."

It seemed incredible that Sueanna didn't simply drag him out by his collar. Instead she frowned sideways at the floor. "You couldn't even get it," she finally said, partly to herself. "I mean, *I* don't even get it, not completely, and anyway you can't imagine."

"I can imagine lots of things."

"Yeah but I'm talking about real things. I just *had* to leave, and then here I was, in Los Angeles with three kids all by myself. It's nuts when you think about it."

"But why? Why did you have to?"

Sueanna didn't answer. Instead her attention drifted, and seconds ticked by. When she spoke again it seemed to come from the middle of her thoughts. "I was always that way I guess. I never could stand it, people telling me who I was. That look in their eyes, like they knew all the answers just from living in that one place."

"You mean Dad?"

"No not him. Well not at first. We had it all planned out like young couples always do, but whenever I wanted to change the plan he got so darned bossy about it, like I was the crazy one. Really I only wanted more options, I mean for all of us, but whenever I talked about us going somewhere else my mom and dad would say the same thing. *This is where you belong*, they'd say. But that only meant I had to shut my face."

Conrad curled up in his seat. "I don't belong anywhere, I feel like," he mumbled.

Now Sueanna sat up and spoke straight at him. "Oh you're just lonely. And whose fault is that?"

There it was! The word inside the word, exploded from within for all time. Why hadn't she said this before? The shock of it made Conrad go quiet for a few beats. But he was still curious. "Aren't you ever sorry?" he asked.

"Oh now there's a touchy question. It hurt people when I left, and it was home, you know? I miss that lake." Sueanna pursed her lips. "I really miss the lake. I never said that to anybody."

"But why not?"

"Well I'm stubborn, haven't you noticed? And saying that, well it's like I'm sorry we came, but I'm not. It's true this city's completely bonkers, I'll give you that. But we're doing so much out here. You can see that, right? You have to see it. Though on days like this your idea about Iceland seems pretty darn nice. Still interested?"

"How about more ice cream?"

Sueanna grinned. "OK one more, but after that it's your turn. And don't tell your sisters."

○ ○ ○

*Oh god it's that freak.*
*Uh, hi Anise. Did you get my pictures?*
*Oh was that it? You put pictures in those envelopes?*
*Well yeah...*
*Well they went straight to the trash. And listen, I need you to keep your distance, hear me? I don't want to catch whatever you've got.*

○ ○ ○

It was time to leave for school but Sueanna was pottering.

"Where did I leave them?" she muttered, rummaging through papers and catalogs layered on various household surfaces.

"Leave what?" asked Conrad, standing with Levy by the door. Levy hadn't spoken much all morning and her eyes were stuck wider than normal.

"Oh here they are!" Sueanna said. "Here you go." She passed

Conrad a still-sealed packet of photos from the roll that was still in the camera on the last day of summer.

"Oh yeah, thanks."

"Well you wanted them so fast I thought you needed them for school today or something."

"Yeah, I do." It wasn't true. He stuffed the pictures into his bag before she could ask to see them and hurried out to the car. But Levy was dragging.

"Levy move your tushie!" Sueanna called.

All the way to school, Conrad found no rest for his hands: propping up his chin, laying flat on his thighs, folded together, stuffed half-under his bottom — anywhere but in his bag. That is, until Divergent came into view. Then fear stilled him entirely.

"Have a good first day!" Sueanna said and drove away. Levy stood facing Conrad as if waiting to be led in.

"Your orientation's in that building." He pointed. "You'll see signs."

"OK." She looked at the school then back at him but didn't move.

He shook her by the shoulders. "Go ahead. And don't forget. *You*... are the *Great* Levinia. All must bow down before you."

Levy pointed at his face and squeaked "that includes you!" as she scooted away.

Now it was Conrad's turn to go in, but he stood staring at the school much as Levy had. Unlike her, he turned and ran.

Near the overpass was a patch of gravel nothing. He sat on it, making it temporarily something, the place where he could be himself, his summer self anyway, for a few more minutes. He unzipped his bag and pulled out the photos. If by some cataclysmic chance the *one* picture Helen had allowed was somehow missing or didn't turn out he would die right there and the Los Angeles Times would struggle to explain it. He thumbed through the snapshots: lake, dock, sunset, moss, lichen, lichen, lichen, lily pads, lichen, bark, salamander, there it was! He pulled it out: Helen, standing next to her bicycle just before he had watched her pedal away — hair still damp, smooth bare arms, hands on the handles. Gravel was a terrible frame for such a picture. He lay on his back and held her up against the sky. That was better... Helen's eyes beamed at the camera, but that warm smile was just for him.

The school hallway came as a welcome escape from the September heat, but it was still a tunnel. Metal door-slams rattled Conrad's head. *Order up!* Putting off going to class, he rearranged his locker as faces new and old tittered by. A few did wave, and he made sure to wave back (even to the one who said "Hey D.P.", because apparently that had stuck and oh well never mind), but nobody he really knew came by — a relief, though an uncharitable relief and he knew it. He should go find the people who knew him best, and pat them on the back like Sal and say 'good to see you!' in a bellowing voice like his dad. He couldn't imagine acting that way, but that was how he actually felt, so why not? He had to find some way, because *fuck this fucking tunnel.* He slammed his locker door as hard as he could.

"Conrad!" said Mrs. Pelora at the studio door. "I heard some rumor you weren't coming back. I am so glad it wasn't true."

"It was true, and then it wasn't," he said, playing the puzzler.

"Why's that?"

"Well I wouldn't want to miss *your* class, would I?"

"Good one Conrad," Mrs. Pelora said. "Take a seat."

Scanning the room for an open easel he saw Gabby, of the mystifying triptych, staring at her empty paper with an equally empty expression. "Hi Gabby," he said and sat down next to her.

Gabby jerked her head.

"Hey I really liked your drawings last year, the ones in the art show."

"Oh... thanks," Gabby said, but reeled herself back.

"I stood there forever trying to figure it out. What made you choose those three things?"

A little smile spread across Gabby's face. "It was just a feeling," she said. "I didn't exactly know how it would turn out myself."

Conrad sat back and stared at his own empty paper. Today he would draw something on it, maybe from a still life at the center of the room, maybe from some indistinct vision in his head, but in any case he would feel only partially responsible for the result. And he couldn't remember it ever *not* being that way, just like his every day had been that way.

So how would today turn out, this first, defining day? It struck him now that despite it still being morning, the upcoming hours were already drawn up in the back of his head: each class on schedule with all the people he would see in turn, leaving out all the *Don't Knows* like talking to Gabby just now. He hadn't seen Joey or Stacy, yet a full round of rehearsals had already been carried out by some over-vigilant division of his mind, because he was more afraid at the prospect of meeting the people he knew than of the indifference of everyone else.

Conrad moved from class to class holding his eyes open on purpose. His blood raced when other people looked back, but for the first time it was good. Then lunchtime came and he was terrified. He stood frozen in the hallway, heart beating fast, until willing his legs to move.

Emerging into the alley, he turned his face up to the sun. *Go ahead, burn me to dust,* he thought, but all he felt was hotter, so he scanned his eyes from one end of the school to the other. It was kind of like Polecat Creek, this busy little place, just a couple blocks long, except he couldn't buy nightcrawlers here. Cocaine maybe. In any case he was hungry.

The benches were gone, as were the trees, all yanked out like molars to make way for a building expansion, so Conrad carried his lunch along the alley to see where he would end up. But pretty soon he stopped to stare: down near the drama building, long reddish curls swung from the head of a gangly male form gesturing at another male form. Conrad had to move closer to believe what he already knew: it was Joey, but he had grown out his hair. This might have been cool except it was ludicrous on Joey in particular. And the other form was Robb Cott, basking in a Hawaiian shirt and flip-flops with a sideways lean that made it impossible that he had ever worn penny-loafers. Robb chortled as Joey spoke — something about buttons getting stuck — but then

Robb pointed with his chin.

"Hey guess who's back."

Joey swiveled. "Well lookee here. Mr. Treetops. Thought we'd never see *you* again."

"That was me on the phone you know," Conrad said.

"Oh yeah, heh heh."

Robb turned to leave with a wave. "Well I gotta split," he said.

"Aw come on man!" Joey called. He turned back to Conrad. "Hey don't look at me that way. He's cool, not like before."

"Isn't that backwards?"

"Yeah whatever. It's *day one*, my son." Joey squinted as if a promised glory was imminent.

"So where do we eat now?"

Joey jammed his hands into his pockets and looked around as if put on the spot. "I don't know dude, they're tearing everything up."

"You got something else going on?"

"No it's OK, it's cool. There's these new bushes they put in back there." He pointed behind the drama building. "All shady."

They went to the back and laid out their lunches by the wall.

"Can't see anybody from here," Conrad said.

"Uh huh." Joey took a bite and chewed, looking away as if he might simply wander off when his sandwich was gone.

"I thought you hated those guys," Conrad said.

"Aw that's ancient history. You know, people change."

Conrad counted the months back to Robb and Todd cheering the fight: five at the most — eons maybe in high school time, milliseconds in Onter time. "So what happened this summer?" he asked.

Joey turned to him with a soporific grin. "Man it was epic. I was at the beach like every day. Babes aplenty."

*It's a robot*, Conrad thought, *locked in a lab closet all summer, hair slowly growing*. But here it was again, wearing the same Van Halen t-shirt and talking at him like it always had.

"Babes, huh." Conrad said. "That's cool." He waited. "So, uh, anything *besides* babes?"

"I did a lot more than you I'm sure, Mr. Moss Photographer."

"Don't be so sure."

"Oh, so what then, did those wild girls finally drag you back to their huts?"

Conrad paused. "I did meet a girl in a hut, actually."

"Christ. Here we go again."

Conrad blinked. It didn't feel right that Joey would snicker so soon. None of this felt right. Had it ever felt right? A stubbornness stole over him.

"It's true," he said. "A girl, in a hut by the road. But she was nasty to me, so I threw a curse on her. Then she showed up at my house and begged me to lift it."

"Uhhh... so did you?"

"Yeah I did." Conrad focused on a distant spot. "I took her through the woods to all the magic places, until the curse dissolved. Then we went down to the lake. But it was strange at first. She just stood there staring at the water, then she started screaming at it and threw rocks at it, and then she fell down crying for the longest time, so I just sat there next to her. But after a while she calmed down, then all of a sudden she stood up and she ordered me to take off all my clothes, so I did, and then she took off hers, and she was so... *so* beautiful. And when we were swimming she kissed me, and she told me I could touch her, so I did, all over under the water, and her hands felt *so* amazing, and we talked and kissed like forever just floating there near shore, and all the way back through the woods we kept stopping to kiss some more."

Joey shook his head. "Dude," he sighed. "I almost feel sorry for you. You went batshit out there, swingin' from the trees all by yourself."

Conrad stared at the dirt between the bushes. He could laugh along like he used to, but this time his insides hotly refused. He could protest and scramble to explain, but he didn't want to do that either, and why was that? It was clear now, his position in this. He slipped his sandwich back into its bag and rolled the top.

Joey squinted. "Lost your appetite?"

"Yeah," said Conrad. He stood up.

"Hey what's up with you anyway?"

"You're full of shit that's what," Conrad said. He turned and walked.

"Hey what the hell?" Joey called out.

Conrad stopped. He turned back to Joey and forced out the words. "I cannot stand your cool-guy act anymore," he said. "Would you just quit it? It's like I'm not even here."

"Sure you are. I see you standing right there like a dumb-ass, just like always."

"Fine then." Conrad moved away.

"Oh, so it's like this, after all this time?"

"I could ask you the same!"

"Whatever man."

Twenty feet separated each drain at the center of the alley, and though all of them were bone-dry Conrad could hear his first day being sucked down through the grates as he passed overhead. He'd flipped out at Joey, his only so-called friend, and with that he had run plum out of so-called friends, though maybe he'd see Stacy — maybe she was still his friend. He wasn't sure. If not, then what? Go around friendless all year? Of course he couldn't make new friends, because that was illegal. And why was it illegal? He'd never questioned this law before. It seemed pretty arbitrary all of a sudden. He stuffed the remainder of his sandwich into his mouth and went to class.

The door to history opened to the previous year's classroom in miniature: fewer students, but packed into a smaller space, with Anise's hair on one side and the last open seat on the other, next to Peter Fronton. Conrad couldn't help chuckling as he sat down.

"Conrad!" Peter burst out. "I've been defending this chair. I was starting to think you weren't actually back."

"Here I am, sir, in all my glory. But look at you. You're all wiry or something."

Peter was indeed different, and he looked at Conrad more directly — though with no less threat of mischief. "The doctor got me doing cross-country this summer," he said. "It was awesome. You should join up."

"What, like run those road races?"

"Yeah sometimes, but mostly we train on dirt, up in the hills. Coach has us going vertical half the time. And those eucalyptus trees smell *so* freakin' good when we come down. It's fun man, come on! You're like deer-boy. We need you."

Conrad found himself nodding. "OK then" he said. "Sure."

"All right!"

"Ahem," came Mr. Sebastien's voice at the door, hushing the room. "Welcome back to 1984," he said as he shuffled to the board, "and thank you for participating in this experiment."

Conrad peeked over at Anise as she straightened up to listen. This was it, the long-imagined moment when he saw her again. And now he didn't find her any less beautiful, even after Helen, though he didn't feel the same. But what was different exactly, what were the words? It didn't hurt, that was one thing. Truly it was nice to see her again, and it came as a relief, though maybe a sad one. *A sad relief.* It was kind of funny to feel that way, he had to admit. But when Anise opened her binder to pull out a paper, Conrad noticed what she had slipped behind the clear-plastic of its cover: Pipsqueak, still mounted on its gray paper rectangle. Anise looked up and gave him a little half-smile, but that was it, and at the end of class she slipped out first.

When the day was over, Conrad went to his locker to gather his things. By this time he wasn't sure anymore how he felt. All he could do was watch.

*Eyes watching outward, eyes watching inward, eyes blinking.*

He zipped his bag and walked to the front. Levy had already run off to a 'first day party' with her new friends, and Sueanna had insisted she would pick him up to take him shopping for a windbreaker he'd insisted he didn't need, so instead of heading out to the bus he leaned near the entrance to watch people leave. An old black Mercedes slowed in front of him.

"Hi Yolanda!" he yelled.

Yolanda nodded just once before continuing down the street. When the car stopped again Conrad saw something strange: Stacy and Anise sitting together, talking and laughing as if in a bubble from an alternate universe. He watched as Anise stood up and shuffled to the car. But Yolanda must have said something because Anise turned and stood taller, then peered over and waved. Then she pointed out Conrad to Stacy before climbing in the door.

Stacy lifted her bag and marched. As she neared, Conrad studied the subtle changes that one summer had made to her face and it hit him with a rush how much he had missed her. "I am *so* happy to see you!" he called out though she was already facing him.

"Me too!" she said, giving him a bear-hug and jumping back. "Thanks for the pictures. Hey look, I made the lichen one my cover for science." She pulled out her binder for a peek and shoved it back in, and then she punched him hard on the shoulder. "Jerk!"

"Ow!"

"I was checking my mailbox like three times a day, and then they just stopped."

"Oh yeah, sorry about that. I kinda got derailed."

"Yeah figures. Well anyway it looks *so* nice there. I totally get it now."

"Oh man," Conrad groaned. "It's so much more. I wish you could see it."

"Yeah, me too."

"Well it's a real place you know. People live there. You could even visit."

"Hmmm," Stacy hummed at the ground, gears turning on this new idea. But then she faced him again. "So what made you change your mind then?" she asked.

Conrad looked back at her, stretching the moment as he struggled. He couldn't say just anything to Stacy, so he couldn't say anything at all. And it seemed to him that behind her eyes the books had moved around somehow. Was this even the same

Stacy? Maybe the old Stacy had been switched out when he was gone. It felt like this with everybody when he came back, but Stacy mattered more. It made him nervous, not knowing what had changed, like he had missed a part of the story. And it was entirely possible he'd become a smaller character, or might have been written out entirely. He didn't want that, not at all.

"I can't really explain it in one sentence," Conrad said. "But maybe I could try sometime, like, if you want to hang out at lunch or something?"

"Yeah, OK."

"Plus I want to hear about your summer. And you're hanging out with Anise now?"

"Oh yeah, ever since summer school. Of course I wouldn't even look at her after you know, but she sat next to me like every single day, and then she practically forced me at knife-point to be her study partner. After that though, oh my *god*, we ran around like nut-cases the whole rest of the summer, like whuh-uh-uh-uh." She bobbled her head.

"But what about Joey?"

"Oh we're not going out anymore. He didn't tell you?"

"No. What happened?"

She sighed. "Oh I don't know... it's weird. I guess it just didn't feel the same after a while. But hey..." She went horsey and shook her eyebrows. "How about you and Anise, huh?"

"Anise?"

"Yeah! We talked about you. I'm pretty sure she's sorry. You still like her, right?"

"Yeah, sure." He gave a little shrug.

"So would you go out with her again?"

"Yeah, I suppose."

"So are you going to ask her out?"

"I don't know, maybe?"

"God Conrad!" Stacy said, turning to her carpool. "You haven't changed at all." With that she waved and left.

Conrad slid down against the wall and hugged his legs. Of course he knew that Stacy was teasing, but still, it stung deep that she had said those words. If they were true then he'd made a terrible mistake: he had chosen to hear them, because he had chosen to be there again — he couldn't pretend that he hadn't, not anymore. And if he was stuck being the same then it hadn't mattered at all that he'd come back, and he'd be doomed to pass through his days there as a miserable exile all over again. He looked out over his knees to survey what he had chosen. *I chose this*, he thought. *And just look at this place!* Hard cement spread out from under his feet to infinity: he had chosen that, and the blistering heat. Helen was far away, and none of his Anise stories had come true, not even the bad one. He had chosen that, too. He had turned himself in, and the trial had begun. And now he squinted from the afternoon sun glancing off the sides of the passing cars, strobing through his eyelids, demanding the truth!

But it was familiar, the wavering light, and as it filtered down through his layers his pulse slowed, and his breath slowed, and his mind slowed to a perfectly empty black, and where the light came to rest it became sunlight on the water, and his eyes glided across its surface like a water-bug zigzagging on a moving stream, and he wasn't done making the choice and he never would be, and he was forgiven. Nothing had ever felt more true, though in another moment it was sort of ridiculous, and with that a new feeling welled up: the fizzing of a cosmic hilarity, inflating him back to his feet.

"What's so funny?" Sueanna asked as Conrad fell in next to her.

"I'm funny, Mom," he said, pointing at himself, "and it's all your fault."

Sueanna gave him a little smile and turned her eyes back to the road.

"OK," she said, "whatever you say."